I0611341

WOLF OF THE WEST

BELINDA BURKE

Wolf of the West
ISBN # 978-1-78430-451-5
©Copyright Belinda Burke 2015
Cover Art by Posh Gosh ©Copyright January 2015
Interior text design by Claire Siemaszkiewicz
Totally Bound Publishing

Published in 2015 by Totally Bound Publishing, Newland House, The Point, Weaver Road, Lincoln, LN6 3QN, United Kingdom.

Totally Bound Publishing is a subsidiary of Totally Entwined Group Limited.

WOLF OF THE WEST

Dedication

For Stella

Chapter One

Marcas stared upward at the sound of an imperative *caw*, and knew he must move faster. Four legs paced under him, swift as the wind, but he could see even from a distance that what had been a battlefield had now become a scavenger's rout. Above him, black crows crossed the sky, first in twos and threes, then a streaming murder.

It is coming.

The twilight darkened into premature night under the shadow of their wings, and from the gore that littered the field came crawling shadows, stick-figures unbending against the light.

Darkness made flesh.

Once, twice, Marcas howled, but the moon was not yet risen and he could summon no light into his service. From the top of a low rise, he could only look down and watch more carnage in the making. Warriors, bloodstained, wounded—waylaid in victory or defeat, they had survived the battle only to suffer something more terrible.

His gaze focused on their widened eyes, the glaring darkness in each overburdened pupil, teeth visible behind lips thinned with fear in each face — yet in none of them did he see what he had come for. A spark of light — the *mark of brightness* that told him the one so marked was meant to survive. That one, he would protect. But where was he?

Wraiths absent of flesh unfolded across the carnage, seeking their prey. The survivors who could move stumbled away from them with all the speed their broken limbs could muster. Marcas' gaze caught on three that moved together, two older, one younger, perhaps a son or nephew of one of the others. The elder two held him back, their hands across his chest at what they must have believed was a final moment of fear — and yet that youth stood forward, his face all confrontation, nothing of terror in the glare of his eyes.

The shadow moved to confront him, the youth painted with blazing light in the dark field of Marcas' mind, and the truth flamed in him, sudden and precise.

This one! This one — now, now!

In a flash, Marcas leaped down the hillside, crossed the blooded grass and buried his teeth in the shadow nearest the youth. Black blood spurted around his fangs, and he felt dark fingers clutching at the fur of his back. Marcas whipped around and lunged at them. He caught sight of the three men behind him, their eyes wider now, if that was possible — watching him, wondering — but there was no way for him to explain.

Like many men before them, they would have to come to their own conclusions.

Growling, spitting, pacing back and forth, Marcas marked a circle with his steps, with his body, with his flashing fangs. He leaped across to threaten any reaching hand, any open mouth, rattle-breathed, foaming.

Three of them, but I can't protect just that one. The boy. The boy wouldn't let me, and it wouldn't be right.

But three men were two more than he had expected. A battle like this one, wounds like theirs — the older men should probably be dead, but there was no accounting for the strength of a heart, a spirit or a warrior. Marcas' quick eyes took in the wound on the younger one — the thigh, wrapped tight, blood soaked but older blood now, not fresh flowing... *Not so bad, boy.* It would be easier to protect him than the other two — closer to death, closer to the enemy.

The crawling multitude of bloodthirsty spirits reached out first for the men, not the boy. For a moment he felt a vain desire to take the boy and leave these fools to their fate. One wounded young man was no match for a wolf of the *faoladh*, no matter what his desires.

But across his mind's eye flashed that first glimpse again — blazing light and eyes with no terror in them at all.

Black energies tore at his back again, gripped his tail and pulled him. He whirled, ears laid back, snapping, tasted darkness and congealed death, but it was neither blood nor anything real. Shadow screeched, a sound like the caw of the crows, but deepened, twisted, broken. He sought the matte jet throats, tore open wounds that spilled nothing, but it was nothing with the taste of ash. Marcas pushed them back with the weight of his body, with his claws and fangs that snapped with supernatural swiftness. Tireless, intent, he fought against the circling foes that increased in number even as he engaged them. They flowed back and receded, then returned to wash around him, a new and stronger tide —

Until the moon rose. The moonlight fell on Marcas' back and his fur shone with a pale light, every hair illuminated. He lifted his head and those of his foes closest to him took a step back. His mouth opened, and out of his throat came an illuminated noise, more than a howl — the true song of the night, safety from all shadow in that one note, even as it was many.

The wolf song shattered the shadow, broke it apart into bits as the moonlight spread and painted the black of the hills and the gore of the field with light. Panting now, feeling the pain of many wounds, Marcas fell silent and stepped back, looked around with wary eyes to see if the night might choose to rebirth its horrors.

There was only silence and stillness. The natural shadows of the night, death in coherent slumber. What the violence had awakened was restful now. *Quiet.*

Satisfied, Marcas turned to face the trio of men he had protected. They, too, were silent, all but unmoving, until he turned to leave.

"Wait."

It was a young voice, the voice of the one he'd been called to protect, but Marcas didn't look back. He turned away despite that call, and vanished into the cloak of the night.

* * * *

The dawn came early, yellow and heavy, sunlight spreading like spilled yolk across the horizon. It was welcome light, which scattered shadow and imprisoned the fears of the night behind walls of memory. The shapes of dark and crooked power that had spilled from what had once been the bodies of friends and foe—the tide of dark within the night—those things were faded, but the memory of that which had conquered them was not.

The wolf.

"Still well, Connor?"

Startled from the thoughts that had distracted him, the throbbing of the wound in Connor's thigh returned full force at the sound of his father's voice. He almost brought up the image that lingered in his mind's eye. *Moonstruck wolf.* But he hesitated, and only answered the question his father had asked.

"Well enough. I'll make it."

They lapsed into silence after that. As Connor limped forward beside the single horse they'd found wandering at the edge of the battlefield, he drew himself out of his thoughts and watched his father over the horse's neck. Silent, craggy, a mountain in motion, he stomped forward as if nothing could—or would—stop him, as if he felt neither the pain of his wounds nor the pain of their journey. How far now? Since the wolf had left them in the blazing moonlight—since they'd found the horse and his father had forced Lord Aran to mount? *Too long.*

There had been an apology on his father's face, as he'd shoved Aran up on the beast, but despite the agony of this stumble through the dark, there'd been no other way to keep Aran moving.

Again, Connor looked into his father's face. His dark eyes were crowded under the clenching of his brow and the poor bandage that was bound there. His father nodded once, approval or encouragement, and Connor set his eyes on the road again, a dusty band that cinched the green hills before them like a poorly tightened belt.

It was good that he hadn't said anything, hadn't brought up the questions that burned in him. When he had asked in the dark after the wolf had left them, his father had shushed him right away, warned of bad luck and spurned blessings. *Some things we should not speak of, even amongst ourselves.* He heard the echo of his father's voice, the only answer he'd gotten, and knew that now wasn't a time to add to his worries — but despite his outer silence, the questions remained inside him, loud and urgent.

What had those things been? Shadow had risen from their comrades and from the enemy warriors both. Was it the power of their foe? *But then, what of the wolf?* Where had he come from? He had never seen anyone fight the way that wolf fought. Focusing on those moments, those memories, he shuddered, stumbled, caught himself and forced himself not to look at his father again. *Some things weren't meant to be faced by mortal men.* He had seen training injuries enough and the wounds on returning warriors — he'd thought he'd known what there was to know of battle and death.

He knew better now.

Battle was not wounds and weapons and warriors. Battle was blood-smoke, a mist of red in the air, so fine the taste of it was in every breath. Battle was stepping forward and slipping and not looking down to see if what was under your boots was mud or the blood-slick guts of someone who didn't know he was dead yet. Connor had learned that the arm could grow so tired it couldn't stop swinging, that a blade new-sharpened could clot in a glut of flesh, chip on a sternum and still shatter a skull. Battle was heaving breath, every muscle burning and nerves dead ended or on fire — no in-between, no pause, no breathing space... And in the lulls, everything too quiet. Every crow's cawing, every breath of wind became a thing that stirred alertness out of impossible fatigue.

He'd thought the end was just another one of those lulls. That there would be another charge, another rush — something else, because it couldn't be over. It would never be over... But it was.

Until night came.

His leg had been long-bound by then and he had done what he could for his father, limping, reaching across the broad shoulders to bind a wound that streamed new flow over the rusty stains of old blood. But it had been Aran who was the worst wounded, by the loss of his sons. Connor had found him, bent over the bodies. Perhaps it had been Aran's cries that had woken shadows out of the dead. *They were loud enough. They went on forever.*

Not that he could blame him. There would be no honored burial, no pyre for those boys, not after this battle. Not when no one survived, no one but them — who would carry the bodies? Who would return to this plain and bring away the crow's feast that remained? They had come to the very edge of his father's kingdom to fight, two hundred warriors seeking to spill blood in the name of an ancient feud long abated. Fifty years of the High King's peace had been broken there, and for what?

Nothing had been won, nothing gained, nothing threatened — a field in the middle of pastureland, and no herds in sight, and now his father's men and the men who had rebelled both were dead.

Connor sighed, licked dry lips and looked up across the endless rolling of the hills and into the sunlight.

How much farther? He took another step, and another, and another...

"Connor? Stop, Connor."

He heard his father's voice, but it seemed to come from a distance. Why would that be? His father was...right there. He turned his head to the left, and the motion unbalanced some precarious state he hadn't even been aware of. His head was light, and his leg was numb. Thigh to foot, he couldn't feel a thing.

"That isn't right..."

"Connor!"

Darkness.

It reached out to envelop him, and for an instant, his heart sped up in fear.

But no.

No worries.

The thought came to him of itself, soothing, silken.

Wolf will protect me.

There was no need to fear the night.

* * * *

When Connor opened his eyes again, he was home. He knew before he opened his eyes, knew by the feel of the mattress under his back and the comforter under his hands, the tiny hole at the very edge that he could feel with his right pinkie. For one moment, there was just the warmth of the familiar place and no memory of the battle or what had come after. Then he tried to turn on his side and felt the pain of the wound in his thigh as if a spear were stabbing him again.

It all came back to him with the pain, and he sucked in his breath and hollowed his cry to a low groan. *Battle...agony...darkness. Especially darkness.*

He moved with more care when he tried again, and the sharpness of his agony was reduced to a pale throb that shadowed his movements, faded to an ache when he was still. When he had his legs over the edge of the bed, he sat without moving for a long while, sorting thoughts.

I must've blacked out on the way back.

Try as he might, he couldn't remember anything more than the thought that had followed him into unconsciousness, and that thought was foolish enough to make him flush even though he was alone. As if he'd ever see that wolf again!

Connor licked his lips and grew aware of terrible thirst. He had a craving for cold water — no, cold milk. That would be rich enough, filling enough...

"*If* I can get out of bed."

A spear was leaning by the side of the bed, the wood of the shaft white with newness, and Connor stared at it for a moment, remembering despite himself the last spear he had seen. His own, worn with wear, coming back at him, sinking into the flesh of his thigh —

Connor closed his eyes, took a deep breath then levered himself to one foot and steadied his good leg beneath him. Half limping, half hopping, gritting his teeth, Connor crossed the two necessary steps and gripped the spear, leaned on it and sighed.

"Much better."

The pain was so much worse now than it had been before he blacked out that he was almost afraid, but the pangs were growing less a little at a time, even if the ache of the wound remained. *How long was I in bed?* He used the spear as a crutch and made his way out of the rooms he shared with his sisters and up to the main hall. Before he was even in sight of it, he could hear noise floating across the *ráth* — the usual feast after a battle, then.

"I couldn't've been out more than a day or so."

Connor drew himself up as he came up the path. The guards at the great doors stood tall and saluted as he passed by, and Connor nodded to them before he passed through the open door into the smoke and noise of the hall. For a moment, what he saw was the battlefield — blood-smoke instead of the smoke of the celebratory fires. The spatter and crackle of meat juices was arrows on shields — spears breaking...

"Connor! My son, on your feet again — good, good! Come, join us, sit beside me."

His father's voice rang out from the head of the high table, struck aside the curtain of memory and left only what was really there. Connor laughed and shook his head at the same time, just at the sight of him, but he still made his way through the chaos to his father's side.

One hairy arm and the whole of his broad shoulders and chest had been swathed in linen bandages. There was linen wrapped around his head and the knuckles of both hands, but he looked no worse for the wear despite that. In his high seat, he was Brádach the King once more. Nothing of the terrified man who had cowered in the shadow of the wolf remained, and Connor was glad. That man...he didn't know that man.

His father was the one before him now, a tankard in each hand, and the plate before him piled high with bread and cheese and roasted meat. Beside him, Connor saw his mother, a slip of a woman, laughing at her husband. Connor stopped behind her before he sat, bent to embrace her and kiss her cheek.

"Hello, Mother."

"*Connor*. Welcome home. Feeling better?"

He grinned at her, then passed behind his father, reached out and plucked a wedge and an untouched loaf from the plate — *platter, more like*. He ducked into the seat beside his father before the hand that nudged his shoulder could unbalance him and knock him over.

"*Half a boar*, Father?"

"Only what's left!" He laughed as he answered,

"No need for that, no need for that, now — there's battles enough to come, and soon enough to come — let me enjoy my time here, boy!"

"More battles to come? Where? Is the enemy moving again?"

His father looked instantly as if he regretted having spoken so openly, so easily.

"You need have no worry about it."

"Don't I? Look at your wounds, Father. If you plan on going again into battle, I have to go with you." Connor spoke quietly, but as if his words were a final thing, and that might have been the wrong thing to do. His father's eyes gained fire, his expression heat.

"Don't test me, Connor."

"Father —"

"I will have no argument on this matter!"

His voice thundered across the hall and there was a moment of total silence, all eyes on them, before natural courtesy and common sense kicked in. The murmur of conversation returned to a dull roar and his father's voice, when he spoke again, was reduced in volume but no less intense.

"Listen to me, Connor. You can barely walk. There will be no fighting for you for weeks. Tomorrow you will go north, away from danger — tend the herds for half a season, eat well, heal — you are young, my son.

There's time enough for fighting in your future, so many battles that you'll grow weary of them."

He leaned back, and Connor sucked in a breath and held it, tried to digest all the hot words he could feel moving at the back of his throat when he swallowed. Something was moving beneath the surface of his father's words, something more than what he'd thought—some battle like the one just past. His father wasn't one to lose his temper like that, not over such a thing, not in public. *What does it mean?* But nothing occurred to him, and he couldn't even think of a question to ask.

His father clapped a hand on his shoulder

"Enjoy the celebration, son. You earned just as much as any of these—more. You fought beside me. You survived, though you did not flee the night."

"It was the wolf that—"

"Have I not said that some things are not to be spoken of? Leave well enough alone, Connor."

His father's voice was raised again, but only enough to cut off Connor's words.

"Drink. Eat. And when you've had your fill, pack for the night, and for the hills, and for the north. You leave *tomorrow*."

Silent, Connor drank the milk he'd wanted. He had thirsted, and it cooled his throat—but it was bitter on his tongue.

What am I missing?

He emptied the tankard and dropped it back to the table with a thud, then turned to the matter of filling his empty plate. As he ate, he tried to convince himself that none of these things mattered. He'd leave in the morning if that was what his father wanted, and that wolf… He wouldn't see it again.

Such things happened only once in any man's life.

* * * *

The feasting — or more precisely, the drinking — went on through the night and into the darkest hours of the morning. It wouldn't end while the funeral fires still burned. At midnight, Connor watched his father slip out of the celebration almost unnoticed, but found it impossible to do the same himself. He wanted to know where his father was going, why he was leaving, but every man he tried to pass wanted to drink with him, congratulate him, question him on the battle — about which neither his father nor Aran had done anything other than report victory.

It was in the chill before dawn that Connor finally escaped the noise and heat of the hall, and limped out into the night in search of his father. Too many cups of ale had dulled the waspish screeching of the wound in his thigh. His discomfort had settled to a whisper of irritation that only grew when he moved too quickly or tried to raise his leg too high, and this only served to reinforce his thoughts, not that they needed it. *If this is enough to hold me back from battle, my father shouldn't be going anywhere.* What moved him with such urgency he couldn't trust any lord under him, needed to send Connor all the way to the northern pastures? Those would be Aran's lands, the wide empty spaces where one village might be a two day's walk from another.

Muttering to himself, Connor wandered in the narrow alleys between the hall and the other buildings in the *ráth*, but there was no sign of his father anywhere, though he caught sight of many other men and women in the shadows. It was slow going, but it wasn't until he came to the northern edge of the compound, away from the noise of the revelry and the light of fires and torches, that he heard the familiar voice coming from behind a closed door—and others, too, not as well known as his father's but well enough. *Niall… Lord Aran…and Lord Cathal?*

With slow, careful steps, trying to make as little noise as possible, Connor made his way to the door and pressed his ear to the crack so he would be sure to catch every word. He was less concerned with being caught than with hearing everything he could. Was it a battle they were talking about, his father and these much-trusted men?

"….he has been failing for some time."

That's Father.

"Age has done worse to greater men."

And Lord Cathal —

"What would you know of it, Cathal? It matters not, a failing king is still a king."

And Lord Aran. Where's Niall?

Connor wished he could see into the room, not just hear disembodied voices.

"And if a king performs acts not suiting any man, and a king least of all?" His father's voice was a low rumble, and Connor had to strain to hear his next words. "I have it on good authority that there is no battle brewing near Magh Slécht. We are summoned to a sacrifice instead."

There was a low drumming—fingers on a tabletop, Connor thought.

"A sacrifice…"

Cathal's words were thoughtful but another man interrupted in darker tones.

"There's only one god to sacrifice to on that plain. Old bent Crom will drink his fill, if Tigernmas has his way."

There's Niall!

"Crom?" Lord Aran's voice sounded more alert in the utterance of that single name than Connor had heard it since the battle had ended. Something of his old sharpness was returned to his tone. "And what would the High King have to do with the crooked one? There's been nothing seen or heard of Crom Cruach since—"

"Since three nights past?" His father's voice cut Aran's to silence. "Since we saw the spirits of our comrades twisted into monsters, shadows—you know what it was that we saw, Aran! The things that men are not meant to see, the reason why no man walks a battlefield past the setting of the sun. Who among us has not heard the old stories?"

"Fireside stories! Tales for children—"

"Yes, for the teaching of youth. And what else were we taught in those stories? *When the dark wind bites, when shadow eats all light—*"

Connor caught his breath and mouthed the words that finished that rhyme as Aran spoke them.

"Call for the wolf of the west and the full moon's bright. I see."

"We were protected once, Aran. We cannot expect such protection to come again, and I will die before I see such a sacrifice as this enacted. No god is deserving of such a price!"

Cathal's voice came urgent and hollow, died cracking on its first word.

"What—?"

Connor heard creaking, heavy footsteps, moved to back away from the door but relaxed when he heard the familiar sound of his father pacing, his tread heavy, methodical, louder, then fainter as he moved past the door and spoke.

"Tell them, Niall."

"Who doesn't know the favored drink of the lord of the mound?"

"Tell them!"

Connor winced, turned his face away. His father rarely raised his voice, but when he did—he heard Niall start speaking and pressed his ear back to the door, his thought uncompleted.

"I have heard from all the priests of all the old gods that terrible preparations have been made at Magh Slécht. It'll be a plain of slaughter for true if what's planned comes to pass." There was a silence, then— "Tigernmas wants the children! The sacrifice, it's the damned children, the firstborn of every man who comes to him."

Connor felt something cold and sickening sink through him at the thought of what had just been spoken becoming reality. *A sacrifice of firstborn.* Bile churned in his belly, already unsettled by too much ale. He had been thinking about following his father when he left, trailing him. *If I had – If I'd done that –*

I would have become a sacrifice.

He pushed himself away from the door and bent over by the wall, retching, terrible images in his mind, an echoing series of words.

Sacrifice…of firstborn.

He heard the door open beside him while he was still retching, then his father's voice, a heavy hand on his back—both unexpectedly soothing.

"So it *was* you listening. I thought it would be."

Slowly, feeling all pain more now, Connor pushed himself up, wiped his mouth with the back of his hand.

"*Why,* Father? To *Crom* –"

"I know. I know, son. You understand now why you cannot come with me."

Connor only nodded—what could he say? A king his father might be, but a lesser one than Tigernmas, and owing him loyalty. Defiance like this—sending away his son, the son that would be sacrificed... Speaking out against the wishes of the High King? *A death sentence.* Something in Connor—the child that he had been—wanted to reach out for his father, demand answers where there were none, demand that he, too, stay. Stay, and renounce it all...

Instead he made his first real, adult decision, swallowed back words and feelings and lied to make them both feel better.

"Then I'll see you when you return." He took a deep breath. "When do I leave? Is the morning soon enough, or—"

A dark-haired figure with flickering torchlight behind him, Niall took a step out of the doorway.

"Go now, if you're going at all. Last night would've been better—so go now!"

Connor looked back at his father, caught his nod.

"Yes. Now—or as soon you can. Niall, a horse and travel gear, and don't forget the—"

"Bandages. Yes. I'll see to it."

The tall man disappeared, and Connor moved to follow him, was stopped by his father's hand on his shoulder.

"Connor, if things go as they have been... There's not time to tell you everything that's going on, but you were there. You saw—and now you have heard. Listen well, Connor, to something only Niall knows. The battle we fought is only one of many that has sprung up across the land like leaks in a boat. Only a few of them had their own purpose—the rest, the High King has *fomented*, undoing the bonds of peace he built. I do not know why. I do not *know*, but the heart of me suspects that the sacrifice we've been summoned to is only the last piece to be moved in a game Tigernmas has been playing for quite some time."

"Father—"

"Don't worry, Connor! I intend to beat him at this game of his—beat him badly. But I want you to be safe. I do not know how this sacrifice will be taken — merely to have you there might be enough to mark you." The weight of his father's hand squeezed his shoulder, heavy, dependable, strong. He met his father's stare, tried hard to memorize the seamed, brown features, timeworn, careworn—the face of a warrior, the face of a *king*. Then he pulled back.

"Niall will be waiting by the gate when everything is prepared. Go with the gods, my son. Only one of us carries the future of our family."

By the time he reached the gate, Niall was waiting for him, bag in his hand and a grim smile on his face.

"Don't come back unless someone summons you, Connor mac Brádach."

He turned away and the gate slammed shut behind him.

Connor took a breath, then turned his horse's head for the north.

* * * *

Free from obligation, free from duty but not from pain, Marcas wandered, paws stumbling beneath him, four feet as unsteady as two—funny, that. He felt warmth through his fur, and wetness. *Blood*, too much of it, his own red living blood and not the black ichor of his foes. *I should have known better. Three men at once!*

A growl slipped out of his throat, rubbed raw against the air and returned to his ears without sympathy.

Tired. That's the blood talking as it goes. Run — hunt and kill and eat and sleep and heal. But first, run.

Like the men he had saved, he could not. Instead, he walked. Through the moonlit hours of the night, into the dull morning — he moved north under a dawn bridled by clouds, from green hills to a forest whose canopy reached out to snatch back the light. He slept in the shade and woke confused at the darkness, confused by the sleep he hadn't meant to take, and pushed himself onward.

One leg...in front of...the others.

In the wild of the wood, the flesh he sought to break his fast ran quick — too quick for him — or hid in deep burrows beyond his reach. The farther he went into the green shade, the more he felt his concentration slipping, his purpose failing him. When the wood faded away, a few straggling trees were all that kept him company as the hills wound up again, until finally, no strength left in him, Marcas made his way beneath a bent rowan and curled into a ball of exhausted pain. *Sleep again, sleep for strength, sleep to wake and fly home.*

He dreamed of the wolf-change, the sleek strength as it had overcome him, the strangeness of *pelt* where for the first twenty years of his life there had been skin. Nothing like what he'd thought it would be, nothing like what he'd been told. Everything the same — everything different — and the words ringing in his new ears. *For seven years you will wear the shape of the guardian, the shape of the wolf. For seven years, you will serve to keep the ancient pact, and guard Crom Cruach's slumber!*

Marcas woke all at once, the name of the ancient foe loud in his thoughts. Pain woke with him and struck out along his nerves with its several messages. The sun was low in the sky, sinking into the west, but enough light remained to guide him forward across the grass. It was cool under the pads of his paws, soothing, and at the bottom of the hill there was a stream. He drank his fill of clear, cold water, stretched muscles gone stiff with hours of stillness as best he could. Again, he turned north. Miles stretched under his paws—at intervals he stopped and licked the blood from his fur, listened for the sounds of any others of his kin who might be near, though he didn't expect to find them.

No. Nothing.

Onward. Soft grass, soft heather, and another night came soft as old wool. How many days? How many nights? *I do not remember.* He was almost ready to lie down again, to sleep, perhaps not to wake, when a new scent came to him, drew him forward. Sweeter, slower meat was near him. Cattle, hiding behind their fences. Rich cows—milk—veal... *Tender.*

The thoughts came not as words, but as images—a sequence of events, legs reaching out of their usual lope and into the short-distance sprint, jaws widening, the sound that's heard like a bone cracking in the head, the sound that is teeth puncturing living skin and mortal tissues, cracking bone... There would be blood. The flowing of blood.

They are close. Close enough.

Marcas felt no guilt as he closed on the fence, began to circle, stalking from the shadow that ringed the enclosure. Deep lowing greeted him, distress in it, his prey aware of the scent of a predator, a free flowing thing in the air. Sinuous, slow, conserving the meager energy that remained to him, Marcas slipped between the fence rails, tasted the air. *Cattle, boy and blood.* All three were familiar scents, a strange thing.

He moved from one side of the pen to the other, seeking the source.

You, boy?

It was the one he had saved. The one who had been *meant to live.* In the clarity of this place, away from the furor and chaos of awakening darkness, Marcas studied feature and form more closely, paring down his earlier judgments to something closer to the truth. A young man, truly, but not more than twenty. Beautiful, as all youth was beautiful, and the red of his hair like blood in the half moon's light.

Marcas laughed, husky panting wolf laughter, and watched the boy as he became aware that he was not alone, that there was something beside the lowing cattle near him, something moving in the night.

More laughter.

Around, and around, unseen, still known, a presence undeniable once it had been recognized — the wolf and his prey. The boy and his charge.

One calf moved away from the protection of the herd, took just a few steps toward the outer portion of the rings, and Marcas took his chance and lunged forward, took the young throat in his jaws and tore at the buried jugular. There was no going back now, no turning around or finding some other direction. The crusted wounds in his body would win — or he would feed and sleep and fight them as he had twice now since the summer moon had widened its grin.

He heard a shout and knew that the boy was coming for him. Marcas wondered what fate had brought them together tonight, what chance had spilled its cup across them—this boy, whom he had protected. How was it that they were meeting again?

I cannot hurt you, boy. Will you hurt me?

Chapter Two

Connor wasn't having a good night, and the previous days and nights had been no better. So long on horseback, even going more slowly than he usually would have, had aggravated the wound in his thigh. If the bone had been broken, he would never have made it, but the puncture he'd suffered was bad enough. He'd changed the bandage many times on the way here, and twice more since stopping, pressing the poultice tight with his forearm, wrapping the linen around, tying it down with gritted teeth.

Each time, he grew more irritated with himself. If he'd only been a little faster, a little bit more careful, he would never have been wounded. *And with my own spear!* It was a lesson he would remember, but he grudged his nerves the pain.

"At least the job's easy enough. There wasn't even anyone here...maybe Father had Aran send them away?"

He stared across the landscape from the top of the hill where the cattle were penned at night. Too dangerous to have them loose — wolf packs, bears, gorges, hunter's traps — and the cows were stupid beasts, the bulls no better. The horizon, red-rimmed like a tired eye, sent up purple shadow, darkened the sky to faultless black. Here and there he watched bright points appear, heralds for the rising moon.

Hobbling, one arm wrapped around his spear, Connor checked the fence one last time. No holes, the gate closed — good. He settled himself by the torch beside the gate, half-sitting, half-leaning on a bale of hay. Nervous lowing came from the cows, then faded. Time passed, minutes, hours. The moon approached the zenith of the sky, shed bars of brilliance down across the grass, the hay, the white oak fence. Watching the moonlight, listening to faint animal sounds, the wind rustling the grass and the leaves of the single tree that grew at the southeast corner of the fence, Connor fell into a daze, almost a doze, but his eyes stayed open, staring outward.

Something is coming.

Susurrus — but that was only the wind again. Or not?

Something is already here.

He blinked himself into a more wakeful awareness, felt a tingling on his skin. Watching, something was watching him!

His first response was terror. His first thought was the crawling shadows, the *slick-click* sound of their umbrous limbs, the black beasts that had surged from the blood of the fallen, seeking...seeking what? He still didn't know, only that everything in him had told him to avoid those things at any cost. And now — and now...

Connor didn't know where the attack would come from, only that it would come. The lowing of the cows was suddenly more distressed, all the cattle milling, then running in circles inside the enclosure, gathering together away from the northern end. There was a low bellow, high pitched squealing.

"Hey—hey, get out of there! Get out of there!"

In an instant, he gave over all his fear of immortal killers for mortal caution—a wolf among his charges! One among them was already wounded by the hunting beast, the sounds told him that, and he went forward as quick as he could through the streaming cows and bulls, scattered from the smell of wolf and blood.

Before he had taken half a dozen steps, he saw the wolf, his fangs buried deep in the throat of one young calf, red streaming over the dark muzzle, the pale throat.

Despite the wound in his thigh, Connor acted without hesitation. Perfect in form, the training of seven years and the words of his father in his ears, he struck, one thrust with his spear—but mid-movement, he looked down into eyes the color of ice, the shade of the sky behind the winter gray, and stopped as if struck. Knowledge confronted him, held him back, hovered between the point of his spear and the heaving wolf-heart, unprotected before him.

"You are *that* wolf!"

Connor tried to take a heavy step back, forgetful of his leg, and fell when it failed to support him. The ground knocked the breath out of him, and he stared across at the wolf as it disengaged its jaws from the calf's flesh and turned to look at him. He saw terrible wounds, gray fur stained black and rust and red with new and old blood, and knew it was true—*this was the one.* He gasped against the pain and tried to think, to understand, could only stare as a throat wide as the night issued a breath of wolf laughter.

The wolf came forward into the narrow brightness of the moonlight, stopped and stared at him. Connor stared back. Those eyes—they acknowledged him, spoke to him, but he didn't know what of. It was more than he had ever seen before in the eyes of any beast, wild or tame, predator or prey. Intelligence. Awareness. *I see you.*

Slowly, Connor reached out again for his spear—more slowly still, levered himself to his feet. The wolf didn't move, only continued to stare at him, smiling—could wolves smile? *This one does.* He licked his lips and took one step forward, speaking almost under his breath, wondering if he'd gone crazy, crazy, crazy.

"Hey...there... Look, I'm not going to hurt you. I'm sorry I came at you like that, but I didn't know it was *you* and I can't just let any wolves that want to eat the cattle—even you should be hunting in the woods, not here—hey, easy, easy! I said I wasn't going to hurt you."

The wolf was baring his teeth and growling now that he was close enough to touch it, but he didn't dare. Instead Connor shifted his weight to his good leg so he could reach out with his spear without falling over. The poor calf, forgotten, was on its knees, blood streaming from the terrible wound the wolf had made of its throat.

Easily, he thrust forward, ending its life—then again, to slit the skin of the belly, one long clean cut with the sharp bronze edge of his spearhead. It was a bit ragged, but that didn't matter—it wasn't for him. He turned and looked at the wolf, steadied himself against the spear and lowered himself slowly, painfully, to the ground.

"Well? Go on, then. I owe you much more than this."

The wolf sniffed at him, the black nose lifting into the air. Its growl descended to a lower tone, a lower volume, but didn't vanish—still, the wolf stood and turned, licked its muzzle before it struck forward and began to gorge on the steaming carcass.

While the wolf ate, Connor studied it, compared it to other wolves he had seen, the packs that streamed through the forest, winter and summer. This one was taller, broader, the fur not the mottled gray that he had seen, but darker, nearly black. Muzzle, ear-tips, ruff and the fur along the ridge of the spine all carried a paler hue, but still it was darker than the coat of normal wolves. How much of that black stain was the color of the fur, and how much of it was blood, Connor couldn't begin to guess.

Some black ichor was mixed with the wolf's redder blood, and he knew what it had come from—the shadows that had caused the wounds. Three great gashes were open along the wolf's hindquarters—another across the shoulders, two on the side that faced him.

All that, for us?

"Why would you do that, wolf? Why protect us? Why get yourself hurt for us?"

The wolf ignored him, only continued to gulp down raw, rich flesh. For a while Connor was content to sit and watch, but curiosity grew to overcome fear, and even caution. This wolf had protected him. Would it hurt him now? Carefully, slowly, he reached out his fingers and touched soft fur that wasn't near any injury. The growl increased, then receded, and Connor stroked the fur of this strange wolf and laughed a little, breathless with the danger, the wonder—was it happening?

Yes.

This is real.

Marcas stood still, only his jaws and his throat moving, gulping again and again. He had only meant to take a little—a few mouthfuls of the undeniably tempting veal, rich and steaming in the cool of the night air, sending out the odors of salt and blood. Out of the corner of his eye he watched the boy that sat beside him as he stroked his fur, one leg outstretched, the thigh wrapped in bandages faintly spotted with blood. Yes, this was the one he had saved, there was no doubt about it.

If I was a normal wolf, I'd have bitten your fingers off by now, boy.

But perhaps it wasn't nice to think that. The boy remembered, recognized him, had said so in tones that left no doubt that he was aware Marcas was no *normal wolf.* There would have been nothing to stop the spear that had nearly ended him—he eyed it warily even now, the point clotted over in dark calf's blood. A warrior, this boy. There had to be strength in him, to have come out of that battle alive—honor, to give up a calf to a wolf, even if the wolf had saved him. *Most wouldn't have done so.*

Red flesh soothed the agony, fed the rush of Marcas' tissues to heal the open wounds on his back and sides. Gorged, replete, Marcas turned away from the carcass and faced the boy. He had kept up a low drone of words, a dull hum about his father, vassal lords, battles just past and battles coming, and all the while the boy's fingers stroked through the ruff of fur at the base of his neck, careful to keep away from anything that might be painful.

Smart boy.

A little at a time, he shifted forward until he was at Marcas' side, a warm presence that was almost comforting. Marcas turned his head, whined a little, licked at the deepest of the gouges in his side. He could see the wounds clearly now — deep, but bled clean except where the shadow-blood stained him.

Moonlight illuminated punctures and slashes, and he wondered how long it would take to heal, how many days and nights before he could take up his duties again. It had been ground into him from the earliest time he could remember, the duty of the clan. *To become the wolf, to fight the darkness.* How many souls would be lost while he was wounded, because he had been so careless as to allow himself to become so?

Marcas closed his eyes, lowered his head until it rested on his forepaws and tried to ignore the blips of brightness in his consciousness He licked again at his wounds. Beside him, the boy spoke again, his fingers still moving through Marcas' fur.

"I could bind your wounds for you — I've got medicine — for my leg, you know? I don't even know if you can understand me, but it would help. It's my fault you got injured. It doesn't feel right, just leaving you like this."

Marcas locked eyes with the boy, read his intentions there — just what he'd said. Guilt, wonder, the desire to do right, to help him, to pay back a debt. He wondered how much help it would really be. Would it shorten the time it took him to heal, or just force him to endure pointless discomfort? Painfully, Marcas tried to haul himself to his feet, to move closer to the boy, make his willingness, his *choice* clear, but he couldn't find a particle of energy with which to do so. There was nothing inside him to draw on, not even the strength to roll over. A dark haze floated at the edges of his vision.

Guilt prodded him, and the fear that all those bright lights in his awareness might go out.

Bright lights like you, boy. Why are you still marked with brightness?

But anything else he might have thought or felt was swallowed by the black tide that rose behind his eyes.

* * * *

When Marcas woke, it was to a great easing of his pain and a great stiffness. At first he thought it was just his healing wounds restraining his movement, but he realized as he looked down his body that he was wrapped in linen bandages almost from head to toe. Around his left foreleg, too—and his head felt heavy...itchy. He huffed and twisted, reached up to paw at the bandage around his head and almost immediately regretted the movement. Agony erupted down his back, along his side—he let his leg fall and dropped his head back to the ground, only to realize then that it wasn't the ground he was lying on.

Where is this?

He turned his head to the right, then to the left. His field of vision encompassed some unknown dwelling, a stranger's hut—furs immediately before him, and below him, the legs of a table to his left, a low pallet with a single figure stretched out on it...

The Boy.

It came to him with a capital letter now, extra emphasis, not quite a name. If he could think of a way, he would get the Boy's name, but for now it was enough to distinguish him from the rest. If he closed his eyes, he could still see the sleeping shape in the landscape of his mind, a single point of brightness like the flame of a candle, one star in a dark night. *Where are the others?* He felt an uneasy, prickling sensation that moved from his spine to the pads of his paws.

What is it?

But there were no answers forthcoming, and he didn't know when he'd have a chance to ask his questions.

Maybe they'll have to wait until the full of the moon.

When it came, his time as *faoladh* would be over — blessed and cursed wolf. Marcas growled low in his throat and carefully, one leg, one protesting muscle at a time, he pushed himself up until he was standing. There was no door keeping him inside, just a leather flap, and he nosed his way past it easily. It was late, the sun moving in the west, falling toward the horizon. An entire day he'd been out, maybe more.

The Boy moved me inside and I didn't even notice. I wonder how he managed that?

Every movement awkward, Marcas lay on the grass beside the door and wondered what he should do now. Stay here? It wasn't done — to interact with normal humans like this, to stay in close contact with one of those who had been marked to be protected. Not once the protecting had been done — *but then why are you still bright to me, Boy?* Had he been called here without even knowing it? Was there still work to be done, despite his success in keeping death from taking what was not meant for it at that battlefield?

Maybe I am just looking for excuses.

It would be easier to stay here, be fed fresh veal, allow the Boy tend to his wounds. They hurt less, now, as long as he was careful how he moved. He would heal faster with care, would be able to return to his duties more quickly — perhaps, by the dark of the moon, he would be ready to resume his service. *But is it right? To stay here…*

A gorgeous scent distracted Marcas from his thoughts. *Boy?* He heard a moan, a low sound that might have been pain, and pushed himself to his feet, turned and thrust his head past the curtain blocking the door. *Oh – gods –*

The noises had been soft murmurs of pleasure, not pain. *Pleasure.* The Boy lay with the covers thrown back from his body, working his cock over with his fist… *Gods, delicious Boy.* Marcas stared through the dimness as the boy teased himself with slow, casual strokes, the thick length of his cock moving easily in his fist.

A dozen arrows of want pierced Marcas in a moment. *Why did I have to meet you now, when I was still the wolf?* He was exactly what Marcas liked in a man – lean, strong, beautiful – he'd known that already, but there was more than beauty here – this was perfection.

He wanted to taste that skin, run his tongue over the dips and hollows of those muscles, over that cock – he would taste just like his scent. Marcas knew he would. *So good.* He wanted his fingers back, to run through the smooth dark hair, see if it was as soft as it looked – to wrap around those slim, strong wrists. He wanted the weight of his own body back, wanted to press the Boy down against his bed, feel skin against skin, bury himself inside.

So deep inside.

The Boy shuddered and moaned, came to his climax as if in tune with Marcas' thoughts. Perfect, so perfect – even now, when he lay panting, sweaty, streaks of whiteness on belly and thighs.

Want. Want, want, want.

But Marcas reminded himself that he was still the wolf, only a wolf, and pulled his head back behind the curtain and moved to lie by the outside wall. *Duty, that's all. He knows nothing more of me than that – and maybe not even that.*

"Wolf? Wolf, are you still here?"

He heard the Boy's voice calling from inside, then fumbling, swearing – something knocked over – footsteps, heavy, limping, and Marcas remembered then that he wasn't the only one wounded. There had been blood streaming down his leg that night, and he was still wearing bandages of his own, wasn't he.

I can do something about that if he'll let me.

The leather blocking the door was pushed aside behind him, and Marcas looked up at a frantic expression with some amusement. He disregarded the fact that he had indeed considered leaving to smile at the Boy, open his throat for panting laughter. The Boy scowled and limped through the door.

"If I wasn't already absolutely sure you were the same wolf, I'd know it now. There's something…there's something strange about you. Not like any other wolf I've seen, I mean…it's not like I've seen lots of wolves, really, but the packs in the forest…" A little at a time, using the spear at his side to help him, the Boy slid down until he was sitting on the ground with his wounded leg stretched out before him. "*Agh*. That doesn't get easier. The packs in the forest – you're nothing like them. I guess it doesn't matter. You can't be anything bad or you wouldn't have protected us, would you?"

He laughed a little, then reached for a bit of leather thrust into his belt, upturned his spear and began to clean and polish the bloody point. Marcas stared at it for a moment, reminded of something, then licked his teeth, let out a little whine, looked up and tried to catch the Boy's gaze. When he did, there was a narrowing of the tanned brow, a crease that appeared for a moment between the red-blond eyebrows then disappeared.

"Hungry, is that it? Well go on—you got out here. You can walk. I didn't move the calf, not like I could if I wanted to. It's all yours."

Marcas levered himself to his feet more slowly than even the first time, unwilling to look more awkward than was necessary. It was a pointless endeavor—with the bandages around his back and middle, his walk was less of a walk and more a slow rock, first to one side then the other. He heard the Boy laughing at him as he made his way from the hut, following his nose to the odors of meat and blood and though he growled a little—just below his breath, wishing he could share a few *choice words*—he didn't look back.

He had to keep *some* dignity, after all.

* * * *

Connor was amused by the wolf's apparent irritation with his laughter—as much as he had been amused by the waddling walk of the bandage-wrapped canine, if not more. When the beast was out of sight, he sat back against the wall again, despite duties he knew were waiting for him. He should have let the cattle out to graze, should have done so hours ago, but the long nights of wakefulness were wearing on him, and the excitement of finding the wolf again had kept him up for hours.

He scowled, thinking. When would his father and the others be on their way—when would the sacrifice take place? He didn't remember much about Crom

Cruach from his teachings as a child, and for good reason. The bent one wasn't a being that anyone liked to linger on—most ancient god, darkest god, the spirit that moved most freely in the night. The thought made him think of something, brought his memory back to the battlefield, the twisted shadows, their crooked figures, the lameness of their movement, the darkness of their claws—that terrible odor, masticated meat, old blood, sulfur.

He shuddered.

"It *could* have been Crom's servants that were after us. Father's right."

And another thing occurred to him, even more terrifying. The lame and the broken were thought marked as the chosen of Crom, and wasn't he lame, now? Without any other knowledge, he was certain of the truth.

Crom Cruach was after me.

Perhaps his father and Lord Aran had only been bystanders, sucked into the darkness because of his presence there. Had the wounds the wolf suffered been only because of him? Had the slime of shadow that crawled out of the bodies of men he had known and talked with only done so because he was there? Because he been a fool, and let himself be wounded? *By my own spear, no less.* The thought was bitter, but no more so than the rest of his situation.

"Father was smarter than he thought, keeping me away. As long as I'm wounded, I'm *marked* for that sacrifice. Just what I always wanted."

There was a riot of noise from the cattle pen and Connor sighed and began the slow process of pushing himself to his feet again. It would be that wolf—he had better not have taken another calf!

"One's enough for a beast that size and fresh enough too, considering."

But by the time he got down the hill, the noise had subsided. The gate to the pen was open, and the wolf stood with his muzzle buried in red flesh, but only of the calf that had already been killed. He looked up at Connor with a satisfied expression, but only for a moment—then he turned back to his meal. Connor looked out across the hill, saw the cattle spreading slowly, tearing up the grass, their heads down to the work of their daily lives.

"Doing my job for me? Are you a wolf or a dog, huh?"

The snarl he received as reply to that comment set him back a step, and Connor almost fell again, smiled sheepishly and rubbed the back of his neck with one hand.

"Sorry, sorry. Wolf it is. But I still say there's something different about you."

The wolf eyes looked at him over the belly of the calf, the blue brighter than he remembered—*if you only knew*, that was what they seemed to say. Connor felt a tingling at the back of his neck. *If you only knew.*

"If I only knew...what?"

There was no answer at all, not even the rough wolf-laughter.

By the time night fell to full darkness, the cows had had their fill and went with docile obedience back into their pen to await the morning. Connor was ready to go to back to bed himself, despite the short day he'd had, but there were things to be done before he could. First, that wolf—and he, himself—had bandages that needed to be changed. Not that he was particularly looking forward to the challenge of tying them on a *conscious* wolf.

"But what the hell. If he wanted to take a chunk out of me he'd have done it already."

Despite his fears, it was a far easier task than he had expected. By the time Connor had the bandages laid out, the ointment for the wounds and his own poultice ready, the wolf had abandoned his meal and come to stand patiently behind him, waiting. It was just one more thing to add to the list of oddities.

When he began to unwrap the bandages, careful where blood and ointment had dried in the dark fur and stuck to them, he had another surprise. Some of the wounds he had treated that morning were nearly closed. Others looked as if they'd been healing for a week since he had last seen them, and not twelve hours. He turned and met the eyes of the wolf, saw patience there, a subtle sense of...fear? A secret. That was it—this was a secret. Perhaps it all was a secret.

"You shouldn't be here, should you? I'm not supposed to know—I'm not supposed to see any of this?"

The wolf looked away, and that was answer enough.

"Don't worry. Don't worry, I won't tell anyone—not even my father—not if you don't give me permission...though I'll be damned if I know how you'd do that."

He eyed the creature for a moment.

"You can't—you can't *talk*, can you?"

The wolf let out a sharp bark, close to a dog's but wilder, harsher, and shook his head.

"I guess that's a no, then. Too bad..."

Connor shrugged, then took a closer look at the wounds, the ointment and blood still caked in the fur around them, and winced.

"I don't suppose you'd take a bath, if I heated one for you—"

There was no bark this time, only a low *huffhuff* of breath. The wolf shifted from foot to foot, looked up at him, didn't move. Connor met his eyes again, wondering—he could be going mad, but again—what the hell?

"You... Do you *want* a bath?"

Again a *huffhuff*, and Connor could only assume that meant *yes*.

"All right, then. Let's...see how this works out."

He thought for a minute about the easiest way to do this—the big tub was outside already, and the well behind the hut...would it be better to build a fire near the well, heat the water there and bathe the wolf outside? An image flickered into his head, his father's hounds after the hunt in the easy days of summer, coming out of the river and shaking, shaking—

"Outside, *definitely* outside."

As if it knew what he'd been thinking, the wolf laughed at him, and Connor just shook his head. The sound was becoming too familiar, despite the strangeness of it.

* * * *

Marcas watched as the Boy went through the various steps that were required before his bath would be readied—build and light the fire, draw the well water and heat it, roll over the big tub—a good thing it was round, or the Boy never would have managed it by himself. He felt a twinge of guilt, watching him go to so much effort. It would be pleasant, this bath, and it might even be necessary, but Marcas thought it would be less of a matter to his conscience if the Boy wasn't wounded.

Or if he'd just wait until moonrise. How much longer can it be?

His gaze moved between the horizon, purple glow of twilight darkening minute by minute toward the night, and the Boy, who was pouring buckets of cold water into the tub to balance out the boiling water he'd heated over the fire. There was still steam rising from the surface in wisps and curls when the Boy beckoned him forward. Marcas stared for a moment at the edge of the tub, contemplating—were his wounds healed enough to let him jump in? But the question was never answered, because in another moment, he felt a strong, warm arm wrap around his body and another catch up his back legs, and lift him.

For a moment, instinct overrode intelligence, and Marcas struggled—but only for an instant. The Boy's shout of pain, the way he wobbled on one leg, on his feet only because the side of the tub was there to support him, dissuaded Marcas from further struggles. In another moment Marcas was still again, his lip lifted in half a snarl, displeased but aware that there was really no other choice.

The Boy was still for half a minute, righting himself, adjusting his balance with the help of an elbow and the edge of the tub. With a groan, he hefted Marcas a little higher, and Marcas felt the strength in the arm wrapped around him, warmth of body, then—from the pads of his paws upwards—the steaming heat of the water.

He whined, low-throated, pain striking anew across every injured nerve as the hot water touched his wounds, but he settled slowly, lay on the bottom of the tub so that just his head was above water. He didn't know about the ointment the Boy had used, but the blood at least would take some time to soak out of his fur.

He huffed at the surface of the water in irritation, looked up at the sky, still dark, still waiting for the moon to rise, then jerked as he felt a hand on his back.

"Easy, easy! Unless you're going to scrub yourself."

Marcas turned his head, but gentle fingers were already working hot water into the fur at the scruff of his neck. *Odd, very odd.* No instinct, no growl waiting in him, no urge to bare his teeth, to snap at those fingers. The Boy was careful, separating the individual strands, easing clotted blood, old ointment and black gore from his fur.

A little at a time, Marcas relaxed, succumbed to the lure of the water, the relaxing touch of the Boy, the murmur of his voice as he spoke—when had he started? Marcas hadn't even noticed.

"...at least you don't have splinters lodged in yours—I thought everything was all taken care of when I woke up, but they found a *dozen* more— couldn't have taken them out when I was out, oh no. Had to wait until I was awake for that. And you know what the worst part is? It was my own spear I was stabbed with. I've had my cuts and bruises, you know, in training—but this..."

The fingers paused, and Marcas blinked and raised his head. The water was still warm, but the steam was gone now and he could see the Boy's face clearly. The line Marcas had seen before was tight and narrow between his brows. His face was drawn with remembered pain. He shifted a little then, and Marcas thought he grew paler—was all the pain remembered, or did his wound trouble him now?

Slowly, but not as slowly as before, his limbs loosened by the heat of the water, Marcas stood and looked back at his body. He was a great deal cleaner than he had been—not perfect, but the Boy was afraid to touch the tender flesh and he didn't trust himself not to balk if he went too far, crossed a line neither of them was aware of. Strong in Marcas' mind was the strangeness of these moments, their mere existence an ultimate improbability. One of the *faoladh*, wolf-shaped protector of the realms of men...he should not be here with this boy.

Boy with the bright light inside him... But for these few days until my wounds are healed, what else should I do? What else can I do?

He turned and faced the Boy, shook his head a little, dampened him with spray.

"All right, all right, no need for that. Water's probably getting cold, anyway. Give me a minute and I'll help."

But Marcas could feel the readiness in his muscles, how far the healing had progressed—and he felt looser, lighter, even with the weight of the water in his fur. He took a step back, then leaped forward, one lithe motion that carried him out of the tub and onto the grass. He was poised to shake before he heard the Boy's voice call out to him, warning him to wait, and he was obliging enough to hold back so that he could get out of the range of the spray.

The shaking stung—badly—and in places he felt newly healed and healing tissues stretch in an uncomfortable way, but when he was through shaking, the water was mostly gone, and he felt cleaner and better than he had in many days. It had been nice, those fingers in his fur. It would be better if he wasn't wounded, if the Boy hadn't had to worry, had been able to reach everywhere—but he caught those thoughts and held them tightly, wrapped them up and hid them away with his earlier desire.

This can't happen again. I'll be healed before he'll even think about such a thing – and he will be, too. Tonight might be a night of crescent moon, a night of waning moon, but there will still be moonlight, and when it comes –

Marcas looked up at the sky. There were clouds, but not many, and the light of a billion stars stood out between them, splinters of light studded into a background of deepest black. He stood still, staring, ignoring the Boy calling out behind him. A little at a time, the clouds moved apart, and he saw the thinnest, barest crescent of the moon, only a night away from the night of darkness. Pale light streamed outward, a silver gleam that fought vain but valiantly against the depth of the night.

It is enough – it will be *enough.* He felt that it was imperative that he heal the Boy *tonight*, without waiting for the moon to pass from new to waxing, without waiting for it to grow easier. He had eaten well. It would be simple, compared to other things he had done. *Like protecting him in the first place.*

He watched another fuzz of cloud pass across the moon, and when he saw that the sky looked to be clear for a while, he turned and looked at the Boy. He had emptied the bath while Marcas was distracted, and now slowly, painfully, he was rolling it back to its place by the side of the hut they'd slept in. Not more than a cattle-herder's hut, but everything about this Boy from the treatment his wound had received to the way he spoke told of high birth and noble blood.

Why are you here, Boy?

The thought touched on the reason why he himself was here, something attached to his binding duty. He knew it, but he could not place the reason why he was so certain of this. It was like knowing he would heal the boy—a true thing, without reason or explanation. Marcas wiped his thoughts clean of all but what he needed to do. What was *now*. What was necessary.

He crossed the space between himself and the Boy quickly—intent, purposeful. The Boy took a full step back, unheeding of his injury, but it was too much for his wounded leg to support and in an instant he overbalanced and fell with a muffled shout of pain. The tub fell beside him, spun awkwardly then toppled upside down with a dull thud. The Boy lay still, gasping, his hands reaching reflexively for his thigh, but Marcas was impatient, if sympathetic.

The sooner he was done, the sooner the Boy would be through with pain for good. He tried to stand, and Marcas did all but tackle him, held him down with the strategic placement of his body weight. Had impatience been wrong? Marcas could hear the frantic pounding of his heartbeat, the gushing blood in his veins, the scrabbling of his fingers against the grass. He shook his head, growled a low rumbling that vibrated through his body and into the Boy's.

Chapter Three

The sound when his tunic tore almost made Connor shout out of reflex, but there was no pain and that restrained him. Only fabric had torn, not his skin — there was pain, but it was only because the wolf had his whole body on top of him. The beast held him still with weight and an unusual sort of prowess, a wrestler's tactics in the wolf-body.

Lifting his head, careful not to seem like he was trying to dislodge the wolf, Connor peered down his body and a low growl radiated through him as a dull, soothing vibration, then froze. The wolf was unbinding the linen that was wrapped around his thigh, around his wound.

The lips were peeled back carefully from the terrible fangs as they took hold of the edge of the bandage and tugged a little at a time, dropping and picking it up again as each loop of linen came undone. There was a moment of pain, as the wolf took delicate hold of the herbal poultice that covered the wound and pulled it off, then spat it away. The expression on his face at a taste that must have been terrible would have been hilarious in any other circumstance, but now Connor could only watch, fascinated and a little sickened by the puncture in his thigh.

The wound, visible now through a thick coating of white ointment, showed no putrescence but too much that was ragged and pink. It was no easy injury, and Connor was aware for the first time that he might never walk right again. The thought was enough to make his heart tight and heavy in his chest. He wanted to be more than the son of a king. He wanted to be known as king and warrior in his own right. Would that ever happen now? Could it?

He looked down his body again and saw the wolf eyes turned back to look at him — storm eyes, moon eyes, lightning-blue bright in them, and a concern that brought Connor back to a greater return of his first awareness. *No normal wolf. Fear no darkness.*

The wolf threw back his throat and began to howl — to *sing*. The moonlight flowed over them, became an open door for some power that flowed down, and down, coalesced like motes of dust out of the air and fell into the raw, puckered depths of Connor's wound like snow. *Cool. Calm. Healing.*

All his muscles went slack with confusion and awe. *What is this? What is happening?* Before his eyes, the torn tissues of his thigh were mending, realigning, growing perfect and whole as if they had never been torn.

The wolf song grew and changed as the minutes passed. The light continued to fall and shatter across his skin, but Connor lost track of it after only a short while, had to close his eyes against the strangeness of watching weeks' worth of healing happening in a few moments.

More than ever, he wanted answers. Why this wolf? Why him? What was the purpose of all this? There were plenty of injured men in the world, and the way his father had been talking, there would be more soon. What made him so special? *But the wolf can't talk. I won't get any answers.*

The tone of the howl raised over him changed again. The music of it was more complex now, infinitely refined, infinitely variable, tones that shifted and told Connor his ears were missing nuances of a song that no man had been meant to hear. He lost himself in listening, hoped he might catch something new as each repetition changed and ascended.

After a time, Connor opened his eyes and saw that the brightness had faded. The wolf-song remained as an echo, an imprint on his ears and no longer a real thing. He shook his head but the ringing remnants of those howls were not to be dislodged. He shifted in his place on the ground, prepared to wince as the motion jarred his leg—but there was nothing. *No pain.* Not an ache, an itch—he opened his eyes and looked down his body past the stretched out wolf, who lay panting now, his eyes closed.

Nothing. No wound, no scar, not a mark to show that there had ever been anything wrong with him.

The wolf lay still, a heavy weight across Connor's body that didn't move, even when he shifted to one side, trying to ease an ache forming in his back where a rock or a root was poking him. Connor stared at his leg, tried to calm his breathing, his racing thoughts. He racked his mind for any piece of knowledge that could help him—light, wolves…Crom Cruach. Strange protection and stranger protector—dark gods and old sacrifices, and now a healing light.

Without even thinking about it, he reached out a hand and ran his fingers through the damp wolf-fur, careful of the tender wounds. A low rumble escaped the wolf, a sound that seemed pleased, so Connor lay on the grass under the weight of a wet wolf and wondered what was going on without any expectation of an answer.

He *wanted* to know—*needed* to know. But who was going to tell him?

"Not you, that's for sure. I wish I knew your name, wolf. I bet you have one, and it wouldn't...hmm. Wouldn't be right to just *give* you one. Still not any more right just to keep on calling you *wolf*, though... You're not like any wolf I've ever heard of."

He got only a faint whine for an answer.

Connor sighed, folded one arm behind his head and stared upward at the blinding sky. Whorls and spirals of brilliance painted patterns of stars and other things—the darkness between and beyond them, mists of color like fog in the blackness, the spray of an unseen shore, some unknown ocean frothing up just at the edge of sight.

"Do you think the sky goes somewhere, or do you think it goes on forever? I've wondered that before—if I could run up into it, catch up to the horizon, would I make my way to somewhere? Or tomorrow? Or...maybe I'd just keep running forever."

Huffhuff.

He blinked, having expected no response at all.

"You agree? That *huff*—that's yes, isn't it?"

Huffhuff.

"Guess that means you can talk—at least a little. But no way for me to know what you're agreeing with unless I ask about everything, is there? I bet you're like me, though—I bet you think it goes on forever.

Whenever I think about it, whenever I'm looking like now, well... How you could believe anything else, anyway? How could it *end*? It's beautiful, though."

His words were interrupted twice by yawns. Connor found himself dozing in his drowsiness and considered how he was going to get the wolf off him before he fell asleep. He was still thinking about it when he did fall asleep, warm under that weight and no fear of the dark in him now, no fear of nightmares. Not with such a protector as this so close, unmoving — and the ice eyes gray in the dark of the night, but open, watchful... Always watchful, even in his dreams.

Connor woke covered in damp wolf hair, the sun shining sharp and bright into his eyes, one leg cold and the other half of his body heavy and hot under an uncomfortable pressure.

Still half asleep, he shoved at the weight pressing down on his chest, grumbled and rolled over. At the same time as he managed to find his way out from under his living blanket, Connor also managed to roll fully into wakefulness and a face full of wet grass. He opened his eyes and stared into the green. A worm was writhing in the black dirt, wriggling its way down, and it took a long moment for him to remember the events of the night before, to look around him and see — yes, the tub was just there, rolled over, and the bucket on the ground beside the well, and the fire burned out...

He looked down at his thigh, and that too was a reality. The wound was gone. Just...gone. Slowly, Connor stood, paced around. The limb felt good as new, as if it had never been wounded.

Connor looked back over his shoulder at the wolf, and saw his eyes focused on him, the mouth open for laughter that he couldn't hear. Then he lay his head down and seemed to go to sleep again, his ears twitching now and then in the warmth of the sun.

* * * *

Marcas paced back and forth outside the cattle pen, uneasy, restless, angry — *why?* The night was moonless and the stars grew bright as the sun sank below the horizon. With the sunset, the Boy had dressed well and gone seeking the nearest village with a certain glint in his eye.

Alone as the night darkened, Marcas paced, disconsolate and unsure of why. Surely he could not be *lonely*. He turned to face the rough path that led down across the green of the hill, a mile or so to the nearest village — not much of one either. A smith — a few shops — hunters, waiting for the season to ripen, and a tavern with a reputation for good mead. He knew the place — in the days before he had submitted to his service as one of the *faoladh*, he had twice crossed these hills, twice stayed at the tavern.

Marcas strained in stillness, all his restlessness focused in the direction he knew he should not go. When he had been human, he had moved among other men seeking information and news, important things for his people. Now…in *this* shape…

He had already been revealed to his Boy as something *other than wolf*, even as he had not yet been revealed for what he truly was. It was not done, to move among men like this, but…there was a tug within him, pulling him onward. Duty, and more. *What is more?*

He licked his lips and tasted starlight, turned his head again to look down the hill. *It might be safe.* He was bandaged—he could act tamer than the best trained dog, if he pleased. Were those not the mark of a domestic creature? It occurred to him that if he was thinking these thoughts, he had already made up his mind. He would be careful—he would be unseen if it were possible, but something within him was being pulled outward. He wondered if it was the urge to protect again, some danger to his Boy, marked still with that special brightness.

Marcas made his way down toward the village in a gentle lope that ate distance but didn't aggravate his wounds. Almost healed, almost gone... Still irritating, though.

When I am healed, I will make the Boy give me another bath. He will not need to watch his fingers, and this time I won't let him stop until I'm tired of it.

It wouldn't matter, would it? It wouldn't break any taboo that hadn't already been broken. And perhaps the Boy would talk to him again—a good voice he had, good to listen to...low, smooth...a harpist's voice. *Maybe he sings. Maybe he will sing for me.* Like everything else that occurred to him, even gaining a name, he had no way to make his desires known, no way to voice his questions, his requests...or his demands. Marcas laughed to himself as he neared the village, and the sound reminded him of that expression—a bend of the brow, one wrinkle between his eyes, a quirk of the lip, half smile, half scowl.

Boy, what are you doing in my thoughts?

At the edge of the village, he was pleased to see that the lights were out except for the yellow glow of the tavern's candles and the red light that fell through the open door onto the road. Voices spilled out, laughing, loud, thick with drink and other pleasures, other vices. A shadow that moved slowly among other shadows,

Marcas peered up through the windows that faced the road, even dared to poke his face around the edge of the open door, but he didn't see his Boy.

He wandered, listening, tasting the air—it was his ears that found the Boy first, the low and pleasing hum of his voice, and Marcas followed that sound and a young woman's laughter to a low building, windowless, the door blocked by a leather hanging.

As he approached the threshold, new sounds came to him, the Boy and some girl of the village—soft mutters, soft groans, soft moans. Marcas pushed his muzzle past the leather, peered into shadow lit by the gleam of a single candle. He saw mouths moving, lips, tongue—skirts overturned, hardness and the pink flesh parting for it. There were new moans, and Marcas tasted the scents of boy-musk, girl-sweet, youth and desire.

There was an ache inside him, a terrible pull that held him there, watching, despite a swell of pain. His eyes locked on the Boy's face, pleasure moving there, shifting the line of lips and eyes, narrowing the line of his throat to a single rich curve in the dark. *Gorgeous.* He turned a little, as if he sensed that Marcas was watching, and locked eyes with him, grinned. Marcas pulled back and walked behind the little building, lay against the wall to wait.

For the first time in the long years of his service, everything within Marcas that was a man had surged to the forefront. It was because of the Boy—because of his handsome strength, his fearlessness... *And don't we fight the same fight, together?*

He reminded himself that the Boy knew nothing, could know nothing. *To him I am only a wolf, not someone to desire. Only a wolf.*

The thought remained within Marcas, echoing. When the Boy came outside, Marcas heard him—and the girl too, laughing behind him. Irritated, angry, instead of peeking around the corner, Marcas ran forward, didn't stop even when the Boy called for him. The girl took one look at him and ran with her shriek strangled in her throat, and though the Boy called to her, chased after her and passed Marcas where he had stopped in the street, she didn't turn back.

Marcas laughed, and the Boy stopped and whirled round, anger on his face. More laughter was all Marcas had to offer—no regrets.

"You shouldn't be here! Four times the size of a normal wolf with eyes like winter, and you think it's a good idea to come running around here, scaring girls? I don't know what you are, but I know you're no wolf..."

The Boy shook his head.

"I don't know why you're with me, what you're doing here. You already protected me once. You healed me, so what's left to do?"

Marcas sat back on his haunches.

"Stay? That's what you're going to do, stay?"

To make his point further, Marcas lay down, forepaws flat on the ground, head on his paws, eyes fixed on the Boy's face. It was a scowling face, and not the humorous scowl which was as familiar now as the face itself, but something else. He was not amused to have had the girl frightened away.

Good. Marcas startled himself with the vehemence of his thought, shook his head to rid himself of it. This closeness, this jealousy... His desire, it wasn't allowed. *I am his protector, obedient to the light. There's no point in wanting more. I must keep the secret, do my duty —*

But jealousy still burned like a swallowed ember in his gut.

Is it just because he's brighter than the others? Because he knows I'm something mortal and not? Wolf and other? It's been so long since anyone human acknowledged me for who I am.

Maybe that was it. Yes, maybe. He looked up at the Boy and saw that his scowl had faded.

"If you're going to stay here, stay *here* — or go back and wait for me. No more scaring people!"

Marcas huffed quietly in answer, turned his face away. His own feelings aside, possessive nature and jealous desire — there was something that had brought him here, a reason against which he would not rebel. All his senses told him that he needed to be here, tonight — beside this Boy whose brightness drew him onward against all reason.

But there is no reason in the work of the gods, only purpose.

The Boy was already walking away, apparently certain that his admonition would be followed. Marcas narrowed his eyes and stood as soon as he had turned the corner and passed out of his sight. There would be no leaving him alone, even if it took more subtlety than he was used to — even if he had to stick to dark corners for a few hours.

The tingling sensation along his spine hadn't abated, and the silence of the road in this dark village of few voices only served to reinforce his unease. Behind buildings, out of sight of doors and windows, Marcas made his way back to the tavern, the only place the Boy could go.

The girl had not returned there, but that didn't seem to matter — already the Boy had a mug of ale and the gleam of his eye directed to some new paramour…which one? The blonde in the blue dress? The redhead, drinking like a man, throat thrown back and the pink tips of her nipples showing through her chemise?

But the Boy had his eye on neither of them, nor on any of the other women in the room. By moving just a little to the left, Marcas could see the figure that had his Boy's attention, and within him he felt something go hot and cold at once. It was another man, older than his Boy but not by much. He had a certain look on his face, a certain heat in his eye—it matched the gleam of the Boy's, and Marcas could see the line of attention as it drew tight and shortened between them, pulled them together, more than companionably close at the tavern's bar.

"You drink like a man, boy."

"I am a man."

"Is that so? A prince, then. A nobleman's son."

"A warrior and a warrior's son."

Marcas laughed at the encounter. It was true—it was all true, but that was how the Boy chose to define himself? A warrior. Not a prince, not the son of a king… A warrior. It opened up new layers of understanding that grew over everything he had seen and heard, but he had no awareness with which to contemplate those things now. The blond man's fingers had risen to the nape of the Boy's neck and all that was in Marcas protested.

Despite himself, the sound of more muttered words pushed him away from the door, away from the sight and sound of things that he did not want to see or hear. There would be an exchange of names soon and despite how much he wanted a name for his Boy, suddenly Marcas couldn't bear the thought of learning it this way.

For a moment, despite the promises he had made to himself and all the trouble he knew could result, he allowed himself to think about what would happen when his service was over. *Soon, now.* What if he left—and returned?

When my duty is done, what then? Not so many days, and I'll be a man again. No more brightness, no more searching the night. What if he came back to his Boy and gave up the wolf persona, told the truth about who and what he was? *He would keep the secret—and I've broken so many rules already.* There were no guarantees. There were never any guarantees, but his Boy was a warrior. His Boy hadn't turned away in fear when a wolf came for him.

Marcas made his way to the hut where the Boy had brought that girl, paced back and forth, lips drawn back, teeth parted, eyes narrowed with sharp awareness. A Boy who had no trouble with his pleasures, a Boy who took his men as he took his women. Again, he felt a forbidden pulse of feeling. Possessive instinct, tremulous desire...the *more* that had hovered behind *duty* for days now.

I could fall in love with him. It would be easy, so easy.

Marcas laughed at himself. Easy, but it would be the worst thing he could ever do. Easy, but he was a wolf, and his duty might call him away before he was even human again. Better to forget it all when the need to be here had passed. Better to move on, let the Boy have other girls, other men, even if Marcas' heart clenched at the thought of it.

As if he had summoned them, the Boy and the man he'd been talking to came together around the corner near him. Marcas had just an instant to pass out of their sight behind the edge of the building. The two of them stepped behind the leather hanging, hands already moving, pushing aside clothes, pulling them away—more roughness than there had been with the girl, more urgency, but the fumbling fingers spoke of mead and darkness.

"Turn over. No, just like that—"

"Oh—*oh...*"

Sounds came richer and thicker, and Marcas found himself on his feet again, nothing before him, no retreat behind. He closed his eyes but that could not close out the odor or the noises. He had been told about the price of service, but this was something new, a more worthy torment for a god.

Fall in love with the Boy and it's just going to kill me in the end.

And the next thought, openly contradictory, the worst sort of hypocrisy.

But only a few days left of this. Only a few days left!

He paced, and endured, memorized moans and sounds of pleasure. After all—it was not so long. Not so long for him—not so long for his Boy. Then... Then, maybe...

I'll hear everything again and make it mine. And the Boy, too. Mine.

He knew he was already giving in, but he couldn't help it. Seven years, and this Boy was the first one who had not been afraid, who had reached out and touched him.

Marcas closed his eyes.

Chapter Four

Crom, Crom, Crom.

On a black throne garlanded with gold and gleaming grain, out of place, out of time, he sat, asleep. *Crom Cruach* — the bent one, the dark god, the blood-drinker. Crom, the ancient one whose sleep had dimmed nothing of his knowledge, even when all other gods or spirits had eventually fallen away, passed out of thought and memory, and finally existence itself.

Crom Cruach. Alone since the dark before the beginning of time, the embodiment of that dark and all that survived of it, all that would ever be of it again, in dreams unending he sat and supped on gifts of power, the old, old sacrifices. The firstborn of kings and nobles, the blood of common men, the souls of warriors stripped of everything but shadow, everything but violence...

His underground was a world to which no light was native but the red light of the central fires, melt-rock, magma — and between the white light of the surface and the red light below, there were oceans of darkness without limit. A realm fit for such a king. Beneath the earth he tasted all things, drank down all things, a hunger wide and consuming as the void of the past. He lived without need, only purposed his desires, shaped them into endless nightmare without form.

Crom, Crom, Crom.

Since there had first been men, there had been sacrifices from those who sought his favor, those who sought protection from his eternal hunger — and from those who thought they could succumb to that hunger and become a part of his very existence. Through long ages, the voices had echoed, called down into the darkness at different times, offering anything, even that which was most precious, to assuage him.

Yet only his enemies understood that nothing could assuage that which was not a need — just a desire. Now, in stone circles across the land above him, a hundred arms were raised in unison. Red blood was spilled by stone knives, stained the growing grass.

Crom Cruach. Crom, Crom, Crom!

One of those times had come now — even in dreams, drinking down the endless victory, he *tasted* what was new. For how many mortal years had he been confined, that now, once again, danger had been forgotten in the face of need — or greed? His essence had been imprisoned, but not his awareness — in the silence, he had slept — but now, to the sound of his name, he stirred...awakening.

* * * *

Tigernmas rode out alone to the plain of Magh Slécht, where the stone circle of the ancient god awaited his purpose. Long processions of men were visible on the roads that led to the gathering place on the plain, and many had already arrived—there were tents and fires burning against the scarlet shadow of the horizon, proof that some of those he had summoned had been waiting for days.

It was with a cynical amusement that he saw that none of those tents had been pitched near the standing stones or the old god's gilded face. Without knowing why they had been summoned—without even being aware of what was come for them, they still knew enough to fear. How many still knew the name of the lord of the dark? Not many, but enough…enough that once it began, it would be known—even if the thing would then be too late and beyond stopping.

Tigernmas shook himself out of his thoughts as his horse brought him close to the stone circle, then shied away. He steadied the stallion and dismounted, regretted for a moment the need to return the weight of his body to his own legs—but no matter. That was the least of what he should worry over. The moment he was off the horse, a crowd began forming around him, the kings that ruled beneath him crowding close, and all of them with questions—where would they fight? Against whom? To conquer, to fend off invasion, to win pride and property?

They fell silent but no answers were forthcoming…at least not from Tigernmas. Behind the others, one among his vassals stood with his features set as stone, immobile lines carved deep and angry in his skin. *Brádach. Brádach, King of Connacht.*

"You will not explain, High King?"

Tigernmas directed a wary stare in Brádach's direction. The man's words and their tone had the sound of too much knowledge—a certain and real awareness of what it was that was about to take place. *How did you learn your truth, Brádach?*

Tigernmas stood tall, his back as straight as he could make it, one hand wrapped tight around the hilt of his sword.

"Of what do you speak, Brádach?"

"I speak of selfishness and what it will cost us. I speak of the lack of battles waiting for us — I speak of the sacrifice, to which you have summoned us!"

There was immediate muttering and Tigernmas did all he could to ignore it, to harden his features, inject something of a warrior's dignity, a king's authority, into his words.

"You would deny me this? The placation of the ancient gods, the rites that are my providence as king?"

"This is no *placation!*"

Brádach turned away from him then, and Tigernmas saw his plans unraveling, the spool of his promises unwinding as Brádach spoke.

"Listen to me, all of you — why did you think those of you with firstborn sons were told to bring them? Why do you think it was no matter if they were newborn or nine years or twenty? Look around you! Do you see the priests among you? Do you see the followers of the bent one, the lord of the mound? This is why we were brought here!"

The High King tuned his attention to many mutters, voices tossing this new idea back and forth.

"A sacrifice —"

"Priests of crooked Crom — they *are* here!"

Tigernmas glared at Brádach, though only a few seemed to understand the import of the man's words. Those who knew the name of Crom Cruach, who had the teachings of the ancient days — he could see in their eyes which they were. Out of the corner of his eye, the High King saw the priests moving forward, knives in their hands and other weapons — weapons of war.

Good.

One way or another, he would have what he wanted.

"You should watch your words, Brádach."

Tigernmas pushed his way forward and stared down into the other man's face, grateful for the extra inch of height he possessed over the younger king.

"How many battles have I fought? How much have I sacrificed in my long life of service to my people? It is only fair that there be a return. It is only fair that what was paid for be received, in one form or another. Tell me, do you think it would be better for me to die without issue, without heir? Would you have me choose one of those who serve me — you, or any of the others — and put him over his fellows and say that he will be High King when I am dead? How long do you think that would last? How long, before war shatters everything that I have spent a lifetime building?"

"Do you think this matters when you threaten all that we hold dear? Our blood for yours — our dreams for yours — our future for yours! For *our* years of loyal service, is this to be the reward?"

"You forget your place! I am not dead yet." Tigernmas stood tall and swept his gaze across the field, the outbreak of fighting in more than one place. "And I will not die until I achieve what I set out to accomplish."

With swift strides, Brádach close behind him, Tigernmas strode to the stone before the gilded idol and took up the knife that had been set before it. The blade was ancient, foreign, some sharp black stone he had never seen before. There came shouting from behind him as he lifted it, the sudden clash of weapons.

He could do nothing and still the blood of many would be spilled, but he had begun this thing and he would finish it.

Six of the young ones were clustered around the stone, hiding, waiting, trembling, brought there just for him, for his moment. He reached out blindly, not caring which one he chose, and his fingers caught in blond hair. He felt youth between his fingertips, and the jealousy within him was more than enough to rise to the surface and fill his arms, his fingers, with a strength he had not felt in years.

Strength enough to fend off Brádach's arm reaching over his shoulder, and the struggling of the one in his grasp as he sought to escape.

With one hand he grasped the blond curls, and with the other delivered a stunning blow to the temple with the knife in his fist. Tigernmas threw back his head and let out a cry that stunned the battlefield.

"Crom Cruach! It is for you!"

He slit the boy's throat, right to left, and pulled his head back so the spurting life-blood sprayed across the gilded face of the ancient stone. His vision wavered as Brádach landed blow after blow on his back, but before his eyes the features of the idol seem to waver, to shimmer, the gold becoming dark. Blackness, utter void, a cut-out a thousand shades darker than the inside of a cave or the spaces between the stars.

The crescent eyes of the idol shifted expression, opened wide. The black smile widened, the mouth an onyx cavern, and from it poured laughter that was all amusement and a hatred so profound Tigernmas quailed before it.

Crom Cruach.

He had come! Warmth spilled down his back, and he knew it was blood, even as he saw Brádach's shadow retreating from the idol. Tigernmas heard the battle ongoing behind him even as he heard the laughter of the bent one as he came forth. Blackness lapped at the blood, a thousand tongues of more than shadow reaching out of the endless darkness beneath the earth.

Breathless, Tigernmas felt that presence come over him, hatred and all black things, crawling and slick with endless agony in the moment he was touched. He had prayed for life, and when that had not been granted, he had turned to death…but it had been the wrong choice. He saw that now, more clearly than he had ever seen anything, ever. He had let loose a terrible force in the world, had summoned it by name, loosed its chains, given it a way to once more fulfill its desires among men.

A voice brought him down into blackness.

"The sacrifice has been made, the price been paid. Now the prayer must be answered. You will not live, Tigernmas, High King. But neither will you die."

Shadow crawled out of the idol's gaping mouth. Tigernmas saw it unfolding, limbs rattling like sticks. The world shook beneath him, and the stars foamed in the sky as the lord of the mound clawed himself from the earth. Void, featureless, without eyes, the great figure stared down and Tigernmas felt the presence of it clawing at his soul—caustic, more ancient than the universe, more ancient than time.

Crom Cruach.
My mistake.

* * * *

Of all the things he'd been irritated by when he'd been wounded, Connor had missed pleasure most — the heat of flesh, seeking motion, sensation... *That wolf, though.* Like a jealous lover, that one. And he was sure the wolf thought he'd not seen him outside the tavern, watching, those eyes always on him and more ice in them than ever. It was why he'd come back here so soon, allayed the long seduction, turned away from the games he liked to play. This uncomfortable feeling was new to him. He chose his partners where he pleased, many or few, for once or for many times — and why not?

This man, now, bent for him, looking back over his shoulder, wanting — this was a good thing, better than the girl. The heat of his body gripped tight around the thickness of Connor's cock, pulled guttural groans out of his throat, and the man below him uttered soft words and whispers of more. *More, yes.*

He heard a howl, loud, immediate in its closeness, and knew who it was from — the man beneath him didn't, but he didn't seem to care, either. There was only heat upon heat, and the tightening deep in his body, surging sensation — more tightening, the man below him thrusting his hips back, crying out —

In concert with those cries, with the white flash of Connor's own climax, there were other screams.

It took him a minute to realize that it wasn't an echo, something in his head — that there were real screams, coming from outside, growing in number, in volume, and with the screams, the shouts of men calling for weapons. He jerked back from the man below him and turned to face the door, fumbling with the tie of his trousers. He ignored uncomfortable wetness on his thigh and the rapid questions coming from behind him. He had only one concern, one sudden thought—that howl, had the wolf *done* something?

If he's caused trouble…

But the wolf was outside, standing directly in front of the leather flap that blocked the door. The man behind him swore.

"What the hell is that! Get back—"

"No! Wait here a minute—don't leave until you're sure I'm gone."

Connor ran out into the middle of the street and was surrounded almost immediately. Everyone was awake, the tavern emptied into the street, and though the screams were less there were still shouts and calls coming from all directions, armed men lining up at one of end of the road. People were coming down in torch-lit streams to the village from farms a mile or more distant, blips of light that vanished and reappeared as they came over the rolling of the hills.

Most of all, Connor saw that every eye was turned south and upward, and many were pointing—yet there was no need. Once he had looked in that direction, he had no need to question anything. Connor felt cold terror for the first time in his life. It slid down his throat, a drink no man should swallow.

The stars were blacked by darkness. Not the darkness that was behind them, not the gentle cloak of the night that had lain smooth and clean over the world since he was born—no. This was *emptiness*. An outline of *nothing* had taken over the sky, man-shaped, enormous, blotting out the horizon with the length of its legs, blacking the span of the sky with the reach of its arms. Its head lifted over the upturned bowl of the sky, crowned for an instant with the sprawl of a billion stars before they were quenched.

A hole had been cut in the night, and he knew its name.

"Crom Cruach."

It escaped him as barely a whisper, but even so much was enough. He knew it, felt the focus of the thing as it fell on him, a raking claw that scarred his consciousness, sent him stumbling backward. Connor reached out his hands for the edges of the blot in the sky, as if he could close it, restore his vision to something unmarred by so much that was unmentionable.

Behind him, steadying, warm, he felt the presence of the wolf. He looked down and his gaze was caught by the intensity of the stare that met him.

Run, boy. Run.

There were no words, just that stare, but it told him everything he needed to know—everything he *didn't* need to know. This was an enemy he couldn't fight, even if he had a weapon. The great shape across the sky was growing—wider, darker, consuming the sky. There was only one thought that kept coming to him, over and over—a truth that he knew without thinking, a truth that had stained his soul the moment that name had slipped past his lips.

The sacrifice. Father failed.

His heart pounded in his chest. Even the night after the battle he hadn't felt a fear like this—but now, now that the lord of the mound was awake, striding across the land…

Would they be buried in darkness?

All he could do was obey that command, still ringing in him without words.

Run!

Connor turned and fled, found his horse and mounted without hesitation. He urged the stallion forward into a gallop that gained ground fast, but he didn't go back up the road toward the hut that stood lonely in the dark. Instead, he fled across the road, through a half dozen thickets and clearings toward the center of the wood. His heart pounded in his chest. Fear forced cold sweat to the surface of his skin along with the sweat of exertion.

It felt like there was something behind him no matter how far he went, no matter how fast he urged the horse beneath him. The trees whipped past at the edge of his vision, and the undergrowth was invisible, a blur of green-gray darkness in the shadow. Were there stars in the sky? Were there stars? Had the blackness eaten them all? Was one of those great hands, the night cut out of existence where it passed — was it over him, even now?

Connor defied his first fear to face this greater one, pulled the panting horse beneath him to a stop and turned in the space between the trees, moved forward until he could look up. For a minute there was only panic, but one by one the prickling brightness of individual stars grew visible. He let out a heavy breath, and realized only then that he was panting, shaking, nauseated.

He threw one leg over the side of his horse and fell to the ground in a heap, his legs unwilling to support him. On his knees he looked back the way he had come, only to realize he had no idea which direction that was. There was nothing to tell him which way was which in the dark of the moonless night. His mind was still racing away from him, terror motivating his senses, every nerve hyper-alert.

He crouched, pressed his back against the nearest tree, laid a hand against the nose of his horse as it nuzzled him. *Calm. Breathe deep. Panic is the enemy —*

fear not a failure – the first foe is yourself. They were his father's words, training words, and now their echo reinforced Connor's will. A little at a time his breathing slowed. His ears grew sensitive to the noises of the night, filtered out the sound of the wind, his own breath, the heartbeat still racing in his ears, the shifting of the horse beside him.

Nothing else, only the sounds of the wood. No screams, no fire, no sounds of men or madness – no oncoming danger.

Just as well, since I've no weapon.

He let his head fall back against the trunk of the tree behind him and slid down to his knees. Most of the night was still before him, and now wasn't the time to start being afraid of the dark. *That shape, though. The sky cut out. It was Crom Cruach, I know it. And He saw me.*

Shadows threatened at the edge of his sight, tempting fear again, but when he turned to look there was nothing there, nothing at all.

"I left...the wolf behind."

Loneliness descended over him like a shroud. It wasn't that the wolf was his, or even that he'd expected it to stay with him – he hadn't. Yet he was lonely, and the thought that his mind hooked on to, was the memory of that pressure against his back, his legs. Warm wolf, and the stare of those eyes that had told him to run.

"Be safe, wolf. Even if you don't come back to *me*, be *safe*."

Connor settled back against the tree and tried to close his eyes, but it was no use. His heart was still beating fast, his thoughts running over and over the events of the night. All he had wanted was a little bit of pleasure, a little bit of fun. Not *this*.

Tonight the sacrifice his father had feared had happened. A sacrifice of firstborn — *blood for the buried god.* Connor shuddered, listened to the warm *huff* of the horse's breath beside him and tried not to think about the drawn and terrible expression he had last seen on his father's face.

* * * *

A drop of dew falling to his cheek startled Connor awake out of a doze, and he tried to stand from his crouching position only to curse and fall over, his legs numb and tingling from so long in the awkward position. When he had slapped some feeling back into them, he stood and paced around a little, tried to warm himself by rubbing his arms and wished he'd thought to grab his cloak from wherever he'd thrown it in his haste to get his trousers untied.

"Not that I didn't have other things on my mind at the time."

He stood close to his horse, and the steaming beast curled its head around to look at him, patient and curious but with none of the awareness he'd grown used to in his other companion.

"And if that wolf's really an animal then I'm a tree."

Connor snorted at himself, breathed on his fingers and finally pulled himself up onto the horse and started forward. He couldn't see the edge of the wood, couldn't remember what direction it lay in, so one way was as good as another. If he was lucky, he'd pick the right direction and find his way out in an hour or so. But he had only gone a few steps before a black shape bounded out of the undergrowth and ran at him — *the wolf!*

"You! I thought I'd seen the last of you."

Connor dismounted, then crouched before the wolf and took the great ruffed muzzle into his hands.

"I hope you know the way back."

He received an affirmative huff and ran his hands back through the fur, leaned his head down to rest against the wolf's forehead. Warm tongue reached out and licked his cheek, but not in the slobbery way of dogs, just heat and dampness, reassuring. "What are you covered with? This stuff…"

The darkness of the wolf's coat was nothing natural, and as Connor looked at it, rubbed it between his fingers, he recognized it as the same black ichor he'd seen before.

Something stared at him from the blue eyes, something strange — pressure that he didn't understand, an intensity almost equal to the moment in which that urge, that order to *run* had been transmitted. A chill touched him, and Connor tried to shake it off, but the feeling wouldn't go. *Those shadows. He fought them. Did they follow? Is it safe here? Doesn't matter. Can't stay — not here, not now.* He *knew* it, without words, without reason. His skin was tingling with the urge to flee

"What about it, wolf? Do you still mean to stay with me?"

The answer he got was a growl that wound up through all the octaves of wolf-noise until it rang out in a clear, true howl, nothing magic in it but the wild of the sound. It was not only an affirmation, but a noise rich with urgency, and Connor turned to face the dark behind him. The shadows were *moving*.

It was time to run.

He mounted his horse without delay, and had no need to rouse the beast to great efforts. It, too, must have sensed the oncoming darkness, but the wood seemed to go on around them forever, shadow in the reach of every hanging branch, every leaf.

There was nowhere to hide, and it was taking too long to get away — and if there was one thing that Connor was aware of, it was his vulnerability to those *things*. Shadow creatures, broken spirits...whatever they were. One stumble, one faltered beat of hooves beneath him was all it took, and there was blackness on them, some jet figure reaching out with terrible claws.

He slipped off the side of his horse as it fell, rolled and took three steps forward. There was a howl, the bright music he remembered from the battlefield. For an instant Connor could breathe, think, *move* without fear...but only for an instant. Shadow swelled behind him, all of it reaching, all of it connected, all of it eager for his death.

The wolf was beside him then, pulling at him, *dragging* him with more strength than Connor had dared to suspect. First his arm, then his shoulder — the wolf had him half on its back before he made sense of the situation and pulled himself the rest of the way up. Connor leaned forward as the wolf sprang ahead, laid his body along the length of that lean, strong back.

Muscles flexed beneath him, and the wind bit at Connor's cheeks so that he pressed his face into the wolf's warm fur. He breathed deep of animal scent, the odor of wild forests endlessly renewed under the moonlight. It seemed to refill his strength, bolster his courage, and he dared to look back...but there was nothing there. The streaming shadows that had accosted them had retreated, or vanished behind them.

The landscape around them was wholly unfamiliar, and he'd been lost in the first place. Now Connor had no idea of where they were, how far they had traveled or in what direction. There was only a sense that he had left everything he knew far behind him. The wolf slowed, until he stopped. A gentle rushing sound that had been growing louder for some time became the visible ocean before them.

Connor slid from the wolf's back with a sigh and sprawled near the water, wondered which coast they had come to as his heart began to slow its pounding in his chest. Beside him, the wolf hadn't relaxed, paced back and forth, his gaze moving from shadow to shadow.

"What's wrong? Aren't we safe here? Did something follow us?"

There was no response. The wolf didn't even turn to face him. Connor had been staring at the stars, but now the sky around them seemed oppressive, a weight of darkness. He turned on his side, then pushed himself back so he could feel the warmth of the wolf as he paced, and stared at the ocean instead. Black water. *Deep*. Many secrets there, old things, dark things...

An uncomfortable prickle tingled at the back of his neck, and he rubbed his hands over it, tried to rub it away. The speed of his heart increased, his breath grew rapid—involuntary responses, but why? Once upon a time, his father had taught him everything he knew about staying alive. He had told Connor to pay attention to his body, trained him to listen to the little things, the small responses. *"Sometimes the body does things of itself out of need. Pay attention when this happens. Look around you before you blame fear."*

"So what's out there now?"

He spoke without realizing, then felt the wolf draw close to him and press against his back.

"There *is* something, isn't there? *He's* watching us."

A low whine answered him, and Connor found his gaze straining at every shadow. Were they lengthening, growing, changing? Was that just starlight off the water, time passing, and the shadows moving...or were the shadows *moving*?

Perhaps an hour passed, not longer. Connor heard a low, unceasing growl from the wolf pressed against his back and started himself out of a doze. As soon as he leaned forward, the wolf let out a low, drawn out howl—no less clear than those Connor had heard before, but different in tone and apparently in purpose.

There was no blinding flash of light, no screaming from the darkness. A subtle glow seemed to flood his companion from nowhere, a dark silver luminance that sheathed him ear-point to tail tip, coated the individual hairs of his fur.

Tense, Connor crouched beside the wolf, uncomfortable with the wide space of the ocean at his back. He had no choice but to trust his protector, and no reason to doubt that trust, but he was used to guarding him*self*.

The attack was swift, as he had expected, and silent, which he had not. For a moment there was a bubbling of warning at the outer limits of the near shadows— that was all, the instantaneous promise of something terrible before the terror itself had arrived.

The wolf drew back and knocked Connor to the ground, stood over him so that Connor looked up at glow and fur, could only see the world vaguely beyond that dark light. Tangles and tendrils of darkness swarmed around them, darted down and hovered, but they wavered near the wolf's brightness and dared not approach.

How long would it last? *Not long.* It couldn't, or there would be no danger. Not for the first time, Connor damned his inability to talk to the wolf and get actual answers. Not for a lack of being understood—he thought the wolf understood *too much*, sometimes, but that didn't help him.

This wolf—he's going to get himself killed protecting me, and I won't even know why!

Connor's heart burned in his chest, made itself known like a flaming spear buried between his ribs, even as around and above him the silver glow was flickering out.

Shadow strained and bit in Marcas' direction, coiled back only to strike forward again. The ropes of blackness came closer each time, as the ethereal protection that Marcas had summoned out of starlight began to fade. He could feel it, the static tingle on his fur vanishing away. When it was gone, it would leave him vulnerable once more—and more than that, more *importantly* than that, leave the Boy vulnerable too.

No such protection was enough. He had known before he called it down over them that it would only be temporary, a few minutes' worth of breathing space, but what else could he do? *Think, Marcas. Think! Where to go, what hiding place?*

He snapped at the darkness as it came close enough, stepped back when it recoiled and urged the Boy to his feet with a shove of his head. He leaped forward and struggled with blackness, heard the boy behind him take a step back—what was he thinking?

Closer to me, Boy, not farther! Don't make this harder for me!

Marcas spat shadow and shook black ichor from his jaws, growled at the Boy and got no response, no approach. He was shaking his head, his eyes on the shadow, every inch of him betraying a slump into despair. Marcas leaped at him, toppled him to the ground and stood on his chest, despite the fact that the Boy was already gasping for breath, all the wind knocked out of him by the fall.

Marcas took the collar of his tunic in his teeth and dragged him across the sand with one defiant dash and tug, then pushed the boy back until he was leaning against one of the damp black rocks revealed by the tide.

The shadow was all around them, black presence forming itself into man-shapes now, not just a writhing ball of rat-tailed ugliness but warriors of darkness, the infinite army of the night. He heard the Boy's voice, low behind him—a revelation of how much he knew, how much he understood—and how little.

"There's no hope! It doesn't matter where we go. He's after me, not you. Don't you get it? What are you doing? Just go—get away from me!"

That the Boy cared, that he would die, here, rather than sacrifice even a nameless wolf for his own sake—it brightened the beat of Marcas' heart, set it pounding in his ears. That he had given in to hopeless thoughts, that he thought the deaths of one or both of them were inevitable—that, too, set his heart pounding, but not because he wanted the Boy. He was *furious*.

Out of his thoughts went every preoccupation with escape, with running, with finding some hiding place in which to wait for the light. Out of mind went the surety of his own failure that had come on him just moments before, the thought that they might never escape, that they might be caught by what pursued them. That tonight, so close to the end of his service, he might lose everything he had gained and everything that beckoned him forward to the future — the idea *enraged* him.

In the Boy's hopelessness, he found hope. In the failure of his spirit, his will, Marcas found his own intensified, magnified a hundred fold. The shadow was reaching for him, tangled fingers of soot and charcoal that clawed at his fur, opened new, deep gashes. He reared back and howled, a sound so loud that behind him, out of the corner of one eye, he saw the Boy wince and press his hands over his ears. Yet it was not a magic howl, summoned down no light, no power — it was a battle cry.

In the next instant, he was the whirlwind. With just the one person to protect, it was easier than it had been the last time. He let nothing past him, relied on claws and fangs and the weight of his presence. Tonight, in the dark of the moon, he had no choice. Not only purpose demanded this of him, not only the defiance of darkness that was his service, his existence. Pride demanded it, and the feeling that was growing in him — the feeling that could be love, if he would let it.

Marcas bared all his teeth at the night, ignored the faceless murmur of the shadow and tore to pieces all that came near them. Free of encumbering evil, breathing hard in this moment apart from battle, Marcas turned and considered the Boy behind him, the flat press of his body against the wet stone, the grimness of his face, his paleness. There was fear in him, and anger, but also shame — Marcas understood.

He was a warrior, but he faced an enemy against whom he was helpless.

He stepped forward and pulled on the Boy's sleeve with his teeth again. He heard a muttered curse before he started to pull back, tried to stand and tug his tunic from Marcas' teeth at the same time. Marcas let go and he stumbled backwards, but Marcas had planned for that and was already beside him, ducking under him so that when the Boy caught himself, he was already half across Marcas' back.

"Why are you doing this?"

The words were soft, aching.

"I don't—I don't understand why you're doing this. I might be the son of a king but I'm just Connor—I'm not—"

He stopped, but Marcas was still, waiting for him to move, his thoughts ringing with that accidental gift. *Connor. Your name is Connor.* Then he felt hands tightening on his fur, the warm weight of Connor's body swinging up and over, settling along the length of his back.

"But if you won't go without me—I've got no choice, do I?"

Marcas huffed softly, looked back over his shoulder and caught Connor's gaze for a single moment. He wanted him to know that despite any danger, there was no chance of Marcas giving him up. *You're mine, Connor. Mine to protect, and maybe – more.*

But the glance would have to be enough.

He took a step back, then sprang forward, east along the southern shore of Eire. He prayed the sun would rise soon, *soon*. Connor's fingers were tense in his fur, the muscles of his thighs tight as corded iron around his back—and yet there was trust in the way he let himself be carried, in the eyes that met his glance, in the smile that spread on his face. It was the smile that made up Marcas' mind.

I will bring you home, Connor. I will bring you to the secret places of the faoladh *before I lose the chance.*

Shadow groped forward again behind them. With a snarl and a gnashing of teeth, Marcas surged ahead, put all the distance he could between himself and his Boy, and the powers of darkness.

Chapter Five

Through the last hours of the night, shadow clinging to the footprints of his thoughts, Connor knew nothing but speed. The world around him was a blur in shades of gray. To look at it stung his eyes with the blistering friction of the wind, and he couldn't focus on anything, even though he knew that the flat black blur to their left must be the sea, and the rolling, shadowed blur to their right must be the hills, perhaps a forest.

He buried his face in the warm fur, breathed deep of the odors of wild and wilderness. He grew accustomed to the rolling gait of the wolf beneath him, the great ribs expanding under him with deep breaths, the streaming fur of the soft ruff blowing back over his face, his forehead. A little at a time he relaxed the grip of his fingers on the thick fur and reached his arms forward instead, over the great shoulders, around the powerful chest.

Now and then the wolf stopped, crouched panting with his eyes on the blackness around them. Connor found himself dozing on these short pauses, startling into wakefulness after a few minutes or many. He had no way to tell. Many times, he thought he heard pursuing footsteps just as the wolf began to run again, a rush of darkness just behind them, but he couldn't turn and look, wouldn't have been able to see if he had.

This was the hour of trust or failure. All he could do now was hold on and hope for a sign, a fraction of sun.

The wolf ran farther and farther into the west, past lands that Connor knew, his father's country — and then again, into a tangled forest that seemed like it should be familiar, but wasn't. They were moving too fast for him to tell if there was a lightening of the horizon, if the deep black of night had yet given way to the softer purple of morning's dusk

After a time their way cleared and straightened, became almost a true path, though Connor couldn't imagine who but his wolf might frequent it. The trees grew so close together overhead that the sky was invisible behind the shade of the canopy, and all around them was an endless rustling of leaves.

Upward, inward, onward, the wolf ran in fits and starts, always with an eye on the shadows around and behind them. They met no overt malice, and after a time the wolf slowed to a calmer pace, almost a walk, but still Connor was glad when he looked up and saw that overhead the sky was brightening. The fear he couldn't repress sank as the dark faded behind him, decreased with every mote of light.

When a hall reared up before them, clean-shaped wood and new thatch, Connor almost fell off the wolf in surprise. Then he was toppled, as the wolf turned sharply and dislodged him.

"Ow! What—"

Connor heard a growl, felt the great muzzle pushing at the backs of his legs, and stood—and still he was pushed, right up the last few feet of the path to the door of the hall, shut tight and all silent within, not a single presence anywhere near. Again and again he felt the wolf's head pushing at the backs of his legs— inside? This was where he was supposed to be safe? What was special about *this* place?

The pressure against his legs vanished and when he turned, there was no one behind him—*nothing* behind him. The wolf had disappeared, as if he had never been, and in that single lonely instant, surrounded by only the promise of dawn and not yet dawn itself, Connor saw the shadow of every moving leaf, every still pebble, as a living thing out for the beat of his heart.

He whipped around and yanked open the doors to the hall. They were unbarred, and he found it as empty as the silence outside had promised. He shut the doors behind him and sank down slowly to the ground, pressed his head into his hands and tried to breathe deeply, slowly.

It had to be safe here. It had to be safe or the wolf wouldn't have left him alone. Wasn't that the point? Wasn't that what the beast had proved to him, even when they had been surrounded by shadow and death and all that sought to end the world? *Safe*. How, or why, those were things he didn't know—but then maybe it was fitting. Maybe the enigma of the wolf required this newer mystery.

In the dark of a stranger's hall, uncertain of where he was or why he had been brought there, deserted even by his last companion, his savior, a deeper truth began to sink past the terror and incomprehensibility of the nights just past.

"Alone — I really *am* alone, this time."

* * * *

Marcas left Connor at the door to his own hall. It was forbidden, what he was doing — by law and custom both. Men of the outer world weren't meant to mingle with the *faoladh*, weren't meant to know that they even existed. *But Connor knows, and what he doesn't, I will tell him.*

He made his way into the wood with disjointed steps. His head felt light, distanced him from his flesh. The green world spun into a yellow haze as the sun came up, and Marcas heard a dull hum in his ears, a sound like nothing in this world. He had heard it once before, seven years ago when he had taken this shape.

Reality dissolved around him into motes of dust and light. The warmth of the sun was tangible, but it wasn't warmth — just a presence of light and brightness, healing energies, all that was growth and life in the world. Marcas had never felt anything so welcome in his life.

He saw yellow and gold and white, all the brightness that there was, and across it a running flame of green that called to him. He bounded forward and found himself staring into ancient waters, across ancient hills, all his awareness painted by a single pair of eyes, brown as the richest earth, black as the night sky when it comes without fear or shadow.

"*You have done well, Marcas.*"

Marcas knew that voice. *The Dagda*. The swell of it, tone pure as the light around them, was a sound that was trees growing, the wind in the leaves and the wind in the grass, the baying of the stag, the howl of the wolf, the hum of the hare's heartbeat and the swift flutter of the sparrow's flight.

"Yet you have not yet done everything you were meant to do."

The Dagda had been the source of Marcas' power. He was the one who had made the *faoladh*, the one with whom they had made the contract against Crom Cruach, the Dagda's ancient foe. What was this? Was this supposed to happen?

"Do more, Marcas."

Slowly the brightness began to fade.

"Do all that you know to be right, as you have done so far."

Marcas felt himself descending out of whatever realm of light and power he had entered, back into the ordinary reality of the living world. The words of the Dagda shone bright as fire behind his eyes, praise and the approval. Suddenly, he was no longer worried about having brought Connor here—about his decision to go to him, to tell him…everything.

He took a deep breath and let it out. No sign of any other presence remained, only the echo of the god's voice in his head. He moved and felt the cool of the dew-damp undergrowth brush over his skin.

My skin. He sat up abruptly, fell onto one side, then pushed himself up more slowly, marveling at the response of every nerve. Marcas flexed his fingers and looked down at his hands, grinned and felt the once-familiar stretching of facial muscles.

As much as it had taken him time to get used to the wolf-shape, it would take time, he thought, to get used to being him*self* again. Slowly, using the nearest tree to aid him, Marcas pushed himself to his feet. It took more than a moment to gain his balance again, to adjust to the strangeness of standing on two feet and not four.

"And the god says *do more, Marcas.*"

He spoke the words out loud and startled himself with the sound of his own voice — like a stranger's, completely unfamiliar. It sounded nothing like the voice he remembered having. Could seven years have changed him that much, even while he was wearing the skin of a wolf?

"Maybe I just don't remember."

A little at a time, balance came back to him and sensation receded, though not as much as he'd expected. His skin felt...new. Maybe it would just take time to get used to the rawness of it. He reached up and ran his hands through his hair — longer than he had worn it before his change, but there was comfort in the weight now, the way it fell on his shoulders.

He passed his hands over his face, the flat human features, no protruding muzzle — over the tanned skin of his torso, the muscles beneath trembling with tension and uncertain mastery, uncertain intention — over taut buttocks...no tail. Up again over long arms, smooth with strength, his eyes taking in the lines of his palms, the tiny hairs on the back of his knuckles.

Experimentally, he took two steps, felt his toes flex against the grass, the arch of his foot a strange curve to walk on. He crouched, then stood again, tried to balance on one foot and fell over almost at once. Thankfully the landing was soft.

Groaning, Marcas let out a breath and brought up one hand to cover his eyes. He breathed deep, thought of the boy waiting for him in the hall at the top of the hill... *Connor.* Would he be asleep? Probably. It had been a long night, and a long day before it.

"But I'm not tired — what's wrong with me?"

Was it the change? Regaining his own skin, wasn't it supposed to be a tiring thing, like all the other uses of that power? He could still remember how it had been in the beginning, when he had first taken up his service and the shape of the wolf with it.

"Slept for three days, then. Maybe it's easier going back to my own shape."

He closed his eyes and breathed deeply, found himself sorting scents automatically—rustling prey in the undergrowth, musk of the wild, green heather, green grass, Connor...

It was only then that Marcas realized the strangeness of what it was he was doing. Sorting scents—how was that possible when he was *no longer the wolf*? It occurred to him that while his sight seemed to have returned to something human—something *normal*—his hearing, too, had not.

The sounds of birdsong and running water were too loud, too clear. He concentrated, just as he had done as the wolf, and heard in the distance falling rock, the footsteps of deer, a larger river—and closer, but still too far for any human ears to hear, he listened to the calm breathing of Connor and the low thrum of his heartbeat.

He heard again the words of the Dagda. *Do more, Marcas.* More—was that why he had retained the senses of the wolf? It occurred to him only then to focus inward, seeking the ever-present brightness that had guided him onward in his service. It had brought him to children, to those lost in the wilderness, to honorable warriors wounded in battle, far from home. It had brought him to Connor, and it was *still there within him*.

There was no denying it when the brightest point that had ever occupied that portion of his awareness was a beaming glow nearby.

It seemed like the change of skin Marcas had been waiting for hadn't changed much. How could he consider his service over if there was still the god's power within him, still the god's purpose hanging over him? As he pushed himself to his feet again, Marcas made the first decision of many that he could feel weighting his way into the future.

He would serve the power that still touched him. He would protect his boy.

"*Connor.*"

He liked the taste of it, the way it came from the tip of his tongue. He took a few cautious steps, and found his balance much improved—the body remembered what the mind forgot. *Good*. He would make the wrong kind of impression if he couldn't even walk in a straight line.

It was time to tell Connor all the things that had been building up inside him for weeks—truths, needs, feelings, what it was that should be feared…and how they could fight it.

Slowly, gaining confidence with every step, Marcas made his way back up the hill to where his hall and his boy were waiting.

There was silence there, the wild noises of the wood scattered by the presence of two men, here where there had for seven years been only rare visitors. Marcas saw that the place had been maintained since it was built, even though he hadn't yet lived there. Even the thatch was new. Slowly, he pushed against the doors to the hall, but only one opened. The other was stuck, and when he slipped through the open space of the right-hand door he saw why.

Connor was sleeping, his back against the left-hand door. One leg was thrust straight out in front of him and the other folded under the first. His hands lay relaxed in his lap, the fingers lightly curled against each other—his head was tilted to one side, so that his hair fell across his closed eyes, and his lips were barely parted, his breathing deep and slow.

For a long minute Marcas stood staring at him, feeling the things focus within himself that he had spent many wolfish days coming to terms with. Even now that he was human again, Marcas was not free of his responsibility, but...

I want you, Connor. I want to love you. Will you let me? Will you turn away, or... What will you give me in return?

Marcas reached out one hand, brushed back the fall of hair with gentle fingers, looked down at those closed eyelids. *Soft, just like I thought.* Then he turned away and slipped silently out of the hall through the open door. It would do him no good to wake Connor like this. After all, he didn't even know who Marcas was, and the truth was something that would take explaining.

Outside, Marcas stretched and looked up at the brightness of the morning sky, rubbed his neck with one hand and considered what to do now. There were things that needed doing—the well would have to be checked and maybe cleaned, and even the short glimpse inside the hall that he'd seen had showed him plenty of things that needed doing. The wolf-hearing he'd retained let him hear the movements of mice, disturbed by his presence...

But Marcas smiled despite that and flopped back on the grass, ears tuned to the sleeping boy of whom he'd grown so fond.

"What will you think of me, Connor?"

He found his thoughts drifting back over the time he'd spent watching over him. The one sided conversations, the questions that Connor had asked and Marcas hadn't been able to answer. He remembered more the more he thought about it, words building up in him, the answers that had been delayed. He wanted to give every opinion he'd been asked and more.

"As long as he doesn't run from me. As long as he stays to listen—even if he laughs, even if he doesn't believe me."

There was plenty of proof, wasn't there? Just answering some of those questions would be enough. And there were other things, which he clung to in his thoughts as truths that would be undeniable. Who had chased away every incarnation of darkness in the immutable night, protected him from shade and shadow?

"I carried him. He'll know me—he has to know me. He won't be afraid, not Connor."

He closed his eyes and visualized Connor's sleeping features, sun-glow on his red hair, eyes moving beneath their lids.

"Wake up soon. *Soon*."

* * * *

Connor woke all at once, as if someone had called him, some familiar voice for which he'd been waiting. He sat bolt upright and fell sideways onto his hands when he tried to scrabble up onto his feet. One leg was dead, the numbness only just beginning to break into pins and needles as he tried to steady it under him. How long had he been asleep for?

The sun was still visible through the spaces in the wall, came through the roof-thatch with a rich golden glow, seeped through one of the doors behind him, open to the afternoon. The tension that had come on him with the thought that he had slept through the day, that the night and all its shadows had come, faded in the presence of that glow — but then he paused, turned and winced at the shot of strangeness that went up his leg as he walked on it.

"The door — I know I closed it."

He stared at it, but it was most definitely open, and he had just as definitely closed it. Had it been the wolf? Could a wolf open a door? If it had been the person whose hall this was, wouldn't they have woken him, thrown him out or offered hospitality? He looked back over his shoulder, wondering.

There was dust on the long feasting table and the long benches beside it. Dust showed silver in the sunlight on the dais at the head of the hall, but no high seat was placed there. There was even dust in the hearth, a hearth swept bare of ashes, which it looked like no fire had been set in it for years. Old black scorch marks were all there were to tell him that a fire had ever been lit. And yet despite the dust, the evidence of neglect, the thatching was fresh and clean, filled the whole hall with the odor of sweet straw. The place was deserted, dusty and disused, but it was certainly no ruin.

Licking his lips, aware of dry thirst and gnawing hunger, Connor turned back to the open door and stepped out into the light. The sun was moving in the west now, close to the horizon — perhaps four hours remained before sunset, or a little more. *Time to think, I guess.*

What would happen when the night came? His memory was full of the struggle just past, the hopelessness of it. Ashamed, he remembered his own cowardice — curled in the dark hollow of some shore-side boulder, tasting blood on his bitten lip, ready to give himself over, give up and give in. *Never again.* He tightened his fists until his knuckles ached and made a silent promise to himself. *Never again. Maybe I can't fight it — the shadow of the bent one. But I will never, ever give in again.*

He wondered, though, if the danger was over. Was that why his protector — his companion — had left him? Connor cast his gaze back and forth across the hilltop and the darker glow of green forest that spread down the hillside and across the level ground below.

"No sign of him." Connor sighed. "I wonder if he's gone for good…that wolf. I guess it's too much to hope that he would've let me know, somehow, if he was going…"

"And why is that?"

The answer came out of nowhere, a warm baritone that sent a ripple up Connor's spine. He whipped around, but there was no one to see, no one standing anywhere near him, at least not in view. He turned his eyes toward the wood around and below him. "Who said that?" There were plenty of hiding places there, plenty of places where a single person or many could stand hidden and not run a risk of being seen. *That open door —*

"There's no point in hiding, I know you're there. Show yourself!"

"I'm not sure I should. You aren't in a good mood, Connor."

Connor stumbled backward a single step, narrowed his gaze in the direction the voice had come from.

"How do you know my name?"

"You haven't guessed?"

Laughter came out of the trees, and Connor froze in place, couldn't even blink. *That laugh.* Panting. Wolfish. Oh, it was a man laughing, but the sound of it carried so much that had recently become familiar. On the heels of the laughter came words that set his heart beating at a speed that was almost painful.

"You were the first man I've ever met that didn't care I was a wolf. Most don't, while the saving is going on. It's afterward, when they have time to think about it, that they run—as far and as fast as they can. If they have questions... Well, maybe they think it will be easier to ask them alone in the smoke and heat of some tavern hall. But not you, Connor. You never ran from me. You called out to me, even the very first night."

There was more laughter, in a different tone but with the same wolfishness, and Connor shook his head—none of this was possible, none of this made sense.

"I don't know who you are, but you're lying! You aren't a wolf. You're a man—"

"Can't I be both?"

There was rustling in the undergrowth, the sound of tree branches being pushed aside—footsteps, definitely human. From the left, not where he had been looking but close to it, Connor saw a flash of tanned skin and turned, fists clenching—

But all the accusations he had intended to fling like weapons toward this stranger playing games with him flew right out of his head. Just the sight of the man in front of him was enough to wipe his mind clean. His lips could only shape a single word, a single syllable.

"*You.*"

Connor stumbled backward, heart in his throat, roar in his ears. His breath came fast, too fast. His vision distorted even as he tried to calm his breathing and himself. How was this possible? It couldn't be — couldn't be possible! And yet he looked across the shortening distance between him and the approaching stranger and locked gazes with a pair of eyes he'd seen before.

I have. I have. I have seen them before.

"Impossible — impossible!"

But they stayed the same — those eyes, ice and gray. *Wolf eyes.*

The man before Connor had gleaming white teeth, visible in a stretch of smile that was so familiar he found himself laughing before he could stop himself, though it came out sounding strangled.

"You *are* the wolf! So many times… You saved me so many times —"

His words ran over themselves when he managed to speak them, repeated the truth that couldn't be yet was. There was no laughter for him this time, just that smile, a grin wider than any man should make.

"That's right. Are you just going to be like the rest of them, now, and start running away?"

"Running…away…?"

Connor realized then that he was backing away — stumbling, more like. He scowled, looked down at the backs of his hands, saw they were trembling and still stopped where he was. He looked up defiantly to find that the stranger — the wolf — the man was closer than he'd thought possible. How fast had he moved? *Fast enough.* In his mind's eye was the speed of those nights of travel, the feel of fur beneath his body and long muscles flexing, bunching, nothing like a horse beneath him, faster than anything living should move.

He took a breath, swallowed, then met the wolf-blue eyes with a challenging gaze.

"I'm not running away. You — you just..."

Aren't possible. But he couldn't say it because it wasn't true. The only thing that was true was staring him in the face.

"You surprised me."

The words came out more quietly than Connor intended, and he looked away, scowling, embarrassed and unsure why that should be so. What had changed? His heart beat faster in his chest, warm ache behind it. There had always been something about that wolf, something more than natural — something too human. Now he knew what that was, why that was, even if he still didn't know *how* it was. Possible no longer meant what it used to mean.

The wolf...the man only smiled and shrugged, some unknown thought or feeling flickering across his face.

"Surprised you? I can understand that."

They were only a few words, gentle words, but they said more than the meaning they carried. Connor felt within himself for a response, but all that came to him was his first and most pressing question.

"Why are you here? Why are you even *with* me?"

"Why did I come to you, you mean? Or why am I here *now*?"

The stranger took another step, and the closer he came, the more Connor could see of the wolf in the man's face. In his expression, in the gleam of his eyes and not just their color, in the prominence of the fang teeth in his smile, the easy way he shifted, every muscle loose and still the strength in him visible.

Something in attitude, in expression, in the way he took each step forward was kin to the padding of a canine hunter after his prey — but all his focus was on

Connor's face, their eyes locked together now. Connor couldn't look away, could barely *breathe*.

"Which is it you wanted to know, Connor?"

Connor flushed, then raised his eyes again, defiant of his own inexplicable embarrassment.

"*Both*. I want to know — I want to know *why* — "

"I came to you because I had no choice. Because you are marked with brightness, and that made you one I must protect. I am here, *now*, because it was this or leave you. I've been close to you, Connor. Too close. I should never have learned your name, should never have wanted to — but I was wounded, and you made it so easy..."

Connor blinked, absorbing this, then asked the question that he thought mattered most.

"What do you mean, 'it was this or leave'? Why not stay like before, be the wolf as long as you had to stay with me?"

The man shrugged, an easy movement that drew Connor's eye.

"I had seven years, Connor. Seven years of service, seven years as the wolf. That's the arrangement that made me *faoladh*. The blessing of the green god of the wood, strength and power, protection for me and mine from the darkness. You know that darkness well enough, now. You have *felt* it."

He paused, and just the mention was enough to make Connor shudder, close his eyes as if to force back memory, but he snapped them open again right away. The blackness behind his eyelids was no comfort at all.

"Those seven years ended last night — this morning, actually. With the light of dawn. I should have left you. This is forbidden, to tell you this, to let you know the real nature of the beast that protected you. It's dangerous for you to know—for any normal man to know. Too many times, gratitude hasn't gone far enough, and so it's our secret. The *faoladh*... We don't share anything we don't have to with the world."

His lips quirked upward in half a smile that faded after only a moment. Connor drew his brows together, shook his head.

"I don't understand. Why would you tell me, then?"

"Because I had questions I couldn't ask, because I— because you were my responsibility, someone who couldn't be allowed to die, and because you still are, even though..." His voice trailed off into silence. He shook his head, shrugged. "Even though that shouldn't be. It doesn't matter, really—and don't ask why, again. I don't *know* why I was called to protect you, why you were made bright to me... Why you still are. The gods do what they please."

Connor rubbed his eyes with his hands.

"Well, you've taken care of what I really wanted to know, anyway."

"Have I?"

He took a step forward, and Connor realized then how close they were and closer now. With so many of his questions answered, no longer beating for attention in his brain, he had time to notice how attractive this naked stranger was, despite the *real* strangeness of him, despite the wolfish gleam, the wolfish grin—or maybe because of them.

Since he'd had his first taste of manhood, Connor had gained a reputation for appreciating all that skin and sensation had to offer. But this was no time for flirting, for giving in to the body's urges, desire and pleasure. Maybe later, he could play those games with this no-longer-wolf.

But his thoughts ran hot between his cock and what his eyes were seeing, and when the stranger took that last step forward, closed the final distance between them, Connor didn't step back.

"I'm not going anywhere without you. Isn't that something you might want to know?"

When the *faoladh* spoke, roughness entered his voice, a wild stirring that Connor heard as the voice of the wolf beneath the voice of the man standing before him.

"You were worried, weren't you?"

There was warmth in the words, but a hint of something *other* showed through, even in that. Connor couldn't find it in himself to mind. If anything, the strangeness that was so visible, so obvious, made everything easier. How could he not believe when the truth was *right there*? It helped him focus, kept his thoughts from straying into wild wonders about his sanity. And this... *He won't be leaving me? I won't be alone here, or anywhere?* Within him something relaxed, even as that newborn ache intensified.

"I'd figured that out already—that you were staying. I'd have to be a fool not to know it, wouldn't I? *This or nothing after seven years,* I heard what you said—even if I don't know anything about it except that you think you have to protect me."

"I *do* have to protect you. Could you fight the shadow, Connor? I had fangs and claws to sink into it—I had the howl and the power and the moonlight to serve me and save you. But it's not just that, Connor. Not just that, maybe that wouldn't have been enough. You think I've carried others on my back—run like that, fought like that, before?"

Connor could only blink, silenced by the intensity in the growling voice.

"Brightness wouldn't have been enough. But you—"

Connor leaned toward him then stopped, every movement arrested by the way that blue gaze raked over his body, caught on his eyes, his mouth, the width of his shoulders, the taut line of his thighs—he could all but read the thoughts in the eyes and the face before him, and was only pleased.

"I've come to want you, Connor. I want you to be *mine*."

Connor grinned, almost a smirk, linked his fingers behind his neck and stretched while the wolf-eyes followed every motion.

"What makes you think I'm so eager to belong to you? To give myself over?"

But even as Connor spoke his eyes strayed, eager—he licked his lips, and got in return more panting laughter. The ache within him blossomed at the sound, arrested his whole being with emotion and heat. He didn't mind. He could see it this time, the way that laughter lit the blue of those eyes, split the white-toothed grin, shook the *faoladh's* whole body.

"Everything about you. Yes, everything about you, leaning toward me—not that I can talk. Not when I'm doing the same thing."

This time Connor knew the *faoladh* laughed at himself.

"But while I'm answering questions, giving up secrets... Connor, isn't there anything else you want to ask me? Anything else at all?"

The same husky warmth that had been in the wolf's first words was in those, and Connor wavered between frustrated irritation and amusement, between silence and heat—but the humor won, and the warmth.

"Only one more thing. What's your name, wolf?"

"*Marcas.* You never guessed." And he grinned. "But it's good that's all you have left to ask." Marcas leaned forward and spoke very softly beside Connor's ear, a breath of warmth that sent a shudder across his skin.

"I've said enough, even for you."

Chapter Six

Marcas breathed deep of Connor's scent—emotions running high in it, the odors of old fear and new arousal—warmth of skin, heat of the silence between them, moments rubbing together, birthing fire in their friction. There was no space between them. They stood toe to toe, eye to eye, sharing breath. He had waited for this, *waited,* and now Marcas heard heartbeats speeding beside him and within him, and considered what he wanted—now, and later. What could he achieve here?

Marcas drew Connor close to him, watchful of the shifting expression on his face. He waited when he felt the soft linen of Connor's tunic touch his naked skin. If Connor resisted, if he pulled back, Marcas would let go. He didn't want to compel him, but it was better to make it clear, here and now, what it was that he wanted—what he meant to gain. *Not a comrade in arms, not a friend, no brotherly relation.*

But just as he had said, everything about Connor was leaning toward him. There were no words, but they hadn't needed them before—why should they now? Marcas lapped at the sin of the skin he could see with his whole gaze, ate it up, wolf-hungry. He smiled, and he knew it was the wolf's smile on his face. Connor stared at him, licking his lips, clenching and unclenching his fingers beside the long, lean muscles of his thighs.

Run, boy, run!

With his stare, Marcas urged him onward, and Connor ran, already laughing. Whipcords of muscle moved in perfect synchronization, flat, shadow-lined cords in calf and thigh. He'd been so right to heal him, so right to be sure that he could run, that he would be perfect like this. Heart pounding in his throat, Marcas sprang after him.

In the body of the wolf he would have run Connor down in half a minute, but now something more like mortal limits contained him, drove him forward with desire but not the special fury of that other shape. Connor had a lead on him that might even grow — there was youth in him, burning in his muscles, and the joy of the run, and lust — yes, lust. Marcas smiled to himself as he ran. If there was to be something more than that which would last, it would start here — with flesh and desire wrapped around this companionable existence, their closeness, their trust.

Love grows strong from that, Connor. Do you know?

Everything stood out with sudden clarity, the pine needles under his feet, the shifting dirt beneath them, the smell of the forest, mulch, moss, water, clean air, silence — and in the silence, the thousand noises of the wood. His own footsteps, the boy running before him, the wind in the leaves and the running of water in the near distance, and the feel of bark against his fingertips as he pushed himself forward after the gleam of blood-tinted hair racing away before him.

Forward, and the only thing he could do was laugh even if he needed the breath. Forward, and this was no easy chase, this was working for everything he wanted. He was falling in love with the moment as much as he was with the boy who was the other half of it. When he finally caught up to Connor, pinned him against green pine, he felt warm, panting breath on his lips as Connor spoke his name, an all but irresistible lure.

"Marcas... I think I like it. *Marcas.*"

Green eyes looked up at him through dark lashes, and Marcas swallowed.

"You have no idea how much I've wanted to hear you say my name."

Warm fingers, lithe and calloused, touched the skin of Marcas' chest. There was hesitation in them, curiosity. He put a hand over them, pressed them against his skin, and reached out with his other hand to run a thumb over pale, parted lips.

"It's just skin, Connor."

"*Just skin.* Do you even know how strange you are? How strange it is to touch you now, and look in your eyes, and see you smiling, and know that you...but it's *just skin.*"

He let out a breath of laughter, and it was a breath that brought a shiver across Marcas' whole body, a breath that crossed his collarbone and ended with those lips on his throat. There was warm, faint pressure, those lips parting until a touch of tongue could lick at him.

"Yes, it's skin all right. You taste like...night."

Marcas lifted an eyebrow, amused.

"Like *night.* What kind of kiss was that?"

The boy was already flush against his body, but now Marcas wrapped one arm around Connor's waist and let the fingers of his other hand roam upward into the thick red hair, smooth against his fingers. Connor shivered when Marcas' fingers stroked his scalp, when he bent and kissed that tempting mouth. *Sensitive...eager.* Heated and wet, Connor's tongue teased Marcas' bottom lip, and Marcas groaned. He laughed at his own response to such a tentative, teasing touch, then returned the favor.

He stroked his tongue against Connor's, tasted mead and the mellow warmth of the earliest morning. There was nothing inhibited in Connor, nothing that waited—his hands were already moving across Marcas' sides, tracing the lines of muscles in motion, the smooth skin so recently reborn and revealed.

His fingers and palms moved delicately, but the touch of them was rougher than the pressure. Connor curled his fingers around Marcas' waist, skimmed the dent of his pelvic bone with the backs of his knuckles, let his fingers slip to the taut curve of muscle at the top of Marcas' buttocks.

It was only then that Marcas knew what it was he had gotten himself into. He should have known, had seen the eager ease with which Connor went to his pleasures. Suddenly he knew that seducing Connor...seducing him would be easy. *But I want more than your body, Connor.* There would have to be something between them, more than just desire and pleasures of the flesh fulfilled. Something else—a bridge of feeling, another way of learning each other.

Marcas nipped at Connor's lip, sucked at his tongue, drank every eager sound and release of breath, but when Connor's hands wandered downward, the sweet touch of those callused fingers seeking for the rigid length of his erection, Marcas caught them at the wrist and stopped him.

The boy was strong and tried to twist out of Marcas' grasp, but Marcas was stronger and had the wildness of the wolf inside him. Calmly, as if it wasn't a struggle, he put a space between them and brought the boy's hands to his mouth, kissed the palms, one at a time, then dropped them.

"Haven't you learned to ask permission from your *conquests*, Connor?" Marcas' lips quirked upward despite himself. "Haven't you learned how pleasing it can be to go *slowly*? If I want you, it's because I've learned you're worth it—but I'll take my time, every inch of the way, and enjoy it all."

Connor stared at him, licking his lips, lust-haze in his eyes, then looked away. A pink flush rose to redness, dusted his cheeks and hid the faint tawny spots that patterned his nose and cheekbones.

"You... I don't... I don't know what you're talking about."

"Don't you?"

"I—"

"You of the wandering hands."

And Marcas grinned, and let his own hands move a bit on their own, down the lean, muscled length of Connor's abdomen, setting up a ripple under his touch, a deep, quick indrawn breath. Marcas' fingers moved away just as they reached the hem of Connor's tunic, and he heard the quick exhalation, the hot, frustrated breath, and hummed in amusement, leaned forward and kissed Connor again, but quickly this time.

"Maybe in time you'll have everything you want, and so will I."

Connor muttered under his breath—*doubtful*—but Marcas still heard, and this time he broke into full and open laughter. The kind that had been denied him while he was a wolf, the kind that shook body and soul.

Human.

Connor blinked, surprised, because when he laughed like that, Marcas seemed, for the first time, completely human. There was nothing of the panting wolf in the sound, just the rich tones of a man overcome by amusement. He bent at the waist, and his cheeks were flushed, and the smile he wore had nothing more wild in it than his own humor. It was both reassuring and disturbing. How could so much that was different exist in one person, one being? And the things he said!

For the second time, Connor felt the flush of his own embarrassment rising to the surface, heating his skin. Had he been wrong, to think that there was something heated, something *wanting* between them? *How could I have been, when he wanted me to run? And that kiss...*

Yes, that kiss. Unconsciously, he licked his lips, tasted Marcas on them. There had been no hesitation there, no pulling back, nothing to suggest anything like *waiting*. Then again... What did he know? There hadn't been *slowly* with his previous lovers. He hadn't had the chance nor the inclination to take his time, whatever that meant. More than lingering over pleasure, obviously, or why would Marcas pull away?

His palms tingled with the memory of those chaste kisses, so strong in contrast to the powerful desire that had been in the lips moving against his mouth, the tongue that played so skillfully against his tongue.

Again, Connor licked his lips. Marcas' laughter faded into a few chuckles that made themselves known between shakes of his head.

"Connor, you've got much to learn. I'll tell you that now—but maybe not so much as I thought, about some things."

"You're laughing at *me?*" Connor scowled. "I don't understand you—my protector, you say. A wolf you were and now you aren't, and whatever that means—for me—isn't to be questioned. You say you want me—and then you say to wait, no argument allowed, no explanation given, and I'm just to be content with that, to live with it." He clenched his fists, desire and anger reinforcing each other. "I'm used to taking what I want, Marcas."

"And so am I. But I won't take anything from you that you don't give, even if I'm sure you'll give it—like just now, Connor." Marcas reached out with strong fingers and tilted his chin up. "If I hadn't stopped you, where would you be right now? What would you be doing?"

Connor struggled to maintain a defiant expression in the face of the knowing grin that spread across Marcas' face. He *had* intended to touch and be touched, to bend what wouldn't be broken. But there was no shame in that, no harm in admitting it—and maybe some pleasure.

"What would I be doing? *You tell me.*"

He stepped forward into the grasp Marcas had on him, forward until his hands, reaching out, had broad shoulders to tighten on. His fingertips danced over the dark skin, traced the lines of faint, old scars on his chest, and fresher new ones. Did this flesh remember the wounds that had been wrought on the wolf? Connor felt a faint trembling in the muscles under his fingertips.

"Can't talk, Marcas? Can't say? *I can.* If you hadn't stopped me, I'd be over you right now, making you beg for what you say to *wait* for now."

In a flash of movement he could neither deny nor deconstruct, everything changed. Connor's view of the world switched from vertical to horizontal. He felt the cool green of the grass tickling the back of his neck, suddenly under him — warm fingers were tangled in his hair, pulling his head back, and back, not painful, just guiding him into position. The whole weight and heat of Marcas' body was over him, pressing him down against the grass, and Connor found himself without any argument against the moment in which he found himself. He tried to move but that only pushed him up against Marcas.

The thigh between his spread legs only let him grind the heat of his erection against unyielding muscle — he couldn't move or turn away. The hand in his hair held Connor's head back, his throat bared, and against the vulnerable skin came open-mouthed kisses, tongue that laved the line of his jugular beneath the skin, seeking out sensitive spots.

He shivered every time Marcas found one, felt the low laughter building in the man over him every time he moaned, tried to pull away and ended up pushing himself closer.

But Connor knew, *knew*, that if he said a word against this, Marcas would pull away from him, let him be, and more humbling than the rest to a prince's pride was knowing that there was nothing in the world he wanted less in that moment than for Marcas to let him be.

And the damn wolf knows it, too. Hot breath blew cold over the dampness at his throat, and Marcas' mouth moved from the point of his pulse along his jaw to his lips, drank the low moan Connor couldn't restrain then returned to his ear.

"You're so right, Connor — and so wrong. If I hadn't stopped you..."

The tip of his tongue touched the curve of Connor's ear, then his teeth. Connor's hips jerked upward against Marcas' body, an all but instinctive reaction.

"If I hadn't stopped you, it would be *you* under *me*. You with your mouth open for my cock, my hands in your hair just like this."

Marcas tugged twice, in play and promise. Connor parted his lips, let out a breath that wanted to be a groan as that rumbling voice stroked over his skin like another pair of hands, all knowing.

"It would be you on your hands and knees, all begging, all heat, all wanting, looking back at me — begging me to touch you, to be inside you, to *give it to you.*"

Connor tried to shake his head, but Marcas' grip on his hair wouldn't let him move that much, wouldn't let him deny the words burning their way into his ears, across his skin, across every nerve.

"*Don't deny it.* The only answer I'll take from you is *yes.* Do you know how much it costs me to hold back now? Seven years, Connor. Seven years I've had no one. When I have you where I want you, it *will* be on your knees. But don't think that doesn't mean I don't know how to give as good as I get... Just that I'll be the one who *gets* first."

He laughed against Connor's skin, licked up the laughter and lifted his head to look Connor in the eye.

"When I have you where I want you, when the time is right, there'll be no getting away."

Connor pressed his hips up against Marcas' and grinned at the breath the other man sucked past his lips.

"What's not right about now?"

Marcas laughed again, but this time Connor knew that he was laughing at *him*.

"You don't want it enough yet. I want more than *this* from you, Connor."

Connor couldn't see Marcas' smirk, but he felt it, the lips stretching, parting against his skin. Again, he felt a languorous stroking of tongue against his throat, nipping teeth, open-mouthed kisses that sucked heat to the surface of his skin to be soothed by that tongue. It was no longer in him to deny anything. He could only capitulate to sensation, his own nerves betraying him with what they wanted.

On your knees, Marcas said, and the image filled itself in his head, more than an image, a whole scenario... There would be the taste of salt and skin. *Give as good as I get.*

He found himself pushing up against the thigh Marcas had pressed between his legs. Connor arched his back off the ground and wished he could get out of his clothes, feel all the burnished heat of Marcas' skin against his skin, but he still couldn't move. He couldn't even get enough movement out of his hips to ease the aching of his cock, so full, so wanting...

What did he mean, didn't want it enough yet? What more was there to wanting than this painful pressure, tingling in his fingertips, his toes, a shiver that turned to a full body shudder when Marcas licked his lips, leaned back over his mouth and kissed him, sucked Connor's tongue into his mouth and stroked it lightly with the tip of his own tongue.

He mouthed his way along Connor's jaw, back to his throat, kissed his shoulder—then bit it, *hard*. Connor jerked upward with an involuntary cry. He had been *so close*—but Marcas was already standing, backing away, grinning.

"That's enough for you—and for me." He drew one finger along the length of his erection, stared across at Connor, and Connor saw blue fire where there had been ice, had to close his eyes to it. "I'm going to get dressed, and then we should decide what you want to do—what *else* you want to do." Marcas amended his words, then strode up the curve of the hill and into the hall, shutting the door behind him.

Connor only opened his eyes when he heard the door close. His shoulder stung where Marcas had bitten him, and his throat was wet where his tongue had touched. He could still hear every word Marcas had said, and the vivid pictures his mind painted for him had plenty to feed on—all that naked skin, the heat of it, the lines of muscles in all the right places, the heavy thickness of a jutting erection that he wanted to touch, to taste.

Rough, quick, biting his lip to hold back a groan, Connor reached under his tunic, worked his fist over his cock, every nerve on fire and the fingers of his other hand digging deep into the grass, deep into the dirt. He spilled white essence over his fingers with a moan and a hiss of breath.

Marcas...

The name was in his head, even if it hadn't passed his lips.

Breathing hard, scowling, Connor wiped his hand on the grass. "*Don't want him enough yet*—what does that mean? I don't know how I could want him *more*."

He sighed then, but despite himself he grinned a little. This was something *new*.

The smile stayed with him until he pushed himself to his feet and came back to the crest of the hill. Behind it in the west, the sun was gradually drawing closer to the horizon, reddening the edge of the sky with blazing promise.

"It'll be dark soon."

The words passed his lips in a murmur. Just the thought was enough to raise gooseflesh on his arms. His memory was full of shadows — what would come with the night?

* * * *

Marcas came back outside dressed and with his thoughts in better order. It had cost him to walk away from Connor's eagerness, but having seen what he'd seen in the honest openness of the boy's face, he knew he was right to wait — at least a little.

Connor was one of those who'd had much of pleasure, but knew almost nothing of love. There was *something* — something more than lust in Connor's warmth, his soft responses…and it was getting hard to deny that his own feelings were no longer becoming. That they had *become*.

But until Connor knew his own feelings, Marcas couldn't let it matter. *Let it be soon, Connor.*

He found the boy sitting with his back to the western wall, staring out at the forest beneath the hilltop and the green of the endless grass below that, its shade shifting from pale moss to malachite with the turnings of the wind. Connor's attention was on the sky, though, not the meadows or the wood, and when Marcas approached him, he jumped a little.

"Don't worry, I only bite for fun."

"Very funny."

"Something wrong?"

Several things passed through Connor's eyes in half a moment, but Marcas had spent time enough with him by now that he could decipher most of them. Fear, and worry, and anger at both those things. *Of course.* They'd been chased here by the first darkness—oldest, eternal, part of the foundation of the world. *And I forgot. I haven't told him why we're here.*

"You can relax, Connor. No darkness can pass the barrier that guards this place, not even the bent one. It was made to keep him out. There's no need to fear nightfall."

With careful movements, ignoring the twinge that came from the last of the wolf's wounds stretching across his back, Marcas sat beside Connor, one leg bent at the knee and his head leaned back against the wall behind him.

"Those *things* that chased us here—they can't follow?"

Marcas shook his head slowly.

"No. I brought you here for that reason. We needed a resting space, time to think and plan. This was the only place I could think of. But…"

He shrugged, but that wasn't good enough for Connor.

"Why wait? Why didn't we come here right away?"

Marcas glanced at him sharply.

"I shouldn't have brought you here at all. It's forbidden. Do you understand? Like everything else I've done when it comes to you—answering your questions, telling you too much. Telling you my name. But, Connor—" Marcas hesitated, then shrugged. "I couldn't do less. Not for you. I could love you, Connor."

He dared the word despite himself, and Connor's lip twisted in a way that was terrible to see, a distortion of the handsome, youthful features. The words that slipped off his tongue were bitter. "Love is...just a game."

The sting of every syllable was just reinforcement to Marcas, proof that what he was feeling was real even if the boy denied it. Another pang made itself known at that thought, but he pushed it aside and focused on Connor and the truth — and saying it, softly.

"A game? No. I've been Marcas all along, a man in the shape of a wolf — seven years I spent alone before I was brought to you, and you... Why not come to prize you?" Marcas fell silent for a moment, gathering words. "I haven't been able to answer your questions, Connor, but I know as much of you as you've showed me in the days I've spent by your side. The first night I was summoned to you, I noticed you — fearless, standing to face a darkness you didn't know or understand."

Connor's lip twitched, and Marcas thought it an encouraging sign.

"I must've looked a fool to you."

"Never. A brave man, rather, fighting out of his depth. Do you know how many turn and run, or try to? Even those who can't—"

"Not warriors, then."

"No? But it doesn't matter, Connor." Marcas closed his eyes.

"I didn't mean... I'm sorry. I'm sorry, Marcas. It's just my father always said that love was a game, and we—" He paused, shrugged. "We're not in some old story. We're not in a song. I want you, you know that. Isn't that enough? "

Again Marcas laughed, this time very quietly — this time at himself.

"Maybe, maybe."

Something about the way Marcas said that last — *maybe, maybe* — Connor turned to look at him — really look at him — not with the eyes of desire or surprise but the eyes his father had trained to evaluate every situation.

He'd had plenty of pleasures in his life, men and women, and none of them had ever made him think about love. None of them had woken it and none of them had mentioned it except the very first — the girl he'd taken in the shadow of the Beltane fires the summer of his thirteenth year. What was her name? *Can't remember.* She'd had dark eyes, but her skin had been pale and her nipples the shade of pink roses in the firelight — and she hadn't been serious. She had teased him with the word as she had with her body.

Marcas. He knew instinctively that Marcas was different.

"Your eyes tell me I should have kept my thoughts to myself — or would you rather tell me something else, Connor?"

The words were quiet, but he jumped a little anyway. *My eyes told him?* What did that even mean? He almost asked the question but as soon as it came clear to him, so did the answer. Hadn't he been learning just such a way with the wolf — how to say things without saying them, how to hear what couldn't be spoken, make the most out of a yes or no answer?

And yet now that this wasn't necessary, now that his questions would be answered and his opinions judged by a mind that he knew was the mind of a man like his own, he found himself silent — not with nothing to say, but no idea how to say it. It had been easier earlier, the play of attraction and arousal. That was a game he knew how to play, and play well. This... There was no easy answer.

"I don't know what to say when you talk about love. Sorry but I don't — I haven't... It's not something I think about."

To his relief, Marcas only smiled.

"What are you thinking about, then?"

Connor opened his mouth, then stopped. Really all there was within him was complete relief that this place was safe — that here, no shadow would molest them. Hadn't Marcas said so? He was having trouble with that, but not with the truth of it, just the casual fact of his own trust in a man he barely knew. He knew the *wolf* that was Marcas, but he didn't know the man, didn't know his likes or dislikes, his allegiances or purposes... To protect, he said. *And love.*

But there had to be more to it than that, even if Connor was forbidden from asking about it or forbidden to know. Things as simple as a topic of conversation escaped him now that Marcas seemed content to be silent, staring across at the horizon, waiting for an answer. Hesitantly, Connor spoke, running his hands back through his hair as he did so, twitching his gaze between Marcas and the grass, Marcas and the last hint of the sunset, Marcas and the backs of his own hands.

But there was only Marcas, in the end.

"You said...we needed a plan."

His words lingered for a moment before Marcas answered.

"I did, but that's not really true, I suppose. You're the one who needs the plan — I'm just here to protect you — somehow."

A hint of a grin flickered on his face, and Connor was confused. "But you said you weren't a wolf any more. I mean, obviously you aren't, but since you're human again, you can't protect me, can you?"

"Not a wolf any more..."

Marcas spoke contemplatively and Connor raised his eyebrows.

"What? Isn't it true? You're not in the wolf. You're the one who becomes the wolf, the wolf doesn't become you."

Marcas chuckled faintly, and Connor caught him shaking his head out of the corner of his eye.

"It's all right. I understand what you mean — and you're right. But would you believe me if I told you I didn't know? Why do you think I brought you here, even though it's forbidden for you to know any of what you've learned? I didn't think I'd be able to keep you safe, and no other *faoladh* has come for you. But you're still bright to me — I might be human in my shape now, but I've still got the wolf's senses, the map in my mind that tells me where the one who needs me is waiting."

He paused, and held Connor's gaze with sharp eyes. "I'm telling you, you are the one still, the brightest light, the only one I can see for miles — if there's any other at all."

"That doesn't tell me anything."

"Doesn't it? Doesn't it tell you that you should be paying attention to your plans because they might matter more than to just you? Doesn't it tell you that someone is watching, that the gods you disregard have an eye on you and your safety? That's a lot more than nothing."

Connor flushed and looked away.

* * * *

In the hours between noon and twilight, the last of the High King's personal servants and vassals fled the new shadow of his service. Crom Cruach watched them go from within the flesh he occupied without a word of complaint. His presence had been a gradual change in the days since the sacrifice that had been held in the moon's darkness.

He was pleased with what he had accomplished, with what had been wrought and gained since he had breached the world and taken possession of this flesh. That possession was completed now, and the flight of mortals immaterial.

The body that had begun as the High King and been of the High King, was now Crom Cruach. He would not share sovereignty. What had been was no more, and what remained was a thing consumed, a man's flesh become an instrument of power. Crom Cruach looked out through the eyes that had once belonged to Tigernmas, down at the flesh that had once belonged to Tigernmas. Though nothing of the shape had changed, there was still a visible difference — mottling, strange writhing where no muscle could produce such motion. And his shadow was nothing like a shadow should be.

It consumed all things, though Crom Cruach did not venture into the light.

The High King had thought he could summon one of the ancient powers of the world, darkness from the foundations of reality, and bend it to his will. Promises had been made, and would be kept, but not in the manner the one who had asked for them had intended. There were terms that must be fulfilled, but Crom would not suffer his being nor his purposes to be twisted. He would not make life where there should be none, would not hold back life from the edge of death when death was all that he desired. *Death to all things.*

Why give life when it was easier to take it, and in doing so still fulfill the terms of the sacrifice that had drawn him into this world? Crom had drunk of the blood and the violence, supped on the bittersweet odors of betrayal, kin-carnage, the finest vintage of fear. In return, Tigernmas had gained an immortal direction. His flesh continued on, and his name would be cursed so that it could never slip into silence. As the night drew on, Crom Cruach summoned his servants to come to him. Out of shadow, drawn to shadow, awed by their own works, they came to lie prostrate before him and promise their service anew. They called him by name, no longer bowing before him with the eager respect due a king, but instead the fearful worship due a god. He was Crom Cruach, and the time of Tigernmas was already tainted.

The eyes of Crom Cruach saw all things where the darkness touched, where danger lurked, where violence blackened the souls of men. He shifted his attention from one place to another, and saw that those who had fled the palace of the High King were spreading rumors of his presence, though they did not speak his name. This and this alone displeased him, for wild rumor was not the same as focused fear. Anger filled him, stretched the features of the old king taut, then passed as swiftly as it had come.

He settled back into the throne of the High King. He would wait. Of all things in this universe, time was the one he had the most of... More even than darkness. There was plenty to entertain himself with in the meantime. Plenty and more than, hundreds of villages... Thousands of lives.

Chapter Seven

After the night just past, the terror and horror of Crom Cruach mounting the world, Connor spent the rest of the evening waiting for something to happen, but nothing did. The night passed quietly. Marcas seemed willing to leave him alone with his thoughts, for now, and vanished quietly in the direction of his hall.

The echoes of the conversation he'd had with Marcas remained with him, prodding him to make some plan, some kind of decision, but his thoughts were confused, wandered in many directions. He had been meant to wait for his father's summons, or that of someone else, telling him the worst had happened. There had been silence for all those longs days in the hills, and now that something terrible had happened, now that the world was broken, the silence continued still.

It occurred to him that there would continue to be silence. He had left his retreat, and there was no message or warning left behind him. Only the destruction that had been wrought by Crom Cruach would remain near the village by Aran's pastures, and what would that tell anyone who came to find him?

They'll think I'm dead – or worse.

"I wonder how far it is… At least a week's travel, I'd guess, and that's if I could find a horse." He let out a sigh and closed his eyes, thought back… Familiar roads, familiar woods they'd passed through on the way here. "We must still be close to home, though…"

As soon as he'd said it, the desire came to him – *go back*. Go back and see if his father was still living, if his mother and sisters were safe. Go back and find out what had happened in the dark of the moon, how it was that his father and those who'd gone with him had failed to stop the High King's sacrifice.

When he opened his eyes, the night seemed darker than it had been just a moment before, the last of the twilight vanished out of the sky. He heard crackling, spitting, hissing, smelled suddenly the odor of smoke…wood-smoke, meat-smoke.

"Marcas?"

He called hesitantly into the dark, and got his answer from the other side of the hall.

"Here, Connor."

He followed the sound of Marcas' voice to flickering shadows, spitted rabbits over a fire set in a circle of stones. Marcas was crouched on the other side, loose trousers tied at his waist but no tunic on and the firelight gleaming on his skin.

Connor grinned at him, appreciative of the view – and the promise of food. Had it been a day since he'd eaten – or more? He couldn't remember, but his stomach wasn't happy with him in either case.

"I didn't know you'd gone hunting. You should've said. I would've gone with you."

Marcas only shrugged. "It was quick work, and you looked like you had thinking to do." He turned the spit, then stood and made to go back into the hall. "Stay, I'll be right back."

But Connor was on his feet the moment Marcas turned his back to him, for reasons that had nothing to do with where he was going. "Marcas, your back!" Midway down his back, crossing at an angle from one side to the other, three dark gashes, black-stained and ugly, were visible in the firelight.

Connor rounded the fire with quick steps, guilt rising in him. They were his fault, those wounds. *And I didn't even notice.*

"Don't worry about it, Connor. It's not so bad."

Marcas was smiling, shrugging, but Connor didn't care. *My fault.* He reached out and held Marcas still, one hand at his shoulder and the fingers of the other touching the unmarked skin between the wounds.

"Don't be an idiot. You haven't even *washed* them—have you got bandages? Clean linen? I can clean them but—"

"*Connor.* You—"

The startled softness of Marcas' voice almost stopped him, but he was too stubborn for that.

"Don't want to hear it—have you got bandages or not?"

Marcas stared at him, silent, contemplative, then shrugged and nodded.

"I do. In the hall—watch the rabbits, I'll get...what you need."

Connor watched him go, his brow knit with confusion and the tangled threads of his own guilt and responsibility. Why wouldn't he want tending? Why leave wounds like that when they might fester?

The black blood of Crom's servants still stained his skin.

With that thought, the dark weighed heavy on Connor and despite what Marcas had told him, he found himself looking over his shoulder, probing the shadows with his sight.

Nothing.

It occurred to him that he should be missing the power of his protector, that he should feel...some sense of loss, now that the wolf with the bright howl was gone, was...Marcas. Instead, he felt the opposite, though he had Marcas' own admission that despite his intentions, what remained of his duty, he didn't know *how* he would still protect Connor. Only that he wanted to.

"I like that."

He liked the warmth of it, too, but he didn't know what to call that, didn't want to try finding the feeling a name.

When Marcas returned with linen and a bowl of water he still wore the same bemused, distracted expression on his face, but Connor didn't care about that. He was still all but lost in his own thoughts.

He took the bowl and bandages from Marcas' hands, then nudged him toward the fire and sat behind him, began to clean the cuts. As he had done when Marcas was a wolf, Connor did now, but perhaps with even more care. Shallow and closing though the wounds might be, he thought they looked much better with the darkness and old blood washed away.

The firelight showed him many other scars crisscrossing the tanned skin, and he touched them with his fingertips, traced them one at a time, wondered what they were from. Some, fresher than the others, still pink and new, not yet faded to silver scars, he knew.

"Too many times you've been wounded because of me."

He hadn't meant to speak out loud, but the words slipped past his lips and drew Marcas' attention.

"You shouldn't be worrying about it, Connor. It was my duty —"

"I know, but that doesn't mean I wasn't useless." He scrubbed carefully at the skin between the wounds. "Worse than useless." Though he couldn't see it, he sensed Marcas' grin.

"You mean against the bent one? All men are, when it comes to that, or why do you think we are *faoladh*?"

Connor scowled, dampened another bit of linen and began to dab carefully at the wounds themselves. Marcas sucked in a hissing breath, and his shoulders tightened under Connor's hands.

"Sorry —"

"It's all right. You were right, anyway, I shouldn't have left these so long. But they don't hurt so much, and I'm not used to..." He paused, the words trailing into silence, and didn't pick up their thread again.

"Marcas?"

"It's nothing. Don't worry about it. Are you — almost done?"

His wince was audible through the words, and Connor looked at his work, sighs.

"You... I can't do anything like this. You need a bath, Marcas." Connor grinned, leaned forward to speak closer to Marcas' ear. "At least you can give yourself one now — if you want to." He had meant the words to tease Marcas, but Connor licked his lips at the thought of all this warm skin, glistening in hot water.

"Actually—that doesn't sound like a bad idea. Food first, though."

Connor's stomach growled in agreement with Marcas' words.

"But, Connor—you know I'm going to need your help."

"*Yes.*"

Marcas peered over his shoulder at him, and Connor looked away from his bright gaze, flush hot on his face. The word had just slipped out of him, and now he wished it hadn't and didn't know why.

It was just that he wanted him, that was all—that was all, wasn't it?

They ate in silence, while water heated on the fire. Marcas was equally aware of the way the night air stung the half-cleaned cuts on his back and the way Connor sucked the meat from the bones, licked the grease from his fingers. There was nothing intentionally sensual about it, but the pink flicker of his tongue held Marcas' attention longer than it should have.

This waiting—maybe it would be more difficult than he'd thought.

Connor seemed distracted, but this time not by darkness—his attention was on the fire, and his concentration had set a familiar pucker between his eyes. He didn't move when Marcas stood and went inside to bring out the bath—not even when he came back with it, let it thud against the ground and moved to take the water from the fire.

Only when he lifted it and splashed steam across the smoke did a startled Connor look up at him. "The water's hot? Sorry, I wasn't paying attention—"

"It's all right. Dump those buckets in for me, will you?"

Connor did as he was told, but Marcas felt his eyes on him as he undressed and stretched. When the bath was ready he stepped in and sank down with a hiss of pain. The hot water was eager for his wounds and he wondered if maybe they were worse than he'd thought. Maybe Connor was worried for a reason.

But the sting receded a little at a time, and he felt Connor's hands on him then, rough cloth moving gently over the wounds and five fingers at his shoulder to keep him still.

"You have good hands, Connor."

There was no reply, but the hand holding his shoulder held tight, then relaxed, moved up the curve of his shoulder, then down his arm.

Marcas let him do as he liked, more pleased than he was willing to show. Connor's hands were gentle, careful, just as much now as they had been when he was an injured wolf. And if Connor's fingers lingered on the smooth skin between the wounds, if his touch crossed Marcas' shoulders, the back of his neck, and threaded through his hair...

Well, there was no harm in that, was there?

A thought came to him that he'd had first as the wolf, and Marcas considered it for nearly a full minute before he vocalized it. "Connor, can you...do you sing?" He was hoping only slightly, but Connor's hands went still against his skin.

"I...do. You want me to?"

Marcas let his head fall forward and closed his eyes.

"I—yes. The sound of your voice, when I was the wolf I wanted... I wanted to hear it. I couldn't ask, though—not then."

There was a moment of quiet, before Connor's hands resumed their work and play against his skin, before he began to sing. He had just the voice that Marcas had thought he'd have, rich and low but not too deep.

He sang old songs, first—the lullabies of childhood, myth-songs, stories of the people that lived under the hill, the beasts of power who had walked the green of the world in ancient times. Of the gods who had stalked them, bound them to service, altered their nature—and of those who had succumbed to it, for in the times of story and song there was always a wildness great enough to conquer even the proudest god, the greatest king.

When he ran out of those songs, Marcas thought Connor invented his own—songs of wolves and trees and green places, nothing of war in them and nothing of darkness. In the warmth of the water, with Connor's hands on his back, Connor's voice in his ears, he sank half into dreams. It wasn't until he was shaken that he blinked his eyes open and saw Connor's grinning face close to his own.

"You shouldn't fall asleep in the bath, Marcas. Finish washing up and I'll wrap those wounds for you, they don't look so bad now that they're clean."

Drowsy, his brain heavy with dream-images, Marcas obeyed. He was amused at the easy way Connor gave him orders, and more so by the flickers of Connor's stare. He caught the heated gleam of the boy's gaze on him when he stood and between rinses—he wasn't shy about it, either, didn't look away when their eyes met.

Want you, Marcas. The thought was obvious in his face, undeniable—not that Marcas wanted to deny it. He dried himself under that *look*, then came to sit by the fire again, at Connor's side. The boy had obviously had practice with such work—his hands were thorough, as gentle with the bandages as they had been when he'd been cleaning the wounds.

Good hands, Connor.

When he was done, those hands hesitated at Marcas' side where he'd tied off the bandage, then made as if to pull away, but Marcas caught them and held them.

"Thank you."

Connor shrugged—*now* he wouldn't meet Marcas eyes.

"It's not anything. I should've done as much before."

Then he yawned, and Marcas smiled and stood. "I think it's time for bed, Connor. For you and me both. I don't know about you, but that run—I could do without another like it." He tugged on Connor's fingers, pulled him up toward the hall, and Connor followed without protest, didn't even try to pull away from Marcas' grip.

It was only once they were inside that he hesitated, and Marcas let his hand go, went forward to the great bed set against the wall and sat on the left-hand side. He stretched, then pulled back the blankets and lay carefully.

"Are you coming? I already said I don't bite, didn't I?"

Connor started, then shook his head and grinned half-heartedly as he came up to the other side of the bed.

"But isn't that the problem?" He sat and stripped out of his tunic, then rolled under the covers and pressed himself carefully against Marcas' back. "I *want* you to bite." Then he pushed himself up on one arm, leaned over and kissed him.

Marcas succumbed to the pressure of Connor's mouth without protest, parted his lips for tongue. He had a moment in which he thought that this might have been a bad idea after all, until Connor pulled back, his eyes dark. His pupils were dilated with desire, and the line of his throat was tense — he licked his lips, and Marcas nearly gave in, almost reached up and pulled him down.

Connor grinned faintly at him, then turned so they lay back-to-back, and seemed to settle in for sleep.

Marcas lay unmoving, fist clenched against the sheets, tasting that kiss and feeling Connors' warm presence against his back until he fell asleep.

He woke with a spray of red hair in front of his eyes, and found that he had turned in the night. Marcas lay now with Connor curled in the curve of his body, back pressed against his chest. He made to move the arm he held wrapped around Connor's waist, but Connor had laid his arm over Marcas' and wouldn't let go.

It occurred to Marcas then that he had no reason to get up — no reason at all. He breathed deep of Connor's sleeping scent and closed his eyes again.

* * * *

Connor woke with a contented murmur on his lips, warmth against his back, warmth around his waist. He yawned before he could get his eyes open, then looked down and froze. *Arm?* The word moved aimless through his mind, until it met and connected with *Marcas.* They'd gone to sleep facing in opposite directions, but now he was pinned by an arm around his waist and his own confusion.

He'd avoided mornings like this for years, had no desire for awkward goodbyes — better to kiss and farewell than kiss and stay the night. *But I did that, didn't I? What's wrong with me?* He wondered if maybe

Marcas' talk of love had made some impression on him after all.

"I could love you, Connor."

The memory was rich with all the tones Marcas had spoken in. His throat felt...tight. Strange. *What is this? What is this called?* Suddenly uncomfortable with his own contentment, Connor shifted forward and felt Marcas stir against his back. He slid his hand along Connor's side from waist to hip, squeezed tight then relaxed his grip enough that Connor could roll free. He let out a breath he hadn't been aware he was holding, pushed the blankets off and sat up.

The air was chill, and he missed the warmth of the bed almost at once, but his head was already filling with the thoughts he'd put aside the night before — everything that had come over him watching Marcas climb into bed and wait for him.

Want you, Marcas.

But it was becoming clear to him, hour by hour, that *want* was only the beginning.

Days passed with a pattern that was easy to grow accustomed to. He woke with Marcas wrapped around him in the morning, no matter how they went to sleep at night. Connor found himself wondering why he'd never stayed with his lovers, why he'd never welcomed this warmth. That Marcas wasn't his lover — at least not yet — that, he wasn't sure how to deal with.

Waiting — he didn't like this waiting. He could kiss, he could touch...a little. But that wasn't the same as what he wanted, and he knew that Marcas was aware. *Does he want me or doesn't he? Why?* But he knew why. A little at a time he was beginning to learn within himself the thing that Marcas wanted, but he wasn't sure it mattered. To care for him—that came easily. But love?

My wolf-protector. I care – I want – but…why?

He just didn't understand why that wasn't enough — not when his dreams were full of heat and the secret future, long hidden within himself, now opening again and again like the flowers that wait to show their petals to the moon. It couldn't be a nightmare, not that desire, but it needed some other word than dream. *A man for myself and the battles I've wanted – no wife, no father looking over my shoulder… Marcas.*

There had been a faceless figure in that dream for a long time, but now it was Marcas. *Always Marcas.* And what could he do about it? How could he make clear that he was beginning to move from want to…need? Maybe it wasn't everything that Marcas wanted, but wasn't it…something? Wasn't it enough?

In the end, maybe the problem was less what he was feeling and more his fear of putting it into words.

Not for the first time, Connor licked his lips of half a dozen confused confessions and left Marcas sleeping in the great bed, wandered out of the hall to explore the woods and hillside.

* * * *

There was uncertainty in Marcas as he returned from another day's hunting, prey in hand. That morning, like a week's worth of others, Connor had been gone when he woke, only a warm imprint in the bed beside him. He had been waiting for Connor to say something, do something—to say whether he would go or stay. To move forward or back. Yet though he remained, he did so without making any of his intentions clear. Not the intentions of his heart—not the plans necessity required.

The hall was empty and quiet when he entered, no sign of the boy anywhere, and he left the meat behind to go in search of him. Scent and the sound of soft murmurs led him unerringly toward Connor, but the way he found him stopped Marcas in his tracks.

Naked, lying with his head propped against a low tangle of roots, one of his hands wandered over his body while the other stroked his cock. His eyes were closed, his breathing was heavy, and now and then small noises passed his lips—words, moans, and Marcas' name.

Every time Connor said it, Marcas was pulled forward another step, until he was standing at the very edge of the tree-line, barely hidden. This sight was familiar to him, he had seen it once before—but now it stirred all the urges he had been restraining almost beyond his control. It reminded him that he had been waiting for a long time, so many days, even before he'd slipped back into his own skin.

That it was his name on Connor's lips—that he could see in his own head everything that Connor must be picturing—that was more than he could take. Before he could stop himself, Marcas stepped forward out of the trees, out of the shadow and into the line of Connor's sight.

"I keep finding you like this."

The moment Marcas spoke, Connor's eyes snapped open and all his attention focused up into Marcas' gaze.

"*Marcas.*" The word was broken with surprise and pleasure both, and the husky tone of it drew him closer. The way Connor's fist kept moving, slower, but without pause — the way Connor's gaze was *fixed* on him — they drew him closer, too.

"I keep…finding you like this. When I was the wolf I watched you, the way you like to touch yourself. I couldn't help it. You're gorgeous, Connor. I started to want you, then. Want you…"

Connor looked up at him with hooded eyes, lustful expression. "Are you just — are you just going to *watch*, then? Marcas…" His voice pleaded for the answer to be *no*, and Marcas couldn't help himself. He took the last step forward. This was still slow, wasn't it? This was still waiting — enjoying — all the little steps, those were on the path he wanted too, weren't they?

Or maybe that no longer mattered.

Closer.

He sank to his knees between Connor's spread legs and licked his lips. "Maybe I'll…help you." And he leaned forward, braced himself on his hands and pressed his mouth against Connor's. The response was instant, insistent. Connor licked his lips, sucked his tongue into his mouth, reached up with the hand not wrapped around his cock to hold him there, fingers twining in Marcas' hair.

They stayed there, tugging him closer, until it seemed Connor was convinced he was going nowhere. Then there were hands on him *everywhere*, slipping down his shoulders, his arms, up again then down his back, so careful of the fresh, new scars. He was more vocal than Marcas had expected, easy sounds slipping past his lips and into Marcas' mouth.

When Marcas finally pulled back, Connor groaned and followed him, leaned up as he tried to pull Marcas down to his mouth again.

"Don't. Don't stop —"

Marcas kissed him again, bit his lip and licked away the gasp that followed. "Who said I was stopping?" More kisses, *his* kisses, harder, more wanton—no way now for Connor to take control. "Unless that's what you want? Just my *kiss*."

Connor pressed up against him, mouth and tongue and cock, reached up and wrapped his arms around him, his whole body straining off the ground and into Marcas' touch.

"No. *No. Please no.*" He kissed Marcas once, twice, stared straight into his face. "Ever since you said it, I can't stop thinking about it—how you'd feel inside me—around me." Connor's tongue darted out to touch his lips. "I've never wanted anyone else like you. I've never wanted anyone to... I want...everything of you."

Marcas felt a warm hand palm his cock, rigid, throbbing, but his thoughts were still trying to wrap around those words. *I've never wanted anyone else to...* What? What Marcas thought the answer might be enflamed him and he drew back, sat on his haunches between Connor's spread thighs, then got on his knees and dragged Connor across his lap, legs parted, back flat on the ground.

The position left Connor open to him, vulnerable, but the boy only stared at him, hot eyed, begging with his whole body.

"You want me inside you, Connor? You want me...but you haven't had anyone else, have you?" Marcas let his hands do what they wanted, stroked the heat and strength of Connor's legs, his thighs. "I remember now—you said *I am the one who takes*, didn't you?"

Connor flushed, and Marcas laughed. He traced the vein on the underside of Connor's cock with one finger, base to dripping tip, brought his finger to his mouth and *tasted*. Salt-sweet, lust and Connor. The boy's cock twitched visibly as Marcas sucked on his finger, wet it thoroughly.

"I won't give you everything, Connor." Something seemed to *break* in the boy's face, but Marcas leaned forward between his parted thighs and kissed him deeply, let Connor rock against him, groaning. "But I didn't say I'd give you *nothing*, either."

Just Marcas' kiss was almost enough to bring Connor over the edge. When Marcas pulled back again, Connor was glad, not wanting to make a fool of himself, but the next moment he thought it might not matter. He felt a single one of Marcas' fingers moving over the entrance of his body, circles that teased with a dip inward, never really penetrating, stimulating nerves new to sensual sensation. His other hand gripped Connor's cock at the base, stroked slowly.

"Marcas — Marcas, please, I'm —"

"*Close?*" The word was a growl that came close to his skin. "*Good*. You like when I touch you, Connor?"

"*Yes*."

"You like when I touch you *here*."

Slowly, the finger penetrated, and there was both pleasure and faint burning. "Yes..." Marcas pressed deeper, and Connor let his head fall back against the ground. "*Oh yes*." The feeling was wholly new, different from any way he'd ever touched himself or been touched by any lover. "Please, Marcas, *more*."

He felt *more* stretching him, knew it was two fingers inside him now, but the slow pace of Marcas' stroking didn't change. *Gods*. He'd been wanting for so long that it was all he could do to keep himself from *really* begging, but Connor's body wouldn't obey like his voice did. He moved his hips against Marcas' fingers, into his fist, reached up to grip Marcas' shoulders with both hands.

He had been teasing himself before Marcas came — what Marcas was doing *now* was driving him to distraction. Connor slipped his hands down Marcas' sides, pressed his palm against the rigid throbbing of Marcas' cock.

"Want you, Marcas. Want more — want *you* — "

The fingers moving in him thrust faster, sharper. The fist wrapped around his cock squeezed tighter, sped its strokes, and Connor lost his words to gasps and moans. He stared up into Marcas' eyes and felt another surge of heat. So good, the fingers inside him, the fist wrapped around his cock — and the way Marcas' looked at him, hungry, panting wolf in the back of his gaze, as if he would swallow Connor whole —

So good.

"Marcas, you — you — *please* — "

The words were barely coherent, but Marcas laughed at him still, his voice almost hoarse with wanting.

"No, Connor. No more than this. Not now." He flicked his gaze up to meet Connor's eyes. "Not unless you want more fingers inside you."

"Yes — *anything*, yes — "

Connor heard Marcas groan, then gasped as he pulled two fingers away and pushed three back inside. It was almost too much, slow burning stretch, deep feeling, but too much wasn't enough.

"So tight, Connor. So tight around my fingers, how will I fit my cock in you?"

Connor squeezed the thickness of Marcas' cock under his hand, felt his fingers inside touch something hot with pleasure. He groaned and bucked up twice into Marcas' fist, fire spreading everywhere inside him, a shattering ecstasy. He felt the wet warmth of his own essence on his chest, his belly, and over him Marcas trembling — trembling so that Connor was able to pull himself back, away from fingers and hand and the heat of his body, and tumble him back onto the grass.

"Connor — don't — "

But Marcas' voice was rich with groaning, and his cock twitched under Connor, where it was pressed against his belly, hot and hard.

"You want me to leave you like this?"

"I'm not going to take you — not now — "

It was Connor's turn to laugh at him. "But what if I wanted something *else*?" He pushed Marcas' tunic up to his chest, then further, until Marcas leaned up under him and pulled it the rest of the way off. "What if I want to taste you, Marcas?" He bent and kissed Marcas' throat, licked at his pounding pulse, sucked warmth to the surface, then bit his shoulder.

Marcas bucked under him, and Connor grinned, lifted his head so Marcas could see it. "Fair's fair." But there was no pain in Marcas' expression, just heat upon heat, and Connor sucked in a breath. "Or maybe not." He slid back onto Marcas' thighs and reached between them for his cock, wrapped his fist around it and stroked slowly.

Marcas groaned and reached out to grasp his thighs, tried to hold Connor still, but he slid back and back, until he was between Marcas' legs, not on them. He pressed his lips to the soft skin of Marcas' inner thigh, then leaned up and wrapped them around his cock.

Marcas jumped under him, then lay back groaning. His hands crept up to tighten in Connor's hair, pulled on it, urging him onward. Connor experimented with the speed of his tongue, the pressure of his lips. This was something new—the taste of Marcas, the smooth skin ridged with veins under his tongue, but he *liked* it. The way Marcas moved under him, the way he grasped at Connor's hair, his panting groans.

Marcas' fingers in his hair guided his head, tightened against his scalp when he found a particularly sensitive place. Connor used his tongue to trace that spot again and again, soft strokes while Marcas thrust into his mouth, until he cried out and Connor tasted salt and bitter heat, felt Marcas' cock pulsing on his tongue.

The fingers wrapped in his hair relaxed, and Connor pulled back and crawled up to lie by Marcas' side, licking his lips and grinning widely.

"Connor...hmm."

Whatever Marcas was going to say faded into his yawn. He reached out and pulled Connor close to his side, onto his chest, yawned again and closed his eyes.

Connor lay quiet, uncomplaining, listened to the heartbeat pounding under his ear and wondered how long this quiet time would last.

* * * *

Crom Cruach had come, summoned by the sacrifice of firstborn sons—summoned by battle, by the thrice-punctured heart of a king. A king's blood, a greedy delicacy, spilled by another king.

Bonds of loyalty broken.

The most pleasant of odors had flowed like a fine wine before all his senses. In the night of his first abiding, he had stretched himself and his power. Now Crom reached out his hands and sent fingers of shadow into the wood, after the one who called his name — the one who was marked by the brightness of his oldest foe.

The Dagda would not possess such a one, oh no — not for him the direct interference, not for him the destruction such a possession would wreak, not unless at the end of utter need. Still, Crom Cruach sensed that a rising tide of conflict was awake and moving. There were changes in this world that the lord of the mound had not seen in years, and Crom was looking forward to the battle, to the glory of his inevitable victory.

To nothing when it comes, to the end of things.

Had he not been called by the king of this land? Had that king not given over flesh and consciousness for the sake of the future, which he could not see continuing without him? Even now the great shadow of his *self* was adapting this new avatar that once had belonged to the High King. His presence was evolving it, changing it, making it a more fitting host for the enigma of Crom's being.

For the first time in millennia, he was moving with a new type of awareness, a new type of *awake*. The world had changed and men had changed with it. The old days were gone — the days of those who cowered in caves with fire their only friend, their only weapon against the darkness — gone, and they would never return. Instead had come the swords and spears of the moonlit night, and the will of the *faoladh* focused bright and deadly as the points of their weapons — the points of their fangs.

Those wolves.

Crom closed the eyes of the High King and looked outward through many other instances of being, seeking...seeking. It was not hard to find the one he sought—the one who called out to challenge him, standing on the last edge of sunset.

Crom Cruach sent out his power, brought out of the bodies of the dead—the shapes of crooked men. They stumbled forward under his prodding at a speed no human had ever achieved. Among all the deaths being sought by his power tonight, amid the ongoing struggle against the light that qualified his being, this one stood out to him, more important and more interesting.

The son of the king who defied me—following in his father's footsteps. The son of the king—Connor mac Brádach.

For the third time, he was being kept from the life of this one boy. Three separate occasions had found him protected by one of those damnable wolves, when it was rare for one man to survive even a single such encounter. *And his father, too, protected him—sent him away.*

You, marked by brightness. Are you more than the others? Are you the hero of this world who will stand against me, the one who has been chosen by my ancient foe? Chosen one, what have you been given? Power? Light? Still, it will not avail you...

Even if one of those wolves ran always behind and beside his prey, waiting, watchful. Even then there would come a time when those eyes would close or look away—and that would be his time.

The time of the stomach, in which darkness would digest the world.

Chosen one, do not sleep easy tonight...or any night.

Chapter Eight

Having gained something of what he wanted, if not the whole, Connor's concern began to turn away from Marcas and his own feelings and back to their greater trouble. Naked still, damp with dew and sweat, he sat up and let out a breath, turned to look eastward.

Connor barely noticed Marcas staring down at him, something like satisfaction on his face. His thoughts were turned inward, firing in the directions his father had trained into him from the time he was a mud-splattered youth, no more conception of the future ahead of him than any of the other brats at play.

"Marcas…"

"Thinking hard thoughts, Connor?"

He shifted his glance to the blue wolf-eyes, a different glint in them now than the heat of lust.

"Yes. You said my plans were important—you said even the gods were concerned. You said I was marked with brightness, but you never said why. Why am I—?"

"*Why* is dangerous."

"Doesn't matter. Do you think I care? If I don't know by the end of this, there'll be hell to pay, one way or the other."

Marcas shrugged and stood, reached for his tunic and pulled it over his head. "The fact remains — in the end, what we do is up to you. I'm only *faoladh*, not the one marked by brightness. Do what you want to do. What you need to do — that's it, I suppose. Do what must be done."

"What must be done…"

The words slipped off Connor's tongue, rolled over in his thoughts and stuck there.

What must be done. What do I do? What must be done?

The questions seemed simple enough but he had no answers, only bits of other questions and half-formed worries. He couldn't wait forever no matter what his father had intended or Niall had said.

Things had changed too much for that, now.

Do what must be done.

The echo persisted and each repetition planted seeds, some of which bore immediate fruit.

What was needed? What *must* be done, before all other things? His resources, what were they? *How do I fight a god?*

Connor heard his father's voice now as if the man were standing beside him, speaking into his ear — calm, steady, the knowledge he had always possessed. *Choose your battlefield. Choose your men. Today's retreat may hold the first steps of tomorrow's victory.*

With his thoughts clear, the first step came to him outlined in light, the obvious thing. He had nothing here but his personal safety and Marcas. Protection against the black terror of the night was necessary, but even Marcas himself said he was uncertain how much use he'd be now, and Connor couldn't stay here forever. *Wolf or not, he'll follow me. Wolf or not, he knows more about Crom Cruach than anyone else, and that's too useful to deny.*

If his purpose was really Marcas' purpose, whatever he chose, that left him only one real option. *I must go home.*

He had put off the decision for too long. In the morning, he would go. He would leave here and go east, out of the forest of the *faoladh* and down to his father's land. If there were consequences because of that, if there was trouble — well, so be it. He couldn't live with the uncertainty anymore, and every day that went by would only serve to reinforce his fears, the near-certain knowledge that flooded his heart.

If my father is dead…

But he wouldn't let himself complete the thought. There was his mother to worry about, his sisters — not to mention all those who relied on his father to be justice and war-leader, lord of the land. There were too many things, too many *people* relying on him for him to stay here, watching, waiting — especially when there was nothing to watch, and he was waiting without a sign or a hope of the future.

The only thing that remained to him were the words his father had spoken as they were parting… Words without hope. *Only one of us carries the future of our family.*

"But I didn't want it to be me, Father…"

"Connor?"

He turned and found Marcas close behind him, waiting.

"I have to go home, Marcas. I have to see — what's happened. You wanted me to make a plan? Well, that's the best I've got. I have to go home, see my mother and sisters… See if my father is still alive."

"You know I'm coming with you—"

Connor pushed himself to his feet and sighed, then smiled faintly. "I was hoping you'd say that." He looked up into Marcas' face, saw the most serious expression he'd yet seen on those features. "You know it's not going to be easy—though it's not far, I'd guess."

"I know. Which is why I must go with you—or did you forget that the mark of brightness that worries you means I have to protect you?" His stare gained heat. "Did you forget that I'd protect you regardless?"

Connor stared at him, lump in his throat, embers crackling in his chest, heart turning over.

"*My protector.* Are you really going to give everything up to me because of that?"

"*Everything.*" Marcas shook his head. "You couldn't take it all if you tried. I've been rewarded for my service, and it's more than one man could possibly need. I will help you, and *not* just because I'm your protector, but because you're the one I've chosen to be mine."

"You're going to start talking about love again, aren't you?"

But Marcas shook his head.

"No. Not when you're mocking it—not when you... No. I've said enough."

Connor shrugged, only a little disappointed, then wondered why he was disappointed at all. *A game, that's all it is. Like the girl in the meadow.* But there was an uncomfortable tightness in his thoughts, in his chest. More than just an ache now. *Something.* He put it aside for later. There were more important things to worry about. He squared his shoulders and faced Marcas with what he hoped was a serious expression.

"You said we were safe here, but how do we leave without being chased by those things? Is that even possible?"

Marcas closed his eyes, and his face went through several changes of expression that Connor could barely track. He wasn't used to the man Marcas had become yet. The presence beside him, the *feeling* of him was the same, but he kept expecting Marcas to react like the wolf. Maybe what he saw was resignation and maybe it was reluctance, but eventually Connor got the answer he hoped for.

"If we leave early enough and don't move in the dark, don't attract attention, don't frequent populated places..." Then he paused, narrowed his eyes. "And maybe there's one more thing. Forbidden, of course. But we need all the help we can get."

"All the help—"

"There are some weapons that can wound the shadow. Not destroy it—even if something could kill the lord of the mound, that would be to destroy the world. But you—if I can't protect you, you'll have to protect yourself." Marcas looked away, then back to meet Connor's eyes. "We'll have a chance. I can't promise more than that."

Connor nodded, steeled his resolve.

"That's enough, then. It'll have to be."

Marcas looked at Connor standing before him, legs apart, eyes locked on his, features set and stern, the expression of a man many years his senior. This time outside the heat of passion, Marcas saw the man in the boy before him. There were hints of wisdom and good thinking, the things that could make a warrior a king. It pleased him, but he kept his thoughts to himself. No easy way to say what he was thinking—no easy way to get out the truth without letting it sour what was coming.

But I think there is something special about you, Connor. I think that is why you are the brightest light I've seen. Chosen.

Marcas looked up at the sky, the last lingering fragments of sunset before the darkness, then turned back to Connor, his mind made up.

"Come with me. I'll bring you to the place — you can choose your weapon."

He didn't wait for an answer, but turned and walked away from the wood and up toward the hall, then down the hill. In the undergrowth, barely visible beneath the reaching fingers of ferns and green bushes, the head of an old path showed as brown dust and a marker stone. Connor came up beside him, still tying up his tunic, and Marcas gestured at the path.

"You'll know when to stop."

Connor cast a suspicious glance into the darkness, then began to make his way down the path. He picked his way slowly, no wolf-vision to help him in the growing dark, and more than once Marcas found himself reaching forward to steady him as he tripped over a protruding root or loop of vine. It was why Marcas had insisted he go first — otherwise the boy would be stumbling along blind behind him. But he knew when Connor had found their stopping place. He stopped dead, so suddenly that Marcas walked into his back.

"Do you feel it, Connor? The sleeping strength in the stone?"

Here, at the bottom of the shortest side of the hill, in a shallow valley more sparsely wooded than the surrounding ground, there was a clearing made bare entirely. In the center of it was a barrow and around the barrow, a circle of standing stones.

In the light of the rising moon, the standing stones glowed gray. They were each one twice the height of a man, narrow and subtly shaped. Marcas watched Connor step forward slowly and raise his hand to touch the nearest stone. He pressed his fingertips against it, then his palm—testing, careful.

Connor looked back at him over his shoulder, and Marcas saw confusion and curiosity mingled in Connor's eyes.

"I feel…something, that's certain. Is this why it's safe here?"

Marcas spoke quietly. In this place, any voice much louder than a whisper felt wrong to him.

"No. The standing stones are here to protect the barrow—and the barrow alone."

"But…"

"Think, Connor. To go down into the earth, down into darkness, would that not be more dangerous than any other thing we could do? And not just us, here and now—all the *faoladh*, since we first took on our task. There's no dawn underground, just the black terror, the bent one's realm going on forever and in all directions."

"Then why are we here?"

"I told you. To retrieve a weapon that will help you fight, if necessary—though I hope it's not."

Connor scowled.

"But why do you keep your weapons in the barrow? Isn't that the worst place?"

"It…wasn't our choice. Some powers must be kept where the one who gave them commands, until they're needed. Then, like you will now, one goes to retrieve what's needed."

Connor tossed his shoulders back and took a step forward, his intent obvious, and Marcas reached out a hand and caught the back of Connor's tunic, jerked him to a stop and shook his head at the scowl the boy threw in his direction.

"Wait for the moonlight."

"The—"

"To touch the entrance. Or would you rather go right into the hands of the crooked king and make it so all that I've done was a wasted effort?"

"I— No, of course not. Sorry."

Marcas relaxed and let go of the boy's tunic. Instead of stepping away, Connor took a step back, closer to him. He peered forward through the starlit darkness into the blacker pit that was the opening of the barrow.

"You won't see anything there—not now."

"Is it...haunted?"

Marcas laid a hand on Connor's back, felt a shiver there and crossed before the boy to stand blocking the sight of the open barrow. "Haunted." He scoffed. "What does that mean? After everything you've seen so far, you still have a question like that?"

"So there's nothing beside shadow and Crom Cruach that—"

"Don't speak his name!"

"I... What?"

"Do you think we call him the crooked king because he rules us, the bent one because someone finds it amusing to do so? The dark god, the black one—all those titles are just to make certain that his name is never spoken out of its time."

"Out of its time—what does that mean?"

"For us, that means never spoken. What purpose would there be to doing so? To speak a name is to awaken a certain expectation. There are always priests who do their best to summon darkness, men who believe that chaos is the soul of order, good the purpose of evil. *They* speak his name. They wake him. They seek him—"

"With sacrifice."

Marcas looked at him sharply.

"Yes—and what would you know about something like that?"

Connor turned a little, met Marcas' eyes almost unwillingly. There was something heavy in his expression.

"Enough. That's the reason for all this. The reason my father's probably dead."

"A sacrifice. *Where*, Connor?"

"I overheard my father talking with Niall and Aran. They'd been summoned to Magh Slécht, to a gathering of chiefs and kings, a gathering for battle—some great war, that was the rumor, the promise. But it was all a lie—so my father told me. It was all a lie, just an excuse the High King gave to summon the hundred kings of Eire and their firstborn."

A suffocating sensation was beginning to rise through Marcas' body, intensifying with every word out of Connor's mouth.

"An excuse…"

"For the sacrifice. My father said the High King intended…that the firstborn—" Connor swallowed and shook his head, vague nausea on his face. "That's why he sent me away." Bitter self-recrimination filled Connor's tone and a humorless kind of amusement.

"Why you were alone when I found you?"

He crouched, tugged at the grass, refused to turn and meet Marcas' gaze.

"That's right."

"Your father saved your life, Connor. And now I know why that great blackness was born on the night of the new moon—he must have done it. High King— the man's a fool, if he's even a man any longer."

His words were grim, and his tone more so, but he couldn't help it. What a fool. What a fool! To summon the dark one out of the secret places and into the open world.

"What do you mean about the High King?"

He shot a glance at the boy looking at him, and Connor elaborated.

"Not that he's a fool, I understand *that*—but what would he be if he's not a man any more? You don't mean that he sacrificed his—"

But he couldn't even finish the sentence, gulped and went faintly green. Marcas shook his head.

"No. The bent one comes out of the dark kingdom under the ground very rarely, only when the summons of the ritual and the sacrifice accords with his own desire for destruction—so the old stories tell us. For a thousand years and more he's been bound by the pact of power that *we* made, the *faoladh*. The sacrifice your High King made—it's woken the most terrible destruction. If he was the focus of the ritual, the one who began the sacrifice, spoke the name of the lord of the mound and summoned him forth…"

Marcas shook his head.

"He will be a vessel of the dark god now. He will be an inhabited being, no longer possessed of his own soul. The man Tigernmas is dead, but his flesh might remain, full of the presence and the power of the bent one."

Connor was silent for several minutes, aimlessly plucking at the grass, staring forward into the distance as if he was sightless.

"Connor?"

"Marcas, can we kill him? The High King?"

Marcas shrugged.

"The flesh that remains might fail, if it's wounded enough. Not from age—the lord of the mound wouldn't let something so paltry affect him. But even if the body is broken, there's still a dark god to deal with, and that's the greater problem." He snorted. "Not that I've any idea what to do."

"You—don't?"

"My work was protecting those like you who were threatened by the bent one's servants—not facing the lord of the mound himself!"

"Then what—?"

Marcas held up a hand to hold back Connor's questions. There was growing gleam visible out of the corner of his eye, and questions like these could take all night. Best to do what they'd come to do before the time to do it in had passed. Tonight, at least, they were going nowhere that wasn't safe enough for relaxed conversation.

"Don't be so impatient. I can't answer all your questions at once. Look behind me, Connor."

Marcas stepped aside and turned, though he knew what he would see. The moon had risen high enough for the pale gleam of its growing light to touch the opening of the barrow, and Connor came closer, stood by Marcas' side and peered at a shining curtain of light as it fell across the opening.

"That's—"

"Power."

"*Beautiful.* Is that what made you a wolf?"

Marcas raised his eyebrows, surprised at the reaction he'd achieved. "Maybe. But you'd better hurry. There's not a lot of time before the moon moves and the light's lost—and you don't want to be stuck down there when that happens."

Connor stared back at him, startled.

"You want me to go alone?"

"I can't pass the barrier—not now. I was down there, once—when I was younger than you, before I began my service. Now that the wolf has lived in me, still lives in me—I wouldn't try it. Not even now that I've got my own shape back."

"But—"

"There can be too much of a good thing, Connor. You can find what you need on your own. You only need to go straight down, take no turns at all. Just don't take too long down there. Light fades fast in the deep places."

"And I can't go in the morning?"

"Sunlight and moonlight are not the same. Go or don't, but make up your mind—and quickly!"

Marcas watched Connor's shoulders tighten, then relax, then settle. The boy's arms were straight and taut by his side, his hands clenched into fists, and he took a first step forward almost woodenly. He put out one hand, and it went through the silver curtain of light as if there was nothing there. He took a deep breath, and the muscles in his neck tightened as if he was going to look back, but he didn't.

Without another word Connor stepped forward, passed through the gleaming veil of brightness and vanished beyond Marcas' sight.

* * * *

On the other side of the curtain of light, its silver radiance extended downward, a glow of light that showed Connor the way underground. He went forward without trepidation along the bright path that was before him, and ignored the dark openings that branched out to the left and right. He counted seven passages as he went forward without turning, as Marcas had instructed.

His journey ended abruptly at a closed stone door on which was a single sigil, blue in the light that had followed him. It looked like an ogham letter, but if it was, Connor didn't know it, hadn't learned it. There were some such signs that were sacred and taught only to those who served the gods, but he thought that this might not belong to them. *It's a sign of the* faoladh.

For a moment he thought about going back, asking Marcas what he was supposed to do. *Was there something he forgot to tell me?* Without thinking, Connor reached out and touched the stone, laid his hand across the sigil. It *sparked*, and behind him the light went out. He stood frozen in total darkness, terror crawling up his spine, along his limbs, on the back of his neck.

Fear sucked the moisture from his mouth. He tried to lick his lips with a dry tongue, failed then tried to take one step back. He couldn't move. His hand was *stuck* to the door. A terrible moment passed before the light returned, thin and fragile, a single gleam that glowed from the crack at the top of the door. A little at a time, Connor felt it shifting under his palm before whatever hold it had over him vanished — quick as it had come — and he was released.

With a rumbling, grating noise, the door was swallowed into the floor. It vanished into the ground as if it had never been, and the chamber that was revealed to him was white with brightness. Luminance gleamed in coils and spirals on the walls, whatever light had made his pathway now clinging to patterns on the floor and ceiling, symbols, more ogham words, picture-carvings... But his attention was jerked away from all those things almost immediately.

In the center of the low chamber that held them was something of far more interest.

"Weapons."

Connor breathed the word and all but leaped forward toward them. His eye picked out a staff, a long-handled ax with a wicked point, another beside it with a double head and a shorter haft...swords, spears, arrows. None of it looked as if it had ever been used. Every edge was keen and bright, begging for battle, and those edges—he'd never seen weapons as sharp as these.

Each blade bore an edge so sharp it was beyond his sight. Aware of the warning Marcas had given him about time, Connor ran a quick eye over each weapon, and finally decided upon a spear. He reached out with hesitant fingers and clasped the pale wood of the shaft. He expected it to be cool, sitting down here in the dark for who knows how long, but the wood was warm to the touch and tingled against his palm when he hefted it.

Thick, sturdy ash, well-polished, but not worn, it had a good weight in his hands, and he turned back and forth, swung the length of it across his body. He made a few experimental thrusts, testing heft and weight and balance.

Perfect. As if it had been made for him. He brought the spearhead close to his face and inspected the gleam of it. Silver, as if the light had clung to it or made it—surely whatever power was in the light was in the point of the spear. The thought brought to mind the memory of the wolf's howl, the radiant moonlight in a burning tide of light and how the shadow had fled from it.

"A weapon that can wound the bent one. I'll make good use of it."

Connor turned to the space where the door had been and made his way out, counting the passages in the dark—yet not the dark. From the head of the spear came a faint gleam, not enough to light the way, but enough to illuminate where he was standing.

He gripped it tight in one hand and made his way up toward the night.

* * * *

Marcas saw motes of light swirling like dust in the wake of Connor's passage, and settled himself to wait by the threshold. He dozed, watching the movement of the motes, and almost didn't notice when the light began to move out of the curtain, went into motion around him. Only when he noticed that the mote of light he was tracking had vanished into the general brightness did he jerk himself into full wakefulness. All around him was light and a familiar presence.

It was like the power that had come over him when he'd been made *faoladh*, but brighter. What was this? This was not supposed to happen—this was nothing like the other time he'd come here—

"*Lovely.*"

The word came from nowhere. Neither was it truly a word—rather, it was an image-sensation that played itself in his brain. What was it? *Who* was it? But in an instant such questions ceased to matter. The light had come close, and now it reached out to embrace him. Marcas tried to stand, to move away, but the radiance that had taken hold of him jerked his limbs out of contact with the ground. Brightness alone held him as fully and closely as a mother holds her child, but the sensation of it was no comfort. His nerves were coming alive as if he were being burned.

Splashed across his brain in brightness, the voice-images came again, shattering in their clarity.

"What would you choose, if you could? To protect? How much would you give?"

Stretched like a thread, Marcas' awareness moved along a track of agony more intense than any other pain in his experience. Even then, he knew the truth. The images came to him with Connor's face in them — *To protect. Choose? How much — I...would give.*

He didn't even need to think about the answer. Hadn't he already told Connor himself? Reason might regret speaking the truth in this place, before this witness, but his heart gave him focus, let him bring thoughts into words, force the words past his lips.

"Everything. To protect...at any price. To protect!"

For a second time, more intensely, more precise, a flash crossed his mind.

"Lovely."

Tears streamed across Marcas' cheeks like fire. He would have begged for the pain to stop, but it was no longer in him to form words or thoughts, to have any coherent process beyond awareness of his stretching nerves, some fundamental alteration of his basic being.

"A gift, for you."

Pain. The word-pictures echoed. Where did they come from? Was there a where, or was the world a dream, and everything a dream but the pain that had come before this moment? He heard a perfect note, endless and piercing, a sound full of *green.* It came to him that it must be his own god that tormented him, and even as he said that to himself, rediscovered words, and the *I* of his being, there was laughter that was as green as the note that had summoned him. The voice tingled on his skin but no longer tortured him.

"So fragile."

The sound of moving rushes. The sound of a river — the scent of the richest mud, and ancient loam, of beasts abounding in the wild nature that opened now before his eyes. Outstretched fingers of oak rustled over his head, and the birds among the branches were flitting jewels with wings the shade of sky and shadow, pearl-throated and singing a music that would have enriched the darkest hovel with the light of a faerie place.

"Marcas of the faoladh, you have been changed. You are no longer the man you were. Having chosen opportunity, will you now ask your questions?"

"Who are you?"

The sound of his own voice was vaguely startling, like a sound that was not meant to be. *Not here, maybe.*

"This answer you know. Does not your power come from me?"

"You are…the Dagda. Then why the pain? Haven't I done as I was asked? You said I had done well. That I should do more!"

"You know nothing yet of pain. You will *do more."*

The words lingered in his ears — ominous, still somehow empty.

"Why can't I see you?"

Laughter surrounded him.

"Do you not?"

It occurred to Marcas then that the *where of his being* might not be a place — that everything around him might be the manifestation of the god.

"You... So you are everywhere. Is there a reason you've brought me to you?"

"To choose. My ancient foe now walks the world. Were I to do as he has done, the world would suffer for it. I would not see all that is life, broken."

"But you said I already made my choice."

"You have chosen opportunity. Will you also choose to take up the purpose with which I would imbue you?"

"What is that purpose?"

"Do what must be done. Chain Crom Cruach once more — protect, Marcas of the faoladh, *as you were meant to do."*

"And I'll have your help?"

"Do you think I offer purpose without power to achieve it?"

Marcas' thoughts flew instantly back to those ringing words, the promise of them, the temptation — *to protect. Connor.*

"No — I... I'll do it. I will accept your purpose."

Lovely, lovely — but it was the leaves, the river, and not the voice that said it this time.

"Come forward, and take the cup."

Green out of the greensward a chalice rose. It had the look of stone, and yet it was light in his palm, light as a leaf.

"Fill it at the river."

The water called Marcas forward as if he were dying of a quenchless thirst that had gone unnoticed to that very moment. He reached down with the cup in his hands, and his fingers trembled as they approached the water, as if it might vanish and leave him — but no, the gleaming currents parted like a curtain for the lip of the cup, and the water filled it. He stood and held the chalice between his shaking palms and waited for the permission, the order, that he knew must come.

"*If you would be true-made,* faoladh, *then drink you now of the god's blood you carry in your cup.*"

And the wind, a wild susurrus, made known the acclamation of his purpose. *Drink now, drink now!*

Marcas put the cup to his lips and drank.

Flowers. He tasted flowers, honey pouring ripe from the comb into his mouth, the freshest clover-fed cream still warm and frothy. Hickory smoke and apple-wood, fish in embers at the shore, sea-breeze, salt breeze. Boar on the spit, and bear stuffed with fruit, spring's sweet syrups and the golden grain of fall — and that was the first draft.

He took a breath, put the cup to his lips and drank again, and the stars poured over his tongue, the light of them crisp as a new apple and sweet as a fresh berry and clear as the finest water from the most sparkling spring. But it was hot, too — hot as the mulled mead of the winter, the cider pulled and let to warm by the hearth.

Marcas felt the cup fall empty from his fingers.

"*Well done.*"

The words had no meaning. The god's blood had taken thought by the throat and shaken the life out of it, and what was left — *what is left?*

"*It is time to return to the world. It is time to return to the one who is waiting for you. Now — now! There is a task to be done. You must drown the dark in light.*"

Night eclipsed the green and Marcas felt the bottom drop out of the world beneath him, even as he licked his lips, seeking the taste of that drink one last time. But those words — *the one who is waiting for me?*

Connor.

With the name came the sight of the stars, the moon in its curve. It hadn't moved much — already Marcas could see the ground below him, and the gleaming curtain of silver light that blocked the entrance to the barrow. He heard the god's laughter in the background of his being, and there was no surprise in him. He knew it as he always had. The Dagda was capricious, despite all his wisdom, his power—just like the moon.

For his own reasons, he had granted Marcas more than any other of his kin, and the greatest of his questions had gone unanswered. *Why?* But already the sound of that voice was leaving him, the memory of that taste, all things and nothing. All that remained was the world and the star-struck night, and over him... Connor's face? He tried to raise his hand, to touch Connor's cheek, to wipe away the concern he saw brooding there.

So you came out of the dark all right. Marcas tried to say it, but he had no voice and no hand nor arm answered his call to action, only the strong length of the foreleg of the wolf.

"Marcas—what happened? You changed back— you—Marcas, you didn't say this would happen!"

The distress in Connor's voice was equal to Marcas' own, and both pleased and angered him. Was this the gift of the god? He leaped to his feet, paced back and forth, a low whine in his throat that grew into an ear-shattering howl. The taste of the god's blood was bitter on his lips, when he thought he'd never tasted mead so fine, honey so sweet—*what now, Marcas?*

The taunt of his own conscience had a sting like a whip. *What now! Look what you've done for power— protect, you said, at any price—well here you have it, the power you wanted, and what do you think of it now?*

Ear-shattering, soul-splitting were the howls that escaped him, and beside him he felt the presence of the one for whom he had done this, the one from whom he would be parted by this, and thought his heart would break. Connor sat with his head in his hands. Had it broken him so completely, to have lost the *man* who was his companion to the wolf again? Something deep within Marcas, underneath all the anguish, was pleased—so pleased, to learn that whatever impact he'd made in so short a time as him*self* was strong.

But I did not mean for this to happen, did not mean to leave you alone this way again!

He was too distressed to notice the change in the pain he felt, heart-wrought pain to the pain of shifting flesh, until it overtook him completely. His bones were wrenched out of alignment, muscles reshaping, ligaments stretching, joints moving, all his flesh in flux.

"What now—?"

Marcas startled himself with the sound of his own voice, and opened his eyes to find himself naked on the ground. He reached out a hand in utter confusion, then looked up and met Connor's gaze and a profound relief and curiosity there.

"Don't—don't ask. I need— Just don't ask. Please. I need some time. To think."

The words jerked out of him in short sentences. Seeking something, anything to distract him, he looked up at Connor and found a few more.

"Did you find a weapon?"

Connor stood from where he had crouched beside Marcas and held forward a spear that gleamed at its point with a familiar and deadly light.

Chapter Nine

When Marcas turned his gaze away, Connor looked down at him and swallowed twice to keep the questions back, because he could feel them building up in his throat like a physical blockage. *How? Why? What was that?* The knot of the request that held him silent was tied around his words. Other than questions, he couldn't think of anything to say. He eyed Marcas and took in lines like the finest work of chain imprinted on his skin.

The marks stood out like scars, silver against Marcas' tan. They ran down his spine, across his shoulders, wound down his arms, across his chest, a subtle tracery everywhere Connor looked. Was it the mark of whatever had happened to him?

Marcas didn't move, didn't turn to look at him, didn't say anything. Connor sighed and began to wander the borders of the clearing. He looked more closely at the standing stones, touched them to feel the vibrant hum that slept beneath their surface. It swished across his skin like a breath of breeze even though the air wasn't moving.

Only a few minutes passed before he turned back and saw that the curtain of brightness was moving. There was no longer a clear path down into the barrow. The darkness seemed to be eating the light, greedily devouring it, and as it did so, not only the shining veil was disappearing.

The moonlight that fell in the circle no longer illuminated it. The stones were gathering shrouds of darkness. The starlight was no longer a clear, clean presence coming down from behind the moon but a choked, chalky light that hung gritty in the air, suspended on the last motes of the moon's brilliance. Connor tightened his fingers on the shaft of the spear in his hand, backed away from the border of the circle until he was all but tripping over Marcas.

"You don't need to worry—or fear."

Connor turned and faced him, saw discomfort on his face as he stretched his legs, pushed himself to his feet, raised his arms over his head then stretched them back, joints popping, settling.

"Nothing will come from outside—didn't I tell you this place was protected? But in there…"

He raised his hand and pointed at the barrow and in the opening, no longer blanked by moonlight, a thousand tendrils of darkness writhed like some tentacled beast from the deep black waters of a nameless sea. Connor jumped back, swore at the sight of it and again because he could barely believe what he was seeing. A thin film, like water but not—like the bubbles that formed in the bath, but infinitely more refined, infinitely more thin, more glowing—held back the blackness.

"In there all the darkness under the world is waiting for someone unwary to go seeking what doesn't belong to them—or what does. It wouldn't care. It doesn't matter. But we're safe here. You can put the spear down, Connor."

Startled, Connor looked down and saw that his hands had brought the weapon up as if some enemy was before him, ready to be skewered. A little at a time he lowered it, tried to relax his shoulders—but the darkness was *right there*.

"*Easy*. In a thousand years and more it's never once been broken. That barrier was set by the Dagda himself, to protect that which is precious to us and that which is precious to him."

Connor was confused until he remembered the other passages he had passed on his way down to the stone door, leading off to unknown places and unknown ends.

"There's more than weapons down there?"

"More, yes. Some things that are ours, treasures that belong to the *faoladh*—and some things that were given to us, gifts to ease our service. And there are some powers that it's said are never meant to be shared among men, that are only for the right times and the right places. They are waiting for their time. They are not for us."

Connor looked back at the seething blackness for a long moment. There was nothing natural about it, nothing *right*—his skin crawled to look at it, to know it existed, and yet he couldn't look away. Was it Crom Cruach? The bent one himself, some aspect of the dark god's power writhing aimless? A long shudder eased its way across his shoulders, down his back. It left gooseflesh behind, a prickling, tingling sensation like a leg gone to sleep.

"Can we—get away from here? Go back up to the hall, something..."

He retreated another step, so that his back was pressed against Marcas' chest and side, and felt a hand grasp his shoulder, squeeze tightly.

"I understand. We'll go back, no fear."

"It's not fear! I'm not afraid, it's—"

And he swallowed, shook his head, looked away from the coiled writhing that again and again attracted his gaze despite himself.

"*Sick*. It's not right—it doesn't belong."

Marcas stared at him, then turned to look into the darkness for a long minute before he turned away.

"No, it doesn't."

He tugged Connor along with him as he moved out of the circle and into the natural night. Connor stared at Marcas' back moving before him. All his rich clothes had vanished, and the silver tracery on his skin stood out in the starlight. A little at a time Connor moved faster, stepped closer, until he was all but tripping on the heels of Marcas' feet.

There was warmth coming off the strong back in front of him, a radiant heat that reminded him more of the wolf than anything human. *The wolf.* For a second time, a hundred questions rose up in his throat and threatened to spill over.

"What—?" He stopped almost at once, even as Marcas paused mid-step and turned to him, expectant look barely visible on his face in the moonlight that ran down between the trees. "Sorry, it's nothing— nothing. You said not to ask and I won't."

Marcas let out a sharp, hot exhalation. "You want to know how I was the wolf—how I became myself again after?"

Wordless, Connor nodded.

"I didn't tell you not to ask because I don't want to answer, Connor. I just don't know..." His voice trailed off, and he turned away and started walking up the hill again, following the path that Connor could barely see. He was surprised when he heard Marcas' voice continue, the words low, quick—hunted and hurried. "While you were below, I was visited. I met the moonlight—I walked in the Dagda's land, drank of his blood... I chose..."

He paused, and when he continued Connor knew that he was not saying what he had begun to say. "Whatever it is that makes the *faoladh*, it has only ever been a temporary thing. But now the wolf—the wolf is still inside me."

They had reached the top of the hill. Marcas strode to the front of the hall and pulled the doors open with a sharp movement. *"Something is changed in me. I'm not a man or a wolf now. Maybe something in between, maybe a monster."* He took quick, heavy steps into the hall, crossed through panels of moonlight to the back, and behind the dais flung open a chest, and then another, looking for something. Clothes? *Yes.*

Connor stared at him, felt...something. An ache. Then he shrugged and shook off the moment of strangeness. He crossed the hall to stand by Marcas' side. There was pain on his face and behind the fall of dark hair, a tightness of jaw and eye that Connor didn't like to see. He reached out with one hand and pushed the hair back, pressed the flat of his palm against Marcas' skin. Marcas jerked his eyes up to Connor's face, but Connor only pulled him straight and kissed him. He surprised himself as much as Marcas, but it felt like the right thing to do. It was the best, the only way he could think of to express what he wanted to say.

Marcas seemed to relax against him, and when finally Connor pulled back, breathing deep, it was with a grin on his face.

"You're man enough for me, Marcas — and you still taste human."

Marcas laughed shortly, sharply. The tension eased out of his shoulders and when Connor moved to step away, Marcas' arms around his waist prevented him.

"*Stay*. Please. Are you…tired?"

Connor shook his head.

"Hungry?"

"I could eat an *ox*."

Marcas grinned. "Well I've broken every other rule… Let's go have some fun."

The curve of his lips was irresistible, and Connor leaned forward to kiss him again, this time just because he wanted to.

"*Fun*, huh? What does a wolf do for fun?"

Marcas looked down at him for a moment, then let him go. "Maybe I'll show you."

His eyes glittered, and Connor's heart beat faster, the blood rushing out from his center, tingling in his fingertips.

"But not now."

Connor let out an irritated huff of breath, and Marcas laughed.

* * * *

Marcas was pleased, now that he had recovered from the shock of his sudden transformation. *So* pleased. He could feel the wolf-pulse in his blood, in his bones, a howl in the back of his thoughts — and yet that was all it was. *A pulse*. He could feel the internal path laid out within him, a leash on which he could pull and call the shattering transition over his flesh. Yet as long as he wished it, he could stay as he was.

And Connor wants me. He wants me, not the wolf I can be – I saw it on his face.

He grew aware that he had been staring while his thoughts roamed the various sources of his current delight. *You kissed me, Connor.* Marcas took his time looking away and didn't speak until Connor questioned him.

"So where are we going that's *forbidden*?"

"I didn't say, did I?" Marcas grinned. "I thought I'd take you home, for now. A mile across the meadow is a valley you can't see from here. My village, the *faoladh* village, is there. A hundred homes, tavern, tanner, meadery, smith—and who would keep cattle better than us?"

Connor blinked at him, curious.

"But the secret—"

Marcas shrugged.

"It's easy to keep. The howls keep strangers away, and the stories from the past...and the shapes of wolves greater than any normal wolf could be, stalking the hillsides, patrolling the borders. Though it's not known that they're borders, of course."

Connor shrugged one shoulder, cast a glance at Marcas out of the corners of his eyes. "Of course."

"You think that's trouble? That there's something wrong with it?"

Connor took a full step backward, confusion on his face now wiping out the earlier expression.

"No, I— Marcas—"

"We don't only protect ourselves from the bent one, Connor. Why do you think everything I've told you is supposed to be forbidden? Men aren't meant to know who or what we are."

Connor was silent for a moment, and Marcas knew it was because the boy couldn't argue with anything he'd said. He pushed his point.

"Nothing good would come of men finding out that the wolves they sometimes have strange encounters with are not wolves but men. If they found out the source of our power, or that it's something over which we have only the faintest control—"

Connor sighed.

"Strength of a beast, mind and heart of a man—they'd want to fight you. They'd want to prove themselves against you."

Marcas smiled a little, but the expression didn't last.

"Most men are easily frightened by things they don't understand. Even men who aren't usually cowards. You're the exception, Connor. Not the rule. And yes, some of them would want to fight us to test their power—is that what *you* want?"

The boy grinned, quick, gleaming, half-lustful even now. "Maybe."

"More would want to kill for the pleasure of killing. A beast like me would disgust and terrify them. It's the reason they run, you know."

He stopped, shaking his head, nothing more to say.

Connor stared back at Marcas. That statement—it felt like it needed some words, some denial, more even than Marcas saying he was a monster. Halting, slow, the syllables still slipped past his lips.

"I never—"

"I know. Or why do you think I've offered to bring you home with me? You—"

But Marcas stopped and turned slightly away. Connor was beginning to see the way the wolf and the man were the same. He thought he knew what Marcas hadn't said, but he didn't understand why he would avoid the words.

You already said you wanted me. You already said you could love me... Awareness sparked in him. *But I said it was a game.* Was it respect for Connor's opinion that restrained Marcas, or just wariness because he had made light of love?

"Marcas." He reached out and caught hold of Marcas' arm, but his words failed him and fell away into silence even as Marcas raised his eyes. What was there to say? Why was he even saying anything? *A game.* So why did he feel like...he was losing something? A dangerous game, that's all — so why did he feel this way?

Marcas reached up and laid his hand across Connor's. "You shouldn't worry so much."

"I — How did you —?"

The wolf-eyes gleamed at him, luminous. "The same way I knew that *this* was between us."

Marcas gestured between them, at the way they stood chest to chest, only a few inches of space separating them. Connor closed the distance, leaned forward so that when he spoke his lips brushed against Marcas'.

"*This?* I like this."

Marcas took a step back, shaking his head, and Connor felt a pang. "I know you do. You know *I* do — but *this* is not all I want, and until you can tell me *something* —" Again, he shook his head, but Connor felt better about it even if those still weren't the things he wanted to hear.

"I don't —" He stopped, swallowed, shrugged, shook his head. He tightened his hands into fists against his sides and, though it was difficult, Connor kept his gaze on Marcas' face, kept contact with the wolf-blue eyes. "I don't have an answer for you, Marcas. Not about—love. But I want so much more of you—"

"*Connor.*"

Marcas blinked at him, apparently shocked by such an answer. Was it the honesty of it? Connor had shaped his words that way on purpose—because he couldn't say no, any more than he could say yes. Because he didn't *want* to say no, and...

Maybe I'd like to say yes. Maybe it would be nice to have someone...to love.

His father wasn't here now to tell him that his days of playing with whomever he chose were numbered. His father wasn't here to tell him that ten generations were his responsibility, that it fell to him to take a bride, continue the line of the king.

"*Pleasure is one thing, but the future is in a wife, and when I find you one, she will not tolerate your boyhood games.*" He had heard the words so many times they were engraved on his mind. Never mind if he had always been more interested in taking someone just as strong or stronger, in finding beautiful men and bending them with a smile and a smoky gaze.

Boyhood games. But, Father, it's not a game to me. It never was. And maybe love — maybe love isn't either. That ache —

He stared at Marcas and Marcas stared back at him, lips parted—for the first time, in contemplating what it meant that he could not say *no*, Connor had a glimpse of what it might mean if his answer was *yes*. Not a game, not just passion, more than lust... The pain in his chest, as it grew, was teaching him its own lesson.

"Marcas."

He didn't know what he was going to say, but it didn't matter. Quick, rough, Marcas leaned forward as if the sound of his name had summoned him and pressed his mouth against Connor's, nipped at his lips until he opened them, succumbed to the stroking heat of Marcas' tongue. He moaned, and Marcas bit his lip, almost hard enough to draw blood. Then he pulled back just enough to speak against his mouth.

"Half the time you say my name, it makes me want to take you, Connor."

"I wish you would—" And before Marcas could answer again, Connor kissed him. "Not now—I know. You just said—but *Marcas*..." He heard the groan under his parted lips and laughed against Marcas' mouth. "I *still* wish you would. And if you don't want me to take things into my *own* hands—"

His fingers skimmed the warm brown skin so close to him, traced the lines of the new marks, silver-dark, quicksilver beneath the surface—collarbone, shoulders, nipples, hips... Marcas twisted backward out of his reach, and Connor was laughing as he finished his sentence.

"You should put some damned clothes on!"

It was the wolf-laughter that answered him this time, but Marcas beckoned Connor into the hall, moved to several old chests and pulled out clothes far richer than those that had vanished during his transformation. The embroidery was fine and shone with gold. The colors were rich in many hues of blue and green.

Unashamed of his own rising desire, how obvious it must be, Connor watched with a steady gaze as Marcas pulled the fine linen over his head, pinned a fine cloak of blue wool with a gold brooch.

"Listen, Connor—while we're among my kin, you can't say a word about the wolf. They'll think you're my lover—I won't grudge them that. Why else stitch my name on your lips?"

"Stitch—"

Dressed now, Marcas came forward from behind the big chests and took a fistful of Connor's tunic, enough to drag him close—Connor thought that he'd be kissed again, but instead of a kiss, Marcas' tongue only darted out, a terrible tease, and touched the place on his lip that stung faintly, the place where Marcas had bitten him. Connor ran his own tongue over the bruises, the swelling marked on his mouth by Marcas' teeth, and grinned a little as he realized what the man had meant.

"I see."

"Those who are wolves will see your brightness, just as I do—but they won't be able to speak of it, even if any of them are near. It wouldn't matter, anyway. The scent of me is all over you, and your own desire too."

"My own—desire?"

"Bittersweet, boy. The scent of you is always tempting, as often as it is that you want me—or think you do."

"That's your fault for not giving in."

Marcas crossed his arms over his chest. "Giving in? You think it's easy? Seven years I've had no one, and now I've got you—and also the bad sense to want more than just a lover out of you."

"Bad sense maybe, but you've good taste."

Marcas scowled at him, a bare twist of his lips, and spoke in a voice heavy with sarcasm. "So modest. But you do understand what I'm telling you, Connor—"

"Yes, I do. You've got anxious kin—I won't say anything to let them know I know your secrets. And if they ask, I'll be sure to convince them of your prowess." Connor grinned at the flush that painted Marcas' cheeks. "Anyway, it's not likely to matter, is it? You're one of them—they'll trust you."

"Maybe." Marcas' voice was very quiet, until he looked up as if something had occurred to him. "Oh— and leave the spear, Connor. You won't need it yet, and they'd recognize it—anyone would."

Hesitant, but knowing he could do nothing but obey, Connor laid the spear on the long table in the center of the hall and turned away. Outside, the summer night was hazy with warmth, the stars nearing their midnight position on the horizon. Marcas was staring up at the sky, or down the hill— either way, his eyes were distant, focused on something Connor couldn't see or hear.

"What is it? What's happening?"

"Blood being spilled—we'll have nothing to worry about from the wolves tonight. There's too many in need of aid, too many…"

"Shouldn't we go help, then?"

Marcas flashed a smile at him, tight and thin.

"No. Even if I were to go, I wouldn't take you with me—and in good conscience, I can't leave you unprotected. Not even here—not even now— especially not now. It was for *you* that I was given this power, not because of the pact of the *faoladh*. I shouldn't even have it, and I'd rather no one who didn't have to know found out, even if they are my *kin*."

Connor stared at him, caught on one thing only.

"For—me?"

Marcas didn't meet his eyes. "The Dagda gave me a choice, asked me what I would give for power—but it wasn't really a choice. To protect you? No, not a choice."

Those words, that truth, lodged like a burning coal in Connor's throat and stayed there, giving off smoke but not enough to choke him. There was a minute of silence before Marcas spoke again.

"It's getting late, and you said you were hungry. We should go, Connor. Follow me—step where I step. I'll guide you as best as I can. There's no path, or I'd send you down ahead of me."

"So when I trip and fall I don't land on you?"

"So *if* you tripped and fell, I could catch you."

Connor blinked, momentarily taken aback. But then, why should he be? *My protector.* And the thought almost made him laugh—but not quite. *Everything. He really meant it—*

His heart throbbed in his chest, and he turned to follow Marcas down the side of the hill.

* * * *

Green leaves shone waxy in the moonlight as it came brief and murky from behind passing clouds, and Marcas strode down the green hillside with great, loping strides, then turned to wait for Connor to catch up. It worked better this way than trying to let the boy come down just behind him—he kept running into his back, and that was enough to send them both falling forward. Marcas had the bruises to show for it.

They were nearly down now, and Marcas was grateful—next time, he'd skip the clothes until they'd come down and bring Connor in wolf shape, carry him on his back.

It's not like there's anything unpleasant about the way he likes to look at me, the way his eyes linger, skip over everything else and come back to me—and he almost laughed to himself, because as much as that pleased him, it would please him more if it happened when he had his clothes on. Then it might mean something. He almost sighed out loud, caught himself and saw that he'd come to the bottom of the hill. He took a few steps forward across the grass, put his arms behind his head and stretched.

"So which way now?"

He turned his head a little, looked over his shoulder at Connor standing behind him, wiping pine needles from his cloak with irritation.

"Ahead. Just a mile and a bit—it won't take more than an hour, even if we take our time."

"What about the wolf?"

Marcas shrugged.

"I don't know. I don't need to be there."

"*Need?*"

"That's how it works. Fast as I can run, it still takes time to get from one place to another. If I didn't know I was needed before the time, I wouldn't be able to help anyone. That's the point of the mark of brightness."

Connor frowned. "*Before the time*? I don't like that. I don't like the idea that things happening to me—"

"That they're out of your control?"

Marcas gestured, took a step forward. Connor skipped ahead a few quick steps and came up beside him as they walked.

"Yes. I want my choices to mean something."

"They do. Didn't you choose to be on that battlefield? To bring that spear, to fight that enemy? To stay beside the other two and not run?"

Connor bridled. "I don't run! I never have, and I never will!"

Marcas eyed him speculatively, shrugged. "You can make that choice too—but I'm not sure it's a good one. There's times when it's best to run...and you've run with me already, Connor."

"Not the same!" The boy spat the words like they were something disgusting. "You did the running for me, didn't you? And anyway—" He looked away and didn't meet Marcas' eyes. "Anyway, I couldn't fight those *things*. Those shadows. But I can now—that's what the spear's for, isn't it?"

"Only at the uttermost end of need. Only if I can't stand between you and the bent one."

"I'm not a child, Marcas! I don't *want* to be protected!"

Marcas reached out and caught hold of Connor's shoulder, spun him toward him and looked into the dark angry eyes.

"Connor, I am not responsible *to* you, only *for* you, and I tell you right now that I *will not suffer a warrior's pride to come between me and my duty*. Not yours—not anyone's."

He took in Connor's clenched fists, the tightness of his back, and let go of the shoulder he had hold of.

"Look, I don't mean that the way it sounded. You're important, don't you understand? You were *chosen*, and I'm the one that was brought to you to make sure that matters, that whatever the lord of the mound has planned doesn't destroy you, or prevent whatever destiny is yours."

Connor's expression grew hard.

"*Destiny*. If it's not my choice, I don't want it. If it's not up to me, I won't *have* it. I don't regret meeting you, I don't regret living, but I won't spend the rest of my life in a cocoon you carry for me, waiting for *destiny*. I want to be able to see what I want of the world, do what I want in the world."

"I was always told there are some ways you can't go. Some lines you can't cross."

"I don't believe that."

Marcas couldn't help but smile, wry and knowing. "I know. I was listening when you talked—all those nights on the hills and the cattle for company. You and your endless sky."

Connor laughed, looked away, reached up and ran his hands back through his hair.

"Aha... Sorry, I was rambling then. I mean, I thought you weren't a normal wolf, but I still thought you were a wolf, you know?"

"I know."

Slowly at first, they started walking forward again. In a little while they came to the edge of the valley and a path that was visible in the green, worn and dusty but not too well trodden—and over the edge, down a steep slope and past the brown curls of the path winding down like discarded snake skin, Marcas saw the familiar lights and heard the noise of talk and living that was the village of the *faoladh*.

"*Home*. Welcome, Connor, where few other men have ever been."

Connor stared down the hill, interest and confusion on his face. Had he expected something more compelling, more magical? Marcas smiled to himself, and led the way down the road toward the tavern at the center of town.

* * * *

Connor looked from side to side as he made his way into the valley at Marcas' side. Voices called out in greeting here and there as they passed fields, then houses.

"Marcas!"

"Welcome home, it's been so long—"

"Is it Marcas? It is. It is, welcome home!"

Marcas only waved at those who were speaking to him, sent his smile in many directions but stayed close to Connor's side, guiding him down the street. All the greetings gave him the impression that Marcas was well-known, and well-liked. Hadn't he said it was an honor, to be made one of the *faoladh*, one of those chosen to walk among the wolves? And they were his kin.

His kin.

Connor felt the heat of one of Marcas' hands lingering near the small of his back, and took comfort from it. Despite the best efforts of their enemy, he still wasn't alone. To distract himself, he turned his attention to the people they were passing, but that only increased his awareness of the stares settling on his back.

"Marcas."

He spoke quietly, hoping not to be heard by anyone else, but Marcas caught his eye and shrugged faintly. The smile that he'd worn since they'd arrived here didn't flicker in the slightest.

"You're an outsider, and not many come here. Wouldn't you be interested if you were them?"

He looked away, turned his attention to studying the houses, the dust of the road.

"Connor?"

An arm came down across his shoulders, pulled him close, and he looked up and saw Marcas' grin grown even wider and a circle of expectant faces staring at him—*children*? And a woman, tall, blue-eyed, beautiful—his heart clenched, thudded, until Marcas spoke.

"Greet my sister, and these her sons and daughters—she only had the one girl when I left, but she's been busy."

"Marcas!" The woman punched his shoulder, then turned to smile at Connor. "Introduce your guest."

"Oh...yes. Connor, Fionnuala, my sister, the wife of Caolán. Fionnuala, this is Connor mac Brádach—one who is mine."

Connor saw surprise on the woman's face, and only smiled. He was almost afraid that anything he said might give away the secret he was not supposed to share—but it occurred to him only then, as he was truly beginning to pay attention, that this might be a village of *faoladh*, but there was no way to tell just by *looking*.

The littlest children were wide-eyed and silent, their elder siblings laughing, prodding Marcas—only the oldest was still staring at Connor, and he was amused by the mixture of attraction and suspicion on the girl's face.

I came from outside. I guess she's old enough to know what that really means. The danger would be obvious to a girl like that, a girl whose uncle had become a wolf and vanished into seven years' service. Looking around, Connor realized then that despite the warning Marcas had given him, there wasn't a single wolf in sight—not a live one, anyway. The only thing that stood out was the brooch all the children seemed to be wearing, and his sister too—bright gold in the shape of a howling wolf's head.

Perhaps Marcas had seen his glance—his explanation was quiet as they said their goodbyes to his sister, walked away and left the children calling and waving after them.

"Those brooches—they mark us for what we are, keep us together, let us recognize each other when we're outside this place—all of us have one."

"When you meet outside... So not just... So you leave here, sometimes?"

"Sometimes. It's good to know what's happening in the world, even if we don't ever really plan on becoming a part of it. Now—to the tavern. It's been too long since the last time I had a good draft."

"The mead's good here?"

Marcas laughed and draped an arm across his shoulders again.

"I'll let you decide that for yourself."

Despite himself, Connor grinned a little, gave in to temptation and looped his arm around Marcas' waist. Marcas was almost a different person here, surrounded by people—more open, louder, gentler... It was strange, but it made sense too. Was there anywhere else in the world where the man was known by name? Even considering all those he had helped?

Probably not.

Marcas led him past several dark houses and turned right onto a broader way. The usual sounds of singing, shouting, laughing, fighting, spilled toward them from the only lighted building as they made their way up the road. Connor felt his mouth watering—good smells were broadcast with the noise, odors of roasting meat, bread, honey...

He heard his stomach growling, and Marcas laughed at him.

"You know, I don't think they'll actually have an ox for you."

"*Marcas.*"

He tried to say it warningly, but couldn't stop from laughing—and Marcas, too, doubled over beside him, shaking his head. Connor stopped, watching him. He looked at Marcas and the sight of his face hit him like a punch in the gut, left him staring and confused. He tried to shrug it off, to make whatever it was go away, but a hot flutter that he couldn't vanish remained.

Connor looked away and stepped toward the open door of the tavern, the square of light thrown out onto the road.

"Well? Are we going in or not?"

Marcas came up beside him, grinning, and pulled him through the door into noise and heat. A shout greeted them, a great *hey!* in many voices, before a swarm of men were around them, then around Marcas, pushing Connor to the side—clapping Marcas on the back, grasping his shoulders, his hands, all of them greeting him, welcoming him back, congratulating him on his success. It was as if they hadn't even noticed Connor was there.

Despite that, he knew they had. Gazes kept moving in his direction, and no one said anything about what their congratulations were really for—no one even mentioned how long it had been since Marcas was among them.

After a few minutes of this, Marcas managed to push back the crowd a bit, and reached out and grasped Connor by the arm, pulled him back close to his side.

"Sorry, boys. I've got my own plans tonight." There was laughter, and Connor shot Marcas a dirty look. "We've come for supper and for mead."

There was more laughter, but this time the crowd parted and opened for them, and Connor found himself being pulled aside to a table near the wall. A pair of foaming tankards knocked the table in front of them the moment they sat down, and Connor looked up, surprised only to see the girl who'd brought them already vanishing back into the bustle. He blinked, then looked back and met Marcas' eyes.

"Good service."

"Only the best for the hero of the day — or haven't you learned that yourself by now?"

Connor snorted, lifted the tankard to his lips, drank deeply. The mead *was* good — the best he'd had in a while. He looked at Marcas over the rim of the cup, feeling inside himself for whatever had happened in that moment outside. It was still there, like a fire he'd forgotten, left burning unattended...and it was tied to the ache that had been growing within him, unnamed.

Marcas spoke and startled him out of his thoughts. He fumbled the tankard and almost spilled it, but Marcas was only talking about mundane things — or maybe he'd gotten the wrong idea from Connor's stare?

"The food's coming, don't worry."

"I'm not worried — about that." His glance slid away from Marcas' face, then back again.

"You shouldn't worry about anything."

"No?"

"Not while I'm with you, anyway, not anymore."

"I think we've been over that."

"What's this, a lover's spat?"

Connor looked up to his right at the sound of the unfamiliar voice, thick with drink. An older man, dark-haired, too much red in his cheeks and his nose. He had the look of a powerful man gone to seed, this one, and something in his smile made Connor's skin crawl. He looked to Marcas to deal with him — it *had* to be Marcas he wanted—and Marcas stood and clasped arms with the stranger, reluctantly Connor thought.

"Tiarnán. Hello—and no, nothing like that."

"Are you sure? Didn't sound like anything good to me, and you've worked fast on this one—I'd hate to see you lose him just as fast!"

And the man, Tiarnán, laughed as if he'd made an excellent joke. Marcas winced a little, tried to laugh but utterly failed—his face looked…strange.

The man stood aside for a moment as the girl returned with the food—two heavy platters, salivating smells coming from them. The moment she laid them down, Connor was on a steaming drumstick, biting through the crisp skin—juicy, hot, he felt grease dripping down his chin and didn't care. He wiped his mouth on the tablecloth and bent to the food again, only half-heartedly listening to the strained conversation going on over his head.

"And where did you…"

"West, and then…"

"And this little one? Fast work, Marcas. Fast work."

"I wouldn't say—"

"His hair, soft like a woman's it must be—and a sweet mouth he's got."

At that, Connor finally looked up, wiped his mouth again and spoke. "What did you say?" His voice was lower than he'd intended, more anger in it—but what the hell! *Soft as a woman's?* Sweet mouth! "I don't stand for talk like that—not from anyone, and not from a stranger more."

His thoughts were running faster than the wolf he'd ridden—anger—embarrassment—a bit of contemplation under it all, because if it was Marcas—*if it was Marcas, and we were alone somewhere together, fire beside us and some cold night…* But no, he'd not tolerate *hair soft as a woman's* ever, not even from Marcas. No, not even from his wolf. This Tiarnán was fumbling with words, but not an apology — something else about *so pretty*, babbling about *treat you better* and *give you more*.

Something in Connor snapped at the sound of, not one of those things, but all of them together and at once. His fist clenched, sent further tightness up his arm to his shoulder, and before he could give the movement a second thought, he had stood and was punching Tiarnán in his too busy mouth.

"Shut up — shut up!"

The man went down hard, clutching at his jaw, and Connor looked down at him, gritting his teeth, and only then considered that hitting the fool might not have been the best thing to do. But when he looked up, his gaze darting around and gauging trouble, he saw people going back to their own conversations, the singing starting up again in one corner, some people laughing — a man came, grinning, and hefted the fallen Tiarnán.

As he was dragging him away, he tossed words back over his shoulder that made Connor relax completely.

"I told him that mouth was going to get him in trouble one day. Good on you, stranger!"

Weakly, Connor laughed, then sank back into his chair. Across from him, Marcas did the same, shaking his head.

"I should have known — didn't you do something like this at the last tavern you were at?"

Connor shook his head. "No, the last tavern I was at was the night the shadow came, the night after you — the night after my leg finished healing. And I didn't go for *fighting*. I went for pleasure."

He saw a dark glitter in Marcas' eyes. *Jealousy?* Somehow, that thought soothed the fire inside him, and Connor grinned, then leaned forward across the table and spoke closer to Marcas' ear.

"Didn't I come with the same idea tonight? But that's *your* fault."

He leaned forward a little more, close enough to kiss—but only reached out a hand and deftly snagged Marcas' drumstick. He sat back in his chair, then held it out of the way when Marcas tried to grab it back—then bit it, and grinned around his mouthful at Marcas' irritated exclamation.

"Connor!"

He was unafraid to answer back. "Get your own."

"I *had* my own—you're eating it!"

"So… Get another one?"

He snickered to himself as Marcas did just that. It amused Connor to no end that his wolf might be one of the more terrifying beings in the world, and yet still was so easy to irritate without consequences. And he stopped dead in the middle of chewing, caught in his own thoughts as if by glue.

My wolf. When did that happen? He'd never felt possessive over someone who wasn't really his lover, and now here he was, not even knowing where the road had divided behind him. He remembered then what Marcas had said, that first night when he had come out of the wood with a man's shape, a man's voice, a man's desires.

You don't want it enough yet.

He hadn't been able to comprehend, not then, but sharp and sudden, in that moment Connor understood.

Chapter Ten

After a certain point, which Marcas found difficulty determining, Connor became very quiet. They finished their meal in silence and left together unmolested, though he was sure there'd be plenty of talk — and more than talk — once they were gone.

Beside him, Connor walked close, always touching — a brush of fingers at the hip, on his own fingers. Marcas leaned against every brush until Connor came finally to walk in step beside him, their legs almost touching, their fingers faintly linked. His throat was flushed, and beneath the dusting of freckles on his skin, Connor's cheeks were dusky, heated. Their steps were slow and time had passed in the tavern. The moon was high before they crested the valley and came out onto the pathless meadow.

Connor was still quiet — quieter than he had been all day, quieter than he had been since those long days and nights of silence when it had been only the two of them and Marcas had been the wolf, even his name unknown. The expression in his eyes was...

What was it?

Marcas wasn't quite sure, but he knew what he wanted it to be and could only hope. *Give in, Connor.* When the boy stopped, became a dead weight tugging on his fingers, he looked up and wondered how long he'd been lost in his own thoughts.

"This is— I know we're going back, but this is far enough because I—"

"*Connor.*"

He was babbling, and Marcas spoke his name to stop him, almost laughing.

"Don't laugh at me. Not now, not even that wolf-panting."

There was a pause, a wide, sharp silence.

"I have something to say."

He was, in that moment, wholly a prince to Marcas' eyes. So formal, drawn up in himself, his shoulders back and his gaze unyielding in the way it sought out Marcas' own. Like a lightning strike, something fled swift and shocking down Marcas' spine.

"Say it, then."

His voice came out rougher than he intended, but he couldn't help it. Connor looked at him with something of a smile on his face, something pleased, something that sought to please—as if he knew the thoughts that had strangled themselves in Marcas' throat behind those words.

"I know what you meant now, Marcas. When you said I couldn't have you. When you said I didn't want you enough."

Connor closed the last step between them, the final distance, reached out and laced his hands into Marcas' hair, pulled him close and kissed him—and oh, what a kiss that was. Every other one that had come before was just a tease in comparison, a game. This passion to which he could only surrender. When

Connor pulled back he was panting and he pressed his cheek against Marcas' cheek and spoke in a low voice that sent a shudder rolling across Marcas' skin.

"I've never been in love. I've never wanted to be. My father told me love was a game, and I didn't want the girls he gave me anyway. But, Marcas, when you laughed before, something went hot inside me, and not the wanting kind of hot. I need—*something*. Marcas, I have this ache inside."

If a heart beats too fast, does it stop beating? Warmth spread through Marcas' chest as if a fire had been lit between his ribs, all the embers he had sheltered flamed by those words into blazing life. Far more gently than Connor had kissed him, Marcas kissed Connor and cut his words to silence. He had to, could think of nothing else that would quiet him. If he didn't do something to stop Connor from talking, those words were going to break him. When he pulled back, he ran his thumb over Connor's mouth, took in every detail of his flushed face—wide pupils, wet lips still bruised and his expression... So open.

"What is you want, Connor?"

"I... Just you. That's all."

"That's all?"

"I want... I want you to teach me how to love you, Marcas. I want you to stop pulling away. I want—"

And Connor licked his lips, looked away—in the brightening moonlight. Marcas could see the intensity of the flush on his face as it increased, until his cheeks were almost as red as his hair.

"I want all those things you said."

Marcas' memory leaped back through the nights behind them to those first human-again moments, and ahead, to the morning they had spent in pleasure on the grass.

"I want all of them, Marcas. All of *you*."

The dark flush faded as Connor met his eyes again. Whatever he saw in Marcas' face must have been enough, because Connor's hands were on him almost at once, skimming his skin, light touches, not teasing but learning. The bare brush of his fingertips was enough to bring Marcas to aching hardness — that, and knowing what it was that was to come. No more waiting — not now. Not after that.

Teach me how to love you, Marcas.

With one hand, he undid the brooch that held his cloak, then let both drop and pulled his tunic over his head with one, swift motion. But he caught Connor's hands when they reached for his cloak, and this time there was no twisting away, no fight, just a questioning look.

"I will undress you."

Connor opened his mouth, but said nothing. He let Marcas do what he pleased, shifted his limbs obediently, reached out now and again once his cloak was off, to skim Marcas' skin with eager fingers. When his tunic dropped to the ground, Connor's hands fell over Marcas' hands and guided them to his erection, begged the touch with such eyes, such a soft *please* that Marcas couldn't deny him, even if he'd wanted to draw it out — but there would be time for that later.

"What is it you like, Connor?"

"What I — what?"

Marcas closed his fingers around Connor's cock and gave him rough, quick strokes, then changed to a slower rhythm almost at once. His fingers snuck out to tease the most sensitive places he could find, so easy to tell by the shudders that ran over Connor's body, the way he moaned.

He leaned back against Marcas' chest, laid his head on Marcas' shoulder. There were no begging words, but when Marcas bent his head and licked at Connor's lips, stroked tongue with tongue, made his way from lips to throat, all his moans became guttural groans.

Connor thrust his hips against Marcas' fist, shameless, wanton—more, the movement said, but Marcas wanted the words. He controlled the rhythm, the pace, watched heat grow in Connor's eyes, on his face, a lusty stain that spread down, past his throat, over his chest.

"Marcas—*more*—*please* I need—*please*."

Marcas let go and took a step back. Connor turned to face him, and Marcas saw a protest forming on his lips, but it died when he untied the trousers he'd worn to cover the Dagda's marks and let them drop to the ground. Then there was silence, Connor's trembling fingers reaching out to touch his skin, run down his chest, grip his hips and pull him close. Low sighs spilled from the boy's lips, one after another. Slow, but not hesitant, he reached out and touched the heat of Marcas' erection.

Marcas spoke roughly, pushed his fingers against Connor's lips.

"*Suck.*"

Hesitant at first, his tongue moving slowly, awkwardly, Connor did as he was told. A guttural growl of a groan slipped past Marcas' lips, and that was enough to make him more confident.

Connor matched the rhythm of his mouth to the movement of his hand, stroking the rigid length of Marcas' cock, until the fingers were pulled away, reluctantly, he thought, and he felt one of Marcas' legs moving between his thighs, pushing him backward until he stumbled. Marcas caught him, even as he let him down, and Connor found himself on his back, his legs spread vulnerably wide.

Marcas hovered over him with a bright glow in his blue eyes. Connor watched him stroking his cock as he looked down at him, slow, steady, one finger reaching out from the others to tease the sensitive nerves along the thick vein on the underside — *looking at me — looking at me like that.*

My wolf.

Connor felt his pulse in his erection, felt a new desire. He wanted to lean up and feel the heat of that steel-satin hardness against his tongue again. He wanted to taste the salt of Marcas' skin, wanted to see his face broken open with pleasure. But Marcas was too close now for him to think of sitting up, and when he felt instead the heat and wet and roughness of Marcas' tongue laving the length of his cock, all he could do was groan and spread his legs wider.

Marcas' tongue sought out the sensitive nerves under the head, teased them with rippling movements, with stroking that matched the wet sucking of his mouth, then stroking that didn't, rough tongue rubbing back and forth. In the midst of this sensation, Connor felt wet fingers press between his buttocks, and one slipped *inside* him, vaguely uncomfortable, almost burning, one finger then two.

When he tightened those muscles reflexively, he felt Marcas moan around his cock, then pull away.

"Do you know how much I want to be inside you, Connor?"

His voice was deeper, wilder than it had been before. In the sound, Connor had a taste of just how much Marcas had been restraining himself. Marcas bent over him again, and his mouth moved faster on

Connor's cock, his tongue a lash of fire that circled and stroked. He thought there were three fingers inside him now, three fingers against which he bucked helplessly, never sure which direction he should move, wanting more of everything. More of whatever pleasure was inside him, more of Marcas' mouth, so hot, an eager torment for all his wanting nerves.

When Marcas pulled back again to breathe, the cool air was a pleasant shock.

"It feels good, doesn't it, Connor? My mouth on your cock?"

"Yes...yes, good—"

"And my fingers inside you... You like that too?"

"Inside me—yes, yes, I want—" Connor looked up at him, licked his wet and lust-bitten lips. "I want you inside me, Marcas—ahh—"

Marcas reached up and began a slow, rhythmic stroking of Connor's cock, light squeezing, generous tugs. Connor moaned, then felt a flash of lightning that connected the fingers inside him with his erection. Every movement of those fingers was a surge of pleasure, a tight thread that attached the motion to the whole length of his cock. No wonder all his lovers had been so eager to be under him. Why not, if this was the reward? And it's only his fingers inside me.

Wet suction closed around Connor's cock again and drove him toward the peak of his pleasure.

"Marcas...so good, Marcas—want—Marcas!"

Marcas' tongue was rough in all the right places, and when he groaned, thrust his fingers deep, Connor couldn't hold back.

Connor's words played again and again in Marcas' head. The taste of him was bittersweet on Marcas' tongue, a goad for his own arousal, and the sight of him—why did I wait? Why did I deny myself? Connor—

More roughly this time, Marcas thrust his fingers back into the wanton opening of Connor's body, needy, grasping, relaxed now in the subtle glow of his climax, just like he'd wanted. Marcas only had to curl and uncurl his fingers to make Connor's hips move in little jerks, to renew his desire.

Connor looked down his body and seemed utterly confused by the way his cock hardened to rigid thickness again so swiftly, the way it twitched and pulsed when Marcas moved his fingers. His eyes were glassy with pleasure, pupils so wide his eyes had all but lost their green.

Marcas could almost have been content to kneel there forever, watching the most gorgeous picture of erotic bliss he'd ever seen. Connor's lips all but bleeding where they'd been bitten, his head thrown back, his eyes closed, his hips pumping steadily against Marcas' fingers, his body squeezing them.

There was a sympathetic twitch in his own erection every time that heat and tightness grew tighter. He wanted to make it good for Connor to be under him, to submit—he wanted only pleasure to haze this memory, not pain—but *gods* he hoped it had been enough. He couldn't take any more of this, waiting, watching, feeling so much he had wanted for so long.

"Connor, I need— I need you, Connor. Will you let me—?"

He bit his lip at the sound of his own hoarseness, but Connor gave him a panting answer that went straight to his cock.

"*Everything*, I want *everything*. I want your cock inside me. I want it. I want... *please give it to me.*"

Slowly, Marcas withdrew his fingers from Connor's body, leaned back and pulled him up as he did so... then down, so that Connor was on his knees between his thighs, his mouth level with Marcas' straining erection. For the second time, breathless now, Marcas gave hoarse instruction.

"*Suck.*"

Connor licked his lips, then the head of Marcas' cock with no hesitation. Soft suction, languid heat of stroking tongue—wetly, he moved his mouth over Marcas' cock and seemed to delight in every low moan that slipped past Marcas' control.

Marcas ran his fingers through the smooth, red hair, kept his gaze locked on the sight of his cock as it moved in and out of Connor's mouth, the soft lips stretched wide around the shaft, those green eyes looking up at him—

A surge of heat tightened his thighs, and his fingers tightened reflexively in Connor's hair. It was so tempting to hold him there, keep going like this, let the slow fire finish building—but no. *No, not this time.* With a groan, almost a gasp, he pulled back and stared down as Connor licked his swollen lips, leaned forward just enough that he could continue to lick the head of Marcas' cock.

"*Gods*—enough—*enough*. On your back, Connor."

Without a word, the boy obeyed, spread his legs wide and reached between them for Marcas, urging him forward. Marcas sank to his knees in the grass and pulled Connor against him, pressed the head of his erection against the opening of Connor's body. *Tight. Hot. Connor*—

Within him, a wolf howled. He leaned on his elbows, his chest pressed against Connor's body, and didn't know if he was speaking to himself or to the boy when the words came rushing out of his mouth, low and thick and groaning, a breathless demand beside Connor's ear.

"Breathe, breathe—*breathe…*"

Under him Connor was wide-eyed, his mouth open in a silent *O*, his legs trembling, his hips rocking up against Marcas' slow penetration, begging more with every movement, but Marcas was holding back with everything he had. *Must go slow. Oh, Connor. Satin inside.*

"So tight for me—only for me—"

The words slid out of Marcas' mouth on a groan. The pressure around his cock was the most delicious friction he'd ever felt, and every slow thrust pushed him swiftly toward the heights of an inevitable peak.

He wanted it, and he didn't—wanted to sustain this moment, this first time—for him, and for Connor. It wouldn't be like this again, even if they were lovers for the rest of time. But below him Connor was growing restless, thrusting back at every movement of his hips, and the things he was saying—*more* and *don't stop* and *deeper.*

"*Harder—harder—please—*" And again, rich, groaning, his hips lifting from the ground, his legs wrapping around Marcas' back. "Please—*please—*"

His voice broke on the second *please*, and so did the final fragment of Marcas' restraint. He thrust as deep into Connor's body as he could go, set a new rhythm of roughness and got cries of pleasure for his reward. He looked down at Connor's face—eyes closed now, mouth open, clutching at Marcas' shoulders so hard he was sure there would be bruises in the morning.

"Marcas—Marcas—Marcas—"

Deeper, harder, biting his lip to hold back the rush he could feel building in his belly, Marcas braced himself on one hand and reached for Connor's cock. One more thrust—one more cry, and there was wetness on his chest, his fingers. Connor's groan went on forever, and this time Marcas felt Connor go tight around his cock instead of his fingers.

Then he was spilling himself deep into Connor's body, his hips rocking again and again, pressing against Connor's buttocks as if there was some way he could get deeper inside.

* * * *

Bathed in a warm glow, Marcas lay drowsing in the grass until he realized that Connor was actually sleeping. He gathered their scattered clothes then shook Connor into wakefulness. Stumbling, slow, stopping now and then for a kiss, they made their way back to Marcas' hall and the great bed set against the western wall.

Marcas slept like the dead, dreamed nothing he could remember and woke early, the first light of dawn barely moving on his face. A warm body was beside him, curled against his side, filling the empty spaces within and without. The memory of the previous night came to him in pulses—remembered pleasure, renewed arousal, the exquisite pleasure of those words. *I want you to teach me how to love you. I want you to stop pulling away.*

Marcas lay still, warmed as much by the memory of the words as the heat of the boy beside him. There were still grass stains on his palms.

Connor. He turned his head and looked at the dark spray of red hair splashed across his pillows, the faint tracery of pale blue veins in Connor's closed eyelids. He lay for a long while, wondering when Connor would wake, soaking in the warmth of his body and watching the sun move across the floor of the room. Brightness crossed the cover, then Connor's face. It tempted him, a band of illumination that floated across Connor's parted lips, still bruised where they had been bitten the night before.

All mine now, all mine.

He smiled to himself, then threw the covers aside and stood. There would be time for *more* — so much more — but for now there were things to take care of.

Pleasant as the night before had been, glorious as was the gleaming warmth within him, the growing hope for Connor's love, there was still a task ahead of him — ahead of them both. A noise outside interrupted his thoughts, and he went to the door but didn't go out. Through the crack he saw only a pair of women, heard their low voices, their footsteps, faint rustling and laughter as they put something down outside the door and retreated.

He relaxed as the sounds grew more distant, and opened the door to find what he'd expected — food. Fresh eggs, a covered pail of milk, cheese, a half dozen loaves, a basket heaped with blackberries. There were a pair of geese, plucked and gutted and wrapped in sweet-smelling hay, and what looked like a rabbit, too, skinned and sectioned neatly.

"That looks good — another reward for service?"

Marcas looked back over his shoulder and saw Connor crossing the floor of the hall toward him, yawning, blinking, peering past him through the open door at the bounty by his feet.

"Something like that — part of why I decided to bring you down last night, so that they'd know I was back — and to bring enough for two."

He grinned and grabbed one of the brown loaves from the basket, found it still warm and tossed it back to Connor, who barely caught it, surprised, then shrugged and bit into it.

"Hm...'s good." He eyed the raw birds, then the blackberries, before he turned his gaze back to Marcas, grinning. "Are you the cook around here?"

Marcas narrowed his eyes. "I can cook, though maybe I shouldn't—"

"Well, don't look at me." Connor took another bite, and another. "I can fight, and straighten a spear shaft, judge a battle or a room full of men—like my father taught me. But you're not going to get much out of me as far as cooking goes."

"So many talents, perhaps I can forgive you." Marcas picked up the eggs, then called back over his shoulder. "Come help me carry this in, you can be at least that useful. And be careful with the pail, it's got our milk."

It was while he was getting the fire going, teasing Connor about his apparent lust for blackberries—of which there were now only a bare handful left—that the first sharp break from the pleasant nature of the morning came over him. It was strong—terrible—not a premonition, just the sense that *something was coming*.

He thought it was a warning, the wolf senses speaking to him in a way that he couldn't yet understand.

"Marcas? Are you—all right?"

Once, twice, he blinked. The feeling did not recede, did not lessen, only grew less distracting as he grew used to their uncomfortable tingling at the back of his thoughts. *Warning. Something is coming.* He wanted to say *yes, everything is fine*, wanted to allay all Connor's fears, but he couldn't lie.

"I don't know. Something is...not right. But not wrong. I don't know what it is. "

Connor met his gaze with a more serious expression.

"I do. You do too."

Marcas held that silent stare for a long moment before he sighed and dropped his gaze. "Perhaps. But *who* and *what* aren't the same thing."

The words came out as calm as he could make them, but inside his thoughts were racing. What to do? How could he protect what he had only just gained — a thing more valuable by far than anything else that it had ever been his responsibility to protect? But all he could think of was to keep Connor close to him as he had done so far, beside him every minute until whatever storm was brewing finally broke.

"You know what this means, Marcas."

"What?"

Connor's voice startled him out of his thoughts, and he looked up to new and burning intensity in Connor's face.

"There's no putting it off — we've got to find a way to deal with the bent one. The two of us alone can't fight the lord of the mound."

Marcas drew the fingers of his right hand together into a fist, tightened it then opened it, shaking his head the whole while.

"Fight him... Connor, that's not the way. That's not — that won't help. If there are men who can stand up to Crom Cruach, it's only my kin — and only the wolves among them, at that, not really the men. The power I have... It's not the usual way of things. Whatever happened to me is something new, and

I…would rather they didn't even know about it. I don't know what it means. I don't want—"

And he stopped, took a breath, shrugged.

"I don't want them to take you from me. I'm not a leader. I'm not a prince, not a king, not even noble born. The honor they do me for my service is one thing, but if they find the one truth, they'll find the other—that you know everything about me, about us. You'd be in danger, Connor."

"But you said the power you had was so that you could protect me!"

"Men don't always agree with gods. Not even men who live in service to one."

Quick steps brought Connor to Marcas' side, and blazing green eyes all but burned him with their ferocious promise. *Which one of us is the wolf?* In any other moment the thought would have made him laugh.

"Marcas, I don't care if you're *faoladh* or *sidhe* or one of the ancient gods yourself. I don't care if your *leaders* are the ancient gods, or think they're acting on their behalf. The only one who will ever *take me away* from you is *me*—and only if I want to, which I don't. Oh—or you—"

"Which I won't." Marcas smiled. "You've got more practice at romance than you told me, Connor."

To Marcas' lasting surprise, he flushed.

"I don't—"

Marcas laughed.

"No, really—I don't! I never even thought about loving someone. What was the point? A game, my father said—and the woman—and I was always supposed to fight and wed and father sons. Marcas, are you listening? Don't laugh! I wanted a man like you—I wanted some kind of life like this, I wanted what's growing between us, just...less shadow and dark gods and more honest battle."

Marcas stared at him.

"You wanted – a man like me?"

Connor snorted faintly, looked down at the table, picked idly at an invisible splinter in its surface.

"Yes, well, I didn't think I'd get to have one. My father –" But he stopped and shrugged. "But it doesn't matter. My father is probably dead, and you're here now – and we've got bigger problems to worry about, anyway."

He fell silent after that and didn't say another word as he helped Marcas with the morning meal in the ways that he was able. When the table was set, and bread and cheese and fried eggs and skewered rabbit laid out beside a pot of honey and the pail of milk, Marcas vanished through a trapdoor in the floor at the back of the hall and reappeared with a pair of foaming tankards full of sweet, cool ale.

He came to the table and saw that Connor hadn't touched a thing, was only looking at him expectantly.

"Well? What are you waiting for?"

"*You*. Obviously."

Under Marcas' eye, he reached out and took a leg of rabbit, a loaf of bread, and cut off a hunk of cheese, but his attention wasn't on the food. Marcas watched him, and it didn't take him long to see what was happening – over and over, the boy's eyes were being drawn to the spear that lay with its point facing toward them from the other end of the table, gleaming like a star.

* * * *

Connor wanted to go back to the beginning of the morning, before his thoughts had filled up with duties and his father's expectation, and the many tangles his thoughts had taken on in the presence of those things. Mostly he heard the old echo — *take whoever you want for your pleasure, son — just as long as you come home with a good woman in the end.* There had been warning in it, always a warning — one he had resented.

Couldn't his sisters have sons, continue the line that way? Couldn't he have sons of his own without bothering about a wife? Oh, it wasn't that he hadn't liked a woman now and then, he *had* — but something in him was never satisfied, always wanted something *other*. Like what he'd found with Marcas, that rough-soft touch.

He stared at the spear lying at the end of the table, considered the future it represented — the potential. *I have to fight against Crom Cruach*. He avoided saying it out loud for Marcas' sake, and out of prudence…and a hint of fear, if he was honest with himself. He hadn't yet forgotten the way that eyeless dark had sought him out with a sightless stare at the sound of its own name. He might never forget.

Again, his gaze was drawn to the spear. *Will it cut him? Will it bite whatever the darkness is made of?* That was its purpose — that was what Marcas had said, and yet it was hard to imagine that pale point doing much to the huge shape of shadow he had seen rising over the horizon. Maybe the body of the High King — or whatever had been the High King — but to attack Tigernmas directly without acknowledged cause would be seen as treason by any of those who didn't know the truth.

"Connor?"

Marcas' voice startled him out of his thoughts, and Connor looked up, saw him standing, bag in one hand and food he was packing in the other.

"If you're ready, we should leave soon — while it's still early."

Connor waited while Marcas took a few minutes to finish packing food and clothes, stood silent with his new spear in his hand. They made it to the road without trouble, and walked for some time in silence. The road was empty and stayed that way, even through a full day's travel.

When night fell, Marcas passed the bag to him and changed his shape, became the wolf and padded along beside him in the dark. Connor slept in fits and starts when they stopped for sleep, but each time he woke and turned, Marcas was there beside him, a bright-eyed and reassuring presence in the darkness.

Connor woke early, sun in his face. The wind from the east was thick with the smell of smoke and burning. His heart sank, but he wasn't surprised when he saw a pacing wolf instead of Marcas' human shape, guarding the limits of their camp.

After an hour's walk, they ran into a line of grim men, ash-dusted, their faces broken in some way Connor had never seen men broken before. They paid him no attention, even when he called out a greeting — their eyes seemed not to see him, looked right through him, even when he was sure he recognized one of them.

Dark-eyed, with familiar, brooding features at the end of the line, surely that was Niall? Brave Niall, who feared nothing, not even his father's wrath...

But the man's name died on his lips as the line passed, and Connor's stare went unanswered, and when they were out of sight, he found himself wondering if he'd been passed by men or ghosts.

Either way, there had been no life in them.

Chapter Eleven

Connor's steps slowed as he continued down the road, weighted by some terrible premonition. He tried to stay focused and alert, but it was hard with nothing to focus on. Marcas paced beside him, steady comfort, and Connor let one hand rest on the broad, furred back.

No one else appeared as he made his way closer to the turn off that would lead to the village and his father's *ráth*, and when he came to it, there was still silence. No one was in the fields and every house he rode past appeared to be empty—no voices, no faces appearing at the doors to see who was riding past.

The quiet was more eerie than any other thing in his experience. Already, his heart weighed heavy in him. *Something terrible has happened here*. He knew it must be true, even though there was no sign of it. No blood, no bodies, nothing out of place.

Slow and slower he went, up through the empty and silent village, along a road he had traveled many times. It curved back and forth across the front of the hill, and at the top he saw finally the reason for the silence.

Fire had visited his home.

Everything was burned — every building, every part of the *ráth* but the walls. It had been days ago, or longer. Only ashes were left and even they grew less and less by the moment, carried away by the wind. He slipped from the back of the horse and down to his knees, staring forward at the ruin of everything that had made up his life.

Time passed. He sat and stared until ash blew into his eyes and set them burning. Slowly, he pushed himself to his feet and made his way from one pile of ashes to another, only then discovering the worst of it.

Bones, but not — only the shape of them. Whatever had burned here was something that had burned hot enough to leave only ash in the shape of bones behind. The charred shapes were everywhere, unavoidable once he had noticed them, strewn through the ashes and left to lie without ceremony or burial.

Some of the bone-shapes were ringed in gold, and he didn't understand how this could be so. A fire hot enough to melt the flesh away and turn bone to dust would melt the gold, too.

"No normal fire did this…"

The worst of it was what Connor came to last. His eyes tracked from one detail to another — there, just there, was the wrecked charcoal shell that had been the hall of his forefathers. And *there,* his bedchamber had been there, and his mother's, his sisters' —

There were the shapes of bones in those ashes too.

No.

He tried to say it, a reflex that went unfulfilled in the dryness of his mouth. Against his will, Connor's gaze was drawn to things that spoke of an undeniable truth. His mother's favorite armband, settled now into the ash, against the shape of a slender bone that wore the bright gold with no flesh to support it. A half dozen rings that belonged to his elder sister — and the others, the littlest bones, black ash and dust and memory, those would be his younger sisters', joy of his mother's heart, delight to his father's eye, twins in their sixth year who would never see another.

Who had done this? Why? Because of *him*? Because his father had denied the High King…or Crom Cruach? On his knees in the ashes of his kin and the hall of his ancestors, he drove his fist against the ground again and again, bloodied his knuckles against the dirt.

What now, Connor? What now? Where? To Tara? To take down the High King?

He swallowed thickly, fell back and sat in a cloud of ash that set him coughing. That was it, wasn't it? He had no enemies, or all enemies, because if he kept the name of his father, the one who had done this would not forget or forgive him.

Connor sensed the cloud of some treachery, some terrible doom hanging over this place, hanging over him. As if to give truth to the feeling, Marcas did not approach the ash or the ruined halls. He stood with his forepaws on the edge of the burned green and paced back and forth, distressed and anxious and unafraid to show it.

Connor drew up a handful of ashes and squeezed them tight in his palm. *The future of this family*, that was what his father had said. "It's mine now. I understand." He stayed very still, staring at the ashes — staring at the gold.

* * * *

Marcas stood with his feet on the edge of the green and held back the whine that burned the pit of his throat. He wanted to step forward, but how could he? Over that ground—dead, all of it, and not nature's death but the death and terror of the darkness. Crom was here. *The shadow has done his work.*

He could taste it in the air, feel it crawling in the ashes before him. If Connor was thinking, he would have realized that something was wrong, but he could be forgiven, considering. For Marcas, there was no denial, no retreat from the truth. Neither natural fire nor the fire of man had burned here.

The wooden beams of the halls, the wool and flaxen fabrics, leather and flesh and bone, all had been reduced to ash and dust in the presence of a power that hated nothing more than life. Metal and stone alone remained, encrusted with dark aura. *That presence…* It was enough to make Marcas sick even standing where he was, never mind going into the thick of it. *And Connor, how could he stand it? But he doesn't know. He only knows his pain, not what caused it.*

As if the world was bent on proving him wrong, Connor chose that moment to push himself to his feet, throw back his head and shout at the sky.

"Tigernmas! Crom Cruach! I'll have my revenge on you—I, Connor, son of Brádach!"

Marcas lifted his head and howled with him.

Connor stood, chest heaving, wetness on his face, his fists clenched around twin handfuls of black ash. When he opened his fingers, the grit streamed out of them like sand and left stains in the creases of his palms. Stiffly, Connor bent and picked a few things up out of the dust. An armband. A handful of rings.

They gleamed brighter than the gold they were in the light of the setting sun, and Marcas looked up at the horizon sharply. Had so much time really passed?

It isn't safe here, not here, not now, not where this power is so strong, not with that name in the air, still on his lips.

Marcas knew with all the instinct of his purpose that this might be his greatest test—to get Connor away from here, to prevent him from seeking his own end at the hand of the shadow that would drive the thirsting spirits bound here. There is no darker power than what's come over this place, these people. Kin or not, they won't remember—they will be nothing of themselves, only shaped by the flesh that once held them. You should not see what's coming, Connor.

A second time, Marcas howled, this time in frustration, then took a step forward. How could he do anything else? There was duty compelling him, the mark of brightness that didn't fade, that only grew stronger. There was the feeling, born he did not know when, inescapable, ever-increasing—even when he had first noticed it, he hadn't been able to deny it, so how could he now?

If Connor spends the night here, there will be nothing left of him by morning. Not of him, and not of me.

Marcas stared at him, hands full of gold, eyes full of tears, skin stained by the black dust blowing into the wind. He whined, barked, howled—none of it mattered, but there was no way he could dare go from wolf to man shape now, with the danger so close.

I want you to live, Connor.

That desire moved him, more even than duty—an equal or greater brightness to the one that marked the boy.

I want you to live.

Holding all those thoughts together was enough to force Marcas forward, will over instinct. His paws sank into the ash, and a shudder of revulsion twisted his flesh, his spine, curved his back—he tiptoed forward in great distress, but forward he went.

When he was close enough, he shoved his head under Connor's arm, jumped up so he could balance his forepaws on Connor's shoulders, press his nose against his cheek. Obviously startled, Connor tried to shove him away and instead ended up shoving himself backward onto the ground. Marcas stalked forward until he could press his forehead against Connor's forehead and stare into his eyes.

He tried to convey the intensity of his purpose, his position—then he took hold of Connor's sleeve in his teeth and started to drag him away from the ash. There was no trouble at first, but Connor struggled free after a moment and shoved Marcas away when he tried to grab him again.

"Enough—enough! I get it. You don't like it here—you don't want me here—I like it even less. But I can't just go."

Marcas shook his head, growled, tried again to drag Connor away. Already, the sun was half set, the world sinking more into shadow every moment. The ash and the boy before him wore the same ruddy glow. There wasn't much time left now, and anywhere was better than here, didn't Connor understand that? Any green place, any stream, any mountain, any plain—anywhere, except where that power had touched.

Mournfully, Marcas sent one howl after another into the air. Connor scowled, winced then finally turned away, cringing, his hands over his ears as the subtle music of Marcas' howls ran over the ends of each other, ate their own echoes in the emptiness, repeated until they were a painful and monotonous cacophony.

Finally he stood and started walking out of the ash, out of the darkness toward his horse and the path that led back through the dead and silent village.

"I'm going now, all right? Enough—my ears are going to break."

Marcas huffed faintly, pressed against the back of Connor's thighs, hurrying him along. He paced impatiently, his eyes on the curve of the horizon, the sinking sun, the fading red glow that was all that illuminated the world now, all that kept back the shadow. When the glow went out, it came just like he had been expecting—the darkness—and he had Connor on his back in half a minute, was running in less time than that.

The sky was full of so many clouds that the moon was all but hidden, and Marcas' gaze could only sip at the landscape. The road was clear before them and the empty village passed by in a flash as they moved up the hill. Connor called to him, confused.

"Where are we going, Marcas?"

Marcas looked back, and Connor looked with him, saw what was behind them—growing shapes in the starless shadow, the reaching fingers of darkness speeding through the trees.

"Away from that. Got it."

Marcas moved faster than any mortal wolf could sustain, only one destination in mind. Connor had seen what he needed to, but he had said nothing else of what he wanted, and that meant it was time to go back home. *Back to safety*. Marcas darted ahead with all the evils of the world at his tail.

There would be a moment, a place beyond which the darkness could not go on. He would watch for it. Then he could slow, stop — but only then.

It came without warning, just as he'd expected. One second the shadow was at his heels, and the next it had slammed against a barrier of brilliance that was not to be challenged. He saw faces in the shadow, and tumbled Connor from his back without pause. *Don't look, Connor. Don't see —*

He shifted, wolf to human, then reached out a hand and pulled Connor to his feet, dragged him away from the darkness and barred the passage of Connor's gaze with his body.

"Go — *go*. Don't tempt fate, Connor."

Pliant, Connor obeyed Marcas' tug, and drifted behind him through the night, up the hillside like an untethered ghost.

* * * *

For the next three days, Connor was silent, overwhelmed by what he had seen, by what he knew now to be true. Guilt was moving in him, the guilt of his family's death, the guilt of a survivor even if he knew, *knew*, there was nothing he could have done. Even if he had died, had gone with his father, had been a sacrifice — would that have saved the rest of them?

No.

Crom Cruach did not distinguish between old or young, man or woman, hated or loved. In the end, the only things left to him were thoughts of vengeance, a vengeance he neither knew how to seek nor satisfy. How many times had he stood before the shadow,

Marcas beside him? And how many times had he been forced to run away?

"Won't win anything that way…"

"Connor?"

He jerked up his head and looked across the hall where Marcas was busy at the fire.

"Sorry, just thinking out loud."

"What is it you want to win?"

Connor sent a sharp glance Marcas' way. "The same thing I wanted to win yesterday, and the day before — and before that. The same thing I've wanted to win since I saw those ashes — since I saw that shadow and it saw me. My father's kingdom — my kingdom now. And vengeance."

"If you want those things, we'll have to find a way to put the dark god to sleep — to entrance him or silence him or ensnare him in something he can't escape from. At least, not without another sacrifice like the one your High King obtained for him."

Connor leaned back, stretched then stood and began to pace back and forth, thinking out loud.

"There's men in the north, and the east — my father's men, and Lord Aran's. There are men in the islands, too, but it might take them too long to get here… And the sea's a darkness, isn't it? Maybe…maybe there will be enough. If we convince the lords and kings that the High King is possessed, taken by darkness, that the lord of the mound is risen…"

"There might be too many dead for that."

Connor paused in his pacing, blinked at Marcas in confusion. "What?"

"The bent one is *here*. There may be too many dead for that. You said it was the lords of the realm, your kings and princes who were summoned to that sacrifice?"

Connor nodded, but slowly.

"Then they are probably all dead, so who will you go to for a king or a leader now? Your lands will be in disarray — or if they are not now, they will be soon. It is one of the things the lord of the mound chooses to feed on." Marcas held up a hand, extending his fingers one by one. "Disorder, chaos, silence, violence, death — the five pointed star of his power. All the firstborn sons are dead, and all their fathers, too, were firstborn sons."

"I... No, that can't be true!" Connor argued despite the sinking sensation in his chest. "I escaped! My father knew what was coming and he sent *me* away — others might have done so too."

"Chance or fate or the power that provides for me made it so that I was there with you to protect you a second time. Made it so that you were there to protect me and balance the scales a little."

Connor had almost begun pacing again, but now he faltered, swallowed a thick presence in his throat, turned and met Marcas' eyes.

"You — you did that, but how did I — ?"

"You could have killed me and didn't. You fed me, bandaged my wounds — that has *never been done before*, Connor. Either because I am the only one of the *faoladh* who has ever been foolish enough to be caught in such a state or because you are the only man foolish enough to heal a wolf that attacks his herd instead of killing it."

"I knew you."

Even now, looking at him, Connor felt the certainty of that first moment, the knowledge that had overcome him staring into the blue wolf eyes. He said it again, more softly, and knew by the expression on

Marcas' face that he had to explain. The truth only came to him one way.

"I knew you, Marcas. The same way I knew you when you came out of the woods in human shape. Your eyes are the same, wolf or human — and you *feel* the same to me. When you looked at me — even when you look at me now." He shrugged. "Sorry, I can't explain it very well."

"No, I understand. I think. Now tell me, what's your plan? If you're going to do this —"

"You'll help me?"

Marcas threw an irritated glance his way. "Didn't I already give you a weapon that can wound your foe? Not that I want you to use it — and less now than before —"

"Marcas, I told you —"

"You're a warrior! Yes, I know. I know — so I, too, will do what must be done."

There was a glittering in Marcas' eyes as he spoke those last words that Connor didn't like. There was a pale edge in the sun-browned features, glittering in those blue eyes, more ice than sky now, and tension, tension in every muscle he could see.

It bothered him and he didn't know why. Maybe because irritation wasn't enough for that dark strain, the spring-hard tightness that had seized hold of Marcas' whole being. And yet…

He was afraid to ask the question. He was *afraid* to *ask the question* that was on the tip of his tongue. Such a thing had never happened before, not even when exploring the dark roots of the being that had destroyed his life. *What is this? What am I afraid of?* But his only answer was a sharp and sudden deepening of the ache in his chest, a furious tightness in his throat, burning in his eyes, some desperate and fragile fire clawing its way out of his gut.

A thought utterly foreign to any previous moment or feeling in his life came to him then, and answered the question he hadn't even wanted to ask. *But, Marcas, I just found you and I don't want to lose you.*

In one movement he darted across the room and pinned Marcas against the table. He kissed him hard, bruising hard, and only pulled back when his lungs were straining in his chest for breath.

"Marcas—nothing will happen to me and nothing will happen to you. It just can't. I… It can't, that's all."

"Connor, if it worked that way—"

But Marcas stopped halfway through the sentence, took Connor's hands and pulled him back toward the bed.

"Who knows? Maybe it does for you—maybe it will for us."

"Do you want it to?"

"Yes. As much as I want *you*."

Connor was torn suddenly between two equally pleasing thoughts, but he knew what he wanted. When he had taken his victory and his vengeance, when he had proved himself—to him*self*—then Marcas would be his, as much as he was Marcas'. But for now…

"Do it again, Marcas."

"Again?"

"Everything—everything you did to me that night."

"Oh no, if *that's* what you want then I'll give you something *more*."

Marcas laughed at him, but Connor only grinned and let his knees give as he was pushed back against the bed.

* * * *

Marcas fell forward with Connor beneath him then pulled back and let the boy pull his tunic over his head and toss it away. He stared at the expanse of naked skin offered to him, filled his eyes with it, but maybe he stood too long, because Connor reached out and hooked an ankle around his thigh, tried to pull him closer.

"Marcas..." Connor looked up at him and used that blazing green to his best advantage. They could look innocent, Connor's eyes, when he was laughing—teasing—but not now. Now they were moss-green, smoky, licked at Marcas' skin, knowing and full of desire.

Marcas stared, and Connor breathed words at him when he didn't come closer, didn't reach out the way Connor wanted him to.

"Don't you want me? You said you wanted me—"

His voice was soft with breath, husky with heat, and Marcas had him against the bed again in the next instant, pressed his mouth to Connor's throat, sucked at his pulse, bit the submissive curve and felt Connor pull in one sharp breath after another under his teeth. He ran his hands down Connor's arms from shoulder to wrist, then back again—all of him, he wanted to touch all of him. He wanted to keep the heat on his face, the bright in his eyes. There had been too many days of darkness and grim expressions since they'd returned from ruin. This...this was better.

Much better.

Connor pressed up against him, pulled his arms free and pushed Marcas over onto his side when he tried to lean up and kiss him again. Connor won just because Marcas didn't want to fight him, wanted his grin, his eagerness, and the boy moved over him, tangled their legs together and licked Marcas' lips.

He held himself between Marcas' thighs, hovering over him, and dipped down again and again to kiss his mouth. Marcas reached one arm around his neck to pull him closer, gripped his hip, his buttocks with the other hand, squeezing the firm curve of flesh. He tried to take his own kiss, but Connor only teased with more tongue, then pulled himself up, straddled Marcas' hips and looked down at him.

"So many marks on you—god's marks and scars."

Connor's fingers followed the branded chains of his service, then moved aside, traced a different path across his chest.

"Like this one—from what, Marcas?"

He had to think back to remember, and when he did he laughed. "That one—a spear. I was the wolf—I brought a girl back to her father, a little one. He was...not like you." Lines of tightness drew themselves around Connor's eyes, and he leaned forward, pressed his mouth to the old scar, licked a wet line of heat across it.

"And this one?"

His fingers moved lower, drew down from Marcas chest, across his ribs to his side. Marcas huffed faintly—it tickled—but he knew that scar.

"A bear clawed me... *Oh*." Connor's lips traced the edges of the scar, three separate slashes over sensitive skin. "Clawed me when I was hunting." Connor hummed faintly under his breath, then leaned back again.

"This one?"

More tongue moved down from his chest, past his navel, stopped with a kiss.

"My first night as the wolf—my first battle, hard-won, too."

"And this?"

Connor murmured against his collarbone, licked the scar, traced the line of it with his tongue, then fastened his mouth over it and sucked.

"Mmm... *Connor*. Fight—tavern. When I was young and stupid—"

"Like me?"

"*Worse.*"

Marcas earned a bite for that, rough-gentle, and Connor moved down, soft lips soothing the tendered skin, and across the ticklish sides of Marcas' ribs again. It quickened his breath, a little pant of laughter, little pant of desire, but he groaned when Connor's mouth founds its way across his hip bone to his thigh. His tongue traced the curve of the muscle down until his cheek brushed against Marcas' cock, "What about this one?"

It was hard to think with the weight of Connor's body sprawled across his legs and the heat of his hands holding his thighs apart. Connor's breath was damp and hot, his lips tingling on his skin, so close to where he wanted them.

"Don't...remember—"

Connor's mouth moved back up along the path it had traveled, licking, sucking, biting.

"Connor—"

"Don't you wish you had more scars, Marcas?" Connor laughed at him, looked up from between his thighs and licked his lips, then turned his tongue on Marcas' cock, licked one burning stripe from the base to the wet, flushed tip.

"Do it again—*do it again, Connor.*"

The sound of his own voice came to Marcas as heavy as if he were drugged. Connor obeyed, then took just the head of Marcas' cock in his mouth. *Tongue*. He let out a sharp exhalation, reached down and tangled his fingers in Connor's hair, made impatient sounds.

But Connor seemed content to stay there, his tongue wrapped around the head of Marcas' cock, tantalizing the sensitive nerves with the heat of his mouth.

"*Connor—*"

There was a growl in the word, but Connor only flicked a glance at him, amusement in it, and pulled back. "Who's impatient now?" He traced idle patterns on Marcas' thighs with his fingertips, turned a heated gaze back up in his direction. "Didn't you say I should learn to take my time?"

But despite his words, he bent his head then and took half of Marcas' cock into his mouth, then more.

"*Yes*—just like that."

The flat, wet pressure of his tongue was hot against sensitive nerves, drew up and back in rhythm with Connor's mouth, then in long strokes that nearly reached the base of his cock. Marcas heard wet noises, his own sounds, Connor's groans vibrating against his cock, and looked down at him, saw his fist working fast and loose between his thighs.

Marcas hesitated, caught between enjoyment and desire, then tugged on Connor's hair, groaned at the renewed vigor of his tongue, a wet lash that traced serpentine patterns over the head of his cock, down, down…then back.

"Connor— Enough, Connor, I want more—I want more than just your mouth."

Connor's fingers tightened on his thigh. He moaned around Marcas' cock, then pulled back, and Marcas sat up and pulled Connor to his feet and forward toward the bed.

"On your knees for me, Connor."

Connor had taken many men the way he positioned himself for Marcas—thighs spread, braced on his arms and his chest dropped low against the bed.

"Yes, just like that."

He heard Marcas' voice from behind him then felt his fingers, suddenly slick and warm, pressing at the entrance to his body. One, then two, pushing deep, stretching—Connor arched his back and groaned, thrust his hips back against them.

Marcas was rougher with him than he had been last time, and Connor liked it—the tightness of the hand at his hip, the eager fingers stretching, curling inside him, seeking…*something*—something—something…

"So good, so good, Marcas, you—but I—"

"*But you?*"

"Need your cock, Marcas. Need your cock in me."

"What if I want to watch you just like this?" Marcas reached between Connor's thighs, stroked his cock with a hand made hot and slick with oil. Connor cried out and ground back onto Marcas' fingers, tried to get more inside him—*need more. Need you, Marcas.*

He looked back over his shoulder, met Marcas eyes and saw him suck in a breath. "I want your cock inside me—*take take take take—*"

Marcas was sudden and hot behind him, bent over him, kissing his back, his shoulders. Connor felt the head of his cock stretching him open, soft burn, perfect, deeper and deeper. He arched up, seeking kisses from the heat of Marcas' mouth as he pushed in. Connor braced himself on one hand and reached down between his thighs to stroke himself.

It was deeper this way than it had been before and Marcas went slow, pulled back until the head of his cock stretched Connor open then sank back in, again and again.

"So tight, so tight for me—"

Connor wanted more, wanted *harder*. He shifted his hips to meet Marcas' thrusts until every stroke was perfect, left him gasping, but still his climax caught him by surprise. Pleasure spread in a flash of heat that left Connor's fingers dripping and his body trembling. Marcas went still behind him, his grip on Connor's hips for once too tight, but only for an instant.

"You—Marcas?" Connor felt him still throbbing thick inside him, so hard, so much, prodding oversensitive nerves. He pulled back at the sound of his name, then thrust in again, smooth and perfect and too, too much with Connor's skin still tingling, his cock still throbbing in his fist, everything inside him on fire. "N-no...more—oh...yes—*please don't stop that.*"

The wolf's laugh answered all his contradictions. Marcas' thrusts were slow, so slow, so deep, filled him up so good—in very few minutes Connor was teasing the head of his cock with his thumb, his head hanging down, while he spread his thighs wider.

Marcas said his name, growling, husky, grasped his buttocks and spread them apart. Somehow he sank *deeper*, and Connor moaned his name or some mangled murmur with the sounds of it, blind with pleasure and hungry for pleasure and Marcas, always Marcas, all of Marcas.

He reached up with one hand, caught a handful of Connor's hair and pulled him back off his hands, onto Marcas' thighs. He kissed him, sucked on his tongue, pulled harder when he tightened his fingers and groaned into Connor's mouth. Marcas' other hand reached over Connor's thigh, pushed Connor's fingers away and stroked him.

"Can't—need—*Connor*—"

Connor felt heat spilling inside him, so much heat, and Marcas shuddering behind him, around him, within him—he thrust his cock up into the oiled tightness of Marcas' fist, pressed his mouth back to Marcas' mouth and rocked helpless from one pleasure to another, gasping, broken. *So good, so good, Marcas. Marcas, Marcas—*

He didn't know if he was saying the words out loud or not, could only hear the blood rushing in his ears, the ringing of his nerves as Marcas' hands moved over his body, calming, easy. Marcas' thumb brushed across his lips, and his fingers under his chin. He turned Connor's face so he could see Marcas' eyes, the look of love there. *Smoldering sea.* Then—then, a kiss. *Soft. This is...very...soft.*

"I love you—I love you, Connor." Marcas' tongue licked against his parted lips, more temptation than touch. "*I love you.*" His fingers slipped across Connor's cheekbones and up into his hair. Then he leaned forward on one arm to brace himself as he let Connor down against the bed and slipped out of his body.

When he lay back, he reached out one arm to wrap around Connor's waist, and Connor relaxed against him, utterly sated. Marcas' murmur reached his ears through a haze of sleep.

"Bath...later?"

Connor could barely blink. *Soft.* "Mm....later." *Warm.*

"*Marcas.*"

* * * *

When Connor woke to the quiet of relaxed muscles, soft skin under Marcas' fingers, fading flush and smiles made warm by pleasure, the conversation that had been strained was easy.

"It seemed so simple, in my head. Revenge... Bloody, but simple. But if you're right, and we can't kill him..." Connor rolled in Marcas' arms, turned toward him, his eyes serious, the green sparking a little, to ask again, to be certain. "You're *sure* we can't kill him?"

"The lord of the mound cannot be destroyed without destroying all things. Before the world, there was the bent one, and when the world has had its time and gone, the bent one will be still. What's light without shadow? What's day without night, sun without dark, stars without a black background to shine against? What is your world without battle, Connor? What's sea, seen to the bottom, or the heart of the deepest wood without shade?" He shrugged faintly, and adjusted his shoulder again under the weight of Connor's body. "Take that away and everything falls apart."

Connor's brow contracted under the weight of a heavy thought. "Does that mean he isn't evil?"

"What is evil? If the *faoladh* know one thing, it's that the bent one desires an end to everything that is not the silence and the dark. Perhaps he's jealous of the purpose of the world. Or maybe he's jealous of the quiet the world disturbed when it was made. Reason, motive... I don't know what those are. *I'd* say that the lord of the mound is evil...but a necessary evil. That evil without which good can't be known."

Connor turned his face away, rubbed his cheek against Marcas' chest.

"I don't believe that. Maybe darkness — maybe we need that. But not evil. They aren't the same thing. But, Marcas, if we can't kill him, what do we do?"

At that, Marcas finally sighed. "I don't know. I know some of what's been done before, other times that the bent one has wandered the world and been sent back to his own kingdom. But all the stories say that the same way will not work twice. In every age in which he appears, there's a new struggle. There was a bard that sang a song to enchant him, a wine so sweet it put even him to sleep. Once, pinned by weapons like your spear until the rising of the sun, he was blinded and cast into the pit beneath the idol...and once, the *faoladh* made a pact with the Dagda. But you've seen what has become of those chains."

Connor frowned.

"No, I don't see — I didn't see. I was with you, and now I know I was right, and I need to go see Lord Aran. He was there with my father — or he should have been — and if anyone survived — if anyone left that place alive, it was him."

"And if he's dead?"

"Then... Then I am really on my own."

Marcas tightened his arms around as much of Connor as he could reach, closed his eyes and clung to the awareness of brightness that told him Connor was his to protect, one of those that was meant to live.

"Never that. You want to go to this man, this Aran? Then we'll go. Until you tell me otherwise, I will be at your side, and even then..." He shrugged. "I will protect you."

Connor felt again the new-old ache, its intensity a growing thing every time he focused on it. "When is it you want to leave, Connor?"

He looked up into Marcas' face and read resignation there, and worry, and behind all those things the faintest flicker of fear. Still, only a fool wouldn't fear the foe that was before them, the enemy against which they had set themselves without even a real plan in their favor. Already, Connor knew that there would be a great chase across the wilderness again. "Soon. I would've said we should leave today, except—"

"We can still leave today."

Connor closed his eyes, relaxed by the slow movement of Marcas' hands on the bare skin of his back, the steady sensation of fingers stroking his shoulders, the back of his neck, down the line of his spine, cool and generous as spilling water... *Leave...today?*

"No...tomorrow."

"Tomorrow—we can't go on like that forever, you know."

But there was no impetus in Marcas' words, no drive to leave either. Connor didn't even need to open his eyes, to look at Marcas' face, to see what he knew was the truth. Whatever warmth he was feeling, Marcas felt it too—the lazy sweetness of a moment that had been drawn out into slow hours now, drowsing, touching—*go on forever like this, why not? Give up everything else...*

But it was only an instant's dream, and the thought itself was like a rush of cold water.

"I know there's things that need doing. I know that. But there's so much to get ready—and I'd be lying if I said I was in any hurry to get up. I like...this."

His fingers traced a line up Marcas' abdomen to his chest, his jaw, his cheek. Rough stubble against his fingers, scent of Marcas' skin filling his awareness, and all was warmth and eased desire and a comforting pressure that came just from Marcas being there, sharing his space, pressing against him skin to skin.

"Have you never held your lovers, Connor?"

Connor shrugged. He didn't want to think about previous lovers while he was lying here. It seemed like…like sacrilege, a violation.

"Connor?"

"Don't ask me that—it's not fair to ask me that. You're not like anyone else I've been with. You're different, and what I feel about you is different, and *this* is different. I wonder why they all said that love was pointless? My father, that girl—"

"If you aren't in it, you fear it—love. Like deep water. You take one step in, and then before you know it you've sunk in up to your eyes."

They were serious words, but Marcas grinned to take the tension from them and wrapped one leg over Connor's thighs, kissed his chest, his shoulder, his collarbone.

Connor peered at him through one eye. "So we stay here today, stay here tonight, and leave at first light?"

"If it's what you want."

"I think it's what we *need*. Time to get provisions, horses—"

"Horses?" Marcas chuckled. "Did you see horses in the village last night?"

Connor blinked, thought back—dark streets, the light from the door of the tavern, but not a single post or stable in sight—no sound of hooves that he could remember, either. *No horses?* There had been such richness in that village that he hadn't even thought twice before making the suggestion.

"I don't understand. Why aren't there—?"

"Too many wolves among us. Those who are human have no trouble, but those who have been the wolf — the true *faoladh* — no horse will bear them again as a rider. Something of the scent of wolf, the presence of it, must linger. It's not enough to frighten them away altogether, and there's always been a few among the farmers who kept one or two around in case of emergency — need of a messenger or a warning, something like that."

"But what are we going to do then? Lord Aran's holdings are on the other side of the island."

"And you think you'll have trouble crossing that many leagues, but you won't. Not as long as you're traveling with me."

"The wolf —"

"Maybe not the most comfortable journey, but it'll be faster than any horse and there's no safer way to travel, considering what enemy it is that's on our tail."

"How fast can you go? You said as fast as you needed to, but —"

Marcas shrugged, and Connor felt the motion in the muscles of his chest, the shoulders shifting under his head. He sat up slowly, pushed himself up onto one arm and looked down at Marcas' face through the fall of his hair as Marcas spoke.

"I've never really tested it, except when I ran with you. How fast was that, Connor?"

He grinned.

"Fast enough that maybe we don't need so much in the way of provisions after all."

"No, and that's good. My kin will bring us what we need, but not much more than that — and those who I'd rather keep uninformed would find out if I was buying things for a journey, whether I wanted them to or not."

Connor slipped back onto his side, back under the blankets, and pressed the length of his body against Marcas. *Vengeance can wait, and everything else there is to worry about.* He put away thoughts of the journey to come and reached one arm across Marcas' chest, pulled himself closer. *Just for today.*

* * * *

The night fell sharp and dark, and Marcas woke at the pressure that came with it, sudden and inexplicable against his inner senses. *Darkness. Something is coming – something is here!*

The thought brought him awake entirely, full of the knowledge that he had to take Connor and go – that terrible things were coming, even if he yet had no reason. *Need.* That was enough, a feeling he had obeyed for seven years. *The bent one is coming.*

Under a concentrated assault of all that was the crooked king, Marcas grew aware of the barrier of the Dagda's power. It had long protected them, had weathered ages of darkness, but no more. Black power squeezed like a fist around it, *squeezed* until it shattered, a gleaming bauble broken into threads of smoke.

Marcas felt it as it died, an enormous power that had hummed in the back of his awareness for years going to trembling dust in an instant.

"Connor!"

He woke the boy with a hiss, shook his shoulder and all but spilled him from the bed when he snatched the cover away.

"Wake up – get up now! There's no time to waste – come with me!"

Marcas dressed swiftly in the dark with wolf-sighted eyes, tossed clothes back at Connor over his shoulder, then boots. He only turned when Connor yelped, and saw that one boot had hit him in the shoulder.

"Sorry—but there's no time! Every barrier is fallen. Do you understand? The protection over this place, the thing that kept us safe from the bent one and from men alike. There's nothing now, it's gone. We can't stay here. I have to go down to the village."

At the door, Marcas stood waiting, looking outward, every sense he possessed prickling, and a growl burning in the back of his throat that he could not contain. He stepped out of the door and a few steps forward, only to the corner of the hall. Was it his imagination or was the hillside in the direction of the barrow darker? *If the barrier is fallen, what about the silver curtain that blocks the barrow-door? Can the shadow come out?*

The hair prickled on the back of his neck. His mouth felt dry, his muscles tight. He found his eyes jumping from shadow to shadow, darkness to blackness, seeking in the umbrous movement some kind of promise that was more than just the natural noise and motion of the night.

He looked up and saw only black overhead, a sky more dark than night. There was only a void without stars, as far as his eyes could see. Connor came up behind him and laid a hand on his shoulder, and Marcas almost jumped.

"Don't do that. Have you got the bag we packed this afternoon?"

"No, you said we were going back to the village so I—"

"Bring it. And the spear, too. I don't— This meeting isn't going to go well, but it's got to be done. They need their warning. They won't know there's anything wrong until it's too late otherwise. You didn't feel anything, did you?"

"No, I—"

"I didn't think so. It's the wolf inside me—but there's no other *faoladh* near."

"What are you going to tell them?"

He heard great hesitation in Connor's voice.

"Everything. Then to scatter and live."

Scatter and live. He could think of nothing else. The true *faoladh* among them would be separated over the whole of Eire, and speed was only useful to those who knew there was need to use it. Most would assume that this place alone was protected, and seek to do all they could elsewhere. For a moment Marcas stood completely still, caught between decision and doubt. Then he undid the tie of his trousers, kicked them off and pulled his tunic over his head.

"Marcas?"

He turned to face Connor and saw that the boy had his hands full.

"What are you...?"

"No point wasting a good set of clothes—and if I'm going to make the revelation, it might as well be with a bang."

He bent and picked up his trousers, gestured for Connor to open the bag in his hand and rolled them up to tuck them inside.

"Are you sure you need to do this? Can't you just go tell them the barrier's been broken and leave?"

"And why would they believe me? The wolves among us have the senses of wolves and more. We are not really wolves, we are *faoladh* – but that is not something that lingers when the service is done—or shouldn't be. Didn't I tell you that what's happened to me isn't *normal*? Even for the *faoladh*."

"But—"

"Does a wolf change its size according to its need? Does it howl down the moon and burn shadow to dust and a different kind of darkness?"

Marcas stared intently into Connor's face, shook his head.

"No, you even said as much—you knew in the beginning I was something other than a wolf. Well that *something other*—it's the only thing that tells me that something is wrong, and the others don't have it. The night feels no different to you because it *isn't* different to you, and it won't be different to them. Did you wake up with a sound like a shattering jug in your ears, only to find out that it was the stars that fell out and not water?"

Compulsively, as if forced by his words, Connor looked up and saw the black sky, the jet absence of luminance, and almost dropped bag and spear both with a cry.

"What the hell is—where are the stars? Marcas! Isn't that enough?"

"Not for them. Not when they believe that they're protected."

He watched Connor draw in a deep breath, close his eyes—when he opened them again there was the steel of a new resolve.

"All right. All right—let's do this. If there's no protection here, we shouldn't stay. We'll give whatever message you want, but then we have to follow your advice, Marcas. We have to scatter and live—until we find the one we have to fight."

"Connor—"

"No! They're your kin. I understand. I'd do the same if I were in your place, and damn the consequences. But there're other fights more important, and I *need you to live*."

Chapter Twelve

Before Connor's eyes, under his hands, the strange change, man to wolf shape, overcame his lover. It was not a *shift*, though it was not sudden, but despite that he found himself unable to track the steps of it, couldn't place the moment when Marcas ceased to be man and became a wolf, and more than a wolf—his greater shape he wore, the size of a horse or larger. When whatever it was that was going on in his flesh was settled, he crouched on his haunches and lowered himself so that Connor could climb onto his back.

Connor slung the bag over one shoulder and mounted, gripped the spear in one hand. With the other, he grasped the dark fur tightly and held on as Marcas sprang forward, moving from the side of the hall down the hillside in great leaps. Again and again he found himself looking back over his shoulder, his neck prickling, his skin tight, cold sweat breaking out on his palms and his nerves thinned into angry slivers that prodded him with false messages. There was no hand on his back. There were no fingers coming up for his ankles out of the grass—only the black of the sky clutching tight to his skin, only dew flayed from the grass sprayed on his calves.

Marcas breached the entrance to the valley and ran down the road that led past outlying farms and through the center of the village. Connor heard voices, shouts of surprise coming to his ears only faintly before they were snatched away by the wind.

There was louder sound and a flash of light, and he knew they had passed the tavern — then Marcas stopped, so suddenly Connor was almost thrown from his place on his back, and had to brace himself quickly against his forearm. Marcas let out a growl of discomfort, and Connor let go of the handful of fur he had been grasping far too tightly.

"A wolf among us — but who have you brought with you?"

Connor looked up and saw that Marcas had stopped in the road because a group of men were in the middle of it, men dressed in finer clothes than Marcas' — finer clothes even than what Connor was used to, and he was the son of a king. *Who are these people?*

As he studied them, they studied him. Intense stares dissected every aspect of his presence. He shifted his gaze from face to face, but he didn't recognize them — yet that wasn't true for the ones who were watching him. From the back, an older man, blond and bearded, stepped forward with an accusing finger leveled in Connor's direction.

"That spear is one of *our* weapons, and you — you are that outsider! You are the one who came to the tavern last night with Marcas — "

In an instant, Connor felt the roiling in the muscles beneath him, the change that he had twice witnessed building again under Marcas' skin. He slipped off the side of the great wolf, stood still beside him with one hand on the wide back and the other hand firmly gripping his spear — *his* spear, whether it was their weapon or not. Would they use it, would they dare?

It didn't seem that way to him.

Beside him, Marcas *shifted* again, the flowing of being that brought him up from four legs onto two, his spine a curve that straightened slowly, muzzle receding, ears vanishing into the dark hair — and even before it was over, all wolfish features vanished into the man that he had come to know, Marcas was speaking, words slipping out of him more growl than voice, steadying slowly with every word.

"He is still *with Marcas.*"

Connor saw every single one of the men before them take a step back, and felt Marcas' fears settle over him like a second skin, hot and clinging, all but a certainty now. *Just looking at him, they fear him. Knowing what he can do, they fear him. Why? They're his kin! I've only known him for a few months and already —*

Marcas stepped forward, blocking half of Connor's view, protecting Connor with his body. A ripple of frustration spread through him, curled around his thoughts. *Still protecting me even after everything I said.* This tendency of Marcas', this way of stepping in front of him, moving into danger's path — it was endearing, and it warmed him, but it had to stop. *Now. Now is as good as ever.*

He ducked out from behind Marcas' shielding arm and stood beside him, shoulder to shoulder, offering all the support he could give while Marcas glared the men before them into silence. Connor saw several of them still looking at him, and returned their stares with contempt. Quietly, without excess or elaboration, Marcas said what he had come to say.

"The Dagda has given me a gift. It was because of this one—Connor mac Brádach, son of an outside king. He was chosen, marked by brightness—he means to lead his people, fight the lord of the mound. The bent one is walking the wilds of Eire in the shape of a man, the one who called himself the High King—the one who summoned him."

A low murmur answered that, and Marcas looked between many eyes.

"Tonight he broke the barrier that protects us. The power is gone—there is nothing now between you and the night. All of you—every last one—must scatter from this place if you intend to live. I think the attack will come tonight. I think it will come here, first—the hardest strike at the point of the strongest resistance. Get out of here while you can, do you hear me? Get out while you can. Scatter and live. Perhaps when the shadow is vanquished—"

"And you think we should rely on this *boy* to vanquish the dark god? This outsider child—"

"I am no child! It's seven years since I was made a man. When the bent one comes for you, do you know what he leaves behind? I have seen it—I have *tasted* it. In my own places, my father's hall and the homes of my kin—ashes, all of it. Black ashes, not the ash of fire but something else—"

"All the life drained out."

Marcas' interruption was quiet but strong, and the murmur from the elders went to silence.

"When the lord of the mound takes, he takes all. Metal is safe from him. Stone. Nothing else—and in the end, not even that. Tell me, what are our defenses? What will you do now that there is nothing hiding us from him? Whether you choose to believe in me or Connor doesn't matter. *You have to leave.*"

Finally, from among them came a voice of reason. "You are serious about this. This is no prank, no—"

"*Prank*? As if I'd ever in my life given you reason to think—no. I'm done here. I have work to do."

"Damn right you do! If the barrier's gone, you have to protect us!"

"Like hell I do!"

Silence, and Connor would have laughed if it were any other situation, any other threat.

"It was never the job of the *faoladh* to protect this place. I have my duty, the duty I was given and the promise of my heart. That's more than enough for one man—or one wolf. Perhaps you'll be lucky, and the others will see the sky gone dark and come to investigate. But I don't think so. I think the sky is dark over all of Eire tonight. I think if you're wise, you'll *listen to what I've said* and get out of here."

Again, the reasonable voice spoke and this time Connor saw that it was the eldest of the men before them, white-haired, bent, all but toothless, his voice strong but lisping, a voice that seemed like it should be no more than a murmur and yet had volume, presence. "Marcas, even if we take the whole settlement to the road, there won't be safety there. Not while the night lasts—"

"No. But there's no safety anywhere now as long as the night lasts—so run while you may."

"You—as you said, you have your work to do. Just the way you came before us, the way you stand here now, that is enough to tell me something is different about you. Did you know your skin is marked?"

"The god's blood did that—and all else."

"I...see."

Again, there was silence. Connor felt an upwelling of awe from the men before them. *God's blood?*

"If you see the others—if you find them on your way—"

"I will send them. But if there are those among our kin who are meant to live—well, you know the way of things. Brightness will be born—and brightness will summon one of us... But it hasn't summoned me."

Marcas turned away, nodded to Connor. *That's all, then.* The painful tightening was entering Marcas' muscles again, the straining of the shift growing on his skin, on his face, but the old man had one last question.

"Marcas, what will you do about the bo—the young man? He knows secrets that were never meant to be shared."

"Connor is mine. Mine."

His voice was the wolf-strung growl again. It stroked Connor's spine, sent a tingle over his nerves—raw possession in every note of his name. It wasn't an answer—not really—the look on the old man's face said that. And yet at the same time Connor saw that all the premonitions of violence and darkness had been for naught, because these men really *did* fear Marcas—feared him in an indefinable, enormous way. It was stamped on all their faces. They feared him so much that they could never defy him.

In another minute Marcas was the wolf, terror on four legs, amusement and sorrow in the blue eyes. Then he crouched, and Connor climbed astride his back again.

"North, Marcas. Run north, swift as you can, and let's prove them wrong."

There was a single shake of the wolf's head, ruff flying in agreement, and Marcas made to speed off into the night—but it was already too late. Over the edge of the village, its feet planted in the farmer's fields, a shadow was growing against the night.

* * * *

In the first instant, Connor felt only the fear — black terror that gripped him like strangling vines. In the second instant, he remembered the promises he had made to himself. *No running. No fear. Turn around. Look it in the eye. Call it by name.* In the third, he was returned to himself. Connor, son of a king, born to be a warrior, to fight — and more than that, to vanquish.

His eyes took in his surroundings, the sprawling night, starless, moonless, creating endless spaces from which their foe could attack. People were coming outside now, throwing screams in every direction, their fingers pointing at the sky. He felt the tension in the muscles of Marcas' back under him, looked back over his shoulder and felt his heart sinking. He had intended to leave, but he couldn't do that now, couldn't leave these people to die — not Marcas' kin, even though they were cowards.

Shadow spilled over the curve of the hills, no tide, no wave, but uncurling figures — stick-like, every movement jerky, unnatural, quickening but not smoothing, knees that bent backward, arms like branches fixed and outstretched forward, fingers bent and splayed into terrible claws.

They came down into the valley, down over the green, and in the faces there were no features. Yet mouthless, they still opened mouths and bent forward gasping, sucking at the wind. Eyeless, they still opened eyes that stared and glared, grasped greedily at the night, at whatever they caught sight of. Connor saw men and women frozen, struck still with terror, his eyes focused on them as if with eagle's sight at a distance.

What the shadow touched, it devoured. When it reached the village, all that darkness would —

All that darkness.

One hand fisted in Marcas' fur, the other holding up the shining point of his spear, he let out a rallying cry.

"*Faoladh*! All you people, listen to me! This enemy will destroy everything. I've seen it — I've suffered it! But if there's one thing I know, it's that Crom Cruach fears the light. Burn everything you can! Houses — wagons — hay, straw, old furniture — burn it all! Where there's light, there might be some safety — or do you want to become like your kin out there?"

His arm shot outward, pointing — all eyes of those that could hear him were drawn past the point of his spear, glinting like a star, to the darkness that consumed and devoured, darker than the night around it and thus visible — how could what was blacker than black be seen? And yet it *was* visible, in its movement, its quick, rattling scrabbles.

There were protests from the elders and from many others, and he couldn't really blame them. But there wasn't time — couldn't they see there wasn't time?

"Fire's our only friend tonight, unless you know how to call back the moon. Would you rather burn what's yours yourself and stay alive or turn to dust with it and die? It's all doomed anyway so *help yourselves while you can*! Move — *move*!"

Around them, where the ears of wiser men had been listening, many people were in motion. Hearths and the houses that held them were already being put to the torch, beginning to burn. Nothing but this threat would have induced these people to give up so much of their livelihood, but overhead the sky sat hollow and horrible, and a terrible stench was coming on the wind from the fields.

Connor had smelled it before at the ruins of his father's hall. *Crom Cruach.* He pressed his lips together, narrowed his eyes at the flickers of fire going up all along the road now. Would it be enough? But he could already tell the answer.

Not nearly.

Fury built in him. He would be grateful to Marcas forever for all that he had done, regardless of softness in his kin and their ideals, but it was only now that he realized how far that gratitude could take him in his understanding.

Not far enough.

Did Marcas know this thing about his people, about the service he himself had undertaken? Did he know how useless it was, how little it really meant, that they called themselves protectors of men? *Or shouldn't they have set guard at Magh Slécht, at all his places of power?*

He tightened his fists in Marcas' fur. *What is the weakness of my foe?* His eyes scanned the village, the fields, shadow that was all-encroaching, all-consuming, a steady tide that increased its speed as it increased its presence.

"No high ground, no place set aside, no way to get them out."

He felt the first touch of despair. *Death for all of them, fools and farmers and faoladh.* They weren't his people, but they were Marcas' people. *I've got none left, but that doesn't mean that he shouldn't either.* And there was a deeper panic in him, because this was the real test, the first battle, and if he failed here —

It was then, the moment when his thoughts, his courage, his confidence, were at their lowest ebb, that he heard the voice of the lord of the mound.

"Is one among you chosen? Does one among you come in the name of my old foe?"

Ice sheathed his nerves, his muscles. He felt straining beneath him, Marcas' will turned to flight, the blue eyes looking up at him, begging him. *Run.* Instead, Connor turned and took in the great and impossible shape of that darker-than-blackness. He met eyes that didn't exist, felt bleak power sucking at his being, heard again that voice, every missing star transmuted into nimble claws that skewered his soul.

For the second time, he confronted the dark god with his name.

"Crom Cruach!"

Terror sprouted within him anew, reached out once more to strangle hope — and yet with it was planted a seed of an idea, a possibility that set his thoughts moving again, salvaged his strength.

"He wants his chosen enemy more than anything. More than any of these…"

Connor knew what was necessary, then. It was just a matter of the doing.

* * * *

Connor's muttered words broke open the worst of Marcas' fear. In an instant he was moving, intending to put as much distance as he could between them and their foe, but Connor slipped off his back easily, just opened his hands and swung his leg over. He hit the ground hard, but not that hard, and Marcas had no choice but to turn and go back to him. Wolf shape became man shape, still bristling, angry, but Connor cut him off before he could even say a word.

"Even if you know what I'm thinking and don't like it, you know I'm right. If I go—you can see it—he's calling for me!"

"Calling for *you*."

The words came low and fragile from Marcas' throat. All his suspicion, all his belief—and Connor wouldn't stop talking.

"You're the one who said that I'm the one that was chosen, aren't you? The brightest light you've known, some kind of blessing—a decision of the Dagda. You have to let me do this."

"You don't know how—"

"Neither do you! Nobody knows, so what am I supposed to do, just let all your kin die here?"

Screams echoed. There was the sound of great destruction, buildings falling in on each other, then all the noise suddenly silenced and in his mind's eye, Marcas could see already the falling ash, the way flesh would vanish, turn to smoke and dust and leave only rings and bracelets behind. *Fionnuala's daughters. Her sons.*

"Marcas."

Connor spoke his name so softly, so *lovingly*—it all but broke him to hear it, knowing what must be coming next to have wrenched such a tone past Connor's lips.

"He'll follow me. You know he will. I have to get him to notice first, that I'm trying to fight him—but he'll follow me."

"Connor, that's *insane*."

"I know. Except that I'll be relying on you to outrun him again, at least for a while."

"I—"

Marcas took a breath, looked away, did everything in his power to still the trembling of his hands and found it still wasn't enough. *So that's his plan. And it has to be for me, as much as for him – Connor.* And he knew then that there was no point in arguing.

"I understand. It's still insane —"

"But there's nothing else we can do. Watch me. Don't let him see you if you can help it, and for the love of the gods… *Don't let yourself get hurt!*"

One kiss, hard, sharp, longing, full of promise. *Live for me, for this,* it said. Because he could, because he had to, Marcas scoffed.

"As if I needed a reminder. Watch your back!"

He watched Connor jog down the street, spear in hand, then let the wolf overtake his being and moved out of the shadow and into the brightest of the flickering firelight. Where else could he hide from the dark? It was harder to see from the midst of brightness, looking out into a night made darker than usual by the absence of stars, but after a time he adapted, peered outward, following the single point of light beyond the fires with his eyes. *Connor's spear.*

He slipped forward from one blaze of brightness to another, staying close but not too close. Connor's plan was clear to him, and it required that all the bent one's attention be on him — that nothing distract him Marcas regretted his word — *chosen. I should not have said it.* Why had he used that word?

He leaped forward into the last patch of brightness and saw before him his worst fear coming to pass. Crom Cruach had taken notice of Connor. Shadow surrounded him, waves and coils of it, dark and gleaming with no natural light. Out of shadow, out of night, an amorphous mass of blackness rose to confront Connor, who faced it, spear in hand.

Then Marcas was running, fast—faster—no more speed than this in the world, his being reduced to a single impulse, a single need. One denial.

No.

From behind Connor, one tendril, poised like a sword, was ready to strike, to end all for his warrior boy who thought to fight honorably against the annihilation of the world.

Marcas dove between that blow and Connor, and it came across his belly, over his ribs, along his back before he could turn and take the darkness between his teeth, shake it to death. Then—*then* came the pain. Numb, in the first moment. Tingling. *Heat.*

Then the heat was fire, peeling away everything, fur, muscles, breath, until there were only nerves, nerves with their screaming messages of pain. Once, he opened his mouth and howled, then fell and felt only the life seeping out of his body, flowing away into the dirt. Dimly, the words like threads of ice, he heard Connor cry out for him—*Marcas! No!*

He turned his head a little to the left, and saw Crom Cruach coming for him, the greater portion of the dark god embodied in flesh that had once belonged to a man. Fallen, broken, Marcas could only watch as Connor failed to flee—as he stood over him instead, his back straight as the spear in his hand.

Connor moved without thinking the moment he heard that howl. He turned before he could stop himself, all his attention taken from the foe before him.

"Marcas! No!"

But it was too late even before he turned, too late before he was aware of what was happening. He caught only a black movement out of the corner of his eye, saw Marcas with his jaws locked tight around a tendril of shadow. A hot spray of blood caught his cheek, his chest, too much blood, far too much blood. It ran wet and salty over his lips, and the way Marcas fell — the way he crumpled — the way those blue eyes stared up at him, begging in them —

For the first time he knew the whole of love, and the price of love. A piercing ember caught cold in his throat. He couldn't breathe. *Marcas.*

He turned and faced his enemy again, squeezed his fingers around the shaft of the spear until his knuckles went white. Before him, the shadow was drawing inward, laughing, a sound like nothing mortal. It *stung*, left his head ringing even though there was no noise in his ears.

"And now you are alone."

He heard the screams of men and women behind him, and the low whine of Marcas' breath — yet the grass was still, the wind silent.

The shadow took on features he knew, but not well, and even so he could see the change that had been wrought. The High King that stood before him was not the High King. If the manner of his appearance was not enough, then surely the rest of him was — the presence that came like a hand around Connor's throat, dried the moisture from his tongue, tried to sap the strength from his beating heart, his lungs.

"Now you are alone and you are mine."

Like the words were magic, tender purpose in the bruise they caused, an eager rage went screaming along Connor's skin. Belong to this monster, this *thing* that had crawled out of some dark pit after a thousand years, seeking destruction? Belong to *him*, when he had taken the flesh and soul of the king to whom he owed his service — had broken the rule of the land —

had slaughtered his father, his mother, his sisters—
Marcas.

Marcas, who was the only one who could say *you're mine*, who had smiled at him, who had *loved* him, who was *dying for him*. He pressed the back of his left hand against his lips, his cheek, felt the spilled blood there, cooling, still hot as a coal touched to his skin.

"Not yours, Crom Cruach—*never yours*. Nothing is yours but death!"

"*So be it.*"

Death was and always had been the bent one's purpose. Connor could feel it clawing at him, reaching for him, a talon that struck at something invisible, the way the voice reached out to touch—but it wouldn't succeed. Not this time—not here, not now, not with Marcas on the ground behind him and the damp of his blood still on Connor's fingers, staining the pale shaft of the spear he gripped in his hand. No running. No hiding. *No more turning away.*

He would have circled, but he was restrained from moving by the tight arc required of him if he was to protect Marcas—and as long as he still breathed, Connor *would* protect him. All shadow retreated, condensed, became the single solid shape of the High King's inhabited body. He grinned grimly. Now he need not worry about attacks from behind, from either side—what a fool he'd been not to guard against them before. *A fool – my fault – Marcas.*

On the tips of his toes, thoughts burning, heart beating like the end of the world, his gaze zeroed in on every twitch of Crom Cruach's unnatural flesh. When it finally came, the strike of his foe was like spilled water, a bar of darkness that came toward him in a solid shot, reaching for his throat. He struck outward with the head of his spear, one perfect blow that pierced the night with a streak of silver and came back haunted. Shadow clung to the shining point, to its edges, then burned away, melted into smoke and nothingness.

Fingers and claws of shadow were thrust outward from the body that was once the High King's, drove toward in him in three places at a time. He dodged the first, but not the second or the third. Together, as if Crom Cruach was aware of his old wound, had some secret knowledge, the tendrils plunged into the healed tissues of his thigh, more than undoing Marcas' healing work.

Connor bent forward, screaming, aware of pain beyond all previous pain in his awareness, darkness churning in the red muscle, down, down — and behind the agony, his own thoughts mocked him, the echo of the dark god in every word.

A fool, and a fool who failed, that's all you'll ever be. What about you is chosen?

"Crom Cruach!"

The name came from him in a roar. On the leg not skewered by a thrust of shadow, he stood, looked up and met the heart of shadow glowing in the eyes of his foe. The head of the spear in his hand gained a glow like white fire as he spun it in his hands and slashed downward. The gleaming metal met shadow and silence and the groaning night, sliced through it and separated the writhing tendrils that had pierced his thigh from the main body of the beast.

It was Crom Cruach's turn to scream.

Connor pulled the bits of darkness that remained from his thigh and cast them aside. On one knee, he watched something that was neither blood nor anything else spew from the wounded stump of what had once been flesh.

The severed portion of Crom Cruach fell to the ground and wriggled there, retracted and writhed, became something shaped like a hand that flopped like a dying insect until finally it skittered and became still, dead, curled fingers lined with age. It was the hand that had belonged to the High King, and it lay in the dirt, bleeding black blood, while the Darkest One howled in agony of his severed being.

All shadow, all blackness retreated, sucked into a single space, a point that vanished, receding without movement, disappearing into the dark. As if a curtain were pulled back from the horizon with the disappearance of the bent one, stars in their teeming billions and the ivory crescent of the moon returned.

Connor stared at them only for a moment, all his attention on the distance that opened between himself and Crom Cruach, the possible return of his enemy — *nothing*. There was nothing. The darkness had vanished, and with it all threat — for now.

In an instant, he was on his knees by Marcas' side, pain pressing through adrenaline but a new fear overmastering both. The wolf that had protected him had become the man he loved. The man he loved, broken. The wounds of the wolf translated to his human flesh.

Love. Marcas. You can't die before I tell you.

Connor had seen men with wounds like this before, but never one that had lived through it. There was too much blood, blood everywhere, and the white bone visible beneath the flow of red — his own injury was nothing compared to this.

"You should have let him kill me." The words fled his lips before he could stop them. "But you had to go and make me a liar, didn't you? Had to be the hero — had to save me again — *Marcas*."

A little at a time, blue eyes blinked open and turned to meet Connor's stare. "I'm...*faoladh*, remember? It was...always...going to end...like this."

"No—not like this!"

Marcas' eyes did all his talking, blue and sweet and crackling with the truth and with regret. Connor could read the thoughts there, the words Marcas no longer had breath to voice. *We are not always what we promise to be. We do not always manage everything we promise to do.*

And within Connor, a cautionary answer walked the edges of a great internal wound. *This is what love is, the price you pay. This is what you give away. This is the price. You pay in pain.*

"You can't die here, Marcas. You can't leave me!"

Connor cut at himself with the words. What could he do? What could anyone do? The wound in his thigh throbbed against his awareness, and the warmth of Marcas' blood, and the brightness in his eyes as it faded. How could this happen? *How is this happening? How is this real? This can't be — can't be...*

His thoughts ran out of words to contain the depth and pressure of his feelings. It was intensity—it was fury—it was an ultimate rage, inexpressible, focused at his own helplessness.

"What am I here for? What I am supposed to do? *Tell me, damn it!* Gods! You want me, you want to *choose* me? I choose *him*! I choose him over everything and everyone. What is it that's so hard to understand? I'm the useless one! I can't do anything without him. I've lost every step of the way and now—"

He screamed at the gods, at the Dagda, at Marcas, dying—at the silence, and the empty space all around him, and the burned out fires and the night.

"I won't lose him? Do you understand?"

Connor tasted salt and blood. He tightened his fists, and heard a snap — sharp, singular, ominous, a perfect sound to break the dullness of the night. Through the swimming of his vision, he looked down and saw that the spear in his hands had broken completely in two.

"What — ?"

The word was hoarse, his voice made rough by screaming. Along the cracks in the wood threads of silver luminance were growing, gaining in strength and pouring out as if the spear had been a vessel and not a weapon, a vessel full of light. Words flamed in his consciousness, burned his ears, his eyes, his nose, his tongue.

"And you, too, are willing to sacrifice everything? Lovely."

Connor saw things that couldn't be, heard sounds that couldn't possibly be real. There was a circle of wolves and in the space of the thirteenth hour, a stag with a human face, an impossible figure, the great rack reaching up, up, seven points stabbing at the stars, joining with them. The wolves howled, eerie, a summons that called for power beyond power, light beyond light. There came a brightness so white that he turned away, squeezed his eyes closed, pressed the back of his arm against them and still was witness to the flare.

"Let it be as you have chosen."

Blinking entirely different tears back from his eyes, Connor could only barely make out two things through the brightness as it began to fade. One was the shape of the great stag, nodding in his direction, the eyes like chips of day-sky set with pupils of jet. The other was Marcas' body, shifting, changing — and *healing*.

Connor watched him become the wolf, saw the crescent of the moon fall into his mouth like a shard of white fire. The terrible wounds were receding, closing, the blood drawing back into his body. Marcas stared into Connor's face with something like surprise coloring his expression as he sucked in a breath, coughed then breathed again.

Connor flopped back weakly, drained suddenly of all strength, and could only laugh—not from heart's ease, but because it was that or cry, and he had already spent his tears.

Chapter Thirteen

Marcas breathed slowly, deeply, tasted the cool night air that he had never expected to breathe again. He had thought he was dying, but now there wasn't a drop of pain anywhere in his body. He smelled blood, but it was old—tasted it, but he couldn't feel the wound it might have come from. He put one hand on the ground, then the other—a little at a time, he levered himself upward, but there was nothing to tell him he'd been wounded. *Nothing*.

"Connor, what did you *do*?"

"I don't—I didn't—*I don't know*."

Connor's voice was breathless. He held up two halves of a spear, the point no longer holding any brightness.

"I don't think I did anything except beg and be angry. It wasn't *me*—I heard—"

But again he shook his head, and despite the lack of information, Marcas thought he could fill in the blanks himself. Fear filled him. Connor had heard...what? That voice, the burning syllables that came from the mouth of the Dagda?

"What did you threaten—? What did you promise, Connor?"

He looked Connor in the eyes and felt heat stab him in the heart. He had known there was something, something that wasn't just lust, but now... *Connor*. His eyes were full and rich with love, all consuming, overwhelming, and in that moment Marcas knew what he was going to say before he said it.

"Threaten? Promise?" Connor sounded almost angry, and Marcas felt warm hands on the sides of his face, warm lips pressed hard against his mouth. "I just didn't want to live without you. I didn't want to *be* without you. I *love* you, Marcas. *I love you.*" The words came hot and furious against his skin, and Marcas leaned up and kissed him, couldn't help himself, didn't want to. What other answer could there be that was better than this?

He couldn't say anything about price or purpose. Nothing existed but this moment, in which the smoke peeled back from the fire inside him like a flower shedding petals.

"Love me, Connor? You love me."

In an instant he was on his knees, pushing Connor back. There was blood on him, his hands, his face, his leg, but Marcas saw no wound, even where the tears in his clothes said that there should be one, so he didn't hesitate, grasped his tunic and pulled it up, down, whichever way it needed to go to be *off*.

The moment Connor realized what he was doing, there was help, eager fingers peeling off his tunic while he kicked off his boots. He reached out to run his hands over all the naked skin that hovered over him. Marcas felt flush with heat, with desire, with love. The words overflowed his lips, so long held back—*mine all mine* and *love, love, love you*, and beneath him Connor matched every movement, gave in to every touch, every minute a higher access of feeling.

"Marcas — Marcas please —"

Connor was pulling him down, pulling him over, wrapping his legs around Marcas' legs, his ankles clinging to the backs of Marcas' thighs, his whole body open, vulnerable, wanting. His erection was strung tight against his body, his legs parted wide, and he beckoned with his hands and his hips and the eager desire of his whole flesh. Marcas leaned forward over him and felt the hot length of Connor's cock press against his own.

"*Marcas...*"

Nothing had ever sounded so good as that, his name rich with desire as it slipped out — all the begging in the world couldn't have given greater heat to his desire. He pressed his body *down*, enriched Connor's moans with friction. He pressed his fingers into Connor's mouth, stared down into his eyes and groaned as Connor's tongue rolled over them, so wet, so hot. He felt his pulse in his fingertips, his cock.

The stroking of Connor's tongue, the softness of his lips set up an echo in the nerves that wanted them most. When he pulled his fingers away, he sat back on his knees and pressed his fingers into Connor's body, wrapped his other hand around the rigid length of Connor's cock.

He sent both sensations spilling through Connor at once, slow penetration, generous stroking. A little at a time Connor relaxed for him and his thighs opened farther, his hips rocking rhythmically against the pull of Marcas' hand and the fingers moving inside him.

"Marcas — Marcas — oh I love you — I love you and — that — yes — Marcas, please —"

"Gods, you're killing me. Do you know how you sound, Connor?"

Marcas heard the huskiness in his own voice and more than that, in Connor's — a deep groan waiting behind every word.

"I don't care — what I sound — *so good* — *Marcas* — Marcas, I want — *I want you inside me* — "

"*Impatient.*" The word growled out of his mouth even as he continued, thrust his fingers deep, three of them now and Connor's panting, so gorgeous to watch, clear beads of want swelling from the tip of his cock, dark flush riding close beneath his skin, climbing across his chest, over his throat, into his cheeks. "I don't want to hurt you."

Lusty, licking swollen lips, Connor stared up at him with eyes shot black with desire, the green-gray ring of his iris thin and dark around wide pupils.

"*So ready, Marcas* — "

"Not yet — not yet — "

Again, Connor licked his lips, and that was one time too many for Marcas. He pulled away from Connor, drank in the eager moans, the begging that came so easy from that mouth now — *please don't stop* and *Marcas, please* and *I want your cock inside me* —

Marcas straddled Connor at the narrow point of his ribs, went up on his knees and took both of Connor's wrists in his hands, pinned them over his head. With that leverage, he moved high on Connor's body, saw the awareness come into Connor's eyes, looking up at him, as he pressed the head of his cock against Connor's lips, then past them.

Marcas took his mouth with slow movements of his hips, feeling tongue against the head of his cock, and as much of the length of his shaft as Connor could reach. Gorgeous, the broken, needy look in Connor's eyes, the eager way he wrapped his mouth around Marcas' cock, and all the while his breath panting hot and cold, and his hips rocking, begging, his hands twitching where Marcas held them, not letting him even think about touching himself.

When Connor learned the rhythm of Marcas' thrusts, he began to move with them, let his tongue match them, pulled a moan from Marcas' lips with every one. When he finally let go of Connor's hands, slipped back down his body, Connor's lips were swollen, glistening. His erection was harder now, twitched as he reached down and gripped Marcas' waist, his hip, then lifted his own legs and bent them at the knees.

"*Connor.*" The name escaped him as a drawn out groan as he moved forward and gripped Connor's thighs. A little at a time, Marcas' cock disappeared into his body, deeper, deeper, and Connor moaned, begging.

"*More. More more more please more – Marcas – *"

Any intention Marcas had of holding back vanished in those words, the sound of his name—the vision before him, Connor's eyes closed now, his mouth open, his breathing ragged, his fist tight around his cock, matching the rhythm of Marcas' thrusts— beautiful. Perfect. And the feel of him, velvet body squeezing tight around his erection, everything hot, everything— Connor' hands were on his shoulders, his back, his buttocks, urging him deeper, always deeper.

"Connor—*I can't – Connor—*"

Everything inside the boy squeezed tighter. His thighs grew tense as iron in Marcas' grip. Wet pleasure streaked across his chest, his belly, and the sight of him, gasping, groaning, head thrown back, his pure submission—to pleasure—to *Marcas*. He drove deep into Connor's body as his climax hit him, shivering contractions flooding every nerve. Slowly, he let down Connor's legs, leaned close to him. Connor reached up and wrapped his arms around Marcas' back, threaded his legs tightly through Marcas' legs—scent of sex, scent of Connor, glow of that green gaze. *Alive. My Connor.*

A little at a time, Marcas grew aware of damp grass under his elbows, his knees. He wondered if he was heavy and moved, lifted himself off Connor and pulled away. Connor moaned a little as Marcas slipped out of his body, removed the warmth of his presence. He blinked up from the ground, then took the hand that Marcas offered him and shivered as he stood and the cool of the night breeze whipped against the dampness the grass had left on his back.

Marcas caught the shiver, searched behind him until he found Connor's torn tunic and used it to wipe the chill from Connor's shoulders, his back.

"What now, Marcas?"

There were a hundred questions in that one—about the silence that had grown in the night, about the enemy that Connor had sent fleeing from them...about Marcas' kin, behind them in a burning village whose outlines could still be seen against the dark horizon, sending up thick smoke. About the journey they had intended before darkness had broken over the world. Marcas let out a heavy breath, reached out and pulled Connor against him.

"I don't know. We'll do what we have to do, one thing at a time."

Marcas tightened his arms around Connor, an embrace that he didn't know how to respond to. No one had ever held him like this, and for a moment there was nothing inside him, no answer. Then there was love and the memory of terror, and Connor's arms came up around Marcas, wrapped around his waist and shoulders and squeezed tight. Connor leaned his forehead against Marcas', looked into his eyes as his thoughts solidified, worries turning into tasks.

"We'll do...what must be done, then."

Marcas nodded as he pulled away. "Here—we should go back before anything else. Tell my kin they should be safe...for tonight, at least."

But there was something grim building in Connor's awareness as he pulled his torn tunic on, squeezed his fist around the blood-damp flaxen fabric of his cloak.

"Longer than that, Marcas. Crom Cruach will be after me now, remember?"

The protest to which he knew Marcas was accustomed died on his lips, and his lips stretched humorlessly at the sight. *Silent now when I say that name.* But how could it be otherwise? How could Marcas tell him not to call their enemy by name when he— *I cut off the hand of the bent one – the hand of my own High King.*

"I remember, Connor. How could I not?"

He spoke sharply, but with humor, then reached out a hand for Connor and tugged him away from the hilltop, the stench of blood and gore and death. *Marcas' death.*

A shudder passed through him.

Their journey to the *faoladh* village was a slow walk that Connor was grateful for, even if Marcas had the power to become the rushing wolf and bring them there in an instant. The warmth of Marcas' fingers closed around his was reassuring. The sound of his footsteps beside him, the occasional word or sigh, though they walked in silence, nothing else, yet, to say. He was still wrapped in the realization that Marcas was alive — that he was *alive* — *and what was that other thing? What did I see? What did I hear?*

He had his suspicions, but they were all impossible. Even so — *the Dagda. Could it have been?* And if it hadn't been — what then? Some virtue of the broken spear, no more than a shaft of ancient wood now?

He kept his thoughts, his questions, to himself, even as he could see Marcas was doing. Yet there was no tension, no secrets. They would talk when the time was right, share everything — he knew it. *So the question is...what do I have to share?* And he thought again of the wolves he had seen howling, the stag with a face no animal could possess, the voice that had granted him his wish. Given him what he had...chosen. *You swallowed the moon, Marcas.*

Connor wondered what it meant, but compared to the other option, it didn't matter. Even if he had given away his soul — but he didn't think he had. He gripped Marcas' fingers tightly, and received an answering squeeze in return.

It took them only a bit more than an hour to make their way back to the smoke and ruin of the village. In the light of flickering fires that had yet to be put out, Connor saw the destruction that had been wrought, not only by the attack of the bent one, but by Connor's attempt to thwart him. Not much was left standing — smoke was rising from every corner that was visible in the dimness.

He reminded himself that it could have been worse, *would* have been worse, otherwise... But it was hard to stand there and see the cost of survival printed in ashes and embers and dust.

Marcas tugged him forward, an arm in front of his eyes to block the worst of the smoke, peering around. Was he looking for someone? *He has family here, remember?* He sighed and followed Marcas from one side of the village to the other, ignoring the stares from the villagers and the choking ash in the air as best he could. The faces around him — those were a different story.

Women, children, a few men wandering here and there — all of their faces were soot-streaked, their arms and cheeks and throats gray, and the little ones gray all over, as if they'd rolled in the ashes. There were red eyes everywhere, and some grieving over bodies that lay broken in the ash...but there was hope here, and determination, too. *Things can be rebuilt. Fields replanted. But unless they were alive...*

The knowledge relieved a weight he hadn't even realized was settling inside him, and when Marcas finally stopped and he saw it was the elders in front of them, the old men of the night before, still in nightshirts blackened with soot, he felt no foreboding. Even when they turned their angry eyes on him — even when they began to speak.

"So you've come back, you —" The man choked back some manner of curse before he could continue. "And you've brought *him* with you! So much for a chosen one —"

"Shut your mouth!"

Connor had never heard Marcas sound so dangerous. The wolf-blue was burning in his eyes, the shining marks, fingerprints of the god, standing out with the same cold fire.

"Do you know what he's done, my Connor? He cut the hand from Crom Cruach! He *wounded the monster —*"

"And what good is that? Who cares for a paltry victory such as that? It is *his* king that is the trouble, not ours. It is his *world* that is in trouble, not ours! An outsider, bringing grief down on us — all that was our lives, burnt up and vanished, and no protection under which to rebuild it! What have we left now, hmm? Ashes? Smoke! What are we to feed our children, *Chosen of the God!*"

Marcas snarled. His body trembled — there was a shift in the outlines of his flesh, not a change but the promise of one, not the wolf's being but the pressure of its presence.

"No, Marcas."

The blue eyes stared back at him, bright glow in them, terrible fury, terrible purpose — *protect. I will protect you, Connor.* Still he reached out, put a hand on Marcas' shoulder, and when he couldn't pull Marcas back, pulled himself forward.

"*No.* Marcas, he spoke to *me.*" And he turned to the man who had addressed him, the anger in his face overwhelmed by fear. Connor saw only a pitiful man, afraid of everything — maybe right to be so, but still pitiful for the fact.

Connor had stood against the lord of the mound, wounded him and survived, saved the only one who mattered to him — the only one he loved. What was one little man now? He saw again in his mind's eye the black and smokeless ashes that were all that remained of his father's house, his family, his past.

"Tell me, old man. What were you planning to feed them when they were dead?"

He turned his eyes on the other elders, each in turn — looked from them to nearby strangers, each one watching with a breathless expression, struck by his cruel words — but he wasn't finished.

"What were you planning to do besides cower and pray not to die—cower, as you have done for how many years, while the rest of the world suffered from the servants of Crom Cruach?"

"Don't say that name!"

"I cut off his hand—I'll call my enemy what I please!"

"And what about the price, boy?"

"*Price*? Price! You have your *lives*. Everything else can be rebuilt. Maybe even the protection you treasure so much—though why, I don't know."

"Because you cannot kill the dark one! He cannot be destroyed—"

"Who cares?" Connor bared his teeth, the grin he'd learned in battle. "Who cares, old man? If you can't kill the darkness, you can drive it out with the light. Wound it. Turn it back—turn it back forever! But there's no excuse for cowardice like yours." He turned to Marcas. "Are we done here? If I go, Crom Cruach will follow me. Next nightfall, or the next—eventually he'll come for vengeance. It would be better in the open—or with warriors behind us. Anywhere but here."

There was something sad in Marcas' blue eyes, something that Connor didn't understand—had it been something he'd said? But Marcas had been as angry at the old fool as he was. Still, there was no more chance for conversation—beside him, Marcas was no longer a man.

* * * *

Marcas let the wolf within him overtake the boundaries of reason. The night was growing old, and dawn would come soon, full of mortal promises and a light that might bring hope, but not safety — not really. Night would fall again.

When it did, he hoped to be far from here, on whatever path they had chosen — he and Connor. He wanted to find a place where the shadow would not come stalking right away, unless perhaps fear might keep the darkness back, keep it from searching for the one who had wounded it... *But that's too much to hope, isn't it?* The lord of the mound was patient, but only in his own time. If it was even fear and not just surprise that had moved him, it was sure not to last for long. Such was the nature of their enemy.

Anxious, he paced back and forth before Connor, showed his teeth to the others who stood near him, looked up and met the boy's eyes. *Come with me. Come with me — no time now. Leave them and come with me. We have to do what must be done. We have to find out what that is.*

Either Connor understood the pleading of his gaze, or he had reason of his own not to stay any longer. He turned and climbed on Marcas' back without wait or hesitation, tightened his fingers in the fur of his ruff, squeezed his thighs at Marcas' sides.

"Run, Marcas."

The words came low and close to his ear, and Marcas tossed his head once to acknowledge Connor's instruction before he sped away from the heat of the fire, the choking ash. There was outcry as they vanished into the smoke and beyond it, but Marcas ignored it. He had to. No time now for kin or old men — he had seen his sister in the mass of waiting people, children clustered around her. The ones he cared for would live. What else was there to worry about?

Crom Cruach had come after his ancient enemies and won a new foe instead.

Marcas bared his fangs at the night as he ran into the north. He intended to work his way inland a bit at a time, farther into the stretches of green hills that spread across the middle of Eire and away from the dangerous coast. He would run until the dark line of the horizon turned white with dawn, a time that wasn't far off now.

The indigo weight of the sky was already a faded bruise of lighter purple and many blues — then there was yellow, and a flush of red light that threaded upward behind banks of clouds blowing in from nearer than the sunrise.

With the clouds came the odor of rain, not yet falling but soon, soon… It would be a dark day by noon, or shortly after. A little at a time, the air grew thick, sweet-dusty, an odor that settled like fog and clung to the ground. Marcas considered all the times he had run over this ground. Was there shelter? No house, no hall that he could think of. There were thickets, though, many nearby that would provide some cover if the sky opened up.

Dawn came, wetly, the first drops beginning to fall as the sun dragged over the horizon. Connor leaned forward as the rain intensified, pressed himself close to the warmth and relative dryness of Marcas' fur beneath him. Fast as he was running, Marcas had to squint his eyes against the raindrops, felt them pelt against his fur like pebbles. It would be harsher for Connor, unprotected on his back, and he sped toward the nearest overhang of dark leaves, waxy and dripping now under the downpour. Deeper into the trees there was dryness still under his paws, the crunching of old needles, old leaves, and only here and there a drop that made its way through the tight-woven canopy.

Connor slid from his back almost at once, soaking himself further on Marcas' wet fur, then stood away and raised his eyebrows.

"If you're going to shake, do it now—I'm wet enough already."

Marcas huffed faintly, amused, but the temptation was there and undeniable. He felt better when he was done, less clinging wetness, even if he was still more than damp all over. *What I wouldn't give for a towel.* But it didn't matter. Connor was already working at building a fire, seeking out dry wood beneath the damp topcoat of leaves on the forest floor.

He was tempted to stay as the wolf, for a while anyway—until he was dry and warm. He would be warming to Connor, too. But there remained the problem of speech, and there were too many things they needed to talk about for it to be postponed. In the silence of their resting time, Connor would talk to him—he always had, anyway—and that would be enough to learn where Connor needed to go, but not more than that. With a sigh that was more of a *huff* in the wolf-shape, Marcas sought inward for the changeling energy, and froze.

There was nothing within him. No power. No sense of *self*, nothing beneath the surface. Where was his human self, the shape he belonged in? *Deeper, reach deeper.* And yet no matter where he struck inward, there was only confusion, emptiness. Only the wolf remained, and no hint of another set of features or a fangless smile. *Where? Where did it go? When did it go?* Fear was rising in him, writhing in him, entangling thought and movement with deadly coils.

No more words. No more of love. Never again to wake beside him. To touch him. Connor —

One after another, high, painful howls pierced the leaves, seeking the sky, freedom for the sound if there was freedom for nothing else.

"Marcas! What's wrong?"

Connor was by his side in a moment, strong fingers steadying the great wolf muzzle. Marcas didn't know what Connor saw in his eyes — *something* — enough that he went from crouching before him to on his knees, new tensions in his fingers.

"Marcas, change back and tell me what's wrong. We aren't running for a while —"

A long, keening whine escaped Marcas' throat. Connor's hands tightened in his fur.

"Change *back*, Marcas."

Shaking his head, drowning in hurt, Marcas pulled his head out of Connor's hands and backed away. Connor went with him even out into the rain, stood under the downpour with his fists clenched and terrible awareness growing on his face as Marcas turned his nose up to the sky and howled again and again, tried vainly to make the change of which there was no sign within him.

Heartbroken, he crouched finally with his legs drawn under him, his eyes squeezed shut and the cold rain pouring down. He heard a heavy thud as Connor sank to his knees in the mud by his side, felt warm arms embracing him through the cold.

"Marcas. Marcas — if you can't change back — what do we do? *I love you.* Marcas, I love you. What are we going to do?"

Even if he'd been able to speak, Marcas would have had no answer, but because he couldn't, the pain of the moment seemed somehow worse. He lifted his head and met Connor's gaze — then, slowly, he pushed himself to his feet, caught hold of Connor's tunic in his teeth and pulled gently toward the thicket. It was too cold and too wet for him to be sitting in the open, and no matter their other problems, nothing would be helped if Connor was ill.

* * * *

By noon, the dim cloudiness of the morning had passed, and Connor looked up at the canopy and the broken light that came through the numerous leaves with exhaustion printed on his face and in his movements. It had been a long night of no sleep, battle and running. It had been a longer morning, fear and pain and heartbreak tangling themselves around…everything.

Despite the returning sunlight, the air remained damp and chill. Connor huddled close to the fire he had built, the damp, warm bulk of Marcas' great wolf shape pressed close against his back, half curled around him. Marcas, too, was not sleeping, though he probably should be even more than Connor. *He was the one who did the work of running.* But Marcas had chosen to sit and look into the fire instead, a steady and unblinking stare.

Connor thought he could guess what Marcas was thinking. His own questions were the same as he thought Marcas' would be, only tinged with guilt. *Why? Why now? Why would this happen? Why take his own shape from him, why trap him as a wolf?* Could it be his fault? Had he done something…? Had it happened with the healing? When the spear had broken — when the wolves had howled out of nowhere —

"You swallowed the moon, Marcas. Is it my fault?"

He was not, at first, aware that he had spoken aloud. Not until he felt the wolf's cold nose press against his palm, looked down and saw sad reassurance reflected in the blue, blue eyes. *Not you. Never you.* And yet he couldn't believe it. Wouldn't it have changed something? Couldn't it have, at least? Did either of them know what had really happened? Connor didn't—not a clue. Only the results were obvious to him, not the process or the power that had made them possible. *So what if?* His carelessness had been the only reason Marcas was wounded. Because he had tried to fight Crom Cruach as if he were a man...and an honorable man, at that.

"Marcas, when the spear broke—when it healed you—there was howling. There were *wolves,* and a stag that wasn't a stag, and—" But he couldn't say it again. *You swallowed the moon, Marcas.*

There were questions in Marcas' eyes now, and a thoughtful grimace stretched the face of the wolf. But even if Marcas had answers it wouldn't matter. There were many things that Connor understood, just in a glance—a look, a huff of laughter, a wry twist of the wolf-mouth. This—this was not one of those things. Sighing, a sharp pain in his chest now, Connor settled himself against the length of Marcas' body and closed his eyes. One way or another, they'd figure this out like everything else. He wasn't going to give up, not now, not easily, but perhaps it didn't matter. There was Crom Cruach to deal with before the unfulfilled future was even a problem. There was battle ahead, even if the thought of planning it without Marcas' input was a trial on its own.

With the warmth of the wolf behind him and the warmth of the fire before him, it wasn't long before Connor succumbed to sleep, though his dreams were far from pleasant. Everything was dark inside him. He could hide neither from the pain nor the fear. In his dreams he was alone, and a wolf stalked his shadow, filling him with grief. In his dreams, the future unrolled before him, his enemy defeated, and the green returned to the world, no fear in the moonlight and the sun gold on the grass in all its seasons—and still no succor, no end to the pain, no hiding place. A wolf at the hearth of the halls of his father's, in the dream restored—a wolf on the hearth, and its fur growing gray in time with his hair. Never again to hear the sound of that voice caress his name. Never again a sweeter moment than what had been. Never again the touch of those rough fingers—not in love, not in lust, neither for comfort nor to compel. A head on his knee, warm, an always-companion—yes, a head on his knee but never again the perfect surrender.

Never again even a kiss.

It was a life that passed before him, the way lives do in dreams, years and decades compressed into the span of a single nightmare. In the dream, he wept for all that he had gained and all that he had lost—the price never meant to be paid.

Chapter Fourteen

Marcas watched tears roll down Connor's face. Whatever he was dreaming, it was no escape from pain. Marcas knew an equal sorrow, but had no expression for it, no tears of his own, nothing but the howl he would not give voice to. Not now. Not while Connor was sleeping—and what would it do but prove to him that this flesh and its powers had become his prison? Restless, he shifted. Connor's arms came up around him, circled as much of his body as he could reach.

He had offered himself to the god and his power, to the future and its protection. To the protection of this one above all others, and yet—*and yet*—this was not how it was supposed to be. He heard the god's voice again, that first and most terrible question, the question that had shaped everything which came after. *"How much would you give?"*

I said any price. Any price, and is this – ?

But he couldn't bring himself to complete the thought, even if it was already there, hovering, its claws sunk into his brain. He squeezed his eyes shut tight, then returned his gaze to the embers of Connor's morning fire, squinted against the smoke when the wind changed direction. He laid his head on Connor's side and listened to the sound of the rain dripping through the leaves. Then he closed his eyes to the world and its broken promises.

When he opened them again, it was almost dark. He woke from a nap he hadn't intended all at once, as if called, his brain fuzzed with sleep and only a single awareness at the forefront of his thoughts. *Night is come.* In the instant between one blink and the next, the edge of twilight that had hovered in the sky when he opened his eyes became true dark, the sharp fall of an ax that cleaved the light from the world.

Marcas unwound himself from around Connor, tried not to disturb him but couldn't help it in the end. The boy was tangled with him, his head pillowed on the soft ruff of fur around Marcas' neck, one arm slung over Marcas' shoulders and the other slipped between Marcas' forelegs, his hand resting on one great paw. *That's not right…*

Easily, as if there had been no trouble in the morning, Marcas reached within himself for the slippery power that was responsible for his change, one form to another. He slipped from wolf shape to man shape and only then remembered in a flash the failure, the fear. *But why? Why now and not then?*

It didn't matter. He could think later—Connor would help him. For now he wanted nothing but to hold the boy in his arms, and so he did. Connor was on the brink of wakefulness already, but Marcas' kisses were enough to bring him up to full consciousness, enough to make him open his eyes.

"*Marcas.*" Such relief in his voice! "How did you—?" He met every one of Marcas' kisses with his mouth, pressed his lips against Marcas' lips, his jaw, his throat, ran his hands again and again over as much of Marcas' body as he could reach. *Warmth.* All the touch that Marcas had been missing, the sensation of skin against skin, rough fingertips, seeking and perfect.

"I don't—I don't know." Marcas' answer came between exchanges of hot breath, between one kiss and the next. Connor's fingers traced the muscles in his arms, the shape of his hands. For a moment, Connor's fingers ran over the backs of his fingers, laced their hands together. Then Connor was reaching out again, his hands grasping at Marcas back, his hip, his thigh, pulling him closer, closer—there was heat between them, instant fire, sparkless, quick-burning.

Marcas became aware of the heat of Connor's erection pressed against his thigh in the same moment that he became aware of the hardness of his own cock, the same moment he saw a single bar of moonlight reflected and broken many times by the relieved tears clinging to Connor's eyelashes.

"*Connor.*" The name sounded harsh to his ears, and the gasp Connor made when he closed his fingers around the boy's erection, bent forward and dragged his tongue along his throat, was sweet in comparison.

"I thought you—that you wouldn't ever—*oh yes.*"

The words came drawn out and unsubtle in their inflection—*ohhh yesss.* There was an equal pleasure for Marcas in the grip of Connor's fingers on his cock, the jerky grasp that smoothed into luscious rhythm, matched the movements of his own hands. Connor's mouth was in constant motion, one kiss after another—he bit Marcas' lip, kissed his throat, nipped at his shoulder, his collarbone, sucked heat to the surface and groaned against Marcas' skin.

"Love you—Marcas—*love* you—"

His fingers were hot, rough, stroked together with Marcas' rhythm. Pleasure coiled and surged under that touch, and beside him, beneath him, Connor cried out and Marcas felt wetness over his fingers, up onto Connor's chest as Connor shook under him. His fingers went jerky and tight, and Marcas stiffened, moaned, thrust against Connor's hand, mindless now, nerves moving him, the slick pulse of his release.

He breathed Connor's name until he was left empty, shuddering as Connor's fingers moved lazily along his cock, then to his thigh, his chest, reassuring himself with the proof of Marcas' human presence. The moment was beautiful in its way, but as his head cleared, Marcas felt the tingling awareness of his wolf self moving within him, warning.

It was night now, and the danger was great and growing. There was no time for sweetness, for *more* — not even time for the questions he had accumulated in a day of forced silence. *Only what's necessary.*

"Connor... We can't stay here for long. Or at all — so before we're off, tell me my direction."

Connor yawned, rolled a little more onto his side, reached out and ran his fingers through Marcas' hair. "To Lord Aran — his hall past the cattle pastures in the north."

Despite himself, Marcas gave in to the touch, its softness, leaned down and rested his forehead in the curve of Connor's neck.

"He was a lord under my father, but he owes me his service now. There was no man more loyal — if nothing else, it'll be a good resting place."

Connor's fingers continued their slow combing through Marcas' hair, but there was tension in them now and when Marcas pulled away and looked up at Connor's face, there was something hard there. *The warrior in him.* But it was more than that. *The king.* Yes. That was it. And how strange it was to contemplate — why hadn't he ever considered it before? *The son of a king becomes a king himself.*

"Connor…"

Marcas mourned the loss of Connor's warmth, his closeness, as the boy pulled away from him and stood. He wiped wetness from his chest, his cock, his thighs with the bloody and torn tunic he'd discarded, then tossed it at Marcas. Anything he had intended to say was circumvented by Connor speaking, going back to the beginning of their conversation as if the rest hadn't happened.

"Do we have time to eat before we leave here?"

Marcas took a breath, then shrugged and pushed himself to his feet.

"Time? No, not really, but we need to regardless. Then…"

"Then?"

For another moment Marcas hesitated, facing his own fear, the terror of the morning. *But there is no other choice. There is no other way.*

"Then we run. We might make your Lord Aran's hall before morning."

"But you — what if it happens again?"

There was true panic in Connor's voice, the same fear that Marcas himself felt. *What if once again I can't change back?* But hearing it in Connor's words only reinforced his resolve.

"Then it happens again. I won't give you up, Connor." Marcas took two swift steps forward, drew Connor into his embrace. "You keep saying you love me. Don't forget I love *you.* That I've loved you since I was only the wolf that watched you. I think I loved you before I knew your name." Twice, bare brushes of his lips, Marcas kissed him. Then once more, roughly, before he pulled away. "Now come on—food and then we get out of here, quick as we can."

* * * *

Connor found hard, dark bread, skins of mead and water, dried meat in quantities that surprised him and a number of sweet, bright apples when he went looking for food in the bag Marcas had insisted he bring with them. There were clean clothes too, and though he longed for a bath, Connor found that pleasing enough for now.

He tossed the package of meat at Marcas, bit into an apple and held it in his teeth as he fished out a clean tunic and tossed it over his head. He finished his bite with a satisfying *crunch* and looked over to see Marcas *tearing* at a strip of dried venison.

Wolf of mine—he laughed, couldn't help himself, but Marcas only looked up at him, raised his eyebrows. *What?* That was what the blue eyes were saying, and not even a lick of shame in them. *But I don't want shame.* He grinned. "I love you, Marcas." Marcas blinked at him, as if wondering what had brought on his sudden affirmation, but Connor didn't care. *This* was what it meant to be in love, to have something more than lust tying you together to the one you wanted, needed—*more*. Whatever *more* was, it was enough for him to know that Marcas loved him, chose him, would stay with him.

He felt the truth settle in him, heavy and comforting and hot. He turned away from fear and worry, tore off a hunk of bread and bit into it, thinking now about the future and now to make what he wanted out of it. They'd go to Aran, bring him the truth of the enemy that stalked them, the truth of what had happened to Tigernmas. *If he's still alive. If he doesn't already know.*

He chewed thoughtfully at a mouthful of apple, gnawed the core down to stem and seeds, then crossed to sit beside Marcas. He snagged a strip of venison, rested his elbow on his knee and his chin on his hand. "Marcas, we need a plan before we get to Aran. Something to tell him, some way…to attack our enemy."

Marcas regarded him for a moment.

"This sacrifice has strengthened him, and taking the body of your High King has strengthened him, and every death since—even to fight him strengthens him."

"He only comes for us at night, does that—"

"You won't find the bent one in the daylight hours. If you can, I commend you—but in ten thousand years, he has only once been dragged out into the light of day."

"And if he's still in Tigernmas' hall, that won't be enough to catch him and call him out?"

"No. You know only where the body he's possessed is—but that is just a body. You proved it when you cut off his hand. You saw, if I did—what happened to that *flesh* once it was separated from the rest of his being."

Connor shuddered. He had seen—how could he not have seen? But he had *heard* too, the scream that was not the scream of Tigernmas, but the scream of what was *other*. The scream of Crom Cruach. He heard again its echo, terrible, the end of everything—

"Connor?"

Marcas' voice jerked him out of the memory.

"It's nothing. Is there any point in asking what's been done before, to hold the bent one back? Since it hasn't worked?"

"Worked?" Marcas frowned. "That isn't the fault of the method, Connor, just a fact of the situation. *The lord of the mound cannot be killed.* If he could, the world itself would unravel. There was darkness before all things, and there will be darkness after all things—"

"I know—you said that. But why hasn't anything been found to put him to sleep forever?"

"Forever is...a very long time. Still, a thousand years, or ten thousand—those are a long time too."

"Not long enough." Connor was growing in bitterness, in anger at the constraints on him—a warrior who couldn't kill his enemy, couldn't face his foe. "Why does this fall to *us*, anyway? The Dagda is the one with power. There was that barrier—why not a barrier like that over...over everything!"

"Because that wouldn't be enough. And the barrier... It's fallen now. A greater one might have done so sooner."

Connor waved away his words impatiently.

"But that's not my point. The Dagda is the source of life. There's nothing else, no other power that's a match for a dark god."

"The source of life..." Marcas echoed Connor's words, then jerked his eyes up to Connor's face. "Connor! There's another access to that power, that *source*. The Cauldron, full forever, never emptied. Connor—"

"Marcas, what—?"

"If there's one thing that could hold the lord of the mound—" Marcas wet his lips, let out a slow breath. "The bent one takes life from things. He wants everything to end. Could there be a worse challenge, something he would want to destroy more than an artifact whose power is the source of life?"

"Marcas *what* are you talking about?"

"The Cauldron of the Dagda. The last of the four ancient treasures of Eire to come to men. But there's no guarantee. He might just destroy it—and then what would be the gain? One of the treasures of the world lost, and we would still be left with the problem of a dark god."

Marcas' eyes lost the spark of brilliance that had come to him with the idea, but Connor shook his head, reached out and took Marcas' face in his hands. "Does it matter? If we all died, would the world care that it had lost such a treasure? It's worth trying if there's any chance it would work." He paused, grinned as a thought occurred to him. "Still, I don't even know what we'd do with it if we had it. Roll it in front of him and try to get him to fall inside?"

Marcas shrugged, smiled a little himself but the smile was listless.

"Connor, *having* it is not the problem."

"We don't have time to go out *questing* for—"

"I know where it is." Marcas' quiet words silenced Connor completely. "You know, too. If you think about it."

Connor's features relaxed the moment his mind made the connection between impossible things and things he should know. *The barrow!* Slowly, Marcas nodded, confirming his thought without a sound.

"We would have to bring it to him. To a place of power—focus all his attention on it. And even to call him..." Marcas paused, and the expression on his face went...strange. "But perhaps that won't be so hard. Blood's needed."

"Blood—" Connor hesitated to continue speaking his thoughts.

"Not a true sacrifice." Marcas amended his words quickly. "But as far as something that will call him there—I don't think anything will work as well as *you*, little as I want to admit it."

"Me—"

"You should have been part of the first sacrifice. You should have died at his hand how many times now? You challenged him—you wounded him. Of all the people in the world, you're one he won't wait on coming for."

"The meat in the trap, then." Humorless laughter slid out of Connor's throat, faded fast. "All right. I'll do it—*we'll* do it. Quickly, Connor packed what was left of the food in its bag, grabbed up both and strode back to Marcas side. "We know what we have to do now."

"Yes."

"Then let's go—let's *go*."

Marcas met his eyes, nodded, and Connor saw the blue of his eyes go momentarily bright, couldn't help himself from reaching out. *"Wait."* He stepped forward, wrapped his arms tight around Marcas, *tight*. When he lifted his head from Marcas' chest, Marcas was already bending to kiss him, one rough and hungry embrace. *Just in case*. That was what the blue eyes said to him. *Just in case*.

Connor was still licking his lips when Marcas stepped back, stood straight and *changed*.

* * * *

The long hours of his run through the darkness were a trial the likes of which Marcas had never known. Again and again, he reached inside himself, touched with relief the sparkling presence of his own image, the transient flesh that was still his own. Each time, he feared the return of the shudder of emptiness that had clawed out his soul the previous morning. *As if my heart fell out of my throat.* But no. *All is as it should be.*

On his back, Connor's weight was a comforting promise. The warmth of his last embrace was continued as Marcas ran, warm arms around his neck, warm body draped along his back, and now and then a warm murmur of breath near his ear as some thought occurred to Connor that he didn't want to lose.

With the speed of a wildfire, Marcas flashed across the grass, past great tracks of murmuring forests. Finally he came to a long river whose banks bore the scents and the prints of many booted feet and mingled among them, from some time past now, was the scent of the man he remembered.

As he followed the river, Connor became more alert, more watchful on his back. He was ready for the grip that tightened when it came, the harsh whisper in his ear.

"Stop here, Marcas. I know where we are, and we're close enough."

Connor dismounted easily and in an instant, as if there had been no doubt in him, Marcas returned to his own shape. At this second change, wolf to man's flesh, there was a relaxing of internal tension, the accumulated worry of the previous day. Something had been wrong, but whatever it was, it had no effect now, no influence over him. *Perhaps I was just…tired.*

He looked across at Connor and saw relief equal to his own on the boy's face, but he bent almost at once and began to dig through the bag of clothes they'd brought with them, tossed a tunic at Marcas with a wider grin than he'd worn since they'd left the *faoladh* village behind.

"Here, put these on. Much as I love to look at you, I don't think Aran will appreciate it as much."

Marcas snorted. "Of course not. And what exactly do you plan on doing, anyway, walking up to his gate and announcing yourself?"

"Yes."

The short answer surprised him, and Marcas lifted his eyebrows, turned and saw for the second time a hard expression on Connor's face, something of himself turned inward.

"What? Did you think I'd have something else planned? My father is dead, and I'm the King of Connacht. Lord Aran is mine, and all his men — even if they don't know it yet. Even if they think me dead."

"Why would they — ?"

"I was wounded and alone — do you think, when I wasn't to be found, that they assumed one of the *faoladh* had come for me, healed me and saved me, or just that I was one of the dead?"

"Connor..."

"So I'll go to his gate, and give his men my name, and wait. There might be trouble, and there might not — some of them know me, his men. More of them knew my father. It's too bad I don't have his *look*."

"I'll be with you, no matter what."

There was a flicker in the dark shield of Connor's features, a softness in his eyes, but it passed quickly.

"I know. I know you will, Marcas. Come on, I don't want to call *him* here. There's been enough destroyed already on my account."

Marcas opened his mouth, but could find no words to respond to that, nothing but vain denials that he knew Connor wouldn't want to hear. He followed Connor out of the shadow of the wood and up onto the road. He paused only for a moment, looked north and south, then began walking north at a brisk pace. Whatever Connor's thoughts were, they were so quiet inside himself that they weren't even visible on his face. Yet still, by the time five minutes had passed, Connor was walking by his side, their fingers caught against each other.

Marcas took comfort from that. No matter what else happened, there was this—there must always be this.

* * * *

The gates of Lord Aran's *ráth* were not as Connor remembered them. Defenses had been expanded and widened, earthworks thrown up a quarter of a mile from where the farthest such protections had once been. Stake-wall after stake-wall was visible in the moonlight. Torches sent flares of light across dikes and ramparts, and the noises of many men became steadily more audible the closer he came.

Unconsciously, he tightened his grip on Marcas' fingers and didn't realize he had done so until he felt the answering tightness of Marcas' grip. *Steady, Connor, steady. You're the son of their king, remember?*

Except that he also remembered that the enemy wore the flesh of Tigernmas, a higher king than his father. Except that he came alone out of the night, no horse, no men, no guards or warriors, no banner or treasure—only his name, and Marcas. *It'll have to be enough.*

"Who is it there? Who comes this way? This land belongs to the Lord Aran!"

The shout came out of the night from a rampart whose torches blinded Connor to the face of the one calling—but he knew the same wouldn't be true for the one who had seen him. His doubts fell away at the sound. What did it matter if all he brought was his name? *That is enough.*

"I am Connor of Connacht, the son of Brádach the King. I've come to meet with your lord—bring me to him!"

His shout was loud enough to be heard by the one who'd called out to him and many more, and he heard loud exclamations of surprise, and disbelief, and confusion.

"That can't be! The one who bore that name is dead."

"I am *not* dead. Bring me to Lord Aran. He knows me, even if you don't!"

There was more noise, words that Connor couldn't pick up, though by the expression on Marcas' face *he* could and didn't like what he was hearing. Though it took some minutes, eventually the clattering noise of the men resolved into a group of white faces, visible in the torchlight. Connor didn't know them, but all of them wore cloaks of dark blue secured with a brooch in the shape of a raven's head. *Aran's men, then.*

They stared back at him, some of them looking over his shoulder at Marcas, and Connor let go of Marcas' hand and straightened his back. The brooches were all bronze, except one—and the gold one, that one would be some captain or commander. He locked eyes with that man, saw fear there and wariness, utter distrust.

"Do you hear me, man? I am your king, and I have need of your lord. Bring me to him!"

Whether it was the words themselves or something in Connor's voice, he didn't know, but the man confronting him relaxed the barest bit, took a step back and nodded. "We can deny no help in times like these. I hope for your sake you are who you say you are—but you haven't said anything about your companion."

"Marcas is mine. Do you need to know more than that?"

More questions formed in the furrows of the man's brow, the downturned corners of his lips, but he said nothing more about Marcas, asked no more questions. Instead he turned and gestured for the men who'd come with him to stand aside. He took a torch from one of them, then gestured at Connor and spoke with obvious hesitation.

"Follow me...my lord."

A tight smile crossed Connor's lips, then faded. As he followed the guard up earthen ramps, past many dikes and walls of stakes and mounds of earth, around and again around the great circular mound of the lord Aran's *ráth*, Connor tracked with his eyes, counting work and men.

There were fires visible on the plains below the great mound of the fortress, the simple dikes and stake-wall that had once guarded the *ráth* hidden behind the fires of many men, stables built quick for the keeping of the horses of many lords... Banners, banners flying in the dark, lit from below by the lights of the fires and torches that showed him the pale faces of many hundred men. He couldn't understand where so many had come from. Surely Lord Aran didn't have such a force at his disposal and most of those banners—

But they passed out of sight of the ground below as they went up the last dirt ramp and past the old wall of fire-hardened oak that Connor remembered from his visits to this place. There was a quiet aura over the roundhouses, over even the main hall to which he saw they were being led. Part of him wanted to reach back for Marcas, pull him close again—reassurance that he knew he couldn't allow himself, not here, not now.

Later, he promised himself. Later, when there was somewhere they could be alone together. There could be no showing of weakness here, nor a moment of uncertainty. Not before this man who didn't know him, especially... And perhaps not in front of Lord Aran, either. A man who had always agreed with his father, about everything—a man who had pushed daughters at him at every opportunity, a man who surely would continue to do so now, when he was not prince but king. A man who would not approve of his feelings for Marcas, his intentions for the future.

Lost in thought, he heard Aran speak before he noticed that they'd stopped moving and the man was in front of them.

"Connor! By the gods—you're alive! You're alive, boy—" The man came toward him quickly, arms outstretched, grabbed hold of both his arms and held him tightly. "Alive, and well too! When there was no one with the herds, we were afraid that you—but you're alive!"

"We? Who is we, Aran? There must be five thousand men outside, and I couldn't understand... But if it's we, then who else lives?"

Connor held the Lord Aran's eyes with a stare that would not relent. Before his eyes, the man seemed to become old—not that he was young, he had never been young, had had gray threads in his beard even when Connor was a boy. But now...no steel in his spine. No steel in his glance and his grip on Connor's arms slackening, the fingers sharper, weaker, an old man's claw and not a warrior's hand.

"We...are your father and I, Connor."

Connor jerked backwards, stumbled against Marcas and felt steadying hands grip his shoulders, squeeze tight for just an instant before they let him go. He felt the imprint of warm fingers longer than the touch lasted, shot a grateful smile over his shoulder, then took a shuddering breath and squared himself.

"My father is *alive*? I thought he was dead—I thought—bring me to him!"

"Connor...perhaps you should bathe and rest first, eat something—"

"Bring me to him *now*."

He set his jaw and held Aran once more with an unrelenting stare.

"Very...very well. And your friend?"

"Marcas is more than a *friend*. I owe him my life a dozen times over. He comes with me."

There was warmth behind him as Marcas stepped close, just his presence, his nearness a comfort. For a second time, Connor restrained himself, did not reach back, but it was harder now. *What has happened to my father?* He had learned too well that there were things worse than death.

One step at a time, he followed Aran as the old man led them away.

* * * *

Marcas followed in Connor's footsteps, out of the hall and to a roundhouse near the southern wall. Already, he could tell that Connor's father might be alive, but he wasn't likely to be so for long. The stench of suppuration wore death as an outer layer and clung to the odor of the man. When they passed over the threshold of the roundhouse, Marcas nearly gagged, but Connor didn't seem to notice. His gaze was fixed on his father's face, yellowish and pale.

Stained linen was bound about his brow, over his massive chest. If he hadn't known this man for Connor's father, Marcas never would have believed they were related, but the red-bearded bear of a man wasting away on the great bed blinked his eyes open then, and Marcas saw a familiar shade of green.

"Aran."

The man's voice was thin, whistling, no strength in it and hardly any breath.

"I am here, my king—and I've brought someone you'll be glad to see. Your son lives." And Lord Aran beckoned Connor closer, but it was unnecessary. Connor was already walking forward, until his legs were pressed against the side of the bed. He reached out for his father's hand, and Marcas was stepping forward the moment he recoiled, gripped his shoulder, held him still. The furs had concealed the truth—there was no hand for Connor to hold, just a stained bandage, a stump that ended halfway down his father's forearm.

"When—"

Gruff, thick, Connor cast the question over his shoulder at Aran.

"The sacrifice. There was trouble—your father's wounds from that last battle were not healed, but you knew that. He would not stay back. Brádach went forward with the front lines, led all those who would follow against the High King, against his men, against the black priests. By the time we got away, there was no way to save the hand, and the other...he wouldn't let us take the other."

Marcas' gaze zeroed in on Connor's father's other arm, elbow to fingertips wrapped in a thick layer of linen — whole, still, this arm, but it was from whatever wound had been inflicted that the terrible smell was rising. Connor, too, was looking, but bereft of the wolf senses that Marcas possessed, he seemed only relieved to find that his father was not totally disabled.

"Connor. My son."

The words were full of breath, almost inaudible, but Connor leaned forward at once, gripped his father's shoulder.

"I'm here, Father. I thought you were dead."

"Not yet. Soon enough." He laughed, a choking sound without humor. Marcas looked away. What a broken man. Alive, but not for long, broken as a man, as a king, as a warrior — did Connor see it? Death in the rheumy green eyes, death curled around this man like a cloak, more than scent, a moving presence. Out of the corner of his eye, he saw Connor shaking his head, and let out a slow breath.

"It's my fault. My fault — I should have been with you. I should have been *careful* —"

No, Connor. Don't hold onto that —

"No!"

There was more strength in that word than there had been in all those Brádach had spoken previously, and the cough that racked him, the pain sprawled across his face spoke of what it had cost him. Still, he continued.

"There is *no blame for you*, do you understand?" He took a labored breath. "Do you understand, Connor? I made... I made my own choices! The wrong ones, maybe, for the right...for the right reasons. I rose up against...Tigernmas. I led the charge — *such a battle, my son*." For a long minute he was silent, breathing shallow breaths with all the effort of deep ones. "Worth a king's death, that battle."

Marcas heard the words, and also the truth beneath them, the things not spoken openly. The summoning of the lord of the mound had been the source of all agonies. This dying man, king that he had been, would be counted rebel or exile by any of those who still counted themselves loyal to their High King—and Connor, too, would be counted such. *How many have seen the truth? How many know what dangers are waiting in the dark?* But Brádach was speaking again.

"I am no king any longer, my son." He lifted the dead stump of his shield arm. "But you, Connor. You have...changed, and you are fit and strong and young—healed, better than I could have hoped."

Connor looked away from him.

Marcas saw many things trembling behind the stubborn, stoic mask that Connor had fitted across his features—awareness of truths, and fears, and the collapse of all the false hopes that had sustained him since he had heard his father was still alive—since he had entered this room. The reality was settling in him now.

Even if a miracle could save Brádach, a king must be a whole man. One who had suffered such a wound as his father would never be seen as fit to lead by the clans and families that must believe in him. He met Marcas' gaze and there was pleading in his eyes and more. Marcas saw the whole story of the last eight weeks settling on the edge of Connor's tongue, and he knew the reason for it. He wanted to share, and he didn't want to lie to his father.

Privately, Marcas considered that the boy might speak later whether he gave permission or not—that perhaps this could be a test...but no. What was the point? Things like that were just the ways that fools with no confidence in where they'd placed their trust acted. And either way, Connor's father looked like he wouldn't last another day. Whether he gave his permission or not, whether Connor said anything or not, the secret would go nowhere.

The other man, Aran... Marcas hesitated, but was there a point in delaying the truth? If he was to be their ally, he would have to know it all, and who better to tell him than Connor? When better than now?

He took a step forward, reached out and squeezed Connor's arm once. "Say what you need to say. I'll be outside when you've finished."

Gratitude glowed from Connor's face. Marcas let his fingers cross past Connor's as he let go of his arm — just once, a brush, the barest squeeze. Then he turned away, nodded once at the Lord Aran and stepped over the threshold and outside. He heard Connor beginning the tale he'd known the boy would tell.

"Father, do you remember the wolf that saved us when night fell on the battlefield?"

He smiled to himself and wondered if either of the men listening would believe it, but as the tale wound on and the night brightened into the morning twilight, there were no interruptions and no pauses longer than it took Connor to take a breath. When he was done, there was a silence that coiled out into the dim air and wrapped around Marcas, brought him to his feet. There were a few low questions then, the rasping voice of the dying man, and footsteps that brought Lord Aran outside to stand beside him.

The man looked at Marcas with a mask of silence on his face, all things concealed, but the question he asked revealed what he wanted to hide even in a toneless voice.

"Is it true, what the boy said?"

"You shouldn't call him that. Connor is your king now."

"Answer the question. That boy is the son of one who is like a brother to me, and the things he says—"

Marcas turned his gaze on the old man, the eyes he knew could reflect the thousand blues of winter or the soul of the savage wolf. It was the wolf he gave up now, the leaping protector, the white of the moonlight, the bright of the stars—a presence he knew could dart like a spear to the heart of any being. It passed in an instant, a great swelling thing, a sealess tide, but what it left behind was *truth*. The mark of awareness was written wide and dark on the old man's face, setting seams and creases into bronze-shadowed relief.

"It's true. It's true! But you—you did not save my sons! Why save me and not them? Why an old man, when they had so much promise?"

Aran's words settled into the silence around Marcas, weighted stones of voice. This time the stirring of the wolf within him was stronger, came from no prodding but that of the man's own questions, his accusation.

"I bear no responsibility for the death of any man. I am only responsible for those who are meant to *live*— and I do not get to choose who those are. It wasn't you, old man—or the one dying. It was Connor that I was sent for—it's Connor I protect. You are alive because he would not have left you behind."

The old man let out a breath. "I apologize. It has not been—easy. I owe you a debt. Your name is...Marcas?"

"Yes."

"I will remember."

Stiffly, his back straight, Lord Aran left Marcas alone with his surprise and walked away into the light.

Chapter Fifteen

Connor watched his father's face after Aran left them—gray, wasted, the red of his beard a strong contrast to the sagging flesh around it. His eyes were dull, tired, every blink so slow it seemed like he might not open them again, and Connor sat beside him, silent now, his tale done, watching the rise and fall of his father's chest. So unexpected, to find him alive like this—but it wouldn't last. Marcas' face told him that, and the way Aran turned his eyes aside.

I am the king now, even before he's dead. Nothing has changed, so why does it feel like everything is different?

"You should be...with your wolf, Connor."

He jerked his head up and met his father's tired gaze.

"Marcas is *faoladh*, Father. I have no ownership of him, not his allegiance either, it's not—"

"Like that between you? Yes...yes, I've been...wounded, not blinded. *My son.*"

There was more affection in his father's voice than Connor had heard since he was a small boy and an implication he didn't want to consider. How would his father know—how could he have guessed? Bed-ridden, dying, and what had he showed? *Nothing, nothing at all.*

But his father was laughing, a coughing, choking sound that faded quickly, too difficult to sustain. There was something between humor and tears straining the corners of his father's lips, and Connor stared at him, didn't understand. Was this appeasement, after so long? The acknowledgment he'd desired—could it be so easy? But it burned bitterly, thinking of it coming here, now, after the years of aggravation and denial.

"I don't want your death-bed blessing, Father. I love Marcas—I'll be with him as long as he'll have me, and I'd decided that before I came here. When I thought you were dead. And I won't change that now, my mind's made up—"

"Your...heart, more like. Be happy, Connor." The force in his father's voice brought him up short. "I've had time to think. Nothing else, lying here, dying every day—no, don't...deny it." Again, the terrible cough. "You think I...don't hear myself? Smell the...arm that's rotting, no—I...haven't got time. For arguments. For...anything. I taught you to be...a warrior. A man—a king. I should have taught you to be happy. To enjoy...what you have of time."

"Father—"

"*Live.* Live through this...and then make a life with him. Your wolf—your *faoladh*. If that is...what pleases you."

There was burning in Connor's eyes and his fists grew so tight he could feel his fingernails breaking into the skin of his palms. His father had said nothing of mother or of his sisters—the black ashes that had been made of their family and the halls they had once celebrated in. *Does he know?* But the words wouldn't come to his lips. *If he doesn't, I can't tell him – not now.*

He took a breath, shook his head. "What about the line of the kings? What if I am happy never to marry, never to touch a woman again?"

"The sons of…many houses died in that sacrifice. Fathers, too—we have…become a land of orphans, Connor. Don't leave them to die. Find the most worthy. Raise them to know…what happened here. Find one you trust…to be king when you are gone. As I trust you."

"Father…"

He reached out and clasped his father's arm, above the bandages wrapped around the stump. But his father was speaking again, his voice tuned to a whisper now, and Connor bent close to hear him.

"Hoping against hope I was, and fearing too—that you were still alive, that you would come here…my son. Trust Aran. He's done more for me than you know."

"I will—I do—it doesn't matter! I'll raise all our men—you know they're still loyal to you, Father."

"They are *here*. Those who will come…all of them…were summoned here. They must be loyal to *you* now, Connor. You must…take everything I've taught you and use it." His father raised a shaking arm, pointed to the corner. "There, Connor. My sword. Take it! Be king—as you were meant to be…"

His arm dropped back to the bed. His eyes closed, and he lay sweating, breathing shallow, heavy breaths. Connor stared down at him for a long minute, then did as he had been told and crossed to the corner. His father's sword—many years he had seen it in his father's hand or at his waist, and now the old, worn leather of the sheath was warm in his hands. The hilt fit his fingers as if it had been made for them... Though it hadn't. *Father.*

He looked over his shoulder, but his father was sleeping now, or unconscious — either way, he needed his rest, and Connor couldn't think of anything to say — at least, not anything worth disturbing him. He clutched the sword tight in one hand, stood for another moment staring down at his father's face.

Then he turned and left the dark of that place and his father's fate behind him. He would help the only way he was able — he would do the thing he had been meant to do, the thing he had been *chosen* to do.

I will defeat Crom Cruach.

Marcas was waiting for him outside, crouched by the threshold, a scattering of many different expressions on his face — questions, answers, promises, hopes. It was only then that it occurred to Connor that Marcas, with his wolf-senses, might have heard all that he had said. *But what of it? What did I say of which I need be ashamed? That I don't want him to know?*

Nothing. There was nothing, even if he'd rather the words had come from him direct, had been a thing he'd said to Marcas face to face. He reached out a hand and pulled Marcas from the ground.

"Connor?"

There were many questions in the single utterance of his name, but Connor only shook his head and squeezed Marcas' fingers once before he let them go.

"Ask me later, Marcas. When we're alone."

The questions didn't leave Marcas' eyes, but he nodded, content to wait. There was warmth for Connor even in so little, and within him everything that had been jolted out of place seemed to settle back where it belonged.

* * * *

Connor found Aran in the hall just as he'd expected and waited at the threshold until he was noticed. He caught sight of his reflection in the burnished bronze of a shield boss, winced at the sight. No wonder the guards had doubted him. Blood and mud and fur, grass stains and the grime of many days marked his skin and the rich clothes Marcas had given him. *Before anything else, I need a bath.*

As soon as Aran looked up and saw him, the man came hurrying forward from the dais at the other side of the hall.

"Your father—"

"Resting, for now."

"I do not know what he told you, but all that is mine, any aid that you need—it is yours. As he told me—as is the nature of things, you are my king."

Stiff and slow, the old man went on one knee before him, and Connor wiped his face blank of discomfort and accepted the moment for what it was. All the eyes in the hall were on them, warriors just woken turning their way, and the guards exchanging mutters behind the shadow of their arms.

"Aran. You've helped me since I was a boy, have been at my father's side since before I was born. I ask nothing more and nothing less than that now." His fist tightened on the sword he still carried in his hand. Then he held out his other hand and pulled Lord Aran to his feet.

"My father said you'd called all our men here."

"Yes. He commanded it—I did it. They understand what's asked of them."

"And you?"

"I have my allegiance, my lord."

"And you choose me over Tigernmas—over the High King? What about *that* allegiance?"

"It died on the field of Magh Slécht, between the standing stones and the bloodstained gold of the idol. It died when the man I had followed, and in whom I had for years had all faith, bent himself to dark purpose. It died the day my sorrow at the loss of my sons grew to gladness that they had died before their lives could be used to fuel his work."

Connor reached out and gripped his shoulder with one hand, held tightly.

"They were good men. They're missed—but you can still do good work here. Your experience is wisdom I don't have."

"After you've slept, we'll make whatever plans you need."

"Good. But for now, Marcas and I need somewhere to rest, something to eat—and hot water. *Lots* of hot water." Aran chuckled, and Connor ran a hand back though his hair and grimaced.

Aran turned and gestured sharply, summoned forward two women who had been kneeling by the great hearth in the center of the hall. "Show the king and his companion to the rooms that were my sons', and prepare the bath—be quick about it, girl!" He turned back to Connor and silenced his attempt at protest with a smile.

"There is nothing to be gained from the waste of space." He looked up over Connor's shoulder and Connor turned a little, saw that Aran had locked eyes with Marcas. Something passed between them that he didn't understand—surely they didn't know each other, hadn't had time to speak—but it passed in the next instant, and Connor succumbed to the tug of the elder of the two women Aran had assigned to take care of them.

"This way, my lord. This way."

As he turned and followed her out of the hall and toward a lower, smaller hall behind it, he caught sight of Marcas behind him and the other girl tugging on his arm. Younger, that one, prettier—fresh, full face, and a head of blonde braids that shone in the sunlight, a shy smile that she turned in Marcas' direction while her fingers stroked his arm.

The strangest sadness Connor had ever felt leaped up in his throat, and in the next instant, meeting Marcas' eyes, seeing the sardonic curve of his lip, the way he lifted his eyebrow, he had a word for the feeling. *Jealous.* And with it the fuel for that feeling, the full awareness of it.

The girl shouldn't be touching him—Marcas shouldn't be letting her. A scowl crossed his features, and the woman in front of him took an extra step, began to walk faster. Connor shook his head, cleared his expression. It wasn't *her* fault.

Both women left them just over the threshold of a richly appointed room. Really it was two rooms that connected, but the open space of the doorway was wide enough for four men to step through and was blocked by no hanging or curtain. In both rooms was a bed, but Connor was pleased to see that either would be big enough for both of them to sleep in.

The moment they were alone, he stepped toward Marcas, surprised him enough with the quickness of his approach that he had the older man pressed against the wall before he knew it. He spared no words, went straight to the point—the hot, sick feeling that had fluttered to life in his gut was something he never wanted to feel again.

"That girl, the way she was touching you, Marcas. I didn't like it." He caged Marcas with his arms, looked into his eyes and saw no laughter there, despite the curve of his lips. "Marcas?"

"I shouldn't have enjoyed that. I'm sorry." Stunned, for an instant pierced by agony, Connor almost missed the rest of Marcas' words. "Not the girl, I mean—your jealousy." The pain was soothed to a sting, but didn't vanish.

"My—jealousy—"

"Do you remember the first thing you did the night I healed you, Connor?"

He blinked for a moment, but the memory was quick in coming to him. "I went...to the village below the pastures. To the inn. That girl—"

"She wasn't as bad as the one you had later."

There was a shadow of pain in Marcas' face and over it a layer of guilt spread thin but tangible. Connor bent his head and did all that he could think of to block out that pain. A kiss, and softness in it—warmth of all the feeling in him, love and apology and desire. Tongue over Marcas' lips, holding him between his arms, and Marcas' mouth opening for him, lip between his teeth, small sounds, utterly desirous.

He sucked up the sounds, traced the outline of Marcas' lips with his tongue, the indentations his teeth had made. With one hand he reached up and tugged on Marcas' hair, pulled his head to the side—with the other he cupped the back of Marcas' head, his neck, ran his fingers against his scalp, felt Marcas shudder against him, and again when Connor repeated the motion, nipped at his lips, dragged his mouth from the corner of Marcas' kiss to the exposed curve of his throat.

Marcas' arms wrapped around Connor's waist and dragged him as close as was possible, held him tight against his body—his hands wandered up Connor's shoulders, cupped the back of his neck and the back of his head. It wasn't long before Connor's eyes were closed, his breathing heavy, his kisses faster, deeper, hungry. He sucked warmth to the surface many places on Marcas' throat, found a spot below his ear that gave his whole body shudders, forced breath from between his lips.

Connor traced a line from that spot with his tongue, found another place between shoulder and collarbone that pulled a moan past Marcas' lips—his head fell back, thudded faintly against the wall, and Connor grinned, took advantage of the moment to jerk Marcas' tunic *up*, part his thighs with a knee and press his own thigh against the hot and hardening length of Marcas' cock.

Despite the vow he had made to himself, there was a part of Connor that wanted to take Marcas *right there*, pushed up against the wall. He was strong. He could pull Marcas up onto him, let him wrap his legs around him. He leaned forward and Marcas groaned at the pressure, rocked against him for the friction, tugged with the fingers still tangled in his hair.

Marcas I want you. I need you like breathing. Insistent, greedy, his cock warred with his silent promise, but the decision was taken from him when the door opened, and the girl who had inspired his jealousy came in with her arms stacked high with clean clothes. There was a certain wideness in her eyes as she looked at them, and Connor only looked back for a moment before he succumbed to Marcas' tugging fingers in his hair, blue eyes still closed and all unaware of their *company*.

Connor licked the seam of Marcas' parted lips, sucked his bottom lip between his teeth and bit it, thirsted endlessly for the soft little pants that were so easy to urge out of Marcas' mouth. *All for me. All for me, do you see?* The bubbling jealousy was subsiding beneath the open response of the man beneath him, the eager rake of his fingernails, the vibration of his moan against Connor's mouth. Once more, he laved those lips with generous tongue, then pulled away and turned to face the frozen girl who stood with her eyes locked on Marcas.

"You are still here, girl? Leave those things, you have other work to be doing."

Beneath him, Marcas started and pushed forward, leaned just enough that he could see the girl around the wall-post, then only sighed, spoke not much above a whisper.

"Connor—"

But Connor ignored him as if he hadn't heard.

"I want my water hot, girl."

Only when she had left did Connor turn back to Marcas' disapproving face, but he only shrugged.

"I don't like her."

"*Connor.*"

But there was fondness in the exasperated tone of Marcas' voice, and affection in his smile—and heat, still, in the blue of his eyes, the dilated pupils—in his hands, that had not left Connor's skin.

When the girl came back again, it was to tell them that the bath was ready, and Marcas found Connor had slipped out of his grasp. Connor tugged him along by his fingertips, a casual catch of touch he couldn't have escaped if he wanted to.

The bath was in a low building of its own, set aside from the long hall that held the rooms they'd been given. It was big enough for five men, the surface steaming and fragrant—blackberry, sage, nothing overwhelming.

More water was ready in buckets set on the floor, and Marcas pulled off his tunic and used the ruined fabric and a bucket of hot water to scrub away the more horrible of the bloodstains dried on his skin. A second bucket rinsed away the worst of it, and he looked up at the sound of splashing and found Connor already getting into the bath.

Marcas allowed himself a moment to enjoy the view, the line of Connor's back, buttocks, thighs as he climbed over the edge and into the water. The hiss he made at the sudden heat reminded Marcas of nothing but the sounds Connor made in pleasure, and he crossed to the side of the bath, was up over the edge and easing into the water before Connor had managed to relax into it.

His skin was flush, his eyes bright with wanting still. Marcas took up the soap, began to lather himself. It had a faint scent of pine, something he had noticed before on Connor's skin. Connor's eyes were on him as he lounged, one arm outstretched along the rim of the tub and his head leaning on it. Connor stared at him, licked his lips, leaned forward as if he could barely restrain himself.

"Here—I'll wash your back."

Connor's voice was husky, his lips faintly bruised, still marked where Marcas had bitten him—something he couldn't regret. *I want to do it again.* The boy stood and slipped behind him, took the soap from Marcas' hands and started at his shoulders. The firm pressure of callused fingers moved down all the muscles of his back, then up again, pleasant strokes of touch. He jerked and almost fell on his face in the water when those fingers grazed the sides of his ribs.

"Connor!"

"*Ticklish*? You? I don't believe it."

Marcas growled at him, almost laughed, but Connor's hands were rich with suds, reaching around to cup the length of his erection, stroke it slowly, and he moaned instead. Connor's body was hot against his back, hotter than the water, and Marcas let himself lean back into his embrace. The hard length of Connor's cock was pressed between his buttocks, and he moved back against it, felt Connor's breath flow out over his shoulders, the grip of his fingers tighten, the strokes quicken. Then he let go and Marcas groaned—the warm hands moved up his chest, over the hard points of his nipples, then retreated.

Marcas turned and closed his fingers over the soap in Connor's hand, pulled him against his body with his other arm, bent and pressed his lips against his mouth. It didn't help—Connor's tongue stroked his tongue in that certain way, so that Marcas found himself pressing him back, and back, water swirling around their thighs, mischief in Connor's eyes, and the heat of him enough to send a shudder over Marcas' skin.

"You're a terrible tease, Connor."

"I was only helping."

"*Helping...*"

Marcas licked the curve of his lip, then backed away and reached for warm water, poured it over his body and sighed as the soap came off—it was good to be clean again.

"Your turn, Connor."

But when he turned around, Connor was on his knees, his hands reaching for Marcas' thighs. As if it was a game, Connor's tongue moved in light and teasing paths over his erection, all but ticklish, following drops of water, and when he leaned forward and sucked Marcas' cock into his mouth, the wetness, the suction, that tongue still moving—they were so intense, so *hot* – hot all over.

His fingers tightened in Connor's hair, pulled *hard*. He almost apologized, but Connor was moaning around his cock, eyelids fluttering closed.

"You like that?"

Connor couldn't answer him, could only moan and send tantalizing vibrations into the flare of sensations his mouth was making. Marcas pulled again at the red hair wrapped around his fingers, forward this time, savoring the feel of every inch of his cock in Connor's mouth, so eager—*every inch* –

"*Connor.*"

He looked down and saw the green eyes lit with wicked spark and still glassy with lust, Connor's lips stretched and wet around the base of his cock before he pulled back and sucked in a deep breath, coughed a little, leaned forward and *did it again.* This time there was no teasing in Marcas' pulling of Connor's hair, only urgent desire, the need to thrust as much of his cock as he could into Connor's willing mouth. The sight of him was almost as intense as the sensation, on his knees in the water, and his cock drawn tight against his belly.

Marcas groaned, then leaned back and pulled away, tugged at Connor's hair one last time, then reached down and pulled him up to his feet. "You have to stop, Connor—"

"But you—that's not—good?"

There was real uncertainty in the roughness of Connor's voice as he stood on unsteady feet and licked his lips, if only a hint. Marcas laughed, tugged Connor against him and kissed him once, hard— harder.

"Good? *Too* good, Connor."

"I like *too good*."

"Obviously." But Marcas smirked while he said it, reached for the soap and dragged his fingers across Connor's shoulders. "Turn around."

Connor did as he was told, relaxed against Marcas' hands. When he lathered his fingers and scrubbed them through Connor's hair, the boy made enough moans and sighs to make sure there was only one thing on his mind by the time he reached for one of the buckets that had been left for them to rinse with and poured it over the red hair.

He stepped out of the bath so Connor could finish, resisted the urge to shake himself and reached for a towel instead. He rubbed the rough fabric over his skin and Connor grinned at him as he rinsed himself, ran his fingers through his hair until it stuck out wildly in all directions, a spiky red nimbus.

Marcas wrapped his towel around his waist and sat to wait while Connor finished, but the boy pulled Marcas from the bath to the rooms Aran had given them, too impatient to bother with drying himself. He came to Marcas with drops of water still shedding from his skin and hair, but Marcas nudged Connor with his shoulder and pulled away.

"Dry off first, impatient one."

Connor scowled at him, but the expression flexed into a smile. Marcas sat in the middle of the bed, pushed himself back and lay across the pillows. He watched lithe muscles in motion as Connor obeyed and rubbed his skin dry, enjoyed the way his glance flicked up now and then from beneath his eyelashes, the green gaze raking Marcas' body. The heat-flush had faded from Connor's skin, and now the red and darker bruises Marcas' mouth had left on him stood out against his paleness.

Mine, all mine. Phantom sensations tightened Marcas' cock against his belly every time Connor's tongue touched his lips, and he thought he enjoyed it perhaps too much when Connor dropped beside him, rolled over and pressed him down against the bed.

Connor licked the curve of Marcas' ear, bit the line of his throat as he turned and twisted, pressed up against the weight of his body.

"Will you get on your knees for me, Marcas? I want your mouth."

Marcas' tongue was a line of fire across his collarbone, down to his nipple. "I don't need to be on my knees to put my mouth on you, Connor."

His lips moved warm and soft over Connor's skin, increasing the speed of his breath, the heat of his desire, but it was only a return for Connor's mischief, a torment, the most generous tease. His muscles trembled under Marcas' mouth, the slow heat of his tongue when he chose to use it.

"*Marcas* – "

"Still not enough?"

Connor pushed himself over onto his side and reached across to touch Marcas' parted lips.

"I want your mouth on my *cock*, Marcas." He slipped his fingers up into dark hair, tugged gently and felt a pulse of arousal remembering – Marcas' hands in his hair, pulling, Marcas' cock in his mouth. Maybe

Marcas remembered too. Suddenly obedient, he slipped down Connor's body, off the end of the bed.

"Marcas?"

He only smiled.

"Aren't you my king?"

Connor licked his lips at those words, the sight of Marcas on his knees before him, glacial gaze dark with lust — teasing, those words, and yet...*not*.

"*Marcas* — "

Marcas caught hold of his ankles and dragged him down the bed, held his legs apart and leaned forward to draw his tongue once along the length of Connor's cock, a stroke of heat that made Connor's leg's go lax, part wider. He pushed himself up on his elbows so he could look down, see what he had wanted — that perfect mouth wrapping around his erection. With one hand, he reached down, and his fingers locked in the dark, thick hair.

"So hot, Marcas, so good — "

Marcas' fingers tightened against his thighs, spread them wider — *oh tongue*. Every time Connor thought he'd adjusted to the pattern of Marcas' movements, started to move toward the peak of his pleasure, it changed, brought him up short — graze of teeth, the slowest rhythm, rough, flat tongue lapping against spots that made his thighs tighten, his legs twitch.

Marcas stood, and his cock was wet with desire, so hard and too close to ignore. For the second time, Connor leaned forward and wrapped his mouth around it, felt his lover jerk against him, thighs tensing, before he leaned forward, one knee on the bed and his hands reaching down to hold Connor's head, fingers of one hand splayed across the back of his skull and the others wrapped into his hair. Slowly, enjoying himself, Connor slid his mouth down until he'd taken the whole length of Marcas' cock.

His hands gripped Marcas' thighs, then his buttocks. With careful attention, he sought out the most sensitive places he could find with an eager tongue. Every sound Marcas made, every pull of his hair sent a pulse of arousal shooting through his blood, but most of all he loved the words when they came, breaking and spilling past Marcas' lips.

"Enough—*enough*—I want...want to—inside you now, *inside you*—"

Connor pulled back, licked his lips and shot Marcas the most commanding look he could summon.

"On the bed, Marcas. Lie down."

For a moment Marcas stared at him, fingers twitching—then, like before, he relaxed and did as Connor had asked. Head on pillows, hands behind his head, he lay with one leg drawn up to the side and looked down his body, met Connor's eyes.

"Do you have more *orders*, Connor?"

He grinned, shook his head. "No." He left Marcas lying there, crossed to the other bed and began to rummage in the piles of clothes that the girl had left. He looked over his shoulder, saw Marcas staring at him with something close to shock on his face, but it faded when he crossed the room again—he had found what he wanted.

From the end of the bed, he moved up Marcas' body, settled himself so that Marcas was made still under the weight of his hands on his chest, his thighs sprawled wide around Marcas'. "You looked so worried—did you think I was going to leave you like this? Leave *me* like this?" He reached down to stroke himself.

With the fingers of his other hand, out of Marcas' sight, he pulled the stopper from the oil he had taken from the clothes. Slowly—because he knew it was cold, because he *wanted* it to be cold—he poured the oil from the flask onto Marcas' cock.

"Connor!"

Marcas' hips bucked *up* under him, and Connor laughed as he stoppered the flask and tossed it aside. He closed his fingers around Marcas' erection, smoothed the oil over the heat of his skin. Marcas lay with his head back, his fingers digging into the bed, and Connor pushed himself up on his hands and moved forward until he was straddling Marcas' waist.

Beneath him, knowing now what Connor was going to do, Marcas shifted, groaned, grabbed Connor's hips and held *tight*. Connor felt his fingers trembling and leaned forward, kissed Marcas once before he brushed dark hair aside, slid his lips against the curve of Marcas' ear.

"Don't you want to be inside me? Isn't that what you said, Marcas?"

Connor rocked his hips forward, then back again, Marcas' cock almost, *almost* penetrating—then he leaned forward again and licked Marcas' groan off his lips. When he leaned back again, pressed against the head of Marcas' cock, Marcas' hips jerked *up* and there was sudden heat inside Connor, stretching him, *almost* painful but the expression on Marcas face, and the head of his cock barely brushing something inside him—it was enough to turn discomfort into pleasure.

"Connor—you—"

"*More*, Marcas. More of you inside me."

He sank back—*deeper*. *Fire*. Marcas' words were swallowed in a groan, and Connor felt his thighs tensing, pushing upward as he moved back until there was no more left of him to take.

"Connor, you — move, *please* move —"

Gorgeous, he was gorgeous, and the tightness of his body — Marcas could barely breathe. Connor pushed downward onto Marcas' cock, his head thrown back, his mouth open, the heels of his palms pressed against Marcas' chest, fingers drawn into fists. Again and again he rolled his hips up, pulled himself off Marcas' cock, then sank down, shifting until Marcas could tell that every movement he made was passing over the right place inside him. At first he stayed upright, let Marcas thrust up to meet him, jar the most beautiful cries out of his throat —

Then he leaned forward and kissed him, and Marcas could do nothing but lie and let him do as he pleased. Tongue against his tongue, moving over his lips, that was almost too much with the heat of Connor's body squeezing tight around him, so tight — but Connor's breathing was heavy now, the rocking of his hips too slow to give Marcas what he wanted.

"Connor — *Connor*."

"Mmm… Marcas, *deeper*."

"That's what I *want*."

There was more growl than voice in his words as Connor rocked over him, kissed him, bit his lips, his throat, his shoulder. He'd never had a lover that liked so much to *bite* him, but he *liked it*. There was pain, but it wasn't pain — it was a liquid flame that sank through his skin, spurred through his blood. He reached up and ran his fingers through Connor's hair, then braced his arms against the bed and pushed *up*. Connor gasped, fell sideways, but Marcas moved with him, pushed his legs over so that he fell on his side, then was up, over him, pulled him up onto his knees and thrust inside him smoothly, easily. Connor pressed back against him, moan strangled in his throat and his fingers clutching the bed cover.

Marcas held Connor's hips in splayed hands, watched his cock as he pushed it deep into Connor's body again and again. He stroked the arc of Connor's back under his hands, and his groans urged Marcas onward — harder, faster.

"*This* is deep, Connor."

But Connor had no more words for him, nothing but the movement of his body as he responded to Marcas' thrusts. Deeper, faster, he moved, heard Connor begging under him — but it wasn't enough, it wasn't *enough*. One more time, licking his lips, he pulled back from Connor's body, closed his eyes and clenched his fist when Connor cried out for him.

"Marcas, don't *stop* — "

"Roll over *now*."

Connor obeyed with rushed movements, and the moment he was on his back Marcas lunged over him and pressed deep, slow this time, savoring the clenching heat of Connor's body as it surrounded him. He looked down into Connor's face, and saw what he'd been missing. Wrecked expression, utterly wrecked — glassy eyes, and his lips half parted, and his heartbeat pounding in his throat. His cock was hard, insistent, pressed against Marcas' belly, and he leaned back and took it in his fist, stroked as he thrust, easy at first then faster as Connor's legs came up around his back and tightened, pulled him as deep as he could go.

"Marcas — I — "

"*No.*"

He closed his fingers around the base of Connor's cock and held tightly.

"*Marcas!*"

Slowly, he pulled back, then thrust *in*.

"*Marcas –* "

"Not the only one who can *tease*, Connor…"

Connor tried to move his hips, thrust into the circle of Marcas' fingers, but Marcas held him still, watched his eyes go *wild* every time he pulled back, almost withdrew, then thrust back in. *Slow*. Hot velvet squeezed around his cock and Connor bucked against his grasp, dug his fingers into Marcas' shoulders. He dragged his nails down Marcas' spine, did all he could to push himself closer.

"*Marcas, please –* "

"Yes. *Yes.*"

Marcas loosened the grip of his fingers, thrust faster. He bent and licked Connor's lips once, only once, and the boy moved in his arms, against his kiss, groaned as wet pulses streamed out of his cock and onto Marcas' chest. Fire curled Marcas' toes against the bed, drove him deep into Connor's body. Blindly he pulled Connor closer, tried to get deeper as the pleasure shot through him.

When it was gone, he sank boneless onto Connor, listened to the rapid beat of his heart as it slowed. When finally he pulled away, Connor rolled over onto his side and looked back at him, reached for him, but Marcas stood and crossed to the damp towels that had been discarded on the floor. There was a jug of water on the table by the bed, and he dipped the corner of the towel in the cool water and wiped his cock, his belly, dipped another corner and brought it to the boy.

Connor didn't move, only murmured nothing and stretched. Marcas' gaze was drawn along the lines of his body, down to the wetness that spilled along the curve of Connor's buttock, slipped down the back of his thigh — Marcas reached out and wiped it away, tried to ignore the twitch of his cock between his thighs, the instant surge of desire. *Mine, all mine.* Connor's thighs parted, exposed his cock, the head still glistening with wetness, pressed against the bed beneath him — and again he moved, so that more wetness slipped from between his buttocks.

Marcas licked dry lips, realized he was stroking his cock, so hard, so ready — Connor looked back over his shoulder, lifted his hips, curved his back, and Marcas lost his internal battle, dropped the towel in his hand and climbed back onto the bed between Connor's thighs, pressed the head of his cock against the tight, wet opening.

"This is what you want?"

"*Yes.* Marcas —"

"*Insatiable boy.*" Marcas gripped Connor's hips and sheathed himself in one motion, and Connor's head dropped forward as he let out a loud, sharp cry.

Again and again he snapped his hips forward, clutched at Connor's back — Connor was crying out under him, *so good*, thrusting back against Marcas then forward against the bed, seeking friction for his cock, but Marcas paid no attention. There was no gentleness in him now, not with Connor begging beneath him for *more*.

He held Connor's hair in his fist and pushed his cheek down against the bed, turned him on his side, one swift, sharp movement that left Connor gasping, stroking his cock so that Marcas could watch now, watch as his fingers tightened, his strokes grew faster, his breath heavy.

"Marcas — Marcas, I want it — I want it —"

Everything was sharper now, every nerve more sensitive, Connor hotter, tighter, a rippling of muscles and intensity.

"Deeper inside me, Marcas."

Four fingernails raked across one shoulder, down his arm, and he felt Connor flying under him for the second time, his groans hoarse now, his legs wrapped with an iron grip around Marcas' thighs. He wanted it to *last*, wanted to see how much Connor could take of what he was begging for, but the desperate squeeze of Connor's body was too much, too soon.

Chapter Sixteen

Connor woke at the sound of the door closing, jerked half upright then was pulled down onto the bed again by the weight of Marcas' arm draped around his ribs.

"'S just the bath girls. They already...came twice already." A wide, full yawn interrupted Marcas' words, and Connor relaxed beside him.

"Good."

"Hmm?"

Marcas blinked at him, sleepy voice, sleepy eyes, the wolf-presence dimmed to almost nothing and the blue equally dim, faded cobalt.

"You made a mess of me, Marcas."

Marcas laughed, the laugh of the panting wolf, but Connor rolled his eyes, leaned back and kissed Marcas' shoulder, then slipped out from under his arm and stood. He hadn't been kidding—he *was* a mess. His bottom lip was still tender, felt swollen against his tongue, and there was other soreness—bruises on his hips, his thighs, the complaints of muscles unused to being stretched. But he stroked his thumb over the marks Marcas' fingers had left on him and smiled. They'd come far from the day that Marcas had said he *didn't want enough.*

Marcas, I think you did it on purpose. Made me love you – terrible wolf.

Naked, he wandered out to relieve himself, but when he came back, Marcas was still lying in bed, his breathing deep, his eyes closed. When Connor sat next to him, reached out to run his fingers through his hair, he opened his eyes, proved himself awake.

"Are you going to get up, Marcas? The bath won't stay hot forever."

"Maybe. Probably." He sighed, groaned as he stretched his arms and legs. "Yes – not like I have a choice. Where you go, I go, remember?" Despite his words, he made no move to get up, pressed his head back against Connor's fingers, blinked lazily.

Connor bent, kissed him, spoke softly. "It's still early, you know. The sun's barely rising –"

"But I've slept enough. We were lucky to get one safe night here, we aren't guaranteed another. Whatever plans you want to make, you have to make them today. There's a run ahead of us, if you still think the Cauldron is the best idea..."

His voice trailed off as he sat up, yawned, and tossed the covers aside.

"It's not a question of best ideas, Marcas. I don't know anything else that has a chance against dark powers, ancient gods – a being that can't be killed. And I won't run from him, this enemy – I've hurt him once and I can do it again if I have to."

Marcas pulled the tunic Connor tossed at him over his head, stood and followed as Connor strode out of the room and toward the bath.

"Connor..."

"No, listen. It wasn't just the High King's body that I hurt, it was *Crom Cruach*. I *felt* that. Since then I've *known* that we can defeat him, even if how is…" He paused and shrugged as he pulled open the door and steam overflowed the roundhouse, a brush of warmth. Behind him, Marcas was still speaking as Connor stripped off his tunic.

"I've been thinking about it, you know. The Cauldron… It gives enough to sate whoever drinks from it. It accesses the Dagda's power directly, the source of life. I think the lord of the mound won't be able to resist trying to destroy it. The question is just whether or not he can succeed — and if he does, how long it will take."

Connor climbed into the bath, settled himself with a sigh and let his head drop back. "That's something, I guess. *We* won't have to deal with whatever comes, but that's not what I wanted. The future… I don't want any future to suffer *this*."

"There's no such thing as forever guarantees, Connor." He heard the water splash as Marcas joined him in the bath, cracked open one eye to watch him.

"Isn't there?" He reached out one arm, and Marcas' fingers met his halfway. "What about what's between us?"

"As much forever as is allowed, just like anything else." Marcas' answer came past his lips easily, as if he'd already contemplated this question a hundred times. Connor wasn't sure he liked that thought, wasn't sure he liked that *answer*, and scowled.

"As is allowed. By *who*? By what? Marcas… Marcas, I made up my mind. I love you, and I'm going to keep you, make you only mine." He lifted his head and held Marcas' gaze, found it a thousand times more difficult than he'd expected. Heat rose in his cheeks behind the flush of the water, but he finished his thought regardless. "Only mine, Marcas. *Forever*. I told my father that — I'll tell anyone who asks."

"*Connor.*"

Water sloshed over the sides of the tub as Marcas pulled Connor toward him, embraced him tightly.

"I mean it, Marcas. I had a dream. You stayed as that wolf — I never got to touch you again, hear you say my name. *I refuse that life*. I don't want to think about permission, about what is allowed. Just be mine, only mine."

Marcas silenced him with a kiss, gentle parting of his lips, more softness than any touch he remembered from his life. "As if there was anything more I wanted from this life. *Amadán*. If it's what you want, we'll make our way." He put enough space between them that Connor could see his face. "If it's what you want, you'll have it."

His kiss grew deeper, his tongue a soothing pressure against the swelling of Connor's lip. His fingers traced a line from Connor's throat to his hip, touched the marks of his mouth and the dark bruises where his fingers had squeezed tightly. The touch was apologetic.

"I was too rough with you."

"Never." Connor grinned. "Just what I wanted — and you, too, which makes it better." He closed his fingers over Marcas' hand, held them against his side for a moment, then leaned against him and took one more kiss before he pulled away. "Let's get out of here before the water gets cold."

Much faster than they had the night before, both of them lathered and rinsed. This time, when Connor washed Marcas' back, he did only that, resisted the lure of warm skin in hot water — yet it was harder than he expected. Marcas hissed when he lathered his skin, and one at a time, Connor traced long, red scratches, the marks his nails had left on Marcas' back, his shoulders, even one arm.

"And you said you were too rough with *me*."

Marcas looked askance at him as he sluiced water from his skin and stepped out of the bath. "I *was*. That second time—don't tell me you don't feel it still." He patted his shoulders dry, his back, rubbed the rest of his skin more vigorously. "You really are a mess, Connor. You shouldn't let me go so far."

But Connor only laughed at him. "My wolf. I wanted everything you gave me. Stop *worrying* about it." With a shiver, he stepped out of the water, caught the towel Marcas threw at him. He scrubbed his skin dry, then his hair, and when he pulled the towel away from his face, he saw Marcas holding the flask of oil he'd used the night before. Connor licked his bitten lip, tasted Marcas, remembered—

"Come lie down, Connor—so I can use this for what it's *supposed* to be used for."

Connor followed without argument, only hesitated at the threshold of their rooms to watch as Marcas got on one knee on the edge of the bed and stayed there, waiting. Connor dried the last few drops of water from the back of his neck and came to lie where Marcas wanted him to, crossed his arms under his chin and propped his head so he could look back over his shoulder. Marcas straddled his buttocks, poured oil into his hands.

"After your nonsense last night, I should let it be cold, but I'm not so cruel as you are."

"I do *not* agree....*ah*." Warmth poured across his shoulders from Marcas' cupped hands, and smooth, strong strokes of his fingers rubbed the oil into

Connor's skin and silenced him. Connor sighed, relaxed as Marcas' hands moved across his shoulders, down the muscles beside his spine and up again. Slow, methodical, the firm pressure of Marcas' fingers stole all the tension from his body.

"Where'd you learn *this*?"

"*Learn*?" He pressed in with his thumbs at the base of Connor's spine, stroked outward. Connor felt deep burning, but it was good, not pain, knots of muscle and tissue relaxing under Marcas' touch.

"Well?"

The question came out as a muffled groan as Marcas shifted his hands to the other side of Connor's back and Connor's face flopped into the bed cover.

"I didn't learn. I'm just as jealous of you as you are of me. Those girls this morning—they wanted to be your *attendants*. I told them no, but that means I have to do what they would have done, doesn't it? *My king*."

Connor shivered, experienced a flash of memory at those words, the tone of Marcas' voice—pure sex, all teasing. How could he be wanting so much, so suddenly, just from the sound of two words? *My king*.

"You were on your knees when you said that last night, Marcas."

Chuckling laughter spilled across his back.

"I'm on my knees *now*."

The words drew Connor's attention to their truth, the strength of the muscled thighs parted over his buttocks, squeezing his sides, the heated length of Marcas' cock hard against his back whenever Marcas leaned forward. When he slid back farther, brought his hands down to smooth the sweet-smelling oil over Connor's buttocks, the backs of his thighs, Connor couldn't help himself, parted his legs enough that he knew Marcas would have an enticing view.

"*Connor.*"

Marcas' hands sprawled open, cupped his buttocks. He dragged one thumb along the seam that parted them, but only laughed at Connor's eager moan.

"You really are insatiable."

Marcas let his fingers continue downward, rubbed oil into Connor's thighs, the backs of his calves, the soles of his feet. It was easy to be distracted by his unconscious rocking, the way he tried to ease his arousal against the sheets beneath him. Marcas could almost forget that there was work to be done here, that this was more than just a calm interlude—that the greater portion of the destruction their foe might cause had yet to be faced.

When the gloss of the oil had subsided to a faint sheen, he lifted himself to one side and nudged Connor with his knee, ran his fingers down his spine one last time.

"Turn over, Connor."

The boy closed his eyes, opened them lazily, pushed himself up on his arms then flopped over onto his back, tucked one hand under his head. Slowly, gaze dragging on every inch of Connor's skin, Marcas pooled oil between his palms, warmed it, spread it across Connor's chest, down over firm muscles, up and along the length of his arms. His nipples grew into stiff peaks that Marcas grazed with his fingers. Untended, Connor's cock pulsed faintly, drawn tight against his body, begging with hardness.

But Marcas moved down to Connor's legs, drew his fingernails across the sensitive skin of his inner thighs, used the pads of his thumbs to rub the oil in and fade the scratches away. He leaned back when he was through, wiped his hands against his own thighs and couldn't help staring at the picture Connor presented — wild hair against the pillow, tongue touching his lips, heavy lids and the green of his eyes dark with lust. It was so easy to provoke him, make him want, make him wanton, and Marcas admitted to himself that he drew a special pleasure from teasing Connor, invoking his desire then stepping back to make him wait.

There was more to it than that — he wanted to make Connor want to take him, wanted to rile him into irresistible urges, feel him *inside* — he didn't understand why Connor waited, had felt his want the previous morning when the boy had pressed him back against the wall.

It pleased him to take Connor, to bend him into new shapes of pleasure, take control of his sensations, but there was the other truth too — he would be just as pleased to be under Connor as over him.

But not now. Now, there's just this torment for you, because you love it so...and so do I. Once, he reached out a single finger and drew it up the length of Connor's erection, watched the muscles in his abdomen tremble, the rigid flesh twitch beneath his touch.

"Do you know how tempting you are, Connor? How much I want to be over you...or under you?"

Connor sucked in a breath that hollowed his stomach beneath his erection, and again Marcas reached out one finger to touch, teasing, drawing back as Connor tried to press his hips up, gain more sensation.

"So you do like the thought of being inside me. Want to take me still...? I thought you'd forgotten, Connor."

The boy let out a shuddering breath, touched the tip of his tongue to lips.

"*Never.* But I promised myself—I promised myself that you would be my *prize.* When we've got our victory, and this world is safe again—"

Marcas lifted an eyebrow. "And you didn't think to ask me?"

Connor pushed himself up on his arms and slid to the end of the bed. "Ask you? When you already said you'd give me anything I want?" He grinned. "You'll be mine, Marcas. *All mine.*"

Marcas tried to feel irritation, disappointment, *something*, but instead there was only arousal and a blossoming of affection.

"I should have known."

And he grinned, but even as he spoke there came the sound of a drum from outside, dull, thudding beats. Loud wails accompanied it, and a woman's voice in keening tones over everything else.

"The king is dead! The king is dead!"

Marcas reached out a hand and seized Connor's shoulder, squeezed tightly. He stiffened, then sucked in one great breath, let it out all at once and with it the sudden gathering of tension.

"Connor—"

"It's all right. No—it's all right." He turned and looked Marcas in the face, and his eyes were dry even if he was no longer smiling. "I knew—when I saw him, I knew. I thought I might get to talk to him today, but—maybe this is better. There'll be no doubt now when I go before the chieftains—and anyway, the gods were kind."

Thickness drowned his voice. The line of his jaw grew tight, before he swallowed and finished speaking.

"They gave me time to say goodbye."

Connor. One more thing taken away – I'm sorry. But he couldn't say it, knew Connor wouldn't want to hear it. It wasn't as if there was anything he could have done. Once, he had saved the man. Once – there had been nothing he could do this time, not for wounds like those – not for a man that close to death. The rest of his strength had to be for Connor. *Now, more than ever.* The heat of five minutes before had gone in its entirety. Something cold lived beneath Connor's skin now, the promise of iron moving into the place where lust had lived.

Methodically, he moved to the bed they hadn't slept on, began to pull on the tunic that had been left for him, belt it into place. Marcas dressed more quickly in simpler clothes, then stood beside him, silent, until Connor asked for his help with the folds of his cloak. Seven folds, and Marcas pinned it at his shoulder with a heavy brooch, gold and amber. There was a band of gold for the arm that was visible, a heavy torc of twisted golden braids, a fillet of bright metal for his brow. Fully dressed, skin and gold gleaming in the dim light of the early dawn, stern expression in his green eyes and the faintest frown on his lips, Connor was the image of a king.

He took quick steps toward the door, but Marcas stopped him before he could pass over the threshold.

"Connor – the sword." He paused. "Your father's sword."

Connor stopped dead. "Yes."

Marcas took the sword from the corner where Connor had left it the day before, girt it around Connor's waist. He reached down a hand and touched the pommel with some reluctance, then squeezed the hilt in his fist and walked out the door. When he was standing in the sunlight, he turned and looked back at Marcas, something strange on his face.

"What are you doing, Marcas?"

"You go to council as a king, Connor. That is one place where *I* have no place."

In an instant Connor was beside him again, fist tight in the rich fabric of Marcas' tunic. He pressed his mouth to Marcas' lips hard, barely a kiss.

"Your place is *beside me* — didn't you say it? Where I go, you go. Don't leave me now, Marcas. Not now."

Marcas bent close, wrapped his hand around the desperate tightness of Connor's fist on his tunic. Far more softly than Connor had, he kissed him, then stepped back.

"Lead on. I'll follow."

* * * *

Connor walked the *ráth* of Lord Aran with burning eyes, one hand tight on the hilt at his waist and the other fisted by his side. There was a part of him that wanted to turn around, take Marcas with him, never face what he knew was come for him now. He couldn't run from grief, but he could run from the eyes that would appraise and seek to compel him, from those who would look to him now as they had looked to his father.

Behind him, he felt Marcas' presence, reassuring, close but never too close, one step behind him and one to his right, his eyes always moving whenever Connor looked back at him. *Protector. Yes.* He remembered the time not long past when he would have been insulted to think of such a thing. Now there was only warmth, the hum of affection that remained as a dull buzz in the back of his consciousness whenever Marcas was near him.

Connor went to the house his father had been laid in, but the white curtains had already been hung at the door, sign that those who tended the body were with him. Things were moving fast for his father now, but then it was summer…and his death had not been unexpected.

Despite there being no way forward, the path was already growing clogged with murmuring people, warriors, lords, women, most of them strangers to him but a few familiar faces scattered here and there. Connor exchanged nods with a few of them. Cathal, who had survived his father's plans when his father hadn't, though missing a chunk of his nose now and three fingers on the hand he lifted in Connor's direction. Aran, at the back of the crowd, watching him with solemn eyes and a question on his face, to which Connor nodded.

The meeting that had been planned must go on. It was a necessary council that even the death of his father couldn't put aside. He stood for a while, Marcas close behind him, and stared at the white curtains, imagined the stillness of his father's face. They would bathe him, bind for the last time his terrible wounds, dress him in kingly raiment, in gold and silk and gemstones — then, not before, would Brádach be brought before his people for the last time.

He took a deep breath, then turned away. He was aware of many eyes on him — of the murmur that followed as he walked away, his name repeated many times, word passing among the people that he was a son of the dead king — *the* son of the dead king. *He lives?* That question, too, was repeated many times, always answered in the positive by someone who knew him, or who knew someone who knew him...or had. There was relief in those voices, and he understood it, even if he knew that soon enough it would fail them.

After all, he was the continuance of the line they followed, but there would be no other after him. He had made his choice with his father's blessing, and he would stick by it. For Marcas' sake—for his own. *No bride, no woman, and so no child.* But since his father had spoken—*a land of orphans*—a thought had been growing in him, a way to make that no longer true.

He looked over his shoulder at Marcas, contemplating, shook his head when Marcas raised an eyebrow in question. *Nothing, for now.* He knew Marcas would understand his meaning—Marcas always understood. *Now isn't the time for the question, but Marcas... I wonder, how many sons could you handle?*

He had a flash of vision, an instant of daydream that flickered out as quickly as it had come—but the memory lingered. Life in the midst of death. A half dozen boys before the fire of a great hall, music in the background and Marcas laughing beside him.

The hope of that moment stood in counterpoint to his nightmare vision, the nightmare of the all-consuming wolf. He knew suddenly exactly what he wanted out of the future—how to satisfy himself and duty both. He tightened his hand on the hilt of his father's sword, and strode now with purpose across the crown of the hilltop, to Lord Aran's hall on the other side of the *ráth*.

Outside the door, Marcas stopped him, a hand on his shoulder, concern in his eyes.

"Connor? Are you—all right?"

And unasked was the thing he knew had spurred this shallow question—the deeper trouble reflected in

Marcas' gaze. *Something changed in you. What is it?* Warmth spread through him. This was what he needed. This one, with whom he was one, no words necessary between them now but the language they had learned because a wolf does not speak.

He did not look around them, see if anyone was watching, before he leaned forward and brushed his lips over Marcas' mouth, the most reassuring gesture he could summon. The girl had seen them — and if she had not told… Well, it still didn't matter. Connor didn't care.

"Everything is fine, Marcas. As long as they listen — everything is fine."

Marcas grinned and pushed open the wide, braced doors with one hand. "If you talk to them with half the strength you threw at *my* people, they'll listen."

Connor was taken aback for a moment, before he remembered what Marcas was talking about. Then he grinned and relaxed completely, his confidence restored. He had been trained for this — bred for this, born for this. For precisely *this* moment, everything that made him who he was had been prepared — and Marcas was right. *I've already done this before…and here all right, all authority, is mine.*

He walked into the dim and smoke of Lord Aran's hall with his features set, his back straight and his head held high.

Marcas walked behind Connor into the hall, but it wasn't just Connor who entered before him, it was *Connor the King*. It was a difference he had noted before, the thing that marked Connor as someone *more*. Every eye in the room was drawn to him just because of the way he moved, the way he walked, the set of his shoulders.

For him, it was proof of the thing he'd known since the beginning. *The brightest light. Chosen.* For what, he was only beginning to gain an idea. Connor's idea was bold — take the Cauldron of the Dagda, confront their enemy in the open and focus all his attention on it...bring him to contest with it.

This meeting — this would be the final chance to turn away, think of something else... But there was nothing else, and no one else, and Marcas knew it. *No one knows the way but me, and Connor will go with me because he must. Because someone must dare to enter the barrow and he'd never allow anyone else. We'll bring the Cauldron to Magh Slécht, because there's no other way to be sure of Crom Cruach...*

But he couldn't see beyond that moment. They could summon their enemy, he was sure of it, but the thing that would happen then? *Connor, you'll do something — say something — I know it.* But there all prediction failed. He only knew that it had to be that way, because Connor was the chosen one. Because within him all instinct, all power, all focus was turned toward this one who was now king.

Marcas lifted his eyes, looked around the room — there were few faces, but those that were present were serious, each of them focused on Connor in a different way. He made note of one man, older, gold weighting his robes, his hair. Every turn of his expression was hostile. *There is one who has heard all the rumors and believes none of them.* The man that Connor knew, and trusted, the Lord Aran — he alone wore an expression both openly hopeful and weighted with grief, but then he alone knew the secret of Marcas' being — that some other help than a boy with a title and his father's sword had come.

It irked him. If it was to be known that he was *faoladh*, if the ancient secret was to be told, here, in this place, then he would make sure it was known that the reason for his presence among them was Connor. *I am not here to fight a war for them.*

Connor crossed to Lord Aran's side and Marcas followed him, heard with no small pleasure Connor's insistence that there be a place at the head of the table for him, a chair beside his. There was no protest from Aran, only a nod of acceptance, and another that brought a bowed slave forward from the shadows to move a seat from farther down the table up beside Connor's.

"Aran, here." He pointed, at the chair closest to the head of the table on the right. "Marcas, you sit with me." The tone of command was back in Connor's voice, but when he spoke to Marcas, it was tempered with warmth. He suffered a sharp glance from Lord Aran and stared back at the other man without a word, dared him to speak, but Connor did before Aran could, whether or not he had intended to.

"It's time now, Aran. Before the others arrive, you'd best tell me what you know about what's happened — and we will do the same."

Marcas saw the strength go out of the old man's body. His shoulders slipped forward, the lines on his face grew deeper. His hands, the fingers curled across the tabletop in pale, wrinkled curves, tightened and relaxed. When he spoke his words were slow, heavy.

"In the last few years, many feuds that had been dropped or thought broken woke to new life. War began to spread like smokeless fire, no warning... No real purpose. Yet the petitions that were raised to the High King were never answered, requests that he do his duty, take up the shield and make many voices speak instead of shout battle cries.

"Tigernmas is old. We thought at first that was all it was, and that was its own worry. Tigernmas has no living sons, no brothers, no brothers with sons — no heirs. We thought he would choose among the kings. We thought...but it was all for nothing." A hard, cold fury moved across Aran's face as he continued. "It was all his purpose from the beginning — we know that now. The sacrifice was only the last step, the final call of a summons he had been making for months, maybe years. The violence...the little wars, the petty battles, those were only to take lives to feed the embers of the fire. The sacrifice was a bellows, and what it brought into the world..."

He shuddered and could not speak, but Connor was not so restrained. His face didn't change as the name slipped past his lips.

"Crom Cruach."

Aran leaned back from the sound of the words, then forward again, reluctant agreement drawn out of him. "Yes. And now the High King has power. Control of some darkness, something that burns like fire but faster, hotter —"

"I saw what it left behind." Connor's eyes grew clouded, and Marcas remembered with him — black ash and bone dust. The gleam of gold amid the gray. *Horror.*

"Did you? Did you." Aran's eyes were dead and lightless. "It was a black flame. It came out of the blood, ignited on weapons — on the grass — on flesh. It burned... I have never seen the like. What do you call a fire that does not throw light, but consumes it? That gives no heat yet burns. Even against the black of that moonless night, we saw it. We saw — we saw —"

Aran's voice faltered, as if he couldn't bear to describe what he had seen, but Connor reached out a hand to the old man's shoulder and offered strength.

"I saw. I know. The bent one arising — a black shape that reached up and blotted out the sky — "

But Lord Aran was shaking his head and his hands, too, were shaking like dry leaves in a high wind, and his whole body, suddenly boneless, sank against the back of his chair as if he might never gather the strength to move again.

"That is what you saw. That is what all those who were outside the circle saw. But you do not know — " He swallowed, or tried to. His throat made a thick, choking noise. "You do not know what became of the shadow. You did not see where it went!"

Connor's face reflected Marcas' own feeling. He did not want to hear. He did not want to know because he already knew — because there could only be one answer, one response that would explain the horror, the revulsion. Yet he had no choice but to listen, to let the words be spoken.

"Everything that was the shadow went into the king. In one breath, the greatest breath ever taken by a man. As if — as if the breath took him."

Marcas closed his eyes, heard Connor's breath escape in a sharp sigh. It was only as he had expected, as he had *seen* — and yet to know it made the reality a more terrible thing.

Chapter Seventeen

Marcas' voice rolled rough into the stillness that followed Aran's words, his necessary-unnecessary revelation.

"You keep speaking of Tigernmas. Of your High King—but he is not a king, nor a man. He's become nothing but the fulfillment of the choice he made."

For the first time since he had revealed the full truth of the nature of their enemy, Aran's eyes grew sharp as glass.

"What do you mean, *fulfillment?*"

Marcas stared across the table. "That man is no more. Whatever was *him*, whatever was more than flesh, it's gone now, crushed under the weight of the bent one. Your High King was a fool, and now he's opened the door for the undoing of the world." His eyebrows contracted, and he frowned. "My people, the *faoladh*—the ancient pact we made with the Dagda bound the lord of the mound in his kingdom, set him in slumber. But what was done, now undone, can never be again. We always knew this—it's why we've worked to keep the Crooked King under the ground.

To keep back his servants, and the dark powers that feed his strength."

"But if you did this once—"

Marcas looked across the table at Aran. "We did this once, and once is the only number of times it could be done. Our enemy is subtle, good at slipping his chains—better at sniffing out traps that might set him in them."

"So that is the way of it." Aran's voice was dull, his words heavy.

"Yes. What you witnessed was the summons that brought the bent one out of his long slumber. Not knowing what he would really sacrifice, your High King still called out for that darkness... And now that he's been eaten by it, no ancient pact, no chain binds the lord of the mound. Only the terms of that summons. Your High King's summoning has bound him to the world."

The old man's hands trembled, but Connor spoke to comfort him, repeated what he had said already to Marcas.

"It's not impossible to wound him, Aran. We faced him, Marcas and I. We fought him—we're still here—and last time, I cut off his hand."

Connor smiled, but the expression was grim and without humor. There were questions on Aran's lips, but he said nothing more. Behind them, at the other end of the long hall, the doors banged open and silenced their conversation. Marcas watched Lord Aran push himself stiffly to his feet, and moved to do the same—these were Connor's men, and Connor was king, and how better to show them that than for even a stranger to show deference? But when he moved, Connor's hand was on his arm, and when he looked up, Connor shook his head, once, sharply. *No. Don't stand. Beside me.*

For a moment Marcas didn't understand but when he did, he flushed, felt the heat rush in his ears, his face, his neck, felt his pulse tingling in his fingers. *Beside him. The king. He wants to...acknowledge me.* And in the next instant, despite suffusing warmth, he had to hold back a snort of laughter. *What does that make me, his queen?*

But his amusement vanished quickly. Men were coming into the hall now, two and three at a time and a few alone, until more than a dozen were assembled, more than twenty, and yet far more *people* than that. They were crowding the sides of the hall, and Marcas thought it was strange. By the sides of most of the men were one or more small boys, most dressed in the raiment of young men. Some were too young for talk, but they wore the clothes of chosen heirs, garments and jewelry marked with the crests of noble houses. *Why? Who chooses an heir so young, holds rights of manhood for a toddler?* But he remembered then. The truth washed over him, clutched at his gut with tight and sickening fingers.

A sacrifice of firstborn, and here was the proof.

With great effort, Marcas lifted his eyes from the small, bright faces, looked at Connor and saw that he too was looking at the boys, coming to the same conclusion. His throat moved. His eyes hardened. There were murmurs up and down the table, but they ceased as Connor fisted his hand on his father's sword and stood. He drew the blade in one smooth motion, laid it on the table before him and looked around the hall.

"King Brádach is dead, but his sword remains. It was given to my hands from him, and it's a sword that's heavy with the weight of its purpose. Do you know why you are here, men of Eire? Do you know why you were called?"

There was a moment of silence, then, "For the death of the king!"

"No!" Connor's answer came quick on the heels of those words, silenced many murmurs. "*No*. You were called because all that is mine, all that is ours, will not last through the season unless something is done to halt the one within Tigernmas. The High King is no more — if you did not know it, know it now! The thing that has cost you your sons and daughters is the lord of the mound, the bent one — the Crooked King, Crom Cruach."

He sank back into his seat as the hall erupted in shouts that made Marcas' ears ring. A hundred things at once were demanded — proof, and how it was that this was known, or if Connor thought them fools — or worse, if he was a fool himself. Out of the corner of his eye, Marcas saw tightness on Connor's lips, thinness slimming the richness of his mouth to a hard, dark line.

"*Enough.*"

If the crowd heard Connor's word, they didn't respond, and he was on his feet again in the next instant, mouth open for a battlefield roar.

"*Enough!*"

For the first time, Marcas saw a hint of the father in the son's face, tension in the line of his jaw, the angry furrows of his brow. Connor took up the sword and drove it into the table, looked various individuals in the eye. Other than Aran, Marcas didn't know them. A few were barely familiar faces, those he had seen acknowledge Connor in passing. But they were all silent now, staring at Connor, settling back from the flush of his authority.

"You'll be quiet, and you'll *listen* and *then you will talk*. Not before."

The man Marcas had noted, the old one rich with gold, stepped forward with irritation on his face.

"Listen to *what...*" and, under the glare of Aran's narrowed eyes, "my king?"

"To the truth. Aran, you were there. Tell them what you told me."

Slowly, more reluctant than he had been the first time, Aran spilled the truth and the terror into waiting ears—hours of words, words that were constantly interrupted. Marcas sat shifting in his chair, eyes darting from one face to another, learning names because there were only a few who stepped forward again and again to challenge or to defend—Aran and Cathal, Fearghas and Diarmuid always on Connor's side—and against him, accusing, disbelieving, Muiredach—that old man—and a pair of brothers he did not know, Cian and Ciar.

The sun was setting by the time Aran had finished and all those who had been in uproar were quieted to a shallow murmur, but the murmur was still full of the same foolishness as what had come before. Disbelief, and fear, and the waiting promise of a special kind of violence. They wanted war, to wield their weapons against a foe from whom they could take their price of blood.

Marcas scowled, but he knew he could hear far more than Connor could of the nonsense passing back and forth in whispers behind the cover of the crowd.

In another instant, the sun sank behind the horizon, the red of its gleam gone for good and leaving the room in dimness. Within himself Marcas felt the presence of the wolf *surge*, sharp and strong and full, a thing he had missed during the day—*the day*. In a moment the truth of the thing came sharp and clear to him. The wolf power—the night! *I didn't try at first, during the day, and when I did—Connor, I'm sorry! I worried you for nothing...*

But his thoughts faded as the rile of noise grew louder again. Muiredach stepped forward once more, passed Aran and Cathal with his glare and turned it fully on Connor.

"Boy, I've had enough of this! You want to be our king, and you come with nonsense like *this* behind you? Ancient gods, not the fall of our High King but the rise of Crom Cruach! Not an army, no, you don't seek to bring us into battle, instead you'd have us rely on wolves of power—and not only that, you want us to believe that sitting beside you is one of them? One of the *faoladh*, a legend, a protector of man! You are either a fool, or a liar!"

"*You* are the biggest fool in this room."

All eyes turned to Marcas as he spoke, a growl in his words that no man's voice could make. With slow, distinct movements that kept every gaze peering in his direction, Marcas took off cloak and tunic, torc and boots. He piled them neatly on his chair, and in the next moment *shifted*. He let himself grow larger, *larger*, until he felt the heat of the hearth on his tail and the press of the roof of the hall on the fur of his back. He was all fangs, all claws, the image of wild terror. He snarled, and knew his open mouth would show them the pit of a throat large enough to swallow a man whole.

Connor reached up, smiling now, all but laughing, and Marcas bent so that he could bury his arm in the great ruff of fur around Marcas' throat. The boy pressed his cheek to the great muzzle and spoke close to Marcas' ear.

"Careful, Marcas. You'll scare them to death."

When Connor turned back to the men behind him, the one who had challenged him, insulted him, was on his knees. A dark patch of wetness was spreading on the front of his tunic, and the sharp odor of urine sprang strong and sudden into the air. Muiredach's face showed the trembling fear of a thousand generations of instinct.

"Get up."

Slowly, Muiredach raised his eyes to Connor's face, no bristling in him now at the contempt in this *boy's* voice and bearing. He moved, one limb at a time, trembling in every inch of his being. When he was on his feet, Connor spared him only a moment's further attention.

"Get out."

Connor turned back to Marcas and reached out to scratch the broad, flat space between his eyes. Marcas closed them, huffed quietly with laughter that put out torches and shook the great fire before the door. Silent, a way parting for him among the others, Muiredach stumbled toward the open door.

This moment was the birth of a new legend. Marcas knew it, had intended it the moment he took on this change before so many men. He would never have seen himself here, now, at any other time, breaking the greatest prohibition that had been put upon the *faoladh* – keep the secret safe! But the secret was already out, and the proof of his presence was for Connor. He could have listened to them spout stupid words about him for a thousand years and not cared, but the fool had *dared* call Connor a liar.

You are not moving fast enough, old man. Learn the lesson!

A wolf does not roar, but when one is the size of the king's great hall, a growl is not a growl any longer. The sound of Marcas' snarl echoed a thousand times, chased Muiredach from the hall and stole the breath from every voice.

* * * *

In the silence that followed the terrible noise of Marcas' snarl, he returned again to his human shape, passed behind Connor and returned to his seat without a word. Connor watched him from the corner of his eye as he dressed again, as carefully as he had undressed, and was forced to hold back a grin. Nothing more perfect had ever happened in his life than that moment. It would last forever—it would be remembered. Who would contest with a king who walked with such a wolf beside him? *Maybe now they'll really listen.*

Without raising his voice, relying on the quiet to hold their attention, Connor continued from where Aran had left off.

"So now you know that everything you've heard is true. But what you fear won't come to pass. I didn't come here talking about vengeance only to put nothing behind it. No mortal or mortal weapon can wound Crom Cruach, but we will face him with the Cauldron of Dagda. It should be enough of a flood of life to drown even the thirst of the bent one."

Even Aran hadn't heard this—there hadn't been time, and Connor saw his eyes go wide with surprise, his mouth shaping the words in silence. *Cauldron of*

Dagda. But it was Cathal who spoke, his eyes hard. "And how will we use this against the false king?"

"I will go with Marcas and take it out of its hiding place. We will face Crom Cruach at Magh Slécht."

A renewed murmur broke out at this. Bring the Cauldron of the Dagda to where all this had begun? To the circle of stone that waited around the gold idol of Crom Cruach, to the center of the contact between man and madness? Two men—even if one of them was *faoladh,* that was foolishness! They wanted to form an army, to go after the *false king,* and Connor shook his head, despaired of ever getting through to them. What didn't they understand about the truth?

"I can call Crom Cruach to me—don't forget that even if he wears Tigernmas' body, he is nothing human."

"But the High King! Whatever mistakes he made, however he's been defiled, at least he was that—" Ciar spoke stubbornly, but there was no real challenge in his words. They'd learned the lesson of Muiredach well, it seemed.

"And now he's dead." Connor made the words heavy, final. If he couldn't get them to understand, then what would the rest be for? Any man who came with them would be just another sacrifice, more lives to feed the bent one, more darkness for him to move in. The spear he had wielded was broken. Even if he went into the barrow and came out with every weapon that he'd seen there on his back, it wouldn't be enough for more than a hundred men—and what could even a hundred men do against Crom?

I live because of Marcas. Only Marcas. And one wolf can't protect an army, even if he would consent to try.

Still, the outcry wouldn't die away.

"We are warriors—"

"We'll fight any enemy, god or man!"

Connor slammed his fist on the table, a shock that sent silence spiraling outward. "You think you can fight darkness at night? You think you can fight shadows?"

He had edged forward just enough that Marcas was behind him, and he felt a hand on his back, his shoulder. Calming. Softening. He heard the growl growing in the base of Marcas' throat, and it rolled around the room, settled the idiots around him into a different kind of silence.

"Enough. It's enough." Connor's words were quiet and not everyone heard them, but that no longer mattered. "If you wanted to fight, and all you would do is spill your own blood, I wouldn't complain. But do you not understand what I said, even *now*? A war will feed the bent one's power—even a war against him—and even if everything else failed, that's something I would never do. Every life he takes is another step forward for Crom Cruach." He took a breath and hoped he wouldn't regret what he was going to say.

"There is, however, another task that needs men. The Crooked King didn't come into this world alone — or even with only Tigernmas' help. The priests that serve him may interfere with any attempt to get rid of him—and more than that, there won't be much purpose to defeating the bent one if he returns in six month's time because of them."

Aran was already nodding. "You wish us to find these priests, to fight them?"

"I want you to kill them. Every last one. Make your plans carefully—do not be reckless—but do what you were born to do!"

There was a shout of acclamation and relief, and Connor let himself relax a little. He had been afraid that only threats would keep them in order, but with something to turn their attention to, an enemy they could actually *fight*, they seemed relieved now to leave the challenging of Crom Cruach to him.

"This discussion is over. I will leave with Marcas *now*, to retrieve our weapon – to confront the bent one. If we're lucky, we may even live through it."

"But my lord! What... How will we know if you've succeeded?"

Connor smiled grimly, shrugged. "If we succeed, you'll know it – and if we don't, you'll know that too." He stood, took his father's sword from the table, slid it into its sheath and heard the sound of the blade sinking home as the tone of finality. It was night already, and there was a sleepless darkness at the heart of Eire – a darkness that might already be probing its way toward them. If they failed, this green land under the sun would come to nothing and fall to ruin. How many were dead already? How many had already been lost?

Father behind the white curtain. Mother – ashes. Ashes.

The thought strengthened his resolve.

"Marcas." In a moment, Marcas was beside him, moving toward the door. He was pulling off clothes as soon as he was outside. By the time Connor crossed over the threshold, Marcas was the pacing wolf, eyes bright with unnatural gleam below the simmer of the stars. Used to this now, Connor mounted easily, settled himself between the great wolf shoulders. Below him, Aran stood respectful, as if Connor had done no more than climb onto his horse like any other king.

"Watch the horizon, Aran. Make sure those fools do what I've said — and if the darkness comes, fly. There's nothing you can do against it."

The old man nodded. "Go well, my king."

* * * *

Marcas brought Connor back to the hilltop that held his own hall, quietly, silently, with such speed that the night splashed by them in a wash of blackness. He didn't know what Connor was thinking — if the boy thought they'd make their way back to the elders or ask for aid from the sleeping courage of his people. He knew only that none of that would work. To ask would only cause trouble, and so he did not intend to ask.

My own kin might try to kill you, Connor. Especially if they knew what we wanted to take.

The thought was bitter, but he knew it was true no matter its taste. The *faoladh* would kill to protect their secrets — to keep their treasures. Only the utter surprise of his own change, the way the god had marked and altered him, had prevented them from trying anything the last time.

In the light of the risen moon, Marcas stood uncertain before the door of his hall, felt Connor slip from his back. The path down through the woods and the underbrush was too narrow, too overgrown for the passage of the wolf, and Marcas shifted back to his own flesh and heard Connor sigh with relief.

"I forgot — I never had time to say. Connor, stop worrying."

Connor looked up at him, surprise on his face. "What? I —"

"*Stop worrying*. I know the trouble — the reason why I couldn't change. It's only the sun, Connor."

"The sun —" His brows contracted, and Marcas reached out, touched his cheek.

"The wolf lives in me at night — so whatever shape I have at dawn, I can't change from it until the sun sets again. That's all. I would have noticed before, except it never happened that I was trying to shift in daylight until — that morning."

"So —"

"So there's nothing to worry about. You'll have me as long as you want me — or as long as we stay alive, at least." He scowled, looked down the dark of the hillside, but one of Connor's hands closed on his arm and pulled him close.

"We *will* stay alive."

"Because you said so?"

Connor shrugged, seemed almost to laugh. "No better reason, is there?"

Marcas only shook his head, smiling now despite himself, and led the way down the hillside, Connor close behind him. In the circle of stones, the dark barrow stood with the space beneath its slanted capstone opened like the maw of a toothless dragon, calling them down into the dark. The moonlight shone full on the face of the opening, but there was no light there, no immortal glimmer like that which Marcas had grown used to.

"Marcas, the light." Connor came up beside him and peered with his eyes squinted, as if there might be something distinguishable from the darkness down there.

"I know. Not only the barrier protecting us fell — this boundary is gone too."

Connor shot him a look, then took another step forward. "Does that mean it's not safe?" He reached out a hand as he was speaking, took another step and laid his fingers against the barrow, shuddered but didn't pull back.

"I don't know. This has never happened before." Marcas, too, reached out one hand for the cold stone, felt it icy and sweating under his palm. "I shouldn't be able to touch it, never mind go past it..."

"You said that last time, but not why."

Marcas shrugged. "Perhaps the gods know better than us that it's not wise to put too much power in the hands of one man. One of the *faoladh*, with access to the great Cauldron and many other such treasures..."

"Too much. I see." Connor pulled his hand away, stepped back. "Well, what does this mean for us?"

"Nothing, I think — except that you don't need to go alone, which is good. I hadn't thought about how I was going to direct you or if you'd be able to remember the way..." Experimentally, Marcas pulled his hand away from the stone, reached his fingers past the entrance of the barrow and into the shadow. *Nothing.*

He shot a glance at Connor, then took a breath and a step forward, reached back across the threshold from within the heart of night. "Are you coming?"

Connor took his hand without hesitation. "As if I'd let you go alone."

There was no path of light, no gleaming spectral fire to show the way to the place they needed to go. Marcas spoke quietly, repeating words that had been locked in his memory for twenty years. *Straight down, past five openings on your right, then take the sixth one. A left, and a right, and the second left, and you will be before the door that guards the Cauldron's chamber.* The directions were heavy in his ears, hanging around him — if he forgot, if he made a wrong turn, they'd lose their way down here forever, never make it out of the dark.

"Stay close, I don't want to lose you down here." In the sharp, dark silence the rough whisper of his voice rushed in echoes away from him, and he heard Connor's affirmation only dimly.

The dirt floor was cold and hard under his bare feet, sharp stones prodding upward against the soles — he made his way forward by feel, one hand trailing along the right hand side of the passage, his ears tuned for the echoes of emptiness so that he didn't pitch off into the darkness beside him whenever he came on one of the openings that led down another path. The sound of his own heartbeat rose like a tide in his ears, and the sound of his breaths and Connor's were like waves in that tide.

"Here, Connor. Turn right here."

He caught hold of Connor's wrist, pulled him close. Almost immediately, he came upon the left he was supposed to take, but the straight passage that opened before him then went on for so long that he began to wonder if he'd missed the turn in the dark. Just as he was deciding that he *must* have, the damp, sick odor of another passage touched his nose, and Marcas stumbled across the opening, reached into it then pulled Connor forward again.

The leftward passages came quickly, the first then the second, and he followed the second to its end at a dark, stone door.

"You must open it, Connor."

"Open *what?*"

Marcas took Connor's hand in his, reached out until they touched the cold, stone surface of the door. He felt it rumbling under his fingertips, then scraping them, sinking into the floor. His eyes went wide in the presence of a sudden odor the moment it began to move—the scent of a thousand summers and all the springs that had birthed them, too.

It was an odor with the faint echo of the god's blood he had drunk in that green place beyond the light, and as the door continued to lower, a faint gleam made itself known in the darkness, a hum of green and gold and white.

A little at a time Marcas shuffled forward, felt the door with his foot—almost gone now, a lip of six inches or less that was still sinking into the floor.

"Careful, the door hasn't sunk all the way. Don't trip on it." Marcas cautioned Connor as he stepped over it himself, stared into Connor's wide eyes by the light of the Cauldron in the blackness.

"Is that—?"

"Yes."

"And inside it?"

Marcas almost shrugged, then realized Connor wouldn't be able to see him. "I don't know." But Connor's question made him curious, and he stepped forward, looked down into the light. He drew in a breath and felt Connor come up to stand beside him, but he couldn't look away, even to see the expression on Connor's face. He was entranced by the glow, the infinity within it. The Cauldron was full of stars—full of snow—the green of the leaves, falling rain, fireflies in the throat of the night—and once again, stars.

"Marcas—" Connor's voice was choked with awe.

"I know. I know—but we don't have time to linger. Reach under the rim. There should be thick rope and a wooden handle—"

"Yes, I've got it."

Marcas felt Connor straining beside him, the tense muscles of his arm and thigh pressed against his side, but the Cauldron shifted only a few inches and Connor let go, panting. In the glow that came off the Cauldron's surface, Marcas looked into his face and saw anxiety and confusion.

"Marcas, how are we going to get this out of here?"

"Thirsty, Connor?"

"*What?*"

"It'll be easier to move when it's been drunk. It stays full until those who've come to it are sated, remember? On that handle—there's a drinking bowl. Help yourself."

Marcas reached under the brimming rim himself and followed the rope until he found the other handle nearest him, unhooked the shallow bowl and dipped it into the glowing liquid, thicker than water, thinner than wine. He brought it to his lips and breathed the hundred rich odors from the surface of the drink before he tilted it across his tongue. *Savory. Sweet.*

Ripe garden, steaming orchard, the cool ale of autumn and winter's hearty fare. The drink coated his tongue, his throat, filled him with indescribable richness. Across from him, he saw Connor's eyes widen over the rim of his own bowl.

A second draft was all either of them could stand, and when Marcas looked down after that he saw that the Cauldron was all but empty now. At its bottom, a few drops of ambrosia remained, bubbling like a spring, and he reached out for the rope, tugged at it and grinned when the Cauldron slid forward easily. It had weight still, but not so much that they'd need more than their own strength to move it.

Despite his estimates, when they lifted it, the going was slow. There was little room to maneuver in the narrow halls, and Marcas was preoccupied with keeping track of the reverse directions. Getting lost on the way out would be worse than getting lost on the way *in*. It might have been an hour later — or perhaps it only seemed that long — when Marcas finally saw a circle of dimmer darkness, the spark of a single star visible through the entrance to the barrow.

He stopped then, a thought occurring to him that should have come to him before, and turned back to Connor.

"Do you remember the way to the room where you found your spear?"

"Straight on, that wasn't hard —"

"Go back there now and find yourself another weapon, Connor."

In the dim light that filtered down from the opening, he saw Connor's mouth open, as if in question — but he said nothing, turned without a word and returned down the dark path that led away from the light.

Marcas pulled the Cauldron the rest of the way out of the barrow himself, and stood under the stars sizing it up, listening with keen attention to the noise of Connor's footsteps as they grew more distant. With one arm, he reached out and tilted the Cauldron, then became the wolf in the next instant and gripped the wooden handle in his teeth. As he increased in size, so did he increase in strength, until he was satisfied that it would be no trouble to bring it with them to the plain in the east.

He heard Connor's footsteps returning then, much faster than they had been going down. Marcas became himself and only waited a moment before Connor burst out of the darkness, a spear in his hands, but the long shaft in two pieces.

"Marcas—Marcas *look at this*. They're *all* like this! Every weapon!"

He could only stare. *Every weapon? Are we to have no advantage in this battle at all?* But then perhaps such violence would be no advantage regardless. He took a breath, shrugged.

"It doesn't matter. We knew we would never win this fight with weapons—"

Connor stabbed the worthless spear into the ground. "Did the bent one destroy these, or was it the virtue of *all* these weapons that saved you, and not just the spear I...broke?"

"I don't know. How could I know?" Marcas spoke quietly, slowly. The thought had not occurred to him, and he sensed in those words of Connor's that the boy had spent more time than was healthy blaming himself and suffering for it, wondering *what ifs* that hid edges sharp enough to cut him.

"Like I said, it doesn't matter now. We'll make do with what we have—with the Cauldron, I can make it from here to Magh Slécht in two days."

"Two days?"

"Two days."

And nights—but Marcas didn't say that.

* * * *

In the dark of the hall of the High King, Crom Cruach sat in waiting for his priests. Imbued with the nature of dark things that came from him, were of him, they possessed powers that moved them swiftly over the land. Yet they were human, and being human could venture where he could not—into the light of day.

"You come back to me... What do you bring me? What...knowledge?"

Out of the group one stepped forward, bowed low before him. "My lord, we have discovered much and little. No eye has fallen upon the one you seek, Connor son of Brádach. Yet it is known to us that in the north, a great gathering of men is growing. They say 'the king is dead', and speak of Brádach as one who has passed, and all across the land goes a murmur, summoning, seeking — there will be war, it is said."

Laughter crawled from Crom's throat, bent the dimness in the room to arcs of shadow.

"If all of them are in one place...the boy...will be there."

"It may be so, my lord. No eye has seen him, and all who are questioned say that the son of King Brádach died before his father — some time before."

Slowly, mobile shadow shredding its amorphous nature in the movement, Crom squeezed the fist that wore a golden gauntlet, the fist that no longer wore a shell of human flesh. There was no truth in the rumor, though it was probably not a lie. The boy and the wolf...*chosen*. In the fleshless essence of his being, there was a pang, the memory of agony. That which had been broken by the boy. *Connor mac Brádach. Chosen*.

"You have done...what is required."

The words inspired a shiver that oozed around the room. As he stood, the abyss expanded from nothing, a gaping mouth that opened a toothless jaw and breathed in, swallowing. *Fire*. In the air and in the touch of Crom Cruach, racing over the skin of the men before him, into the fabric of their robes, rich or ragged. Hair smoked, crisped, vaporized — skin vanished, and the soft tissues, left turning skeletons in a wake of ash that hung suspended.

Time to go north. To find those who would defy him—to find the son of the king.

Chapter Eighteen

Connor wasn't sure why, but Marcas seemed distracted as they prepared to leave the barrow, lifted his head again and again to the wind, breathing some scent that was beyond what Connor could detect. The wind came from the north, and that worried him — what kind of death might Crom Cruach be working on the men they'd left behind, no one and nothing to protect them? But he knew there was nothing that worrying could do.

Marcas bent for him to mount, then swelled to even greater size beneath him. He took the Cauldron up by the rope wrapped around its rim, delicate movements of teeth that left the great Cauldron hanging in mid-air, suspended from enormous fangs.

Marcas ran then, and the air in Connor's face was cold and strong. It almost blew him off Marcas' back until he found a steadier grip on the fur beneath him. He couldn't do much more than squint against the wind, but he trusted that Marcas knew the way, and he was surprised when they stopped just before sunrise. The purple of the night was still heavy against rose fringe of the dawn. Carefully, the wolf put down the Cauldron, crouched and took on a smaller size.

Almost before Connor had slipped from his back, Marcas was changing again, and from up close, Connor thought he could almost *see* muscles and bones reshaping, reforming, fur vanishing to leave silver-marked skin behind.

"It's so strange…"

Connor couldn't keep himself from reaching out, running his fingers over the lines of silver script that flowed over Marcas' muscles, uninterrupted, utterly seamless.

"The change?"

"Yes." Connor felt Marcas shiver under the skim of his fingertips, stepped closer. "Why did you stop?"

"I'd rather not run through the day, even if I could. That thing is *heavy*, Connor. And if I didn't stop now, change now—"

"I remember. How could I forget? I'd rather be able to talk to you. Anyway, the day is safer, for sleep, and—"

Marcas laughed, but only a little.

"No more *and*, Connor. Not now."

The faintest disappointment trembled through him, not lust abraded but something else. He didn't know how to ask for other closeness—he hadn't been lying when he'd told Marcas he had no experience, no talent for romance. His experience was flesh and feeling, nothing more. *But a warrior takes what he wants, doesn't he?* Hesitant still, he leaned forward, hands still on Marcas' shoulders, and kissed him, slow pressure of his lips. There was all the time in the world for Marcas to pull away, but he wrapped his arms around Connor instead and pulled him closer.

"You don't need to be afraid of touching me, Connor."

"I'm not! I only—I want to be close to you, just be near you. That's all."

"You could say that, you know."

"I just *did*."

Marcas kissed him again, hands on his face, slipping back into his hair, and Connor let his eyes close, relaxed more with every touch. When Marcas' mouth moved to his cheek, his jaw, he sighed, leaned his weight into the circle of Marcas' arms, looked up and drew his thumb over the arc of Marcas' cheekbone. "*I love you*." The words came of themselves and slipped past Connor's lips.

"Connor?"

"What?"

He met Marcas' eyes as if that utterance of his name had been a challenge, but all he saw in them was softness—acknowledgment, maybe. His lips were parted, as if there was something he wanted to say, but he said nothing, closed his mouth and when he opened it again was also smiling.

"Nothing. It's nothing. I love you."

For another minute, Connor stayed still in Marcas' embrace. When he pulled away, his fingers moved over Marcas' skin again, reluctant to let go. When he sat, it was closer than usual, and he was pleased when Marcas made no move to reach for clothes or pull away. Instead he lay flat on his back in the cool grass, his head in Connor's lap and an arm over his eyes to keep out the sun.

"Tired?"

"You try running with that thing in your mouth."

Marcas yawned, and for the instant of his silence Connor contemplated that thought and burst out laughing. "No, I think I'd rather not. Sleep, I'll keep watch. I think we're safe as long as the light lasts." He reached down one hand and ran his fingers through the dark hair spread loose in his lap. The sky held his attention for a while, the shift from golden glimmer to full brightness. When he looked down again, surprised that Marcas had never answered, he saw that he was already asleep, lips parted, breathing steadily, one leg drawn up and folded under the other.

Almost without him noticing, his fingers began again to stroke through Marcas' hair, against his scalp. *I would like this to continue.* Connor closed his eyes and leaned back onto one hand, felt the warm breeze move his hair and sighed. *I would like this to go on forever, just like this.* Drowsy, he blinked at motes moving in the light. This was reason enough to keep moving forward — to gain victory and vengeance, to make the dark safe again...

He wanted to bring Marcas to the forests of his youth, where he had run behind the hunting party, where he had chased fireflies in the twilight. He wanted to bring him to cool lochs under the moon, show him that all that was heat came from flesh, from skin against skin... And after, in some warm place where there were furs and fire, to hold him close — to keep him near so they could wake together.

"We've only so few mornings like that, Marcas. So few mornings that were calm, and easy...I hadn't even told you I loved you then."

The words fell softly from his lips, tangled in the fingers that had woven themselves into Marcas' hair. He bent over Marcas' sleeping face, kissed him once, a bare press of his lips against Marcas' lips, and returned to his perusal of the sky.

Time yet before they'd have to make their way to where it had all begun. *Tonight we'll find the plain and see what's left of the summer's carnage. Tonight we'll bring Crom Cruach something to slake his bloodlust.*

He wondered what it would look like, in the end. Would the glow and scent of the Cauldron's immortal mead be enough to enrage their foe? If he drank it, would it be poison? Maybe so much that was life would act as a slow toxin to death and emptiness. Would Crom leave a body behind, the flesh of the king he had conquered with whispers and terror? Would he vanish the way he had come, in shadow and black fire?

"Anything, so long as he doesn't ignore it."
This has to work.

* * * *

Marcas woke in the heat of the afternoon and found Connor sprawled beside him. At some point he had taken off his cloak, and lay with his head pillowed on it. He hadn't moved Marcas from his lap, had only stretched out with one hand curled against the top of Marcas' head, and Marcas pulled away slowly, yawning still, and tried to judge the time by the sun in the sky. Not more than an hour past noon — plenty of time, still, and they couldn't move until dark, even if they wanted to.

Without doing more than that, he pulled himself up by Connor's side, stretched out an arm and laid his head on Connor's chest. The sound of his heartbeat was white noise that drowned out all other things and fast enough, Marcas fell asleep again. He dreamed unsettled dreams in which that sound went quiet forever and woke to barely remember — only enough that he swore to himself that such a thing would never happen.

It was dim at his second waking, darker beneath the trees where they'd gone to sleep than out on the hilltop beside them, which still showed the orange of sunset reflections.

The time had come.

"Connor, wake up." Marcas pushed himself up onto one elbow, bent down and kissed Connor once. "Wake up — the sun is setting."

He pulled away and stood, stretching, heard Connor roll over behind him, groan and stretch, joints popping as he moved. Even knowing what was coming, what they were about to attempt, Marcas felt only good things about this moment, the sounds and scent of the boy behind him, the warmth of sleep still clinging to his skin. They had won every other challenge that had presented itself to them thus far — they had beaten Crom once, avoided him until they were ready, found a tool that might aid in his destruction.

We'll succeed. We'll do it or die trying — and I won't lose him, so that's not even an option anymore.

Somewhere along the line, Connor's absurd optimism had infected him. Why else would he now no longer even contemplate defeat? Behind him, he heard Connor going through the routine of the morning, turned finally and caught him mid-change, tunic half over his head and one arm tangled in the length of it.

"No one told those women I was going to battle, apparently." He girt the tunic to his knees, slung his father's belt on his shoulder and stowed his cloak in the bag. Marcas shook his head, almost laughing, then caught a tempting scent. "Did they pack *mutton* in there?" It was Connor's turn to laugh at him.

"Of course. Aran's got flocks here and on the islands, the most famous wool. What else would he send with us?"

He tossed the bag across to Marcas, let him fish out what he wanted for himself. There were subtle odors in the clearing that told him the cauldron had grown full again with that sparkling ambrosia, but he had no need for that kind of fullness. He wanted to sink his teeth into something, and the wolf was hungry for meat. Connor's *friend* had sent mead with them too, and dark ale. It was the ale Marcas chose, savoring the bitterness. He let his thoughts clear while he drank, breathed deep and watched the sunset draw on to twilight and deeper darkness.

"Marcas? Are you ready?"

He looked up when Connor called to him, met his eyes and nodded once. "Yes. *Yes*, and may this be the last time."

The boy came close to him, a hand on his shoulder, a hand cupping his face—the sudden tenderness that Marcas had grown accustomed to, the tenderness that marked his fear. "Whatever else comes, you know I—"

"Those are the kind of words that get people killed."

Connor blinked at him, confused. "What?"

"When they think they've said their goodbyes. When they think they can die unburdened."

"*Marcas*. I won't die—or let you, either. We're more than a match for Crom Cruach—haven't we proved that already?"

Marcas took a breath, nodded once, sharply. "Yes. We have." He pulled Connor toward him, kissed him. Then he was the wolf, all his senses awake and probing the flood of the night as it fell around them.

Connor climbed onto his back without a moment's delay, and Marcas felt him shifting there, settling finally between his shoulder blades as he called on the power, grew taller, broader, more massive than any mortal beast or monument.

Delicately, he bent and caught the rough, thick rope that bound the Cauldron beneath the rim. The moment he had it in his grip, he pushed ahead with all the speed he possessed. Connor rocked on his back, then tightened his grip and hung on.

Marcas knew the way. He had known it since the beginning—or at least the beginning as all this had come to *him*. The first night he had spent in wolfish form, he had been guided by others of the *faoladh* to the stone circle at Magh Slécht. He had seen the golden idol with its gleaming crescents of closed eyes.

As he drew close to the plain, a terrible odor began to make itself known, and when he had thought about it for a moment, he knew what it would be. The lord of the mound did not clean his messes, and who else was there who would do it for him? Those who had fled the sacrifice that had summoned him had left all behind—the scattered remnants of their camps, the traveling courts of little kings, and the bodies of the dead, both friend and foe.

When he came out of the hills and onto the plain, Marcas saw from a distance that everything he had suspected was true. In daylight, he thought the circle of stones might be painted red, and the odor was enough to bring up the gorge in his throat and send him three steps backward as the wind gusted across the trampled grass.

The farther forward he went, the more he saw to disturb him, and he heard Connor's muttered exclamation clearly in the silence that had infected this place.

"Gods—"

Chaos was smeared across the world in front of him. The plain of Magh Slécht, the remains of the sacrifice, showed a bloodbath worse than any battlefield he'd ever seen. Crimson mud had been gouged up in great rivets from the blistered earth, and wherever the black fire had touched the grass, the trees and the ground itself were smoking ruins. The bodies of the dead lay scattered like broken dolls on a madman's playground, and over it all lay a pall of black ash that blew about lightly in the wind, filling out the static embrace of terrible odors.

Marcas paced straight through the carnage and stopped only when he stood before the golden idol. It gleamed incongruous at the center of the destruction, the only thing clear of gore, as if the gleaming surface had sucked up whatever spattered on it—and maybe it had. Black eyes glittered at him, gathering the starlight and throwing it back over the gaping maw of the mouth.

Marcas put down the Cauldron only a few feet in front of the thing. A little at a time, the bubbling drops at the bottom were beginning to fill it again, the immortal mead appearing from whatever *other* it came from. He backed away, shrinking, crouching, let Connor slide from his back and turned to look at the dark iron curve of the cauldron behind him. Connor's face had gone grim and quiet, and he stepped forward without any hesitation, jerked the sword at his waist from its sheath and faced the idol, stared into its mocking, tenebrous gaze.

"To bring an end to it—"

He pulled the edge of the blade across the palm of his left hand, hissed as it cut him and reached forward with splayed fingers to grasp the idol by its face.

"Crom Cruach! Do you smell it, the blood you hunger for? It's here—*I'm here*! The chosen one you wanted—I've come for you, Crom Cruach!"

Connor's voice was a roar that demanded acknowledgment, and slowly, that acknowledgment came.

Crom Cruach's voice came first, a gurgle that breathed its words in wheezing shudders from the mouth of the idol.

"So you...have come...to me."

Connor sensed laughter, though nothing was audible as the voice had been. Slowly, uncertain of the purpose, sure only that he couldn't do *nothing*, Connor drew his father's sword and felt the tight, old leather wound about the hilt settle firmly into his grasp.

He heard a howl and spun to see that behind him, Marcas grappled with a black dog, his hands holding back snapping, translucent jaws. In another instant he had taken on the shape of the wolf and locked jaws with the beastly shadow, but Connor couldn't spare his attention to see more than that, was forced to look forward as a shape that was familiar to him coalesced out of the night, stepped forward until they stood face to face.

"Connor mac Brádach. *The boy king*."

The words were mocking, but Connor straightened his back and stared forward fearlessly into a blank and broken gaze.

"More a king than *you*."

Decay had printed itself irrevocably on the features that had once belonged to Tigernmas. Crom Cruach stared back at Connor from eyes that were wide and white, showed no iris and only a pinprick of a pupil, a needle's view into the void. A bright glint caught Connor's attention, and he looked away from the face and down. The glitter was a golden gauntlet where Crom Cruach was missing a hand, the fingers crushed into a tight, bright fist. It was a reminder he needed, both of his danger and his potential for success.

His gaze flickered to one side—the Cauldron was close, the glow of it brimming in the presence of such as a thirst as Crom Cruach's. Connor's fist tightened further on his sword, and he turned his back on the idol, saw streaming shadow flowing forward from all directions. Each shadow, Marcas swallowed with moonlight, but it seemed as if he only sent them back into the greater tide.

One gleaming howl fled Marcas' throat, and like an arrow shot at the moon, the sound prevailed against the blackness, summoned a flare of light that beat back the dome of darkness growing all around them. *What now? What now* —

He was a warrior, but this was an enemy he could neither fight nor kill. Defend himself—maybe. Wound—oh yes... But that had been when he wielded a spear blessed by the god, and even now he wondered if such a thing would have been enough— here, in Crom's place of power, his origin point. And Crom wasn't looking at the cauldron, had cast his glance toward it only once, the High King's face twisted into a sneer...

Connor realized then the weakness in his and Marcas' plan, a thing that might have occurred to him sooner if he hadn't been so focused on *ending all this*. He had attracted Crom Cruach's attention, but now the bent one was more focused on him than anything else. *Too focused.* Connor had defied him once too often maybe, or perhaps the memory of that wound and its agony lingered, defeating any other intention.

Is all I can do die and leave it all to Marcas?

Out of the corner of his eye he saw Marcas struggling with the shadow, pushing back against waves of shapes cobbled together out of crooked sticks of form and meaning.

No.

It was a resounding negative, defiance that encompassed his whole being.

No. I want that future – I want it to be mine.

Connor took a step forward, then to the left. He circled around the still figure of Crom in the High King's flesh until he could reach out with one hand and grasp the rim of the Cauldron. The tips of his fingers touched the light that brimmed within it, and he felt an electric tingle sing across his skin, then deeper. He knew suddenly what he had to do – he could see it all in his mind's eye, printed there as if it had been placed by some other consciousness. A memory – something Marcas had said, the words clear and rich in his thoughts.

"Your High King's summoning has bound him to the world."

The summoning. That flesh – would it prevent the cauldron's work? Would it keep him in this world? *The chains that bind him now.*

In that instant, Connor knew what he had to do. Crom Cruach was fixated on *him*, and would be so until he died – or worse. He must *use* that fixation, just like he could use the stiff and stumbling movements of the frigid flesh in front of him.

"Crom Cruach, you forget. I'm not just a king. I'm a warrior."

Laughter gurgled at him for a second time, but Connor lashed out without waiting and felt the blade of his sword hack deep into flesh, crack the thick bone of the thigh. He pulled back and struck again, despite more laughter. Without the blessing that had made that spear a burning weight in his hand, he could not hurt Crom himself, but Connor was achieving his purpose regardless. His second thrust skewered the arm that had already lost a hand. He gave the blade a savage twist, and this time the crack of bone was audible. There was a faint *thump* as the arm separated below the shoulder and fell to the ground.

"This flesh...feels...no pain, Connor mac Brádach."

"You'll have no problem with me taking off the other arm, then!"

Black blood globbed out of the wounds he made, clung to the blade of his sword and spattered on his skin, the odor rotten and nauseous, still no more than a footnote. One piece at a time, he disassembled the body Crom Cruach had stolen for himself. The body that bound him to the world, restrained the shadow and shackled it at the same time...but not in the right prison.

He was glad for the darkness when his sword struck deep into visceral flesh and lodged there. Connor didn't want to see what was spilling from the broken core of that dead flesh. With one last blow, sensing the time had come, Connor took off Crom's grinning head.

Chaos erupted.

The void vacated the flesh of Tigernmas in an instant, an explosion that burst outward with shattering force and rent what was left of the old king's flesh into scattered bits. Even as Connor processed the successful accomplishment of his purpose, tendrils of shadow were lashing into cohesion, coming together. He didn't even see the blow that caught his shoulder and sent him spinning back to crack his head against one of the standing stones.

Connor blinked twice, then saw only darkness, all things vanishing, the sight and the smell and the sudden sound of Marcas' howl last of all, one terrible cry.

In the instant Connor fell, Marcas was moving, and in that instant, no shadow, no outpouring of malice was enough to hold him back. He saw only Connor, the way he lay, eyes closed. Was he breathing? Did he move at all? In the swirl of shadow he couldn't be sure. In the noise and cacophony of a thousand attacks, he could hear nothing of Connor, and only the pounding of his own heartbeat in its fear.

Around him, behind him, the darkness grew thick and cloying. Shadow clotted where the full moon's light fell on the standing stones and sent the long fingers of their reaching shapes across the plain. Howl after howl poured out of his throat, and though he did not intend to call down the light, called only for Connor, again and again, the brightness answered him and struck like spears of brilliance from the sky.

His shape was changing even as he came to Connor's side, so that he knelt naked beside him, touched his cheek, the side of his head, felt wetness there, smelled blood.

"*Connor.*"

Behind him, there was a flare of shadow, the laughter that he had heard taunting Connor. As he had once before, he saw a gleaming tendril slick as oil darting through the shade of the night, but this time, possessed of rage, of an agony of grief, he neither stood before it nor tried to move away. With a hunter's reflexes, he caught the streaming shadow, held tight to it and *pulled.* The great mass of Crom's being heaved toward him, but only a breath's worth of space. In a moment Marcas had to let go, panting — there was no point to it. He could not *move* all that was darkness in the world!

Fury rushed through him, and frustration, and fear — not for himself, never himself, only for Connor lying behind him, breathing — oh yes, breathing, and there was a rush of relief in that, but not much. *Not enough. Connor, you are the one who was chosen! You are the one —*

He stood, and placed himself between Crom Cruach and Connor. He eyed the umbrous shifting, wondered where it would move next, and in that moment had the glimmer of an idea. Beside him, almost within reach, the glow of the Dagda's Cauldron showed over the iron brim. Not the metal but the magic, that was his need. Could it be enough if he — ?

There was no more time for thought. The bent one *moved,* and Marcas moved with him. One swift step to the right, his heartbeat bristling at the vulnerable opening, the path to Connor behind him. One swift step, and his hands clutched the rim of the Cauldron. One swift step, and he took hold of iron and rope and with one great heave tipped it over.

Out of the Cauldron came a river of light.

Marcas saw a flicker of the green *in-between* where the Dagda had granted him a *faoladh's* power a second time. His skin tingled, and he looked down at himself and saw the gleaming brightness of the Dagda's silver markings with more light in them than had been since the moment they were branded into his flesh. The odor of all good things was in the air, overwriting the smells of carnage and darkness and death.

The brightness flowed against Crom Cruach, unceasing, not a shallow trickle but a flood, as if the Cauldron existed only in the moment in which it had first been tipped, full to the brim and never less than that, even now. The darkness that was Crom seemed to draw itself up, a process as endless as the flow of light. There was birthed a swallowing maw that sucked down the streaming nectar, vanished it into nothingness and crept forward.

All that was Crom Cruach was a greedy swallowing mouth and a pair of hands that reached out to grip the Cauldron's rim. Yet the hands could not complete their journey. No void could compete with the power that spilled forth, endless, an improbable ocean whose source was the very source of life.

Though Crom Cruach tried, grasping, reaching, vainly struggling against the light even as he sought to draw it in, it looked to Marcas like he was losing this battle.

"Mar... Marcas."

Faint, too much breath in it, the interruption was still Connor's voice, and despite the strange convulsions of shadow and light going on before him, Marcas' head whipped round at the sound. To the everlasting relief of his seized and aching heart, he saw Connor blinking at him, pushing himself up, first on his elbow, then to his feet. He swayed, steadied himself on the stone beside him, and Marcas was beside him in an instant, a hand on his shoulder and one at his waist, holding him—too tight, he told himself, but even then he couldn't make himself let go.

"What's...happening, Marcas?"

Connor reached up, touched the side of his head and winced.

"I spilled the Cauldron—I tipped it over. To keep him from you, mostly, but—"

"But?"

"*That*. Whatever *that* is." And he paused to look once more at the tide of light, moving in a whirlpool now, the spilled nectar of the Cauldron flowing toward the standing stones. Marcas pulled Connor back with him, until they were just outside the circle.

"Why did you do it, Connor? Why did you—"

"Hack up the old king? Because of what you said—don't you remember? That the body Crom Cruach had stolen would bind him here…"

But Connor fell silent, distracted by the activity within the circle.

The shadow that was Crom Cruach had shrunk to a dense and writhing knot of viscous shadow, penetrated by no light, not starlight, not moonlight, not the so-bright glow from the spilled Cauldron, still brimming over. It washed outward moment by moment like the tide at the shore, no sign of ceasing or slowing, slowly reaching out to encapsulate the black. At that moment Marcas knew the answer to the riddle, how the puzzle would be solved, and watched as that answer fulfilled itself.

"You forgot the first lesson, Crom Cruach. In the beginning there was darkness…until there was life, which could not be blotted out or consumed. You should have known—but now you'll have the rest of time to understand."

There was a wail without sound, a clap of thunder in the noiseless air—the drowning of all immortal shadow as it was sucked within the flow. The flood lapped at the edges of the circle, beat against the stones and returned. Daring the light, Marcas dashed forward and put his shoulder to the rim of the Cauldron. With effort, he hoisted it upward against the tide of spilling light.

"Marcas?"

Connor's question was hesitant and when Marcas looked up, he saw Connor standing beside him, one hand pressed against the side of his head but his eyes bright as he stared down into the green-gold glow.

"Is it...done?

"It's done."

Marcas let out a breath and dared to test a smile. The world did not collapse. No struggling darkness reared out of the night to bite him. The shadows the moon cast remained only shadows, nothing to fear in them, and beside him Connor let out a sigh and took a step back, set his spine against the nearest standing stone and slid down to the grass.

"Thank all the gods for that."

Marcas took two steps and sank down beside him, let his head rest on the cold, damp stone and tried not to think about what the dampness was.

Right now, it didn't matter.

Chapter Nineteen

Connor lay limp beside Marcas and let the stone behind him do the work of supporting him while he tried to ignore the pounding pain at the back of his head. He probed a tender spot with careful fingers, but he couldn't feel much more than a bump and drying blood.

When the ground started to shake, he thought at first that it was the beating in his head, but Marcas was moving beside him almost as soon as it began. "Marcas, what—"

"I don't know—I don't know!"

With one hand Marcas pulled him to his feet and yanked him to one side. The stone behind them was trembling on its foundation, and all the others too. The earth had gone unsteady beneath their feet, and the golden idol cracked at its base, but the statue did not fall. The dark eyes in the golden face were closed now, no more than sleeping slits, and at the foot of the idol a great pit was opening, a cavern that cracked into existence, expelling damp breath from the fetid depths. Within the earth, Connor had a glimpse of black, darker even than the face that Crom Cruach had showed to the world.

All Connor could think was *terror*, more than a thought, the consummation of his existence. Was it the return of their enemy, all their planning, all their work failed and nothing they had intended come to pass? For that instant, the future was a thing once more out of reach and his vengeance meaningless currency, a price owed and never to be redeemed.

Then came a voice that he knew — the voice that had spoken on when all that was precious to him had lain bleeding in the grass.

"Well done."

Marcas' hand on his shoulder tightened painfully, then relaxed. Connor recognized then that all his suspicions were the truth, and that Marcas, too, was aware of who it was that spoke. A sense of *presence* grew around them — green, growing, the whole of which the Cauldron's powers were only a part and yet the same in essence.

"Lord, are you taking the Cauldron now?"

The answer to Connor's question came from nowhere, everywhere, a voice as distinct as the blades of grass beneath his feet.

"Yes. This is your sacrifice, for the slumber of your foe."

"Our foe, you mean. Will you restore the barrier that protected the *faoladh?"*

"The barrow will be protected. The rest is up to Man now. The wolves of the west are your responsibility, Ard Ri."

There was, not the sound, but the sense of laughter. With a snap that cracked through the air and left his ears ringing, the presence vanished, and the Cauldron with it. The great pit into which it had been sealed, vanished as if it had never been. Once more, the great stones stood silent vigil around the wounded idol.

Connor sucked in a deep breath and found as he did so that despite the noise, his headache was gone. In one moment all the tension fled his body, left him feeling boneless, almost giddy—*almost*. Those last words—*Ard Ri. High King*. But he shook them off as he turned to Marcas and couldn't control his grin.

"Do you think you have the strength to run again?"

Marcas too was smiling, almost laughing as he answered.

"*Strength*. Back to your friend Aran? I could run there and back twice before morning, but I'll be just as happy never to see this place again." For an instant, the blue of his eyes was shadowed. Then it cleared, and he nudged Connor away with his shoulder, let out a breath and *changed*. Connor climbed on his back without hesitation, gripped with his thighs, leaned forward and pressed his fingers into the soft ruff.

Marcas leaped forward, surged away from carnage, chaos, blight—and as he ran Connor was possessed of a wicked thought, until he couldn't contain himself. He slid just a little farther forward, as far as he could safely go, and leaned over so his mouth was beside the tufted ear.

"Run faster, Marcas. I want my prize."

He expected the panting wolfing laughter, but Marcas only looked back at him, blue fire in the great wolf eye, and raced the wind.

* * * *

There were still hours left in the night, and Connor's cheeks were burned red from wind-friction when they reached Lord Aran's *ráth*. They found a place that looked as if a tide of destruction had washed over it in their absence. Fires still burned here and there in the ruins of buildings and halls that they had stood in only two days before. Black ash was everywhere, but so were people, and after the first shock had passed, Connor saw the pale shapes of many tents spread across the plain.

He slipped off Marcas' back and turned to look at him over his shoulder as Marcas shifted from wolf to man's shape. "I don't understand. This looks like what happened to home, but if Crom attacked here—"

"They should all be dead."

They shared a glance that passed confusion between them, but there were no answers to be had without questions. Slowly, they walked forward out of the shadow of the wood at the top of the hill where they had stopped and down to the edge of the valley. From this angle, Connor could see a thousand fires, the great army that had been summoned by his father.

"We should find Aran, Connor."

Connor flicked his gaze up to Marcas' face, nodded slowly. It was impossible that Crom had come here and slain *no one*. Perhaps they had acted just in time, gone for him just as he had sought to turn his attack in this direction? But it sounded too convenient even in his own head, and Connor sighed, sped his stride. *Aran, must find Aran...*

He didn't get far among the men gathered on the plain before he was noticed—and Marcas beside him. Whispers followed them as they walked past many fires. He didn't need to ask for guidance—a path opened for him, a way down to the center of the valley, half a mile's walk along which pointing fingers and low voices urged him onward.

"This way—"

"This way."

Word of his presence seemed to go before him into the crowd on the plain, until not only warriors but the women and children who had come with them were pressing near, hands reaching out, brushing against Connor's skin but too hesitant to dare touch Marcas. In the short tunic he had tossed on while they came down the hill, the marks of the God were visible on his skin, the silver script iron dull in shadow, bright in moonlight.

"Connor? Are you all right?"

The words were so low that Connor barely heard them and knew no one else did. Faintly, he shrugged, and Marcas came closer to him, stood so near as they walked that Connor felt the heat of his skin, the brush of his arm as he moved. The touches from those at the edges of the crowd died off then, and when he looked back, Marcas wasn't looking at him. His eyes were scanning the crowd, bright challenge in them instead. Connor grinned and turned his face back the way he was walking.

Suddenly it was easy to remember that whatever came after this moment, Marcas would be with him — king or no king, accolades or not. Connor walked faster, lifted his head and called out as loud as he could manage.

"Aran! Aran, where are you? How much farther do I have to walk?"

Some of the tension around them dissolved in laughter among those who heard his shout, and others passed it forward. In only a minute, there was a call from ahead of them, the familiar voice ringing over the rush and mutter of the crowd.

"Connor! My king, you've returned — and your quest?"

"Victory, Aran! As you know — or I wouldn't be here now."

A heavy hand clapped down on his shoulder, and Aran's smile was equal parts joy and relief.

"Well done! Well done… And you, sir. Marcas of the *faoladh*, I must thank you for what you and your kin have done for us."

Connor looked up at Marcas and saw quiet confusion there to match his own feeling. Marcas had certainly done enough to help them — had, in the end, been the one to defeat Crom Cruach, even if Connor had done his part. *But his kin?* Aran answered the questions on their faces as he gestured for them to follow him to his own tent.

"You may have heard the rumors as you came across the valley — word that passed from the council we held before you left passed swiftly, and there were many that heard the howl of the great wolf. But there was a difficulty of belief until *other* wolves came to save us from the shadow."

Marcas stopped in his tracks, jerked Connor to stillness with the grip he had on his hand.

"Other wolves?"

Aran smiled, nodded. "Oh, yes. They're in with the sheep now, but I don't grudge them anything, no more than either of you." But even as he spoke there was an outcry, a scattering of people as Marcas shifted without warning, became the wolf and surprised even Connor.

The reason was clear in a moment, when four other wolves ran out of the night. They came close to Marcas at once, pressed near his body in a display of wolfish affection, touched noses with him. He howled once, and Connor sensed a question in the sound, but there was no audible answer.

One by one the *faoladh* drew back from Marcas, paced around him and came to stand before Connor. Each wolf bowed before him, then turned and ran into the night.

"Marcas—what? *Why?*"

He had thought he was done with all strange powers, all such beings but Marcas.

Ard Ri.

A laughing god.

He shivered. Behind him there was wind and movement, the rush of Marcas' change, then the softness of his voice.

"The wolf sense still marks you with brightness, Connor. You will have their respect, and their protection—did you forget? The first thing that drew me to you was duty."

"I...remember." Connor was still unsettled by the drama of the moment, by the way Aran was looking at him now—*even Aran? Aran who knew me as a child*—but once again there was the firm pressure of Marcas' presence beside him, and all tension relaxed. Once again, the swelling sense of his own purpose filled him. One last time, he would do *what must be done*. Whatever came from that—whatever was *tomorrow*—he could take it as it came, one day at a time.

I must be king.

"Aran, I want a bath for Marcas and I, if such a thing still exists here. Tomorrow night will be the funeral feast of my father, and I will take his place. Let the men know."

Aran seemed to hesitate before he nodded. "Of course. Allow me to offer you my tent, my king. Crom Cruach wrought a great deal of destruction, but it would be wrong of me not to give you the best I can. And I'll call for hot water at once."

He was gone before Connor could protest, bowed as he walked away—the first time Connor could remember him doing so. Just for a moment, Connor stood still, peering around him at the activity resuming in the dark. Then he turned, pushed aside the flap of Aran's tent and pulled Marcas in behind him.

* * * *

Aran's tent was dark, lit only by a hearth whose embers had burned to low and glittering coals, but that was more than enough light for Marcas' eyes. He saw only the things that mattered to him despite that—the low bed by the leather wall that moved in the night breeze—Connor's face, the smile that still turned up his lips. Outside, there was sudden shouting, loud noises of celebration.

"Aran has announced what you commanded for tomorrow." Marcas pulled Connor close, bent and kissed him. "I wonder if they're more pleased that they've got a king or a feast?" He grinned. "I know what pleases *me*—"

Connor leaned back into his kiss, took control of it, injected heat into the stroking of his tongue. "That I'll be inside you tonight? That tonight you're mine, all mine, just like I've been waiting for, just like I've been wanting? *All mine, Marcas.*" He kissed Marcas again, commanding with his hands at the back of Marcas' neck, tangled into his hair—bit his lip, sucked the groan from his tongue then stood back.

"Well? Does it *please you*, Marcas?"

Marcas rocked his hips against Connor's body, let him feel the rigid erection those kisses, those words had provoked. "What do you think, *my king*?"

But they were interrupted by the opening of the flap of the tent, and the entry of a whole line of women. The first merely bowed in their direction before she turned and held the flap out of the way for those behind her. Four girls strained under the weight of an enormous empty tub, which they settled on the ground, well to one side of the bed. Again, there were bows — then more girls bringing towels, oils, clothes and soap and last of all the water, steaming hot and cold in measure until the tub was full.

Marcas watched Connor watching the girls, amused by the glower lurking in the back of his stare whenever one of them dared raise her eyes. He could read the thoughts in Connor's head just by the shifts of his expression — what right did that one have to flushed cheeks, she wasn't carrying hot water. And why should they linger once they'd done what they were supposed to do? And that one — wasn't she the one who'd looked at Marcas the last time?

Under the weight of stares like those, none of them lingered, but Marcas didn't complain. He stripped eagerly out of his tunic, noticing again now the black and red stains of the battle just past. Across from him, Connor too stripped out of his clothes, crossed to the tub and stepped in after he had tested the water with his fingertips. Marcas joined him, wincing at the heat as it lapped his thighs, but Connor was already sinking down, disappearing under the water until he was completely submerged.

Amused, Marcas sat more slowly, let the heat work its way into his muscles a little at a time. Connor came up dripping, took a deep breath and wiped his hair back out of his eyes. A long sigh accompanied his relaxation, until his head lay back on his shoulders, leaning against the edge of the tub.

"Are you actually going to *bathe*, Connor?"

Connor's head lolled forward against one arm, but he only opened one eye to look in Marcas' direction. "Maybe." He sank a little lower in the water, sighed again, and Marcas laughed at him. Eager to rid himself of black stains, Marcas lathered his skin, scrubbed hard. As he washed, the black gore that had come from Crom Cruach seemed, not to rinse away, but to *evaporate*, ceasing to exist. Sweat and his own red blood he washed from his skin, but that was all, and as he looked at Connor, he saw that the same thing was happening to him. *So it's all done with then. Really over.*

A final bit of tension he hadn't even been aware of evaporated with the darkness, and Marcas rinsed off the clinging suds, then crossed to Connor's side. He nudged him with a shoulder and grabbed the soap.

"Sit up, Connor." Connor obeyed, faintly grumbling, but the noise faded as soon as Marcas' hands were on his shoulders, moving down his arms, lathering his back. Connor looked back at him with a lazy expression, and let Marcas move him as he pleased, twined their fingers together as Marcas washed the back of his hands.

"This would be easier if you were standing, you know."

Connor shrugged, stretched out his arms, took the soap from Marcas and scrubbed his face. He sank under the water again, then stood when he resurfaced, shedding water, his eyes fixed in Marcas' direction.

"Well?"

For a moment Marcas just gazed up at him—*beautiful boy.* Slowly, enjoying himself, the skin under his fingers, shifting muscles, Marcas continued from where he had left off. His gaze wandered freely, and he listened with special pleasure to the shallow breaths Connor sucked in when his hands moved up his thighs, lathered the length of his cock with slow, firm stroking—but after a moment he stood, continued upward, lingering touches that enhanced the subtle heat in Connor's eyes.

"Marcas."

There was a growl under his voice, not begging, but *more* was in it—demand, not request. He stepped back, and Connor rinsed again, stood a second time with beads of water clinging to his skin like molten crystal and enough heat in his gaze to have melted it. The languor had left him completely, and instead of returning to the water Connor stepped out of the bath, reached for a towel and slung one over his shoulder at Marcas.

"In a hurry now, Connor?"

But his glance silenced Marcas' humor, and Marcas recognized that this moment was different, something blazing in Connor like wildfire. Everything he knew of being under, giving in, Marcas had taught him, but this, *this* was only Connor, all of Connor, the man who knew nothing of gentleness, who know only hot and rough and lust. As if he had read Marcas' thoughts, Connor's hands were on him, pulling him across to the bed, pushing him down—

He knew what Connor wanted without asking, but still Connor reached out and threaded his fingers into Marcas' wet hair, tugged him forward so that when Marcas licked his lips, his tongue brushed over the head of Connor's cock. He tasted salt drops and skin, then leaned forward farther. He couldn't quite take it all, but he wanted to—all taste, all sensation, while in the back of his awareness was the way Connor's fingers stroked through his hair, against his scalp, urgent and rough while his hips rocked forward and his eyes closed.

One low moan after another slipped past his lips, slid down Marcas spine and settled like pinpricks of heat, until Connor spoke.

"I want to be inside you, Marcas — *now*."

Marcas suffered a pulse of want that struck through him like fire. Since when had Connor had a voice like that?

Connor fisted his hands in Marcas' hair, tried and failed to keep his hips from thrusting his cock further into Marcas' mouth despite his own words. "*So good, Marcas.*" It was all heat wrapped around him, perfect wetness, and Marcas' tongue moved with his mouth, back and forth on the head of his cock, under, short licks of the pointed tip then strong suction that had him bucking forward again. "Marcas — *oh yes.*"

It wasn't enough, but *enough* wasn't what he had wanted — not from this, anyway. Connor let his head drop back onto his shoulders, bit his lip, closed his eyes and savored the slow lapping of Marcas' tongue, everywhere, eager. When Marcas finally pulled back, he was a panting mess, wet lips, dark eyes — Connor stared at him, drinking him in — but the moment passed in an instant. He had waited long enough.

He pulled Marcas up with one hand, then shoved him back onto the bed, commanded him with a groan. "Back now — *now.*" Marcas obeyed, and Connor parted his thighs and knelt between them, leaned forward and pressed two fingers against Marcas' lips. "*Suck.*"

Marcas' cock twitched visibly when Connor uttered that word, seeped drops of wetness that Connor licked his lips to see. Connor knew what Marcas was remembering, and reached down to smear those drops across the rigid flesh with his thumb. He felt the vibration of Marcas' groan around his fingers and jerked them back.

"*Connor—*" But the sound of his name was cut off partway by Marcas' cry as Connor pressed his wet fingers against the tight opening of his body and *inside*. The cry became a groan, low pants one after another, some of them with words that went straight to Connor's cock.

More, always more Marcas asked for, and Connor's eyes were fixed to the sight of him, fists tight in the bed sheets, thighs spread wide and beckoning, rocking back onto Connor's fingers until he couldn't take it, pulled his hands away and pressed the head of his cock against that tight entrance instead. Slowly, so slowly, savoring this moment that he had waited for, fought for, he watched Marcas' body open for the head of his cock.

Marcas moaned under him, pressed his hips up toward Connor's slow thrust. Marcas closed his fist around his cock, stroked slowly, up, down, and Connor pressed forward until he was buried in Marcas, throbbing in such tightness that he could barely breathe.

"*Please.*"

He was so focused on the rippling sensation of Marcas' muscles squeezing around his cock, the clinging velvet and the heat, that it took him a moment to register Marcas' word. When he did, he only smirked, rocked his hips a little and treasured the sharp gasp Marcas couldn't restrain.

"*Please*, Marcas?"

He was rewarded with a stream of words, with the rocking of Marcas' hips as he tried to move himself on Connor's cock. "*Please—move—*I want it so much,

Connor, so much—inside me—*oh gods, please move.*" Connor's throat went dry. He licked his lips and pulled back as slowly as he could manage, thrust in once more the same way. Marcas' frustrated desire was gorgeous to see. He had never expected Marcas to be so willing under him—not from how he had acted at the beginning, so eager to take everything Connor had to give.

"I like when you beg, Marcas. *Do it again.*"

The words flowed out of him and Marcas sucked in a breath, eyes glassy now, his fingers tracing the sensitive clusters of nerves beneath the head of his cock. Connor felt everything hot inside him burning at its brightest. He thrust slowly, just as much to hold back the glistening tide that threatened to overwhelm him as to draw out Marcas' pleasure, but when Marcas obeyed, easily, no restraint in him at all, Connor was lost.

"*I want it, Connor*—I want it harder—more and more, I need—*please.*" And he licked his lips and focused the wide, dark pupils of his eyes on Connor's face, wrapped his legs around Connor's hips. "*Please, just give—please—please—*"

Sharp, hard, rough now, giving in, giving over, Connor thrust deep into Marcas again and again. He leaned forward and pulled Marcas *up*, held his face in the sprawl of one hand, then let his fingers slide back into his hair and pulled, kissed him hard. Marcas arched his back, his neck, pushed back onto Connor's cock with eager movements of his hips. "Connor— Connor—" The sound of his name in Marcas' pleasured voice was always lovely, but now it was a perfect thing.

Connor pounded his hips against Marcas' buttocks, changed the angle of his thrusts until Marcas' groans were punctuated by a cry and a gasp every time he drew back. He rolled his hips and Marcas *jumped* under him, a string of plucked tension. His toes curled against Connor's calves. The fist that was wrapped around his cock jerked erratically, and Connor pulled back just enough that he had a full view of Marcas spread open beneath him, threads of slickness connecting his cock to his belly.

Connor dragged his hands along Marcas' body, traced the dip and swell of muscles, the hollow of his hipbone, up to the dark points of his nipples. He was distracting himself now, trying to pull his attention away from the impossible tightness squeezing around his cock.

"So tight—so good—so good inside you, Marcas." The words slipped off his tongue, filtered into the sound of Marcas' moans, the soft and constant begs for *more*, more, until Connor curved himself over Marcas' body, reached down one hand and closed his fingers around the fist Marcas had wrapped around his cock.

"Wanna watch you—wanna see—just for me, Marcas. *For me.* My cock so deep in you—"

Marcas' groan wound out of a growl and into a cry. He took Connor's cock as deep as he could, and Connor felt his toes clench against his calves, his cock twitch in his fist as surge after surge painted Marcas' chest. The sight was just what Connor wanted, more than enough to send him over the edge he'd been teetering on since the first moment Marcas had squeezed tight around him.

"*Marcas—*"

Marcas. Ecstasy. Connor held Marcas still while the pleasure racked him, pumped his hips again and again into the perfect meeting of flesh. When it was gone, *nothing* remained, a blank and boneless haze that brought him sinking down onto his wolf, into the swift and sudden circle of his arms. Connor pressed his lips against Marcas' throat, one open-mouthed kiss after another, and all the while he muttered the only truth that mattered.

"Mine—oh mine—*Marcas, all mine.*"

* * * *

Connor slept like the dead, but still woke before Marcas—woke tangled in the lean, muscled limbs and grinned at Marcas' groan when he pulled away, at the way he groped across the blankets seeking him before he peered up from under the pillow that had slipped across his face.

"Con—nor..."

The word was broken by a yawn, and Connor reached across the bed to tug the pillow back onto Marcas' face.

"Go back to sleep. I'll wake you when the bath's ready—I'm going to call those girls."

By the time they had bathed and loved and dressed, slow and soft in the early morning, Aran was waiting outside, his shadow visible on the flap of the tent. There was a certain reluctance in Marcas that Connor didn't understand, but he shook away the feeling, kissed him once before he summoned Aran inside.

"Good morning, Aran. Is everything being made ready? I suppose I've got some rumors to fix."

Aran hesitated visibly before he replied.

"It is...no longer a matter of rumors, Connor." He hesitated still further before he continued. "It is not just your father's men who want you to be king. While you were gone, after the darkness passed, there were meetings—there was talk—and there were many who said that if you returned, you would have proved your right to a place of some contention. Now you *have* returned…and it is not your father's place but Tigernmas' they want you to take. They would crown you High King, Connor. They would bring you to Tara and set the whole of the land into your hands."

Connor felt a skipping in his chest, a shattering of intentions. In Aran's face he saw a certain understanding. Behind him, Marcas was growing more tense by the moment, an electric presence he could feel as easily as he knew he would see the strained expression if he turned, but he did not turn. Connor's mind whirled with the suddenness of this, and how stupid he had been not to have expected it.

Tigernmas had died without an heir and with Marcas' help, he had vanquished Crom Cruach and avenged him. *Avenged all of them, fatherless, brotherless, sons stolen. I should have guessed.*

He blinked, and realized that Aran was speaking low and urgently, and all his words were wise.

"…do you think I would wish this on you, who are the son of my friend, if I thought there was another way to go about it, another man to choose? But there is not. There is only you, who are a hero to them all now—who no man can deny has won the right to the High King's crown."

Connor did turn then, and saw that Marcas' eyes burned steady as coals, stared into the old man's face. Connor saw layers and layers of tension there, building and washing away like waves on the sand. Then it dissipated, passed out of existence as if it had never been, and in that instant Connor's decision was made.

"I'll do it."

Aran took a step back, surprised by the abruptness of his decision. "You — will become the High King?"

Silent, Connor nodded, and Aran broke into a relieved smile, began to babble. "There's no doubt they'll be well pleased to know the line of the king continues on — but they'd be more pleased to know it will continue to do so. You should take a wife at your coronation —"

"No."

And there it was, the thing he had been expecting and which must now — and for all time — be made clear. His word was a flat denial. Connor had already put too much thought into that very thing when he'd had only his father's kingdom to worry about, could feel Marcas tensing behind him at just the suggestion. His mind was made up — the ache in his chest, the heat of his desire, everything he was had been tied to Marcas the moment the wolf that had protected him had become a man, and laughed.

It was nothing he could explain and even if he could, he knew it wasn't an explanation that Aran would accept. *Duty. Duty over everything — but not this.*

He would give up his life to become king, but he would not give up his love. *How do I make it clear? How do I stop the offers that are sure to come — the girls who will be groomed for me, sent to tempt me — as long as there's no bride by my side, I know it'll continue.*

Aran was still standing silent beside him, wearing a rebuffed expression, and Connor allowed his lips to curve a little, shook his head and met Aran's eyes as he took Marcas' hand. He saw the disapproving expression flash across Aran's face, and a moment later resignation — the first Connor had expected and the second he had not, but he spoke to make himself clear just in case.

"Do you see this, Aran? This is the bond between us, Marcas and I. My father saw it—maybe you did too—"

"*Heard it*, more like."

Connor stumbled over his own words for just a moment, felt heat flush his face in an instant and dissipate just as fast as a thought swept through him. *So the girl didn't need to talk.* But he put that thought and the smirk that came with it aside for later, squeezed Marcas' hands tighter and forced a shrug.

"So you know. Marcas is the only *bride* I'll ever have. You understand? I won't let any woman come between us—not now, not ever." A resolution crossed his mind then, the answer to his earlier question and something he thought might make Aran—make *all of them*—understand. "Tonight, when I stand on the dais where my father once stood, when I receive the oaths and vows that are rightfully mine, when they offer me the crown of the High King and I accept it—there will be no empty seat beside me. *Marcas* will be there. *Marcas will always be there.*"

Marcas' grip on his fingers tightened, became almost painful, and to Connor's lasting surprise, Aran laughed, a sound that came from low in his throat.

"I see. I see. Well—I will not argue with you. If the line of kings is to be broken, it should at least be for love."

"But it will *not* be broken, Aran! How many sons left without fathers are wandering with only ash of the inheritance that should have been theirs? How many fathers without sons? My father said Eire had become a land of orphans—I won't have that."

Surprise softened the tension on Aran' face, and he nodded slowly. "It is…well done, my king." He looked away, something glittering in the corner of his eye, and Connor gave him a moment to compose himself. When he spoke again, his voice was rough but his words were clear.

"I will tell the others…what you have said."

"I know. Make sure you tell them all of it, Aran."

Aran nodded slowly, then shrugged. "You think it will matter? They have seen your Marcas now, as I have. They know his power and his name. You will be their High King, Connor, the *Ard Ri* of Eire—and your wolf… They will make a place for him because they can do nothing else. Because they know that behind those eyes the wolf that aided the defeat of Crom Cruach is waiting."

Marcas stepped forward then, pressed close against Connor's side.

"Make sure they know I will *always* be waiting, old man."

Connor laughed. Of course he would say that—his one, his *chosen*, his only.

Marcas.

About the Author

Belinda currently lives on the New England coast with her fiancé, their room mate and her cat. When she's not writing, she's working toward degrees in Philosophy and English, embroidering or reading.

Belinda writes in several genres, but a little lust and love always work their way into her stories.

Belinda Burke loves to hear from readers. You can find her contact information, website details and author profile page at http://www.totallybound.com.

Totally Bound Publishing